Tally's knife flew across the table. It landed in the dirt floor, vibrating, point down, beside Michael's bare feet.

He cocked an eyebrow. "Did you do that on purpose?"

"If I'd done it on purpose it would be in the top of your foot, and not on the floor. . . . You certainly seem to bring out some weird klutzy thing in me."

"Pent-up passion."

Fork halfway to her mouth, Tally looked at him. "Pent-up passion?"

"Sure. It has nowhere to go, so you fall over your own feet and fling cutlery at me. Perfectly obvious. You need to get rid of that sexual tension inside."

"Didn't I do that last night?"

"Sure, but that was yesterday's tension."

"Of course. Hmmm. I'm going to have to give this serious thought, doctor. . . ." She bit her lower lip and opened her eyes very wide. "I'm afraid I must disagree. My problem isn't sexual tension, it's a deep-seated homicidal tendency." She smiled at him sweetly and picked up her fork. " If I stick to my medication and stay away from you, I think I'll be better in no time."

"You're a dangerous woman, Tally Cruise."

By Cherry Adair
Published by Ballantine Books

KISS AND TELL
HIDE AND SEEK
IN TOO DEEP

IN TOO DEEP

Cherry Adair

IVY BOOKS • NEW YORK

An Ivy Book
Published by The Ballantine Publishing Group

www.ballantinebooks.com

ISBN 0-7394-2734-2

Manufactured in the United States of America

To Maureen Child

"Thank you!" she cried, waving her wooden leg.

Acknowledgments

Fabien Cousteau
My expert on all things nautical.
For answering my questions so
good-naturedly.

and

The people of beautiful Tahiti
Mauruuru

and

Michelle Davison
Timekeeper Extraordinaire

An enormous THANK YOU!

Any mistakes I've made are all my own.

Chapter One

"Turn around, lady. I can't see what the hell you're saying!"

From the deck of the *Nemesis,* Michael Wright attempted to lip-read the conversation onboard the *Serendipity* four hundred yards away while his boat pitched and yawed with the swell of the waves.

Tally Cruise and Arnaud Bouchard.

The daughter and the right-hand man of his archenemy, Trevor Church.

Now here was an unholy alliance.

The high-powered binocs brought the woman up close and personal. Plain little thing. Stubborn chin. Dark hair. Blue eyes. Surprisingly sensual mouth.

Her timing sucked. Hell, Church wasn't even around. Yet.

Michael had three days before Church's return. Three days to bait and set the trap. Three days, after eleven months of meticulous planning.

Anticipation had kept him motivated. But he wasn't alive. Lieutenant Michael Wright had died on Paradise Island last October. Now the living ghost of the man occupying his shell was ready to write the last chapter and close the book on Church once and for all.

It was as personal as it was unofficial.

Even off the books, this would be his last mission for Uncle Sam. He needed no accolades, no medals, and no acknowledgment. He and his partner had started this a year ago.

And failed.

Now he was back. Alone.

Failure was not an option.

He was ready. Focused. Intent. A heat-seeking missile targeted on Church's destruction. The long months of preparation had come down to mere days. The hours ticking away like a metronome in his brain.

Bouchard grabbed Tally about the waist and tried to kiss her. Ms. Cruise pushed out of the guy's arms, then hauled off and slapped him. Hard.

"Ow." Michael winced. "That's gotta hurt."

Apparently it did. She shook her hand, her slender shoulders stiff as she turned away. Gait unsteady because of the rough seas, she continued gesturing as she paced.

Talking. Animated. Pissed.

He readjusted the binoculars for a better view. "Better" being the operative word. He almost didn't notice the absence of his left eye.

Almost.

The increasing swells three miles out from Paradise Island sent the two yachts bobbing like opposite ends of a teeter-totter. The cork action didn't help Michael's lousy depth perception. And according to the National Oceanic and Atmospheric Administration, things were about to get worse.

Considerably worse, if NOAA's prediction of category three monsoon winds slamming into the French Polynesian Marquesas Islands by late afternoon was accurate.

As soon as he'd learned of the approaching typhoon, Michael had integrated it into his plans. What he hadn't incorporated was the presence of the young woman on the other boat.

"Damn. Turn around again, honey, so I can see what you're saying," Michael complained. "Not that you don't have a sweet ass." The view from the back, in fact, was prime. Her slender hands punctuated her words. She stormed all the way to the rail near the bathing platform at the stern, then made an about-face with military precision and started the circuit all over again.

Her curly black hair bounced around her head in the gathering wind. Navy slacks hid the shape of her long legs, but did great things for a truly spectacular ass. The wind pressed her neatly tucked white shirt against small, high breasts and a flat stomach.

His libido had flat-lined way back. But it wasn't dead after all. Not if he could still appreciate a great ass. The shrinks had talked to him about depression before the navy cut him loose. Hell, he wasn't depressed. For months nothing had held his interest for long. If he'd had the energy to be *anything,* it would've been *pissed.*

At least now he was doing something about it. He lacked the official backing of Uncle Sam, but he had other players on his dance card if he needed them. None of whom had to play by the rules.

Michael's fingers tightened on the binocs as he readjusted the focus on Bouchard's reaction to the boss's daughter's harangue. Bouchard laid a conciliatory hand on her shoulder. She swatted it away. "Honest to God, Tal, I do"—his hand went up to sweep hair off his face—"believe me?"

"Yeah. Yeah. Yeah," Michael bitched, wedging the fishing pole between his feet to keep it from sliding to the deck. "Whatever you're selling, she's not buying, pal. Kiss her ass and call it a day."

Michael had taken time early that morning to batten down the hatches and trim the sails in preparation for the building storm. He anticipated nine- to twelve-foot storm surges and hundred-mile-an-hour-plus winds. The sooner he got out of the direct path, the better.

He'd made a huge pot of coffee, stored it safely in a large Thermos, and had built a pile of man-size sandwiches and sealed them in a waterproof Baggie.

The *Nemesis* consisted of forty-five feet of high-tech beauty. Built of fiberglass, with an Airex foam core, she was lightweight and strong. While he prepared for this trip, Michael and his inventor-of-cool-gadgets-brother-in-law, Jake Dolan, had outfitted the *Nemesis* with some exceptional toys. Consequently, Michael was ready for anything.

He'd meticulously scripted the next couple of days: limp into port, drag out repairs, reconnoiter the small island, find his target, and wait like a fat, hairy spider to ensnare Church in the web he'd meticulously woven.

Running into the daughter and the second in command, like ducks in a shooting gallery out here, might prove to be a bonus. Especially if they'd cooperate and say something interesting.

"Come on. Come on. Come on. Give me a frigging clue what you two are up to, would you?" Ten minutes. If they didn't reveal anything useful, he'd call it a wash and head into the shelter of the harbor, and go from there.

He wasn't prepared to risk the *Nemesis.* Church had already taken way too much from him as it was. If those two wanted to sink in the coming storm, they could have at it. Two less people for him to keep tabs on later.

Michael had intentionally positioned the *Nemesis* to be as inconspicuous as possible as a silhouette against the horizon. And although it was only early afternoon, the low, dark sky gave every appearance of dusk. He slapped the binocs up to his eye.

"Say something worth listening to, damn it. I don't give a crap if you drown. But it's my frigging worst nightmare. So turn the hell around and talk to me."

He attributed his accelerated heartbeat and sweaty palms to the relentless approach of the typhoon. The wind felt cool on his wet skin. Hell. Even a rational man would give pause when faced with a monsoon.

Thanks to Church it was fucking more than that for Michael. He kept his gaze locked on the other boat and not on the broody, malevolent, almost black water that stretched into infinity. The sea wasn't a woman to him. It was a man-eating, man-mutilating monster.

Merciless. Amoral.

Greedy. Unforgiving.

Christ, he'd lived with night sweats and day demons for months, and in the process developed a phobia bigger than the *Titanic*.

Michael snorted. A Navy SEAL afraid of the sea. . . .

Ex.

Ex–Navy SEAL.

Well, screw *that* for a joke.

"Danger, danger, Will Robinson," Michael muttered, getting a firm grip on the seat of his chair as the *Nemesis* went up one side of a wave, and down into a deep trough before bobbing back to the crest. The fishing pole clattered to the deck as a frothy wave washed over the side, dousing his legs with water.

An icy sweat formed on his skin. He ignored it.

Que sera sera.

If this trip didn't cure his irrational fears, nothing would. He'd purposely surrounded himself with what he feared the most: water.

It was a last-ditch, drastic act. The sea was either going to kill, or cure him.

And right now the former was a distinct possibility. . . .

Water foamed across the deck and drained back into the ocean, leaving a malevolent gleam on the boards. He swallowed hard.

Tally turned. Michael could once again see her face. "—So full of it," he repeated, reading the lady's furiously moving lips. She had a pretty mouth. A mouth that was going to be sucking up seawater if they didn't hurry up and do whatever-the-hell they were going to do before this storm hit.

Tally fell into her erstwhile lover as a wave broadsided their boat. She shoved away from him as soon as she caught her balance.

"Six minutes and counting," Michael guesstimated aloud. "Then I'm outta here. What the hell kind of name is 'Tally,' anyway?" he asked the three-legged cat, who'd jumped onto his lap, walked the plank of his thighs, and now stood, legs braced, on Michael's outstretched legs. Sharp claws dug into his shins. Black fur combed by the stiffening breeze, Lucky's ragged ear twitched in response.

Michael repositioned his feet on the teak railing; Lucky adjusted his weight accommodatingly. "Tally Ho? Tally up to the bar? No, that's belly up to the bar, isn't it? Which is where the hell we should be right n—pull in your claws or get off my damn leg, Cat!"

Tally Ho said something. Bouchard shook his head and put an arm around her shoulders. The lady didn't like the contact and shoved him away.

Bouchard abruptly left her side and went below. Tally braced her arms on the brass railing of the *Serendipity* and glared up at the grayish purple sky. The movement did interesting things to her breasts. Michael let the rising wave shift the binoculars to where Bouchard had disappeared.

He'd be a hell of a lot happier watching this storm from inside a comfortable hotel room than this up close and personal. He had a few other kinks to work out over the next several days other than recon.

The hatch on the other boat opened. Tally ignored Bouchard as he emerged and skulked around the wheelhouse and out of sight. What was he up to? And where was the crew needed for a boat the size of the *Serendipity*? There had to be at least one, preferably three, hands aboard. Probably below, keeping out of the danger zone. The *Serendipity*'s sails should've been set an hour ago, but they billowed with the force of the wind, straining at the anchor and mast. Those poor fools. They should've headed back to the island before now. It didn't make any sense for them to be this far from shelter for no reason. Not in this weather.

"Dumbshits," Michael muttered, standing up. "No reason why we have to be out here risking our asses to keep tabs on morons, is there, Luck?"

But, damn it, Bouchard was up to something. A sixth sense prickled. Pins and needles for Michael's atrophied soul. He leaned forward, raising the binocs for a final look before heading out to sea to race the storm.

With no warning, a ball of flame erupted from the sea, blowing the *Serendipity* to smithereens.

"Jeesus!"

The boom of the explosion beat back the wind a fraction of a second later. With a screech, Lucky flew off Michael's legs as the *Nemesis* leaped in the violent backwash caused by the explosion.

Flaming wreckage flew high and wide, until the luxury yacht was nothing but floating debris burning on the water.

Michael braced himself as the *Nemesis* rocked violently with the impact. "Sonofabitch!" He sure as hell hadn't seen that one coming.

Dazed, Tally fought her way to the choppy surface, lungs burning, vision blurred, heart pounding. She rode the swells gasping for air and trying to figure out what had just happened.

One moment she'd been standing at the railing, waiting for Arnaud; the next . . . she was in the water. "Arnaud?" she shouted. "Hey! Arnaud!"

Chunks of flaming boat bobbed several yards away. She kicked off her remaining shoe and frantically scanned the charcoal-colored waves for a sign of Arnaud's bright head. And what about the crewman who'd been below? With his black hair and dark skin the other man was going to be almost impossible to spot. Oh, God. What *was* the other guy's name?

Lu!

"Lu! *Haere mai!*" *Oh, God. Oh. God.*

Tally did a full circle, riding the waves, trying not to panic as she searched for the two men, and kept as far away from burning bits and pieces as she could. She didn't want to think about how deep the water was, or how high the waves had become. Or what might be swimming in the murky depths beneath her.

Terrified, she swam as close to the fiery wreckage as she dared. Cold water chilled her body even as the fire heated her face. There was no piece of flotsam bigger than a surfboard. And pretty much everything that wasn't burning was sinking—fast. Most of the flames came from floating fuel, which did not reassure her.

She spat out a mouthful of water, coughed, and pushed her hair out of her eyes. A thrill of trepidation shivered through her at how tired she was already. She hoped to God there weren't any sharks around. She might not be a *good* swimmer, but she was a strong swimmer. Of course that didn't mean she could outswim a hungry shark.

Tally drew up her legs reflexively. Waiting for a wave to crest, she kicked upward and tried to spot Arnaud and Lu.

Both men might very well have died in the explosion. And if she trod water much longer, she'd be equally dead. Since Arnaud's favorite expression was "every man for himself," she reluctantly started swimming toward one of the boats she'd seen earlier. With help, she'd try to find him. If the adage "only the good die young" held any truth, Arnaud Bouchard was healthy, happy, and already swimming to shore. Tally hoped the crewman was with him.

By the time she reached the other boat she was exhausted and out of breath. Dark, storm-tossed waves pummeled her as if trying to shove her away from the boat. Salt spray blinded her; water rushed down her throat. She reached out, smacking her arm into the side of the craft.

With numb fingers, Tally gripped the rim of a porthole. Now what? She couldn't scale the side of the boat without assistance. She cried out as a wave dashed her painfully against the hull, then dragged her beneath the surface. Coughing and spluttering, she fought her way back to the top, lungs on fire.

"Help!" Futile. The wind howled, the waves slammed against the hull, and the world sounded like it was ending in a roar. She spat out a mouthful of salty water and held on. Out of the corner of her eye she could see the flames and black smoke of the *Serendipity* smudging into the low, dark cloud cover.

Tally shuddered, really, really frightened now as the waves buffeted her and the muscles in her arms trembled from the strain of holding on. Her fingers were beyond numb. She couldn't hold on forever.

She did a visual search of the length of the boat, trying to figure out how she was going to climb aboard. Where the hell was the ladder? Her grasping fingers slipped off the porthole. She kicked frantically to stay afloat, ignoring the ache in her thighs. Should've kept up that gym membership.

From this vantage point the boat seemed enormous. Not as big and fancy as Arnaud's, but it loomed over her, large and white and solid. And currently impenetrable and unscalable.

With any luck they had a swim platform on the back. . . .

"Hey, lady. Life preserver. Behind you!"

Startled, Tally looked up. The dark silhouette of a man leaned over the railing. He pointed behind her.

Bracing a hand against the glassy smooth side, she turned to glance down the trough of the wave behind her. There indeed was a white and blue life preserver. Thank God. She reached for it. Went under. And, thanks to the waves, came up ten feet farther away.

So near and yet so far.

Her arms and legs threatened to give out. Her lungs felt waterlogged, and her eyes burned. Tally flailed toward the life preserver and finally managed a two-handed death grip on the ring.

A sharp tug nearly wrenched the ring from her puny grasp. She held tighter. The strength of the man hauling the rope zipped her through the water. Within minutes she was airborne and landed with an ignominious splat on the deck at his large feet.

For several moments, panting took every ounce of energy she could muster. Not even the cool wind slapping her wet skin induced her to move. Cheek flat on the smooth wood of the deck, she didn't bother opening her eyes when she felt a tug on the preserver. Straightening her fingers was all she could manage, and even that, shakily. Her lungs filled with the scent of varnish, salt, and the oily smell of smoke.

"Were you burned?" the man asked in a rough voice.

Tally lifted her upper body off the deck, feeling as if she weighed two tons. She coughed. "I—uh—don't know. I don't think so."

She looked up.

Up long, hairy, tanned, muscular legs, past ragged Hawaiian shorts, past a flat, bare belly to skim a broad, tanned, hairy chest. Good God. No wonder he could pull her out of the water with a single tug. The man was a giant.

Ignoring her, he braced against the roll of the waves and walked a few feet to stow the rope and life preserver in a locker aft, then turned and came back. "Are you hurt anywhere?"

Tally coughed up seawater. "I don't think so," she repeated. Frankly, she had no idea. She was just happy to be out of the water.

"Then rise and shine. There's a category-three monsoon bearing down on us. We're clearing out."

Tally staggered to her feet and spread her legs for balance. "Lord, yes, let's," she said to his back. "Thank heavens you were out here. I don't think I could've kept on swimming much longer."

"Fortunately for you I was catching my supper before the storm hit."

"My lucky day." Tally rubbed her frozen upper arms with her equally cold hands. "I'll never turn my nose up at a fish dinner again. You saved my life." She grabbed the railing to steady herself as the yacht rocked and rolled with the waves. Spray soaked her already sopping wet clothes. She shivered.

"Don't start the French fries, honey. It's not saved yet," he told her with a quick glance at the darkening sky.

He turned to fully face her, and Tally sucked in a sharp breath and took an involuntary step backward. For a split second her heart almost stopped beating, then lurched into a heavy rhythm that made her entire body feel hot and prickly.

Ye gods and little fishes!

A pirate!

A black patch covered her rescuer's left eye. The elastic holding it in place drew a thin line between his dark brows and across his forehead. His dark hair was wet, and slicked back off his lean face. His strong jaw was hazed with dark bristle. His face bore the austere lines of a man hounded by demons and comfortable with danger. He looked scruffy, unkempt, and strangely appealing. Tally attributed her reaction to being delirious with shock.

"Seen enough?" he asked dryly as she continued to stare. "Or do you want me to turn around?"

By all means, do. "Sorry. I wasn't really looking *looking*—I zoned out there for a second." *Very smooth, Tallulah. "I wasn't looking looking"? Oh, brother.* She blew out a sigh.

He wasn't quite a giant, but he was solidly built, and towered over her own not insubstantial five foot nine by a good five or six inches. Six foot four of sheer power, hard muscle, and sex appeal. His broad, darkly tanned shoulders gleamed with moisture. Salt water glittered like tiny diamonds in the hair on his chest and on the silky dark hair on his thickly muscled legs. His hands and feet were enormous.

"Understandable." His mocking and enigmatic gaze took in her clinging clothes, bare feet, and grim hold on the railing as his boat rode the swells.

There wasn't a thing she could do about her appearance, so she didn't bother fiddling. Besides, she didn't want to draw attention to the wet transparency of her blouse. Not that he looked the type to be crazed by lust. Especially for a woman like her. Perversely disappointed, she realized that far from being crazed with lust at the sight of her size A boobs, the pirate hadn't even noticed he could see right through her shirt.

That one, piercing, whiskey-colored eye locked onto her,

and Tally's stomach did a weird little somersault. Adrenaline still raced through her body at a furious clip.

She took a deep, shuddering breath. "Tally Cruise." Pleased she sounded coherent under the circumstances, she thrust out her hand and smiled.

"Michael Wright." He took her hand, not with his right, but his left. His thumb brushed the back of her knuckles. Little zings of electricity shot up her arm. "You've got a few scrapes here."

Surprised, Tally glanced down. His hand was dark and so big, her pale fingers almost disappeared inside his grasp. Her knuckles were red and scratched. Probably from trying to cling to the hull of his boat. "I can't fee—they don't hurt." As lovely as it was standing there holding his hand, Tally gently extricated her fingers. The electrical charge went away. "I'm okay. Really." She took a deliberate step in retreat. "Did you see what happened?"

"Hard to miss," he said dryly. "Your boat went kaplooie."

Tally blinked at his easy dismissal of two lives and a million-dollar boat. "Is that the technical term for it? Did you happen to see if anyone else was thrown clear?"

"Nope. You're it. There isn't even a fish alive for a three-mile radius." He reached out and touched her upper arm. "You *were* hurt," he said roughly. "You're bleeding."

She twisted her shoulder a bit and glanced down. The sleeve of her white blouse was stained pink. She hadn't noticed it before, but the moment she saw the seeping blood, the wound stung like fire. "Damn, my stitches must've opened."

"I'll take a look when we're clear of this storm."

"It'll wait. The salt water was probably good for it."

"I'll check, anyway." He turned his back and started doing something to a rope and pulley nearby.

A take-charge kind of guy was exactly who she wanted to be with if she was with anyone in this weather. "Do you work for my father?" she asked curiously.

He threw her an amused glance over his shoulder. "Do I look like I work for anyone?"

She tilted her head, water dripping icily down her neck. "Looks can be deceptive."

"Can't they, though."

She rubbed her hands up and down her upper arms, chilled to the bone and shivering in earnest now. "My God, what could've caused the boat to explode like that? A leak in the engine or something?"

"No."

Hmm. "What can I do to help you?"

"Know anything about boats?"

"Other than one end is pointy? Nothing."

"Then stay out of my way."

"That I can do."

While the pirate heaved and ho'd, Tally's mind raced.

Arnaud was a wealthy man in his own right. He had hot and cold running peons to do his bidding wherever he went. Yet he'd taken the *Serendipity* out without a full crew—except for Lu, who'd remained below the entire time they were onboard. It wasn't until they were well out of the harbor that Tally had even noticed they were alone.

And knowing Arnaud, she'd immediately become suspicious. He'd tried to make a pass. Had he decided that if he got her out on the water he could force himself on her? To what purpose?

Tally frowned. They hadn't seen each other in years, and their last meeting hadn't exactly been stellar. She'd politely declined his proposal then, as she'd done his proposition today.

He wanted something from her. Something important enough to make him ignore the danger of a storm. But, what? Not sex. Sex was the package he wrapped things in to make them appear more palatable.

She shivered, and used both hands to pull at her shirt, which clung uncomfortably to her wet skin. She might never know what Arnaud had in mind.

The boat bounced hard on the waves. Reflexively, Tally shot out a hand to brace herself on the closest stable object.

She stared in horror at her own pale fingers gripping the front waistband of the pirate's shorts.

His purple Hawaiian shorts were now riding low, very low, on his hips, as the weight of her hand dragged the fabric down.

And down. . . .

Chapter Two

Tally yanked her hand away and stuck it behind her back. "God. I am so sorry." She'd *touched* him. Felt the heat of his tanned skin, felt the crisp hairs at his groin . . . felt . . . oh, man.

"Nice try, but no cigar. Want to go for two out of three?"

Tally closed her eyes and blew out a breath. "Oh, this day just gets better and better."

"It's certainly looking up for me." With an amused glance, the pirate hitched his shorts back over the sharp angle of his hipbones. There'd been no sign of a tan line. "Hold on to the rail until I can get you hooked up."

With long, perfectly balanced strides, he went to the stern, where he lifted the top of a teak bench and dug through the contents.

Tally gripped the slick rail with both hands. "Can we go look for them before they drown?" she shouted to be heard over the pounding of the waves. She forced her gaze off the pirate's broad, tanned back and spread her feet for balance instead of sacrificing herself to Poseidon.

"No point." He returned and handed her a life jacket attached to a harness. "Put this on." He snapped something on the back of the jacket and connected it to a line running along the deck.

Tally was grateful beyond belief that he wasn't going to say any more about her grabbing on to his dipstick. "Of course there's a point. Arnaud and Lu might very well be trying to stay afloat as we speak."

"Doubt it."

"Oh, come on! I made it. Lu's lived on Paradise all his life. He must know how to swim, for godsake! And Arnaud's a much better swimmer than I am. That water's *deep*—they must be exhausted by now. We have to hurry."

"Lady, you're just not getting this, are you? Your boyfriend didn't make it. Consider yourself lucky."

"He wasn't my boyfr—who cares *what* he was. Is." The creak of torqued wood sounded eerily like a woman screaming. Tally hunched her shoulders. "I'm sure they were thrown clear just like I was."

"Didn't see anyone else thrown clear."

"Did you see me thrown clear?" Tally demanded, fastening the front of the jacket with numb fingers. The life jacket came almost to her knees and smelled faintly fishy. But it was dry, and it cut the wind. She felt the hum of an auxiliary engine beneath her feet.

"Yeah, I saw you."

"So Arnaud could've—"

"He didn't."

The possibility of Arnaud being dead refused to register. Just a little while ago he was at her side—strong, vibrant, healthy, invincible, unscrupulous, and lying through his perfect white teeth. Damn it. He was too oily to drown. He must be floating out there somewhere.

Tiny, stinging whips of wet hair blew against her cheeks. She shivered despite the jacket, and tucked the short strands of her hair behind her ears. A quick glance skyward showed how low the dark clouds had dropped. The wind howled. Waves pounded at the boat as if demanding entry.

Angry white foam danced along the lip of water, spraying across the teak deck. In the few moments she'd been aboard, the waves had grown and the wind had picked up. Sea spray sent needle-like stabs at her exposed skin. It was obvious, even to a landlubber, that they were in for a major storm. If the waves had been this high when she was in the water, she would have drowned.

Despite his words, she staggered over to the rail, leaned into the wind, and searched the sea for signs of life. Wind and waves had torn the remnants of the elegant yacht to shreds, then swallowed the pieces whole. The choppy water surged, drowning the flames still struggling in the wind. A dwindling flame garden of burning debris and whitecaps. The *Serendipity* was gone as if it had never been.

"Hey." Her host grabbed her by the back of the jacket and hauled her upright. "I'm not fishing you out again if you fall overboard."

Their eyes met. He wasn't kidding. "Not exactly a people person, are you?" she said.

He grimaced and released her. Tally turned back to the rail, oddly disconcerted by his touch, even through the jacket. She didn't lean as far out this time, but she strained to see in the growing darkness.

Tally suspected Arnaud's boat was probably Trevor Church's boat, and if that was the case, her father was not only going to be absolutely livid about the loss of property, he was also going to blow his stack if she didn't at least make an attempt to find Bouchard. Damn it.

"I'll pay you to help me find him," Tally said briskly, turning to face him.

An eyebrow rose. "Yeah? How much?"

"A thousand dollars." He didn't so much as blink at the offer. "Are you for real? Okay, two thousand."

"Only two? He couldn't've been very important to you."

She considered Bouchard a slimy turd, a necessary evil. On the other hand, the pirate wasn't going to risk life and boat if he knew she felt that way. "Five? Ten? Twenty thousand? How much will it take?"

"How much you got on you?"

She held her arms out. "Not a whole hell of a lot. But I have traveler's checks back at—I'll buy your boat from you." She narrowed her eyes when he didn't answer. This was nuts. She was standing out here in the middle of a typhoon negotiating with a pirate to save the life of a man she'd just as soon drown herself. "You rat. Okay. I'll pay you to captain it. *And* I'll pay you to help me find Arnaud."

He folded his arms across his massive, hairy chest. "Hmmm."

"Is that a yes?"

He paused for so long, she thought he'd gone into a coma with his eyes—*eye*—open. "Keep a sharp lookout. This is going to be fast and dirty." He strode past her, heading for the wheelhouse.

Fast and dirty, it was. While she doggedly clung to the railing in the prow, he guided the boat within feet of burning timbers and bits of the *Serendipity,* weaving in and around flotsam. There was nothing to identify the bits and pieces floating on the waves as a luxury, seventy-five-foot yacht.

She felt a chill that had little to do with the wind. If she hadn't been thrown clear, she wouldn't be alive to tell the tale.

It was obvious Arnaud and Lu were gone. Dead.

Her fingers tightened on the polished wood rail as she strained to check every piece of debris floating on the surface of the choppy water, anyway. Occasionally a sudden rebellious flare, or the smoldering glow of embers, or a lacy froth of phosphorescence broke the turbulent, black water, but there were no signs of life.

A relentless wave pounded the hull, then crashed around Tally's bare feet. She staggered, braced herself, and held more tightly on to the solid railing. Not only was it now almost fully dark, she realized she was out to open sea with a man she didn't know. And no one knew where she was.

Had she jumped from the frying pan into the fire?

Had she had a choice?

The skies opened, releasing a torrent of rain that raced across the surface of the water like a thick gray curtain. Big, fat drops fell closer and closer together in heavy sheets. Tally lifted her face. The rain stung her skin, and tasted sweet on her tongue, making her feel gloriously alive.

Out of the corner of her eye she saw a bright light blinking, and turned to see Michael Wright in the wheelhouse aiming a flashlight beam at her as if she understood Morse code. She got the message. He wanted her inside.

Tally moved away from the rail. The swells had grown stronger, more erratic, more furious. It was as if hell had risen up from the bottom of the ocean and was now having a temper tantrum. She held on to whatever she could for the few yards she had to traverse, grateful for the line anchoring her to the deck as her bare feet slipped and skidded on wet wood.

The door to the wheelhouse flew open. Michael grabbed her arm and hauled her bodily inside. The wind slammed the door behind her.

"God Almighty, woman. Do you have a fu-fricking death wish or something? Unhook yourself and get below." He gripped the wildly vibrating wheel, then shouted over his shoulder, "Use whatever you can find. Tie yourself to the bunk. And *stay* there till I come for you."

The warm, stuffy air inside the wheelhouse contrasted sharply to the bite of the clean-smelling storm. A monstrously huge black cat lay curled on the instrument panel above the wheel. He opened one green eye and twitched a chewed-up ear at her.

"Hey, Cat."

Ears back, the animal hissed at her.

Lovely. The pirate kept a pet demon.

Tally stared back at the beast until its eye closed, then concentrated on undoing the clasps on the front of the bulky jacket. Her fingers were stiff and clumsy. She swore under her breath and tried again.

Michael held out one hand and made a "come here" motion. "Turn."

Without taking his intense focus from the open sea ahead, he swiftly unfastened the safety harness, then swiveled her face front and worked the closures on the jacket. Cold air bathed Tally's wet clothing and already chilled skin. His fingers felt warm through the wet cloth of her shirt.

"Th-Thanks." Instead of feeling the cold, she felt a rush of heat and stepped away. All this fear and adrenaline rushing around inside her was screwing up her normal, logical self. Her response to the man was as unexpected as it was intriguing.

Apparently, by the look on his face, *he* hadn't felt anything. "Get below," he said, voice grim, jaw set. He moved about on bare feet. Moved fast, but efficiently.

"Should I take your cat with me?"

"Don't *have* a cat."

The black furry thing right in front of him blinked.

"What's that?"

"Snap to it, sweetheart. We've got about seventeen minutes before the tail end of that typhoon hits us."

Tally almost smiled at the precision. "Exactly *seventeen* minutes? How could you *possibly* know that?"

"Want to stand there and debate it with a stopwatch?"

"No. What can I do to help?" She had to shout, and even then she wasn't sure he'd heard her.

"Told you. Below."

Waves crashed violently over the deck, foaming and grabbing, as though trying to suck the boat down. Tally gripped onto a bulwark and held on. The boat did a dizzying lurch, then rocked unevenly as the water rose and dropped like a free-falling roller coaster.

She staggered to the hatch and pulled at the door. The deck bounced beneath her feet, and the heavy door slipped out of her grasp with a bang. Off-balance, she smashed her leg into something sharp and she stumbled again, this time into a solid hard body. She threw her arms around the pirate's waist and held on as the yacht did a fandango on the waves.

Pain radiated up her thigh, stinging like fire. "Ow. Ow. Ow!" Eyes squeezed shut, she pressed her face against his warm, bare back and clung like a limpet.

"Jesus, woman. What are you? A Jonah?"

He plucked her off his back like a piece of lint. "If you

won't go below, then hang on to something that's not me, and stay out of the way."

Tally grabbed the back of the chair he wasn't using. The cat gave her the evil eye from the dashboard. She figured the pirate's familiar had already done the curse thing. The boat plowed sideways into the mounting waves. Sky up one minute, the black sea the next.

One of the windshield wipers, protruding like a mutant eyebrow hair from the windshield, snapped off as a wave broke over the wheelhouse. Tally flinched and held on tighter.

Her stomach protested vehemently, and she swallowed the nausea through sheer will. The boat rocked and pitched, the movement uneven and terrifying. Desperately Tally searched her brain for a prayer. Any prayer. *Now I lay me down to sleep*... No! Not that one. Hail Mary something, something. She wasn't Catholic. Oh, God, she should've gone to church more often. And Jesus, now definitely wasn't the time to blaspheme.

Fingers completely numb from gripping the chair, she kept her gaze pinned, with manic attention, on the pirate's large, strong hands on the wheel. Backlit eerily by the red lights on the instrument panel, those few teeny, tiny red lights were all that held her together.

She hated the dark. Hated, hated, hated it.

She wasn't that fond of roller coasters, either, and this was about seven hundred times worse. Putting the two together was overkill and proved that God had a sense of humor. Maybe she didn't want to pray after all. The boat hit a trough with the force of a ten-ton cement truck slamming into a granite mountain. Every bone in her body jarred.

Dear God, how long could the pirate ship last in this onslaught? Her brain pulled up every water movie she'd ever seen. *Titanic. The Abyss. The Deep. Jaws*... Oh, Lord. *The Perfect Storm*....

There were things she still wanted to do in her life. Off the top of her head she couldn't think of a one right now. But topping her list was dying in her own bed in Chicago. Dry. Of old age.

The noise was deafening. Liquid thunder slammed against the hull. Again and again. An incessant creak and crack of distressed wood torqued unmercifully. Giant fists of rain pounded the roof of the cabin. The low pulse, more a sensation than an actual sound, of the engine beneath their feet, throbbed like a primal animal roaring death throes.

Tally's stomach rose with the next wave, leaving a terrifying feeling of free floating, then came crashing down in the next plunge as if all her internal organs weighed a thousand pounds.

As terrifying as it was, the sheer power of the storm was exhilarating. The experience was surreal, and her thumping heart and racing pulse seemed perfectly timed to the frantic beat of the water below the boat and the rain pounding on them from above.

There was no doubt they were doomed.

Tally did what she always did when she reached the end of her rope.

She sang.

Loudly. Cheerfully. Defiantly.

"The sun will come up, to-mor-row . . ."

If the man battling the elements heard her, he gave no indication. She finished the songs she knew from *Annie,* then started on *Phantom of the Opera.*

Tally sang to keep the fear tamped down.

She sang to defy the storm.

She sang to make sure God knew where she was since she couldn't think of an appropriate prayer.

And she sincerely hoped He liked show tunes.

He should've let her drown.

Tally Cruise had the most God-awful voice Michael had ever heard, and he'd heard some doozies in Asian karaoke bars. Fortunately the violence of the storm, and the thunder of the waves, drowned out most of it. He ignored her just as he did the pounding of his heart, faking himself out that it was the rush of facing off against the bastard Sea making his blood race and his palms sweat.

Vibrations shimmied up his arms, cruising his muscles bulge and strain. He ignored the ache in his legs from trying to maintain his balance, and the sting in his eye, half-blinded by sweat. The damn ocean fought for control of the boat. A lesser engineered vessel couldn't've survived this long. *Thank you, Jake.* Michael held on, fingers welded to the wheel.

He was *not* going into that goddamn, black water. If they went down, it wouldn't be for lack of trying on his part. *Ah, Jesus . . .*

Almost numb with shock seconds after hitting the icy water, Michael moved into action with an instinct born of countless hours of training. God, he loved this. The danger. The adrenaline. The immediacy of cramming your whole life into a single second.

Even with his illuminated Tac board, which combined compass, depth gauge, and watch, visibility was limited to six inches in the inky black water. Beside him, swim-buddy, Hugo Caletti, shared the danger as they made their way down toward the night's target. . . .

A mighty *CRACK* brought Michael back. Mouth dry, heart manic, he shook his head to clear it of the flashback. He had enough trouble in the here and now.

"Shit and double shit." He'd lost the main mast.

For a moment, the sixty-two-foot pole hovered overhead, as if held by an invisible hand. Then, with a wrench that sent the *Nemesis* gyrating, it twirled into the wild, wet wind, rigging and lines trailing like tentacles. "Hell!"

"When you wish upon a star . . ."

Behind him, Tally continued warbling, her voice not only hideously off-key, but hoarse as well. Great. Just great. Why couldn't the mast have knocked her out before it blew out to sea?

An hour crawled by before they escaped the full fury of the

monsoon. By then, thank the Lord, his passenger's voice had faded to nothing. The waves calmed to rolling swells, the wind died down, and the rain drizzled to a stop.

Shafts of amber sunlight filtered between the thinning clouds. He drew his first easy breath in what felt like a year.

"Is it over?" she asked, voice thick and husky.

Michael peeled his numb fingers off the wheel. "Looks like." He set the boat on automatic pilot and turned, taking in her appearance. Soaking wet, shivering to beat the band, her face dead white, lips tinged blue. "Go below and find something dry to put on. We'll be out here until she blows through, might as well get comfortable."

She didn't move. Her white-knuckled grip appeared permanently attached to the back of his chair. She licked the teeth marks on her lower lip. "What about you?"

"I'll do the same. Hey, Luck? Here, boy." The cat crawled from beneath the wheel and limped over on three legs to be picked up. Both man and beast headed toward the door. Michael pulled it open. "After you."

Tally passed by him, careful not to make bodily contact. She was acutely aware of him, all her senses ultrasensitive and almost vibratingly alert. Darn it. It was pitch black down there. "Is there a li—" He reached over her head and hit the switch. "Oh. Thanks."

The salon was small. Too small for the two of them. The storm had tossed everything he owned all over the place. Clothes, shoes, papers, and open books littered every flat surface. A sock hung over a wall light. A pair of sunglasses lay in a corner as if crushed underfoot and kicked aside.

He caught her perusal out of his good eye. "Maid's year off. Here." He bent to gather a scatter of papers off the floor, then opened a locker, shoved them inside, then locked it. Why he bothered with those when the place was a shambles Tally had no idea.

He opened another locker and handed her a rumpled, hopefully clean, pair of Hawaiian shorts, and a creased white T-shirt. "Head's that way." He turned her toward the back of the boat by her shoulders. "I'll take a look at that arm when you're done."

A buzzy electrical current passed from his hand through her body and sizzled tantalizingly just under her skin. Tally refrained from flinging herself into the pirate's arms and holding on to his hard body. Tightly. It wasn't lust, she told herself firmly. She would've flung herself on any man who'd managed to keep her alive through that storm.

He was big. Solid. Unafraid.

Strung as tight as a rubber band, heart still in her throat, Tally craved a little of that confidence rubbed off onto her. Instead, she drew a deep shuddering breath and stepped away.

"Make it snappy," he told her as she opened the narrow door to the head. "And don't take all the hot water."

Door closed, Tally sank down onto the closed toilet seat and buried her face in her hands. Emotions on overload, she sat for several minutes. Now that she could breathe again, she had trouble drawing air into her lungs. She couldn't move. Couldn't assimilate all that had happened in the last few hours.

Arnaud had been a louse, but he didn't deserve to die alone, and in the dark, like that. God, he must've been terrified. . . .

He pounded on the door. Tally jumped to her feet fighting a fresh surge of adrenaline. "Up and at 'em, honey. If you're not going to shower, let me in. I'm freezing my ass off out here."

Tally turned on the faucet and took the fastest shower on record. She emerged five minutes later, slightly warmer, and extremely self-conscious in his baggy orange shorts and T-shirt. Her Wonderbra had been far too wet to put on again, and she held the bundle of wet clothes against her chest as a shield. "That did the trick. Thanks for letting me go first. I was as quick as I could."

"No problem." He gave her an ironic look. "If you hang on to those wet things like that, the shower will prove useless.

Toss everything in the dryer. Sandwiches and hot coffee in the galley. Help yourself."

The door to the minuscule bathroom closed with a click.

Lord, how was she going to handle her father when he got back? As slimy as Arnaud might've been, he'd played the role of intermediary superbly. So superbly he'd once managed to slither right into her bed. Tally shuddered. That counted as one of life's Big Mistakes.

"I'm sorry you drowned. But I am so freaking annoyed with you, I could *scream.* And just so you know—the sex was lousy. And to top it all off, you never did tell me why my father sent for me, you creep."

"Meow."

The black cat sat regally on the table staring at her out of unblinking eyes. He meowed again. She stared back. "I'm going to have some hot coffee. Is that all right with you?" The cat cocked its head and continued its unblinking, malevolent green stare. "Well, aren't you just charming?"

She paused to refold an open map, spread half-on, and half-off the table. Moving through the cabin, she inserted a Post-it note into an open book as a bookmark, closed the novel, and returned it to a secured shelf above the sofa. Next, she gathered broken pieces of his sunglasses before someone stepped on them again.

The galley was small and efficient. Forcing herself to think only on the most superficial level, Tally found a compact washer and dryer cleverly hidden, and tossed in whatever clothing she found littering the floor. That done, she made quick work of the few dishes and utensils in the sink, before she wiped crumbs and butter off the Corian countertops.

Tidying up helped her focus on something outside herself. And right now that was a blessing. Satisfied with her contribution to his housekeeping, she folded the damp dish towel and hung it over the handle of the oven to dry.

But when she reached for the Thermos, the cat, sitting on the stove top, hissed at her. "What? You want a cup, too?"

Lucky gave her a superior look before contorting to lick himself.

"I'll have you know that children, the elderly, and small animals usually love me," she informed him as she poured hot, fragrant coffee into a mug. "You're just being perverse."

Tally went back to the table, then stood for a few moments admiring a beautifully rendered framed watercolor hanging on the teak wall above the sofa. The small rustic cabin nestled in snow-covered pine trees seemed an odd choice for artwork on a boat.

She slid onto the cool leather seat, the thick mug cradled between her hands, and inhaled the scent of good French roast. She let the heat swirl down inside her.

While compact, the boat had everything a person could possibly want—other than dry land. Her father's boat had been bigger, more expensive, flashier. Trevor Church loved the sizzle as much as the steak . . . which, she supposed, was why his too tall, unattractive daughter was such a disappointment. . . . Tally looked around for a distraction. All she needed were a few minutes to slap patches on her self-control.

She could always polish—but the gleaming teak didn't need it. The curved banquet seat on which she sat was covered in royal blue, tufted leather, and a blue and tan plaid carpet covered the floor. All the comforts of home.

Her stomach jumped, and her pulse refused to settle down. It made no sense. No sense at all. Boats didn't just blow up for no reason. She shuddered, lifting the mug to her mouth.

The bathroom door snicked open.

The room immediately got smaller as the pirate emerged wearing nothing but wrinkly fluorescent lime green shorts and steam.

Lord, he was yummy. Tally had a disconcerting urge to rush over and rub her face on his six-pack abs.

"Are you warm enough?" Michael asked.

She was hot all over. And it had nothing to do with her

shower. Tally pressed the mug to her mouth for a moment before she remembered to take a sip. "I'm like the baby bear. Juuust right."

His lips twitched. "Okay, little bear, take off the shirt so I can check your arm."

"I don't need to remove my top—my arms stick out the sides, in case you haven't noticed."

"Honey, I've noticed everything about you, up to, and including, this little mole right here." He brushed a finger under her right ear, and the small hairs all over her body stood to attention.

Tally discovered there were other ways to drown. And she was going under for the second time.

Chapter Three

The injury to the back of her arm was long and raw; several stitches had pulled out, probably while she'd been swimming for her life. Blood seeped slowly from the four-inch gash on her pale olive skin.

Michael held her gently by the elbow as he inspected the wound. "The salt water did a good job, but some of the stitches should be replaced. Is there a doctor on Paradise?"

"I don't think so."

For a plain little thing she was profoundly sensual. Except for her wounds, her skin was clear and creamy, eminently touchable. Tousled, damp, black hair framed her face. Guileless blue eyes watched him with misplaced trust. The longer he held her gaze, the faster the pulse at the base of her throat throbbed.

Michael felt a twinge of admiration for her as she maintained eye contact. Unable to resist, he brushed a thumb over the soft skin of her inner elbow. Her long, black lashes fluttered, and she drew in a sweet, sharp breath at the contact but she didn't look away. The rush of lust he felt was a surprise. He'd felt nothing in nearly a year.

Perfect.

Not only would she make a powerful weapon to use against Church, seducing her would be a pleasure. Michael abruptly released her. He wasn't interested in *feeling*. He'd smile and say the right things. He'd play to her emotions until those big blue eyes of hers shone with anticipation . . . and then he'd lower the boom without a qualm.

All he had to do was remember another time and another set of trusting blue eyes.

There'd be no deviation from his chosen path. In the end, Tally Church Cruise would be just another casualty of war.

"I have some butterfly bandages in my first-aid kit. Should do the job."

Her lashes dropped as she inspected a scratch on her thigh. "Great. Thanks."

About to rise, Michael glanced down at her legs. "Jesus," he muttered, noticing the abrasions there for the first time. "What the hell happened to you? Were you in some sort of accident?"

"Several," Tally admitted wryly, blue eyes ironic as he gently touched her leg.

The secret, Michael warned himself, was to gentle her to his touch without getting sucked in to the sensual haze himself. He could do that. All he had to do was ignore how soft, how sweet, how . . . shit. He rose. "Stay put. I'll get the first-aid supplies."

"I'll be right here."

He paused, unable to resist brushing her cheek with one finger. "Try not to damage any other body parts while I'm gone."

Tally smiled. "I'll do my best, Captain. Will you be gone long?"

"All the way to the galley and back."

"Six whole feet? I'll try to restrain my party instincts in your absence."

"Are you a party girl?" he asked from the galley.

She chuckled. "Hardly."

Her husky laugh went right through him. Michael shot up a mental block. The woman was Trevor Church's daughter. A means to an end. Nothing more. "Do you always sing when you're scared?"

"It's a lot easier and more convenient to sing than to lug around a cello."

His lips twitched. "Can you play the cello?"

"Not as well as I sing," she said with a smile. "And it sure beats screaming."

He smiled, because her unfortunate singing voice was pretty damn close to screaming. "Yeah, I'm sure it does." He returned with a small first-aid box and crouched at her feet.

"I can do tha—" He looked up at the same time, and she jabbed him in the eyebrow with her outstretched hand.

She jerked back. "*Caray!* I am *so* sorry . . ."

He glanced up, angling his head because she was on his blind side. "Honey, I only have one eye as it is. Want to just sit still and let me take care of this?"

"Sorry." She sighed. "I can't believe how clumsy I've been lately. I used to have perfect balance. I even learned how to walk a tightrope once. Of course, I was only seven at the time."

The scrapes on her knees were several weeks old and didn't require much attention. Michael made busywork as he listened. "Not something every kid learns," he murmured, dabbing on the antiseptic both of them pretended was needed. "Did you want to run away and join a circus?"

"Nope." She smiled. "My mother and I stayed outside Paris for about a year. One of the other boarders was an acrobat. He gave me lessons in his spare time."

"Have you used this unusual talent since?"

She grinned, blue eyes filled with amusement. "There's not much call for acrobatics in my line of work."

"Which is?" There was a fresh scratch on the back of her slender ankle. "Does this hurt?"

"No—yes, a bit. I'm a translator."

Michael applied antiseptic to the cut, then smoothed on an unnecessary Band-Aid. Her calf muscles were long and firm and led his gaze to her thighs, and beyond that to . . . *Knock off this shit, Lieutenant.* "Do much traveling?"

"Not if I can help it." Her voice was dry as she shifted to allow the cat to step onto her bare legs. Green eyes stared at Michael unblinkingly, as if the animal were saying, "See? I'm where *you* want to be." The cat draped himself over Tally's thighs with a put-upon sigh.

"I'm the proverbial homebody," Tally said, stroking Lucky's dense, black fur.

A homebody who got blown off yachts, was covered in scrapes and bruises, and whose father just happened to be the meanest, most sadistic son of a bitch Michael had encountered. And in his occupation—*former* occupation—he'd run into the worst.

"Where's home?" he asked, realizing that he'd been cupping the back of her calf while listening to her. He stroked his thumb rhythmically across the sweet curve at the back of her knee and watched with satisfaction as her eyes hazed.

It took a moment for her to answer. "Chicago. What about you?"

"You're sitting in it."

A nomad. Tally mentally shook herself out of a sensual fog and almost sighed. It figured. The first man she'd been attracted to in years was just passing through.

She relaxed against the thickly padded seat while Michael inspected her legs for injury, his breath warm on her shin. The feel of his slightly calloused hands on her skin was more arousing than it was soothing, but if he felt the same way he was much better at hiding it than she was.

"This poor cat doesn't look too lucky to me," she said dreamily, enjoying the sensation of the cat's silky fur beneath her palm. Loving the feel of Michael's hands stroking *her,* Tally almost purred more loudly than the cat.

"Are you kidding? He'd just used up his ninth life when I ran across him in a back alley in Hong Kong."

And what, Tally mused, had Michael Wright been doing in a back alley in Hong Kong? "Not literally, I hope?"

"Nah." Tally heard the smile in his voice. "Didn't bother him that he was cornered by the biggest, ugliest mutt in creation. He maneuvered just fine on three legs. Once we'd shown the dog who was boss, Lucky followed me back to the *Nemesis*. Been on board ever since."

"Ah. I love a happy ending."

"Not a lot of those around."

"No, I guess not. But it's nice to believe in them. Arnaud and Lu could've used one." She ran her fingernails over the cat's head, across his back, and to the tip of his tail. The cat arched under her hand. "Thanks for rescuing me and giving me a shot at finding a happier ending than they got."

"No thanks necessary. It's the law of the sea."

"Is that anything like the code of the West?"

His grin revealed even, white teeth. "Sort of. Speaking of the sea, what brings you all the way to Tahiti? Vacation?"

"First in three years," Tally admitted, trying not to wince at the icy sting on a particularly raw spot on her left leg.

He glanced up. "You're a workaholic?"

"No. Well, maybe." She really, really needed to do something about her boring social life when she got back. Work had become a replacement for the family she so desperately wanted. How pathetic was that? "I enjoy my job, and usually let the employees with families take the best vacation weeks. Don't get me wrong—I'm not completely altruistic, really. It's just that when vacation time comes, I'm not that enthusiastic about going anywhere. I usually end up staying home and fiddling about in my garden. I can do that weekends, so why take off weeks and weeks?"

"And this time?"

She smiled. "My father sent the ticket and invited me to come for a visit."

"Are you close?"

"Not really," Tally said wistfully. "He left when I was five. We've never had an opportunity to connect, but maybe we can now that I'm an adult."

"Parents divorced?"

"Never married. My stepdad adopted me when he and Bev, my mother, married years later." God, Tally thought, not for the first time, she'd used up so much time yearning for her "real" father that she'd wasted what should've been wonderful years with the man who'd treated her as his own.

"What better place to connect than an island paradise. No distractions. Sea and surf. Sounds ideal."

"I hope so. And not a moment too soon, either. I swear I've become my own worst enemy in the last couple of months. My boss almost forced me onto the plane. He claimed I'd better leave town before I got run over by a bus." She smiled.

"A run-in with a bus did all this?" Michael motioned with the pink stained cotton at her scrapes and bruises. His slightly too long hair had dried, and she noticed how the sun had bleached the shaggy ends. She resisted the urge to touch. His hair. His bare shoulders. His face.

"Thank God, no buses involved. This one"—Tally pointed at her left knee—"was when I tripped *up* the stairs going to the El. This one when I bumped into some guy in the dark and wound up tumbling down the stairs at the movie theater. You'd think I'd just learned to walk. If I wasn't falling over my own feet, it was near misses with falling flower pots and eating the wrong mushrooms at the deli."

She wasn't intrinsically clumsy. Although over the last few weeks she'd begun to wonder if she had some sort of hex following her, because she'd suddenly become accident-prone.

Three years without a vacation was too long. This break in her routine was way overdue. Of course having the boat blow up could hardly be attributed to exhaustion and the need for a vacation. By surviving, Tally reckoned she'd broken the jinx.

Unfortunately, close proximity to this man made all her nerves and muscles jump to attention like a hormone-driven adolescent. Since she'd never experienced anything like it, she was as fascinated as she was perplexed. Was there such a thing as survivor's lust?

"Sounds dire."

"It isn't. I just need a long, relaxing vacation, and where better than Paradise?"

"The ideal place to relax," he agreed. "Turn around a bit so I can get at the scratch on your arm."

Tally let out a little shriek as the antiseptic bit into the open wound.

"Sorry," Michael said gruffly, then blew on the sting. Tally almost melted into the cushions. "This is healing fine. A little seepage where the stitches were pulled. The butterfly bandages are tucked into the left side there." He nodded at the first-aid box sitting open on the table. "Hand me one, will you?"

Tally sorted through the contents with her fingertip until she found the bandages. "From what I've heard, Paradise isn't that big. What does your father do way out here? I imagine he's not old enough to be retired . . . or is he?"

Tally pulled the paper off the bandage and held it stuck on the end of her finger until he was ready. "No. He's a boat broker. Buys and sells luxury craft."

"They say the prices they sell those boats for are sheer piracy." He took the adhesive strip and applied it gently to her arm. His hair brushed against her chin as he bent over her. The masculine smell of him made her heart beat faster.

Lordie Miss Claudie, she had it bad. Tally smiled. "I guess so. He's not going to be happy about the *Serendipity* going kaplooie, I bet."

He nudged her bare foot, and an electrical charge shot up Tally's leg. She jerked out of his way and bumped her knee on the underside of the table. Her elbow connected with her still full coffee mug. Hot liquid spilled over the table and dripped onto the floor.

"Easy."

Right. Her cheeks felt hot. "Let me get a rag—"

"Stay put."

"Do you have any stain remover?"

He glanced up and gave her a wry look. "You know, I meant to ask Martha Stewart for some the last time she dropped by, but—"

"Fine. Liquid detergent should work. Shall I—"

"It's only a carpet."

"If you use regular soap, it'll make the stain permanent, or at lea—"

"Relax, okay? What were you and your friend doing away from harbor just before a typhoon?"

"We weren't aware there was going to be a typhoon. Trust me, if I had known, no one could've pried me from dry land."

"At least this'll give you something to talk about when you get back home, right? What I did on my Tahitian vacation . . ."

"Or, how to survive a yacht explosion and live to tell about it," Tally said dryly. "Same goes for you, I suppose. Where were you headed before the storm broke?"

"Sailing around the world to see what I can see. I'd planned to stop at Paradise to replenish supplies and take on fresh water." He shrugged. "Hadn't considered staying any longer than a couple of hours, but now it looks like I'll need to make time to have some repairs done, and to order a new mast before continuing." He ran a finger lightly over her abraded knee, and Tally sucked in a sharp breath as a shot of pure lust traveled up her leg.

"Paradise is about twenty miles from here," Michael said conversationally, holding her eyes. A surge of heat traveled along her nerve endings, and her mouth went dry. "Well, it was a hell of a lot closer before the storm hit. Still, we'll head back there—that's where you're staying, right?"

Tally licked her parched lips and blinked, almost hypnotized by the intensity and heat of his gaze. *Whew*. "R-Right. It's pretty small, and private. But a beautiful place to stop off for a few days if you have the time."

"I'll make the time." He gave her a slow smile, and her pulse rate went up. "Will you be spending all your time with your father? Or did you show up on Paradise with a lover? Boyfriend?" He frowned. "Husband?"

Between his touch and the flattering assumption she'd traveled with a lover, she didn't know whether to moan or laugh. "None of the above. I'm alone, with about a hundred and fifty of my father's—of the inhabitants."

"Your father?"

"Trevor Church. He owns Paradise Island."

"Impressive. The boat selling must be lucrative. You didn't answer my question."

Tally wasn't sure what the question in his eye was; she wasn't adept at reading that kind of heat. "It seems I've arrived for our shared vacation ahead of my father. Apparently he's been delayed for another two or three days."

"And they say no good deed goes unrewarded," Michael said, still smiling, although his eye seemed shadowed.

"I thought it was 'No good deed goes unpunished'?"

"Not in our case. My reward for being there when you needed rescuing is having you to myself for those days. This is perfect. You can show me the sights while my boat is being repaired, and you wait for your father."

Be still my heart. "I'm not sure how many sights there are to see, although it's breathtakingly beautiful. It's barely six miles long and three miles wide," Tally said dryly. "And while I'd love to play tour guide, I wouldn't be much good. This is the first time I've been there myself."

"Is that right? So this is a new acquisition for Daddy?"

"I think he bought it ten years ago. The timing was just never quite right for a visit. But here I am, so I'm going to enjoy every moment. We can explore together, if you like."

He paused what he was doing to look up at her, his large hand resting lightly on her thigh. "I like."

Tally had left the small reading light on when she'd crawled into the V-shaped bunk in the forward cabin. Now the light was out. She toggled the switch. Nothing. She fumbled in the dark and felt for the tiny lightbulb. Twisted this way, then that. Nothing. Damn.

She blinked back panic. The oddly shaped alcove felt microscopic, the blackness thick and weighted. Her heart began to race, and her skin felt clammy. "Here, Lucky," she whispered, hoping the cat would hear her and come bounding onto the bed to keep her company. "Come here, pretty boy."

Not a peep from the perverse animal. He was probably curled up on the foot of Michael's bed, dreaming of fat rats and endless ear rubs.

Michael Wright slept only ten feet away. There was absolutely nothing to be frightened of. As illogical as her fear might be, Tally's heartbeat escalated to a frantic rhythm, the precursor to a panic attack.

Not now! "I'm okay," she whispered. "I'm okay. I'm okay."

She swung her legs over the side of the bed. Perhaps if she sat on the sofa in the stateroom, the feeling of space would negate the attack. Perhaps. She wiped a hand down her damp face with a shaky hand.

Past the kitchen, hand on the counter to aid her, Tally found the leather sofa across the small room. It wasn't any lighter in here.

Had she been home, all the lights would be on. She'd rattle around in the kitchen, make a pot of tea, curl up on her sofa, and read until she got sleepy. *You're not in Kansas anymore, Dorothy,* she thought dryly, staring into the darkness.

It had literally been years since she'd had a panic attack. And damn it, she wasn't going to have one now, either. *Breathe in. Breathe out.*

All she required was a faint glow to ground her. She squeezed her eyes shut and tried to imagine the flicker of a small candle flame. She managed to conjure up a slim white taper with a glowing halo of light. The imaginary flame flickered, then died.

She jumped up and felt her way into the tiny galley and opened the oven door. No hope there, either. The power was out. Beneath her feet the boat gently rose and fell. If she really wanted to freak herself out, she could imagine she was riding on the back of a giant sea serpent. . . .

"Stop it!" Frankly she was more afraid of the oppressive darkness than at the thought of being gobbled down by an imaginary beast.

Holding on to the counter to orient herself, she paced back and forth. "Here comes the suuuun," she sang under her breath.

God she *hated* the way her heart threatened to pound right out of her chest, and how damp her palms were. She hated the fact that she was frightened of the dark like a little kid. She banged her shin on the table as she passed.

"Ow, damn it. Here comes the s—this is *not* working." She wiped her clammy hands down the side of her shorts. That's it. She couldn't stand this.

She felt her way across the room until she stood outside the door to Michael's cabin. The door slightly ajar, she rested her hand on the latch. "This is a bad idea, Tallulah, a bad, bad idea," she whispered. "Be a brave little toaster and go back to your own bed."

She pushed open the door. She couldn't hear him breathing. Was he even in here? Her heart skipped a beat. Then another.

"Can't sleep?"

A relieved sigh slipped from her throat. Next to light, the second-best defense against the darkness was good old human contact. "The lights are off."

He'd heard her singing under her breath out there, and tamped down the ridiculous notion that he found her God-awful singing oddly charming. "Power's out because of the storm," he lied. He'd turned off all the electrical a few minutes ago. She couldn't snoop in the dark, and it served another purpose. He could take several days fiddling with the generator when they limped into port tomorrow.

"Oh. Sure. Right—do you by any chance have any candles?"

"On a boat?" he asked, amused.

"Flashlight?"

Several. "Nope."

"You're not real good in emergencies, are you?"

"Just go to sleep. It'll be light in eight hours." He could barely make her out in the doorway, and his night vision was terrific.

Silence pulsed. She didn't move. "I-I have a bit of a phobia about the dark."

Yeah. He'd noticed. How to use the knowledge to his

advantage? "You could always come in here with me," he offered lightly. "I'll keep the boogeyman away."

She gave a small hiccuping laugh. "I'm not all that sure *you* aren't the boogeyman." But she didn't retreat shrieking in protest.

Michael patted the mattress. "Come on. It's a king-size. I'll stay on my side, if you behave yourself and stay on yours."

"This is probably not a good idea," she said in a husky little voice, taking the first step into his web.

"We're both adults. I'm not going to ravish you. We both need to get some sleep. If having company facilitates that, then go for it."

She padded over, bumped her legs on the foot of the bed, and felt her way around to the other side. Michael considered throwing the sheet over his nakedness, then decided not to. It was obvious she had lousy night vision.

The mattress depressed as she sat down, then swung her legs up. She lay flat. He almost expected her to cross her hands over her breasts like a Victorian maiden. Instead, she surprised him by rolling onto her side and facing him. "Thanks."

"No problem. Do you usually sleep with the lights on?"

"Pretty much." She was quiet for a moment. "I know it's silly. I just hate the dark. I normally have a night-light. As long as it's not pitch-dark, I'm okay."

"Some traumatic event in your past?"

"Not that I remember."

"Some traumatic event in your future?"

She gave a little laugh. "I don't think so."

"Will you be able to sleep now?"

"Hopefully. Thanks."

"No problem. 'Night."

"'Night."

Michael stacked his hands under his head and stared at the ceiling until he heard the soft sound of her even breathing.

Once, she'd known she was safe. She'd fallen asleep as quickly as a child.

Which was laughable. Without knowing it, Tally Church Cruise had presented herself like a sacrificial lamb stretched right out on his king-size altar. That Michael was going to use her was a given. He just needed to decide *how.*

Tally didn't usually remember her dreams, but even as she dreamed, she hoped she'd remember this one. The bed was incredibly soft, the darkness somehow comforting and not the least bit scary. Her back arched as a man's hand skimmed, soft as a whisper, across her naked breasts. The sensation was achingly familiar, as if she knew the man intimately.

There was no doubt this was a dream. Tally hadn't had sex in so long, she frequently imagined her body parts closing up from disuse.

Clever fingers found her nipples, pinching, rolling until the nubs felt engorged and tender. She moaned. It felt too good. His slightly rough hands were featherlight on her skin. He cupped each breast in turn, taunting her nipples until they ached.

The mattress shifted as he redistributed his weight. Then his hot, wet mouth closed around an aching peak.

Tally found her fingers tangled in the silk of his hair, holding his head against her breast. He sucked hard, drawing the nub into the furnace of his mouth. Tally cried out as sweet pain shot from her breast to her groin.

She was wet with desire, aching with need. She shifted her legs restlessly. Wanting him inside her, but knowing the anticipation was more titillating than the actual consummation. Tight as a bowstring, Tally arched her upper body off the bed when he bit down lightly on her left breast. Oh. God.

She grabbed his head and drew his face up to hers. The kiss was hot, out of control, a frantic mating of tongues and teeth.

Too good, too *real* to be a dre—

Chapter Four

Michael dragged his mouth away from hers. Tally moaned a complaint. "Is that a yes?" he demanded.

She breathed in the scent of him. Man. Heat. Need. "Y-Yes."

"Sure?"

In answer, she pulled his head down, and kissed him again.

Michael's knee nudged her legs apart as he slid over her; he rocked against the very heart of her desire, pushing inside the juicy opening of her body.

And slipped inside like a homecoming.

He was huge, rock hard, and moving the moment he sheathed himself. The sensation felt incredible. Unbearably aroused, Tally wrapped her arms around him. The muscles in his back were hard under satin-smooth skin. She reveled in the feel of him. Inside and out. Desire pure, sharp, and out of control made her arch her hips off the bed. He plunged all the way to her cervix, then withdrew. His mouth opened against her throat. He plunged again, sinking his teeth into her neck. Not hard enough to break the skin, but hard enough to send a bolt of pure sensation directly to where they were joined. His large hands clamped under her bottom, drawing her tightly against him as his fingers spread her cheeks.

"Wrap your legs around me," he demanded, breath hot against her sweat-dampened throat.

He withdrew; Tally followed the movement, raising her bottom off the bed, wrapping her legs high around his waist, opening herself for his penetration. He plunged deep.

The shocking intensity of her orgasm went on, and on, seeming to last forever. Tally's body trembled as each ripple of sensation ebbed and flowed, echoing back on each other, drawing out the pleasure until her mind blanked. Brilliant colors showered the darkness. Her arms tightened around him as the planet slipped off its axis.

When she finally came back to reality, head hung off the foot of the bed, she was as limp as an overcooked noodle, and Michael was still deep inside her.

"W—" Tally moistened dry lips, and tried again. "Wow. You're really good at that."

"I'm a man of many talents." His voice came soft against her ear, his breath brushing her cheek, her throat.

"How many talents?" she wanted to know. Just to be prepared, of course.

"How much time have you got?"

She smiled into the darkness. Hey, she didn't have a problem with his ego. Judging by what she'd just lived through, he wasn't bragging. "What happened to my clothes?"

With his weight on his elbows, Michael moved his hip in a maddeningly slow glide in. Out. In. "Technically they were *my* clo—Jesus. Do that again."

Tally contracted her PC muscle again, and had the satisfaction of hearing Michael groan. He withdrew, then pushed into her again. She was ready, her vagina tight and slick, as she pulsed around him. She relaxed the muscle until he was almost in to the hilt, then tightened it sharply. They groaned in unison as he pumped into her tight opening hard and fast.

He came in a hard, shuddering rush, then collapsed on top of her.

For several minutes the sound of their harsh breathing filled the darkness. Tally mustered enough energy to raise a heavy arm and stroke his sweaty face. Her fingers brushed his eye patch, but didn't linger. Poor, wounded warrior. She raised her head and pressed a soft kiss to the cool fabric of the patch. Michael captured her face between his broad palms and realigned her mouth downward.

"I love a woman with good muscle control," he told her thickly before crushing his mouth down on hers.

Tally demonstrated again just how controlled those muscles were. Michael groaned as he lifted his head. "Anything else you're afraid of?" he asked laconically, bracing some of his weight on his elbows.

Too weak to move, Tally's legs fell open on either side of his narrow hips. She liked the weight of him pressing her into the mattress. He was still semi-hard inside her, and her muscles flexed spasmodically around his shaft. "Thank God, no. And if I'd come up with this cure years ago, I probably wouldn't be afraid of the dark anymore, either."

She felt the brush of his hand against her sweat-dampened hair. "Not going to scream bloody murder because I took advantage of you while you slept?"

"Sorry, you can't take all the credit. I was awake for most of it," Tally said dryly. "I can't exactly claim maidenly modesty when I climbed into bed with you in the first place, can I?" Actually, she *was* embarrassed, now that it was over. Embarrassed that she'd been so uninhibited, embarrassed that she was lying, quite naked, beneath this stranger. For once, she was glad it was dark.

She wasn't in love with the man. Didn't know him. Yet it was the best sex she'd ever had. And she'd had some pretty good sex. Okay, that had been at least five years ago. But she hadn't forgotten. Still, this had felt *waaay* better. Comparatively speaking.

He began to move again, his thick shaft engorging impressively as he pumped inside her, keeping the pace maddeningly slow and even.

"Geeezzz," she whispered on a half moan. "What kind of vitamins do you take?"

"Strong enough for a woman, but made for a man," he said, and she heard the amusement in his voice.

"Amen." Tally squeezed her eyes shut, stopped talking, and went with the flow. There'd be plenty of time tomorrow for self-analysis and recriminations.

. . .

The sky was a clear, cerulean blue the next morning. The water calm and well-behaved. It was as though the storm had never been.

Under normal circumstances Michael abhorred using women as pawns in his ops. But Tally Cruise had been dropped into his lap like manna from heaven.

She was a bonus. And eventually a prisoner of war.

Nothing, not even a soft-skinned, wary-eyed female, was going to stand between him and his objective.

Nothing.

Church was going to watch as Michael took away everything he held dear. Then the man was going to die.

A surge of adrenaline supercharged him.

He'd left nothing to chance; yet, like a good soldier, he knew how to incorporate unexpected diversions seamlessly into his plans.

He guided the *Nemesis* through the deep channel in the reef and into Paradise harbor with consummate skill. Tally stood at the outside rail, shading her eyes with her hand.

"Isn't the clarity, and color of the water *amazing*?" She hung over the rail giving him a delectable view of her butt. "Oh! I can see tiny, bright yellow fish darting about down there."

Her short hair ruffled in the breeze, and her long legs were spaced apart for balance. His orange shorts flapped about her knees, and his much-washed white T-shirt effectively hid her small breasts. Her breasts were sensitive. The nipples quick to peak when he sucked them into his mouth—

"Did you say something?" Tally turned to glance at him over her shoulder, oblivious to the havoc she'd caused.

He'd groaned. The sound should've been him pounding his head against the deck. "Just concentrating as I navigate the reef."

"Okay. Just ignore me as I *oooh* and *ahhh.* No wonder my father calls his island Paradise. The name might not be original, but it's appropriate. Look at it. It's breathtaking. I wish

I were an artist." She babbled on as he eased through the channel toward the small marina. "Wouldn't it be amazing to be able to capture all the blues and greens on canvas?"

"Take a picture."

"I don't have my—a photograph isn't the same. It doesn't have the same heart as something done with brush strokes."

"Don't tell my brother that."

"He's a photographer?"

"Yeah. And a good one."

"I bet if he came here he'd want to pick up a paintbrush."

If Kane came here it would be to retrieve his older brother in a body bag to take home for burial.

Michael brushed off the thought. Dead or alive, when he left Paradise, his job would be done.

Paradise Island. Sleepy. Picturesque. Inauspicious. Home and headquarters of the Scourge of the North Pacific, Trevor Church. Island population, 132. So small, the damn thing wasn't on the map. It didn't look any different now than it had a year ago. Only this time, Lieutenant Michael Wright was no longer a Lieutenant. And *this* time he was upright, healthy, and ready to finish the war they'd started.

Despite being in a protected inlet, the ire of the monsoon could be seen in downed trees, uprooted shrubs, and debris littering the beach and shell road leading into town. The small marina was a hive of activity. A dozen or more men were busily bringing various-size boats back to their slips.

Michael eased the boat into an empty slip, then jumped onto the worn, weathered dock to tie her off.

"Thanks for getting us back to terra firma safely."

"Did you go to boarding school?" he asked lazily as he tightened the bow rope, then let it drop to the deck.

She ran her fingers through her curly hair as she glanced around, then turned to look at him. "Frequently. Why?"

"Frequently?"

She grinned. "Often. Recurrently. Periodically."

What a strange little bird she was. She swore in ancient languages, was as polite as a schoolgirl, was a sailor's wet dream in the sack, and couldn't hold a musical note in a handbasket. "I know what 'frequently' means." He motioned Lucky to stay onboard. The cat blinked, then gracefully jumped onto the wharf and began licking himself.

Michael glanced back at Tally Ho. "I asked because you're so charmingly polite." He smiled. *Don't look at me with trust and hope in those baby-blues, sweetheart. I'm a son of a bitch. I'm going to destroy you along with your scum-sucking father without a qualm.* "Too bad you can't control what your eyes are telegraphing. Which is something altogether different."

"That's your imagination." She dismissed the accuracy of his statement, but lowered her lashes fractionally, anyway.

Michael's smile widened.

"Of course I'm polite. How ungrateful would I be if I didn't thank you for saving my life?"

He held up his arms so she could jump down, and she leaned down to rest her hands on his bare shoulders. Michael made sure he slid her all the way down his front. Very, very slowly. Then enjoyed the way her cheeks pinked, and her blue eyes sparkled as she looked up at him. "I did a little more than save your life," he reminded her.

She took a small, retreating step out of his loose hold. "Um, yeah. To be frank, I'm trying to figure out how I got myself into a situation where I feel as though I have to apologize to you for"—she waved a slender hand in a vague description—"I'm . . . oh, damn . . . I'm embarrassed, all right."

"Yeah? Well, don't be. We're both grown-ups. The pleasure was mutual."

"Well, yes, it was . . ." She paused, then said in a rush, "Was I gray in the dark? Wait. Never mind." She put her hands over her face. "Oh, damn. I can't believe I asked you—forget I asked. Stupid. Stupid. Aggh! Forget it."

Michael cupped her shoulders with his hands. She was as stiff as a board. "Are you trying to ask me if any woman would've done last night?"

"Yes. No. Of course any woman would've done. We don't know each other. I was available—could we *please* change the subject? I'm really uncomfortable Monday morning quarterbacking."

"Done it often?" he asked silkily.

"No." She ran her finger through her hair self-consciously. "If I had, I'd be better at this, don't you think? Shoot. I didn't even remember until this morning that we didn't use"—she glanced around the busy dock to make sure no one was within earshot—"protection."

Nice to know she'd been too hot to notice. "Yeah, we did."

Those big blue eyes widened, and a slow smile curved her lush mouth. "We did? Oh. Ah . . . good."

He lifted her chin with his finger. Her lashes fluttered. Oh, she wanted to block out the sight of him, but Tally Ho was just too straightforward. Too *honest,* for subterfuge. She reluctantly dragged her gaze to meet his.

"I haven't had sex in more than a year, honey. And it's been offered. Plenty of times." He cupped her hot face and ran his thumb over her cheekbone. "Believe me. You weren't any shade of gray in the dark. I knew who you were. And you were glorious Technicolor."

"Bless your heart." She smiled almost shyly. "You are *such* a gentleman, Michael Wright." Her pink cheeks made her eyes appear bluer. She pressed a soft kiss to his palm. "Okay. End of subject. Come up to the boardinghouse. I'll spring for breakfast."

"I'll take a rain check on that. I'd better see to repairs on this old tub before I get settled."

"Oh, shoot. I forgot my clothes in the dryer. May I?"

"Go ahead. I'll wait for you," he said absently, staring at her mouth.

He quickly helped her back aboard. He was getting into the act a little too enthusiastically, Michael thought sourly. Screw it. She wasn't recreation, she was a pawn. Nothing more. The charming act was for her pleasure, not his. He'd better damn well remember that.

He did a visual scan of the area. The marina, and a long stretch of sugar white beach, nestled in the inner curve of the island. A village comprised of a handful of small, white-washed houses was tucked in the valley formed by the base of the volcano. Spectacular emerald green folds fanned out around the base of the peak like pleats in a velvet skirt. Several small hills, like bumps on a spine, trailed off to the south.

Coconut palms swayed and rustled in the warm breeze, and scarlet hibiscus grew wild and lush in every direction, bright among the lush tropical foliage.

Paradise Island was a grandiose name for a tiny, bean-shaped island in the middle of nowhere. To the north, the cone of a small volcano reared out of the lush vegetation. High, steep cliffs on three sides made it impossible to breach. The island might be small, but it was impossible to approach without being seen from any direction.

And an unwary sailor would ground his boat if he didn't know exactly where the channel was. Church's precious cargo hadn't been brought in by tanker. The channel was too narrow, too shallow. No, the cargo had been transported bit by bit onto the island. What Michael was looking for couldn't be far inland. As small as the island was, there was no form of transportation, other than a few bicycles and some golf carts. Whatever was removed from the ships had to be carried. And what had been carried was extremely heavy. So. What he was looking for was close. Close to the marina.

"All set." Tally tossed him the bundle of her clothes and accepted a hand down. "Thanks." She smiled up at him. "I'll see you later."

A burly guy in khaki shorts and an open-neck shirt came down the jetty to meet them. "Made it through the storm, I see," he said unsmilingly to Tally.

"Gee, Brian." Tally brandished a smile so friendly, it should've raised all sorts of warning flags to the guy. "I'm glad to see you, too. Yes. We did. Michael Wright," she said,

"Brian Kenyon. Brian runs the marina. Michael was kind enough t—"

Kenyon shot an annoyed look at Michael. "This is a private marina, then, mate. You'll have to shove off."

Not unexpected, Michael thought, sizing up the Australian. He stepped closer to Tally. "Now is that any way to treat a guest, *mate?* I just saved the lady's life, and in the process my boat took a beating. What you want me to do, limp outta here and head for Bora-Bora?"

"What were you doing out there—"

"Good grief," Tally interrupted. "What is this? The Spanish Inquisition? The *Serendipity* ble—sank. Michael saved my life, that's all anybody needs to know."

Brian stuffed his hands into his pockets, his eyes still on Michael as he said to Tally, "Where's Arnaud? Still onboard, then?"

"He didn't make it."

He shot Michael a suspicious glance. "Is that right?"

"Nor did Lu," Tally informed him. "Poor man. Did Lu have a family?"

"No. Fact, we were getting ready to have a service for *you.* Thought you'd gone for fish food. Lucky this bloke happened to be in the right place at the right time, isn't it?"

She shuddered. "I'm sure my father will be grateful to him for saving my life, *and* welcome him here for as long as he'd like to stay."

Brian glanced at her. "You think so, do ya?"

"Yes, I do. In fact, I'm quite sure you want to help with the repairs to Michael's boat. Don't you, Brian?"

Michael bit back a grin. He'd seen wrestlers mat their opponent with more finesse. But she'd got the job done. He couldn't have planned this any better if he'd tried. Having Church's daughter as his advocate was going to be the cherry on top of Church's downfall.

Tally gave the Australian a speaking look, then said to Michael, "I'll let Auntie know to expect you up at the hotel."

He mock-saluted her and watched her stride along the wooden marina toward a small, ramshackle town nestled in the green hills about half a mile away. She gave every appearance of a woman dressed for high tea with the queen. Except she wore his most disreputable pair of fluorescent shorts, and an old T-shirt. And no underwear. The thought of her going commando was enough to elevate his blood pressure several uncomfortable degrees.

"Homely, scrawny thing, ain't she? Nice arse, though." Brian watched her for a long minute, then lifted a dirty hand to scratch his whiskered cheek before turning back to face Michael. "Still, not my cuppa. Too much trouble on the hoof for my likin'."

How fortunate for you that I don't put you first on my kill list, Michael thought savagely. "Since I've spent the last dozen or so hours with her," he said with spurious calm, "I'll vouch for that a hundred percent."

"Let's agree you'll be outta *here* in the next twenty."

"I'll split the minute my boat's fixed, how's that?" Michael offered cheerfully. There wasn't a damn thing Kenyon could do about it. Other than the mast, Michael had orchestrated what was broken with meticulous care. The *Nemesis* wasn't going anywhere until he said the repairs were done.

"I'll be sure you get all the help you need then, mate."

Michael grinned companionably. "I'll *need* all the help I can get. I'm good with a line and sail, but all thumbs with anything mechanical."

"Is that right?"

" 'Fraid so," Michael lied again cheerfully.

"Mosey up to the building over there and ask for some help, then. Tell 'em Brian said to give you top priority. I'll order your parts this arvie, after they've told me what you'll be needing. We'll have ya shipshape in no time."

Michael took his sweet time walking toward the marina building, feeling Kenyon's suspicious gaze stabbing him between the shoulder blades. No more mention of Bouchard.

Either Kenyon didn't give a rat's ass his boss had drowned, or the Australian was holding his cards close to his chest. Either way was irrelevant. One less person to deal with.

The marina was well-equipped. A boatyard, with a Quonset building off to the side, doors open, housed the equipment to maintain and repair some good-size boats.

Three eighty-footers bobbed inside. Tucked into the slips were half a dozen yachts and boats of various sizes. All top of the line, and well-maintained. Of course there was no sign of the tourists who under normal circumstances would've owned them.

Among other, far more sinister activities, Trevor Church's Paradise Island was a glorified chop shop.

Michael shaded his eye and looked around. His gaze climbed the hill and settled on the overblown white monstrosity nestled with a bird's-eye view of the bay. Church's home.

Bile backed up his throat.

Hugo. I'm back, man. The bastard's gonna pay. I swear to God, that son of a bitch is gonna pay in a spectacular way for what he did to you.

He overheard a smattering of French, the pidgin English the locals used, a bit of Australian-accented English, and some guy swearing colorfully in German. Michael waited a few seconds for his eye to adjust to the relative dimness, then approached two guys painting a brand-new, hundred-foot Mangusta motor yacht with the words *Beautiful Dreamer* on the bow.

The boat was magnificent. Big bucks, big ego, small dick kind of magnificent.

"G' day, mate. What can I do ya for?"

"Hey," Michael said companionably. "Michael Wright. How're you doing? That's my Oyster out there. Needs some repairs. Just talked to Brian, and he said a couple of you could give me a hand. I have a list of what I think I might need."

. . .

Tally squinted, shielding her eyes with her hand. The sun shone directly overhead, shortening shadows and beating down on her unprotected head. Not a breath of wind disturbed the grasses and palm trees on either side of the path. Hard to believe less than twelve hours ago she was clinging to the side of Michael's boat thinking she'd drown at any second.

She rubbed a hand over her tired eyes. Oh, she was glad to be away from Michael's force field. She felt hot and prickly all over just thinking about last night. God. What had she been thinking to crawl into his bed like that?

She grinned. *Technicolor, huh?* A gallant lie, of course. But sweet of him to say it, anyway. Men didn't normally drop at her feet like autumn leaves in the fall. She was usually the one men confided their love lives to. The little sister, the friend, the office Dear Abby. The one whose advice they asked before they went out with someone else.

But Michael Wright . . . Tally groaned. He must think she was a moron. God only knew, she was probably going through adolescence at twenty-seven. He literally made her hot. Tingly. And because he was so . . . male, he made her hyper-aware of *herself.*

Tally sighed again. What did it matter? He was only here for a couple of days. They'd go their separate ways and never see each other again. Besides, he was the *last* man she should get attached to.

Not that she hadn't had her share of dates over the years. She'd even had two fairly long-term relationships. Rory Foster had lasted almost a year. Until he'd taken that job in South America building the dam two months after he'd returned from Central Africa building a bridge. Then there'd been Ben Collins. She'd adored Ben. But so had many other women in airports all around the world on his international flights.

In the last couple of years she'd made a pleasant home for herself. Built a comfortable environment. She was ready to share her life with a man who was equally stable and responsible.

Michael Wright? She snorted. Not even close.

Obviously she was a sucker for traveling men. Not a good thing when a woman wanted hearth and home, two point nine children, and pot roast on Sunday nights.

Of course there'd been her brief walk on the wild side with Arnaud that time in London when she'd been a nineteen-year-old virgin. Tally groaned. The unmentionable-never-to-be-thought-about aberration when she'd spent several sweaty hours in Arnaud Bouchard's bed. Ugh!

It seemed that the men she attracted, when she attracted men, were the *wrong* men. She really needed to get a handle on that when she got back to Chicago.

Tally trudged up the hill to the small village on the rise overlooking the marina and the picture-perfect bay.

Hotel, boardinghouse—either was a rather grandiose name for a bar with a couple of bedrooms above it. Still, it was comfortable for a short stay, and the bathroom was large, with plenty of hot water. If her father wanted her up at the house he'd correct Arnaud's mistake when he arrived. Arnaud had indicated that Trevor might prefer that Tally stay with Auntie.

Not being welcome in her father's home had hurt. Her father had invited her, not Auntie, a woman she didn't even know. The fact had nothing to do with comfort and everything to do with what was right and hospitable.

It was impossible not to feel an ache when, once again, her father had given with one hand while he had taken away with the other. She'd fantasized about living with him since she was a small child. God. This was only a *visit,* yet he still kept her at arm's length.

They'd had an uneasy relationship her whole life. He was a mystery to Tally, and she was clearly a disappointment to him. It no longer hurt as it had when she was a child. Just because they had a biological connection didn't mean they had to have feelings for each other. But it was past time for her to at least attempt to forge some sort of link with the stranger who was her biological father.

Her relationship, or lack thereof, with Trevor Church had

colored her life in countless ways. One of which, Tally was sure, was her relationship with men. Her mother's example of loving Trevor unconditionally, almost obsessively, through the years had saddened and confused Tally.

How could her mother so adore a man who was never there? Because that, and a million other questions, had confounded and puzzled her forever, she pushed aside her mental list until they were face-to-face.

She wasn't sure having a sexy stranger stranded here with her was going to make it any easier.

When she returned to Chicago she'd reshuffle her life a bit. It was getting a little staid. Even for her.

Until then, she had Paradise. Her father's Tudor mansion was nestled at the base of the inactive, she hoped, volcano. The white walls and black trim of the medieval architecture looked incongruous looming over the small, whitewashed houses and surrounded by tropical vegetation. Although a road wound up to it, there didn't appear to be any vehicles on the island besides a few golf cart-type thingies like the one Arnaud had driven to pick her up at the landing strip. . . . Could that only have been three days ago?

The air was redolent with the heady scent of flowers—just breathing was intoxicating. Tally narrowly avoided a confrontation with two feuding chickens as she walked. The chickens cackled around her feet for a few moments before dashing off in the opposite direction.

"Hooo-eee!"

Tally glanced up to see the woman who ran the hotel bearing down on her with open arms. "Baby girl! *Haere mai!* You be alive!"

She found herself enveloped in Auntie's ample arms. The Tahitian woman smelled of white ginger and the minty hand lotion she favored. Though Tally had only met her three days ago, she was delighted to see that the other woman was hale and hearty.

Today, "Just-call-me-Auntie-baby-everybody-does" 's muumuu was bright blue with yellow plumeria on it. Deep ruffles flapped over her ample, coffee-colored bosom and bare feet. She had arms like a sumo wrestler and a heart as big as her beloved island.

Tally hugged her back, needing the human contact, then let go. It didn't pay to cling. It was a lesson she'd learned early and well. She gave Auntie a smile and blinked back the moisture in her eyes. "*Eaha to oe huru?* Are *you* all right? Did the storm damage anything here?"

The large woman tucked Tally's hand under her arm and started up the hill. The sun shone brilliantly, reflecting off the white walls of the buildings. "Everything A-okay. Big mess to clean up, but nothing too bad broken." Her wide, white grin exposed a gold tooth. "Not people, anyhows." She grabbed Tally again for another squeeze. "Everybody say you drownded, baby girl!"

"Reports of my death were greatly exaggerated," Tally said. "Arnaud and Lu didn't make it. It was quite an adventure. Walk with me, and I'll tell you all about it." *With a strategic bit of editing.*

From her second-floor bedroom window, Tally had a magnificent view of the bay. French doors led to a long, narrow lanai that looked too rickety and fragile to bear the weight of anyone over six years old. Yet it was obvious someone carefully tended the pots of flowers and greenery scattered higgledy-piggledy between the rattan chairs and wobbly looking tables placed to catch the shade and any breeze.

The view was just as good from inside her room.

Tally ran her fingers through her salt-sticky hair and winced. She desperately wanted a shower, but the incredible view from the window was a siren's song. Directly below were Auntie's gardens, which surrounded the two-story building in a wild profusion of exotic colors and scents.

A shell path wound down the hill, flanked by shrubs, fern, and wild orchids. It divided, one branch headed to the marina, the other to the beach.

She'd done enough traveling as a kid to last her two lifetimes. As beautiful as Paradise might be, she much preferred home and hearth to foreign ports and exotic locales. Been there, done that. "Got the neurosis to prove it."

"Talking to yourself?"

Tally spun around. "I thought so. If I'd known I had an audience I would've been more amusing." Just looking at Michael Wright put a lilt in her heart.

"Door was open. I'm going to take a shower."

Now didn't *that* invoke lascivious thoughts. "Thanks for the update." She returned his smile. "I'll alert the media."

The pirate gave her a slow, wicked smile. "Want to save water?"

The room got a lot smaller as he advanced inside. Tally crowded against the open window and clutched a handful of bright cotton drape. Then she realized she must look like one of the heroines in an old 1920s movie. All she needed was to be tied to the railway tracks and have the words spelled across the screen at her feet . . . "No, Black Bart, not *that.*" She could practically hear the piano music. She dropped the drapes.

"There's no shortage of water. Knock yourself out. Did Brian help with your repairs?"

"Yeah, finally. More thanks, I suspect, to your intervention than to my dubious charm. Looks like I'll be accepting your father's hospitality for a couple days or so until they get the parts ordered."

"The beach looks worth a lengthy visit."

"I'm not that much of a sun lizard. Dinner, later?"

Tally felt each separate beat of her heart under the hand she had up to her throat. "Sure. I'd like that."

Said the fly to the spider.

Chapter Five

The new mast had to be ordered from Papeete.

Although it had pained him, Michael had made sure there were fist-size holes in the stringer-reinforced GRP hull; the rigging was FUBAR; the ship's radio appeared shorted out, and several dozen 6mm stainless bolts were gone; the sail-drive unit, if anyone was interested enough to check, was out; and he needed a new backup 88-amp-hour, 12-volt battery.

Appearances were deceiving.

Right this minute the *Nemesis* could outsail, outrun, *outwit* anything in the water.

Her owner was as adept with a screwdriver as he was with a Sig Sauer automatic. By the time he'd spent an hour "helping" Brian's guys fix his boat, they had all but begged him to go away and leave them to their jobs.

Now all Michael had to do was wait.

There was plenty to do. A thorough recon of the island was in order. He had to know *exactly* where Church had the arms hidden. It was tempting to blow the entire island to hell. But there were innocent civilians living here. And he wasn't a murderer. He was here for justice. Not wholesale slaughter.

Michael rolled over on the fiber mat, the sun hot on his back. Anyone looking would believe he had nothing better to do than laze about all day. Later he'd continue romancing Tally Ho.

If ever a woman was having second thoughts it was Church's daughter; he'd seen it in her eyes. Oh, she'd enjoyed the hell out of their wild monkey sex last night. But in the clear light of day she was remembering she wasn't "that sort of girl." It wouldn't be hard to change her mind. Last night had merely whetted her appetite. He had a few more tricks of his own with the pubococcygeal muscle he was eager to show her.

However innocently it had begun, *she* had instigated their first mattress tango. What man wouldn't say hoo-yah to waking to find a half-naked woman sprawled on top of him?

Yet her morning-after honesty had surprised him.

He'd expected recriminations, and the excuse that she'd been too sleepy to think clearly; or that he'd forced himself on her. Instead, while she'd been sweetly embarrassed by her enthusiastic response, she'd been clear-eyed and frank.

A small part of his brain reminded him she was as guiltless as the islanders. But he pushed it aside. He could have no qualms about using Tally Cruise in whatever way was necessary to make Church's downfall a reality.

The sex was an added bonus he'd not expected.

He hadn't had sex in over a year. Hadn't had the interest. Even though he'd met all shapes, sizes, and colors of women in his travels. He hadn't given enough of a damn to make the effort.

His focus was revenge. Blood lust had blinded him, and had effectively turned off his sex drive.

Yet here was plain little Tally Cruise, with her lush mouth, and innocent face. And a year's worth of pent-up lust rushed at him like a freight train. Go figure.

He could turn it off, of course. But why the hell should he?

Just thinking about her taut, toned, lanky body and those small, firm breasts brushing his chest last night made him hard.

This op was getting sweeter by the minute. As long as he didn't let himself get distracted by Tally's sweet little ass.

The island was only six or seven klicks from end to end, and about four across and was surrounded on three sides by sharp, inhospitable cliffs. The small town was *it,* as far as accommodations went. Not exactly a hot cosmopolitan resort. Even at a leisurely pace, and with Tally slowing him down, he could cover what he needed to see in a day.

He had two.

Plenty of time to search the island, play at repairing the *Nemesis,* and fuck his archenemy's daughter.

Tally stood on the lanai of the island store—the only store-slash travel agent-slash island hotbed of gossip—and stared blindly at the sugar white sand and placid turquoise waters of the bay.

Being so far away from her own little nest, from the familiar routines of her life, was enough to make her want to swim to Papeete. Okay, she couldn't. Shouldn't. She'd come this far. She had to see this visit through to the end. Her father had never invited her before, and Tally had stopped asking many years ago.

So what *could* she do until her father arrived? Tally snorted. If a girl had to ask herself that question when she was on a tropical island paradise and there was a good-looking guy around who obviously wanted her body, she was in bigger trouble than she'd thought.

It would be foolish to come all this way and then turn tail and run before her father even got here. Besides, she wasn't that eager to attempt the long flight from Papeete again. Not for a while, anyway.

Besides, there were no scheduled flights in or out. Not that Paradise had anything resembling an airport. Just a narrow airstrip near the lava fields on the south shore. According to her loquacious pilot, it had been built as a marine landing strip during the Second World War. Now it was only used to bring in supplies once a week.

The six-hour flight from Papeete alone had almost given her heart failure. Yet here she stood, wishing she could climb aboard that rickety twin-engine six-seater that had seen better days. It had wheezed to a rocky landing on the dirt strip on Saturday morning, helped no doubt by her rendition of "Fly Me to the Moon."

Only three days ago. A lifetime.

Tally glimpsed the pirate lying on the beach when she walked back from the store. He didn't seem particularly perturbed that his boat couldn't be fixed right away. He'd worked on it for a couple of hours, then gone to the beach, where he'd barely moved for the rest of the day.

Tally watched him from her window.

He was delicious to look at. In fact, just looking at him, coupled with the tactile memories of last night, was enough to make her feel decidedly warm.

Other than that patch over his eye, and several nasty scars, he looked hale and hearty. *Extremely* hale and hearty.

Her reaction to him was as troubling as it was bewildering. He was so not her type. Tally didn't exactly regret having had sex with him. But she was surprising herself. It had been 100 percent her fault. Still, that didn't mean she'd play vacation bed bunny for the guy for the duration of his stay. Acting out of character just once and, damn it, *enjoying* it, was enough.

Maybe it was the danger of the storm coupled with her attraction to him that had made her lose what was left of her mind and crawl into bed with a stranger. Maybe it was . . . it didn't matter. She'd done it. Didn't regret it.

And wouldn't repeat it. Once was incredible, but enough.

What did Michael Wright do for a living? Anything? He seemed to enjoy sleeping on the beach all day. For a beach bum he certainly had an extremely nice boat with lots of nice guy toys on it. He'd probably cashed in everything he owned to buy the boat, and a man probably didn't need that much money to bum around the world. He probably worked odd jobs here and there to pay for supplies. Feasibly he could sail around the world forever.

It was a twist of fate that they'd bumped into each other at all. The adventurer and the homebody. Oh, yeah. Now *there's* a scenario with a future.

At seven, she applied makeup—the whole enchilada: foundation, blush, eye shadow, and mascara. It wasn't a case of gilding the lily. She'd never be a beauty, but a girl did what a girl had to do to look at least halfway attractive. Thank God for makeup. She spent some time with a curling iron straightening the natural curls out of her hair, then took out her travel iron and ironed a pair of oatmeal-colored linen slacks and the matching blouse, ironed *his* fluorescent shorts and plain white T-shirt and folded them neatly at the foot of the bed to return to him later, and sat in the chair by the window.

He was going to burn to a crisp. Silly man.

The ocean stretched to infinity. Teal and turquoise. Calm. Benign. The storm, and her near-death experience, just a chilling memory. Tally shivered and rose to put the finishing touches on her attire before going down to dinner.

Gold earrings, discreet gold chain, crocodile belt, matching flats. Classy armor. Clothes made the woman. She was as ready as she'd ever be.

Auntie served dinner between eight and ten. Tally always ate dinner on the dot at six, and her stomach was growling by the time she ventured down to the bar at 8:05.

The sliding shutters that made up the entire front wall of the room had been opened to the evening air and trade winds, giving an incredible vista of the masts of the boats bobbing in the marina, and the faint shimmer of the starry skies on the ocean. The scent of evening blooming jasmine and other exotic fragrances vied with the yeasty smell of beer.

The mingled aromas were as intoxicating as champagne on an empty stomach.

The tiny bar was crowded as Tally stepped through the door at the foot of the steep cement stairs. Every head turned. Silence descended as the door closed slowly behind her. There were a few women about, but most of the patrons were male.

It would have made an interesting picture—that open-mouthed curiosity—if she hadn't been the focus of their gawking attention. Tally kept her spine straight and looked around for a vacant table. There wasn't one.

Auntie padded around from behind the bar, a big welcoming smile on her face. "Hoo-ee!" She gave Tally an up-and-down look and clasped her hands over her monstrous tummy cloaked in a searing orange print muumuu. "You lookin' A-okay, baby. *Ua poia anei oe?*"

"Starving. But there's no—"

"You come with Auntie, quick, quick. Fixed nice, special place for you on lanai. Come on. Hey! Henri? You go on, get behind the bar, Ethan needs a beer. Go on, you. Come."

Tally followed. She felt a little leap of her juices when she saw who was waiting for her outside at a romantic, candlelit table for two under the stars. *Ye gods and little fishes.* Did the man never wear clothes?

"Ah, wearing your formal black shorts this evening, I see," Tally teased.

"You bet." Michael looked her up and down. "You're looking particularly . . . hot."

"I'm quite comfy." Seeing him half-naked, "hot" didn't begin to cover it.

Talk about hot . . . She paused to collect her thoughts. Did she need to say this? Yes. She did. "About last night—"

"Movie. 1986, I think . . ."

" '85," she corrected just to tease him, and he gave her a surprise grin that punched at her with the force of a closed fist. Oh, boy. "Look, Michael, the sex last night was great." She paused, thought about it for a few seconds, and amended, "Okay, *really* great. But it was a onetime thing. Okay? It's not my style to have one-night stands, even on vacation. It was terrific. But not something I'm going to repeat." Oh man, she was babbling. Not a good sign. She hated when she babbled.

"I just wanted to make that clear so we weren't awkward with each other for the duration. I mean, not that you would be awkward or anything, but I would, and this way I won't and, besides, it's better this way all around, don't you think?"

"Take a breath."

Tally dragged in a gulp of fragrant flower-scented air and let it out slowly.

"Good girl. Hmmm. No more sex."

"Right." Probably *ever,* if she used last night as a yardstick. Who'd be able to compare, really?

"Unless you get scared of the dark again."

"I have a night-light."

"Extra bulb?"

Tally's lips twitched. "Two."

He sighed. "I'll try to keep my lascivious hands off you, then."

Her gaze dropped to said hands clasped over his flat stomach as he leaned back in his chair, and her brain short-circuited with the memory of those hands on her body. Down, girl. "And I'll keep mine off you," Tally said briskly. That hadn't been as difficult as she'd thought. Although the fact that he'd taken it so well was a relief, a little part of her was perversely ticked off that he'd accepted her edict so readily.

"Now that that's settled, would you like to take a little hike with me tomorrow? Auntie tells me there's a beautiful waterfall on the other side of the lava fields. I'd like to see it."

His eye glinted wickedly. "A waterfall sounds dangerously romantic to me. I'm not sure we could keep our hands off each other with that kind of provocation."

"Of course we can. Pass those rolls, would you? I'm famished."

He stretched out his arm without sitting upright and shoved the basket across the table so she could reach it. Sprawled out in a large rattan chair, bare legs extended, spine slumped, a cold beer by his side, he looked as relaxed as a man could get without being in a coma. Unfortunately, just looking at him made Tally salivate. He hadn't bothered putting on a shirt, still wore the black shorts he'd worn all day and was liberally salted with sand.

Michael gave her a lazy look that made her blood curl inside her like smoke. "Anyone say anything about the explosion and/or Bouchard?"

There was a surefire way to cool her off. "No. Not to me,

anyway. I feel awful about it—especially about Lu. He was only about twenty years old. What a hideous way to die."

"Amen."

"I was damn lucky." She rubbed her upper arms.

"What was the story with him?"

"Story?"

"The two of you. Out there. Oblivious to an incoming storm. Romantic."

"Hardly. I—" *Think he was up to no good.* She didn't want to think ill of the dead. But Arnaud had been up to something.

"What were you going to say?"

Tally shrugged. "He wanted to show off the new boat."

"Couldn't wait until the typhoon blew over?"

"*I* didn't know there was going to be a typhoon."

"As a sailor, *he* must've." He took a pull of his beer. "Seems odd that he'd risk a multimillion-dollar craft for a joyride."

"Yes. It does."

"I imagine his boss will have a few questions," Michael said dryly. "So if that's Daddy's house up on the hill, why aren't *you* up there?"

"Auntie's is fine." She bit into the sweet roll.

"Sure, it is. But why not stay up there?"

"I—" *Don't feel welcome? Comfortable?* Shoot. *Wasn't invited.* "We're not that close. Since he's not here, I don't want to impose."

He frowned. "How can you impose? He's your father."

"You don't know *my* father," Tally said dryly.

Yeah, he did. Trevor Church was a cruel, sadistic bastard, the Scourge of the North Pacific. "Apparently not Father of the Year material, huh?"

"Hardly."

Candlelight softened her features and made her blue eyes appear luminous and mysterious. She was one of those women whose looks improved with makeup. And God only knew, she'd gone whole hog. Michael cocked his head. Strangely, he preferred her without the war paint. He liked her skin clean and fresh, and her large, blue eyes were thick-lashed and striking without the goop. She'd also done something to her hair. All the cute, bouncy curls were gone. Now her short dark hair was straight, and sleeked back off her face and tucked neatly behind her ears. He didn't much like it, but it suited her. She looked sophisticated and in control.

She hadn't been in control last night. Michael found he missed the uninhibited woman who'd come to his bed. However, he recognized camouflage when he saw it. Cammy and war paint. Tally Cruise drew her trappings of civilization around her like a protective cloak.

He'd like to see her naked again.

The beige outfit could've used some color. Red would look dynamite with her pale, creamy olive skin. Hell, he'd better have another drink if she was starting to look that appealing.

Michael balanced the cool beer can on his midriff. "So," he said lazily. "What kind of translating do you do?"

"I work for the Federal Reserve Bank in Chicago."

"Interesting?"

"It can be. I have a talent for languages, so it's a perfect fit. Growing up I did a lot of traveling with my mother. It was practical to use my skills in my career."

"Who was doing the growing up? You or your mother?"

God, her eyes were pretty when she was amused. Incredibly blue and sparkly with mirth. "Both of us, I think. Trevor, that's my father, took off when I was about five. My mother was barely eighteen when she had me. They weren't married, but she loved him passionately and was devastated when he left. My grandfather compensated by paying for her to travel wherever she wanted to go. We jet-setted from one place to another for the next thirteen years. By the time I was nine I could say Kaopectate in seven languages." She smiled. "Languages became my hobby. I was a quick study, and it was a game to me to see how much I could pick up before we were on the go again."

"Is that where the boarding schools came in?"

"Sure, when I could convince Bev to let me enroll. She didn't much like traveling alone.

"It wasn't until I got into my mid-teens that I realized she was traipsing all over the world searching for my father, which was incredibly sad. Because of course he didn't want to be found, so that proved pretty fruitless. Eventually she gave up."

"And did you?"

"Did I what?"

"Give up looking for your father?"

She shrugged, her eyes clouded. "My mother eventually remarried, and I like my stepfather."

"Yet you came all the way here to see him."

"He invited me. I was curious."

"How long since you last saw him?"

"Six years. Can we change the subject? I'm kind of stressed about this meeting, and it's worse because he's not even here, so I have to wait for him to get back. Kind of like anticipating pulling off a Band-Aid."

She was too open. Too easy to read. Her father's defection had hurt, and she was reaching out to him. Michael could've saved her the time. Trevor Church cared for no one but himself. If she had an inkling of the man she was hoping to connect with, she'd charter a flight off the island tonight and never look back.

"Mind if we talk about something else?" she repeated.

"Sure. What would you like to talk about?"

"You. What do you do for a living, Michael Wright?"

"I'm a sail bum."

"That's it?"

"That's it."

Tally flinched at the sound of a bar fight breaking out inside the bar. Michael figured if he got really antsy he'd go check that out later.

"No goal to sail around the world faster than the last guy?"

"I'm in no hurry," he said lazily, and watched the shades come down over those expressive blue eyes.

She had pretty hands, with long, slender fingers and bright red polish, which he found a real turn-on. Her toenails sported the same color. She was perfectly groomed, apparently perfectly in control, and he was starting to get perfectly pissed off.

He'd preferred her off-kilter, slightly untidy and passionate, as she'd been onboard. He wondered who was the real Tally Cruise.

"What about hobbies?" she asked doggedly.

"I sail. I eat. I sleep." *Your father's been my hobby for the last year. Ask me anything you like. Chances are I'll know the answers. Not that you'd like to hear any of them.*

"No TV?"

"Nope. Not in years."

"Movies?"

"Nope."

"Friends?"

He picked up his fork and balanced it on a finger. "Nope."

"Don't you get lonely?" she asked, big eyes serious and full of compassion he didn't fucking well need.

"I don't think about it. Do your friends make you less lonely?"

"Of course."

"How?"

"How? We talk, and go to the movies, and do things together. Shop. Go to the gym. Laugh. Cry." She gave an eloquent shrug. "Things."

"And then you go home," he said, looking at her. "And you're alone. How do your friends keep the loneliness at bay then?"

"It must be pretty lonely sailing around the world all by yourself," Tally said, not answering his question.

"It's not," Michael said flatly, tossing the fork onto the table with a clatter. He preferred to be the one asking questions. She'd neatly turned the tables on him.

"Dinner here!" Auntie caroled as she waddled out onto the lanai, hands full, followed by a beautiful Tahitian girl carrying more plates.

Auntie set a platter before Tally—who of course looked suitably horrified by the enormous portions—and the plump, sloe-eyed girl sidled up to Michael to deliver his dinner personally. By the look in her dark eyes she'd have liked to serve up something a lot hotter than mahi mahi.

Michael smiled.

The girl smiled.

Tally snorted.

"This be Leli'a. My sister's baby, come to visit her old Auntie. She take good care of you. You just sing out you want something. You hear?" Auntie departed in a froth of bright fabric and bouncing body parts.

"I'd like another nap—"

"I'm off duty," Leli'a informed Tally swiftly, and spun on one bare heel to follow her aunt inside. There were a lot more interesting bouncy body parts on the niece. Her legs were a little short, but her yellow pareu had done little to cover a great expanse of milk coffee–colored skin, and some very nice jiggly parts.

Things were definitely looking up.

Tally's knife flew across the table.

It landed in the dirt floor, vibrating, point down, beside Michael's bare, left foot.

He cocked an eyebrow. "Did you do that one on purpose?"

"Of course not," she said with a straight face. "If I'd done it on purpose the knife would be in your foot, and not in the floor." She picked up her fork and stabbed her dinner with considerably more force than necessary. "You certainly seem to bring out some weird klutzy thing in me."

"Pent-up passion."

Fork halfway to her mouth, Tally regarded him thoughtfully. "Pent-up passion?"

"Sure. It has nowhere to go, so you fall over your own feet and fling cutlery at me. Perfectly obvious. You need to get rid of some of that sexual tension inside."

"Didn't I do that last night?"

"Sure, but that was yesterday's tension." There was humor in the way he said it, but enough truth to be flattering. It was hard not to appreciate the combination.

She put her fork down on her plate and opened her eyes very wide. "Really?"

"Absolutely. You need sex and lots of it. Administered by the right person, of course."

"Of course. Hmmm. I'm going to have to give this serious thought, Doctor . . ." She bit her lower lip and opened her eyes very wide. "With careful deliberation . . ." She cocked her head and gave him a sultry look. "I'm afraid I must . . . disagree. My problem isn't sexual tension, it's a deep-seated homicidal tendency." She smiled at him sweetly and picked up her fork. "If I stick to my medication, and stay away from attractive, half-naked men wearing eye patches, I think I'll recover in no time."

"You're a dangerous woman, Tally Cruise."

She met his gaze head-on without blinking. "I have no illusions. I know what I am, Michael," she said, all seriousness now. "And all flirting aside, I'm really *not* going to sleep with you again. I know I instigated it, and I'm certainly not sorry, but that was it. I don't respect women who say one thing and do another. I enjoy the flirting part, but I have to make it clear that it's hands-off for the duration."

"Honey, you have the final say, and I certainly appreciate you spelling it out for me. I'm just curious why, when we have such obvious chemistry, you want to put the kibosh on a good thing?"

"You're far too rich for my blood, Michael. I can't handle recreational sex. Trust me when I tell you this sophisticated facade is paper thin. Inside, I'm still that insecure little kid being dragged from pillar to post with my mother, and never quite fitting in."

"You fit me rather nicely last night."

"Yes. Let's cherish the memory," she said with a demure smile.

The mahi mahi was tender, cooked to perfection, and delicious. She dug into her meal with delicate greed. She wouldn't sleep with him again. Unfortunately. Tally knew herself too well. Michael Wright was charming, amusing, and sexy. She was halfway in lo—*lust* with him already.

One taste had been incredible; another would involve a part of her anatomy she wasn't prepared to give up to a wanderer. When she gave her heart completely, it would be to a man who had both feet firmly planted. She'd had precious little stability in her life, and over the years she'd carved out a place for herself. A place where she felt safe.

As sexy and attractive, and downright appealing as Michael Wright was, as incredible a lover as he was, he *wasn't* the hearth-and-home type.

Tally wasn't going to settle for anything less.

No matter how tempting the package.

"This is delicious, isn't it? Do you have a big family?" she asked curiously. Michael wanted to vault over the glass table and lick that sheen off her lush lips. He took a swig of his beer instead. The taste wasn't even close.

"No, wait," she said, sparkly eyed, before he could speak. "Let me guess."

"Go for it."

"You're how old? Forty?" she teased.

"Thirty-four."

"Oh. Hard childhood. You were an orphan. Foster families, cruel, inhumane, of course."

"Of course."

"You were a runaway, always in trouble." She cocked her head. "Hmm. What kind of trouble? You're too in control to do drugs. Numbers running? The ponies?"

His lips twitched. "Are you finished?"

"I don't know. Was it better? Worse?"

"What gives you the impression I was an orphan?"

She shrugged. "I read a lot. The hero always has some sort of angsty background."

He went still. "I'm no hero."

"Am I right about *any* of it?"

"Not even close. I have a kid sister I adore. Three brothers I'm crazy about, and a father I get on with very well."

"Oh. Well, I'm glad you weren't an orphan, anyway." She picked up her water glass and took a drink. "Can anything be done about your eye, or is it a permanent injury?"

Michael stared at her. No one. *No one!* Had ever asked about his eye. Even his family only knew the barest of details. "It's permanent. And I don't talk about it."

"Perhaps you should."

"I. Don't. Talk. About. It."

"Does it hurt?"

"No."

"You'll work through it, you know."

"What the hell are you? A psychiatrist?"

"Brooding doesn't appear to be in your nature—or at least not intrinsically. I imagine you're going through a learning period. A time of adjustment. When you've come to terms with it, you'll adjust beautifully, and go back to whatever you were doing before you decided to hide, while sailing the seven seas."

"Jesus, Tally Cruise, are you for real?"

Chapter Six

Tally rolled over and punched her pillow. She'd upset Michael with her questions about his eye. Why couldn't she learn to shut up? Sometimes her brain disengaged from her mouth, and she just blurted out her thoughts before filtering them.

She'd like to blame him for her open-mouth-insert-foot comments. Damn it, he'd sat there, bare and delicious looking—and *reasonable!*—and had expected her to have a rational conversation? Tally groaned. This was absolutely the most ridiculous, the most *inappropriate* behavior. She'd been shocked at the salacious thoughts dancing through her mind while she'd watched him eating.

At one point, when he'd dropped that slice of melon on his chest, she'd stared at the damp spot it left behind and had fantasized how the combination of Michael and melon would taste.

She rolled over again. Too hot. Too wound up to go to sleep, and punched the stupid, not down, pillow. "Get out of my head, blast you!"

She tugged the front of her pajamas away from her far too sensitive nipples, and scissored her legs to find a cool spot on the tangled sheets. *That* was a bad idea.

She rolled over again, eyes squeezed shut. *You are getting sleepy* . . . horny was more like it!

Sleeeepy, damn it. Verry veryyy sleeeepy . . .

Nope. Wasn't working. She wasn't the least bit sleepy.

Self-hypnosis was a bust, and she didn't want to count sheep. What she wanted was Michael Wright in bed, inside her.

She stared at the ceiling, softly lit by the dim glow of the night-light, and tried to convince herself that not repeating their sexual encounter was the right thing. Okay, fine. It had *felt* right at the time, but now she was reasonably rational, she had no excuse.

She turned over on her tummy. It wasn't as though the man *meant* anything to her. How could he? After such a short time? Women needed emotional involvement as well as physical release. At least *she* did. . . .

Tally groaned. Was she trying to talk herself into taking the easy road and sleeping with him again? God only knew, her body was rarin' to go.

Sleeepy.

Nope. Cold turkey was the right thing to do here.

Why was *he* so blasted intriguing? Tally flopped over onto her back. She'd never lost sleep over any other man, but then, she'd never felt this kind of erotic heat in her life. She liked the feeling too much, so it couldn't possibly be good for her. She wriggled onto her side, punched the pillow, groaned, then turned on her stomach.

Not only was it inappropriate to say the least, the feelings weren't reciprocal. Which basically made her pathetic.

Michael Wright had slept with her because she'd crawled into his bed and let him do whatever he'd wanted with her. And, God help her, let her do whatever she'd wanted to him. Her cheeks flamed. Holy cow, she couldn't believe some of the things she'd done to his body. Michael Wright knew what he was doing in the lovemaking department, that's for sure. But she wasn't sure he was fully engaged in the exchange.

Sleeepy. Very, very sleepy.

"Oh, for Pete's sake!" She was ready for this night to end. She buried her face in the pillow. She wanted to sleep. She needed sleep. Tally lifted her head and flipped the pillow over to the cool side. It didn't help that it was barely ten P.M. when she'd come to bed. Far too early. No wonder she couldn't—

Her eyes flew open as a barely audible sound superimposed itself over the faint hum of voices from the bar below. Was that Michael coming upstairs to bed? Her entire body tensed, as if for action. Would he stop outside her door, hoping she was awake? Would he be tempted to come in?

"You are such a wuss," she whispered. "Get a grip." She didn't hear the noise again and tried to relax.

Her bedroom door snicked open.

Wait a minute . . .

Her door?

Oh. My. God. Tally's eyes flew open, and her heart almost stopped as realization struck: *He's come to my room. Be still my heart.*

Oh, Lord. She'd categorically told him no more sex, then flirted with him. She'd given off completely mixed signals, but damn it, that was because she was *feeling* mixed signals. Her body wanted va va voom, and her brain was sending a Klaxon call of warning.

Tally froze, listening to his stealthy footsteps approaching the bed. She didn't know what to do. Sit up and say, "Come on in," or pretend to be asleep, or yell at him for crossing the line she'd drawn in the sand.

His footsteps stopped, and the soft, comforting glow in the room was suddenly extinguished. He'd unplugged the small night-light by the door.

Fear tangled with desire and damn near squashed it. *I wish you hadn't done that.* Dark was the last thing she needed right now. She was already overstimulated, and the man hadn't done anything. Yet. Tally squeezed her eyes tightly shut, pretending she was bathed in candlelight.

It helped. A little.

Her heartbeat sped up, and every sense vibrated as Michael crossed from the door to the bed.

She opted for pretending she was asleep. Cowardly, perhaps,

but nonconfrontational and safe; the best course for this time of night.

His footfall was quiet, a soft shift of bare feet on wood. She wanted to roll over to greet him. With open arms.

No, she didn't. What was she *thinking?* This would be a good time to "wake up" and tell him to get the hell out. This would be a perfect time to get her body and her brain to cooperate and come up with a definitive N-O. How the hell could she make it clear to him when it was as clear as mud to her?

Tally lay still, barely breathing, her body humming with anticipation. With sheer, unadulterated lust.

The footsteps stopped beside the bed.

Under the pillow beneath her head her fingernails bit into her palm. If they made love again, there'd be no going back. If she managed to get a grip on her raging hormones and tell him her decision had been final, that would be that.

To holiday fling, or not holiday fling. That was the question.

Make up your mind, Tallulah!

It was now or never. She started to roll over. The movement was arrested by a large palm slapped roughly over her mouth.

"Heyth!" The callused hand tightened painfully. Tally struggled to sit up even as she tried to shove the restraint away. He was strong and determined. She couldn't even manage to lift her head from the pillow.

The son of a bitch hadn't taken no for an answer after all.

Infuriated, Tally tried to break his grip on her face. One of her arms was pinned beneath her head. The other trapped against her body by the sheet he was apparently kneeling on.

The nerve of the man. The unmitigated *gall.* How *dare* he come in here and just grab her after she'd . . .

Oh, God. This was not *Michael.*

He bent over to whisper something in her ear. Tally hadn't a clue what he'd just said. It sounded like French. Did he think that phony accent would turn her on? The man was crazy.

He put more of his considerable weight against her shoulder, squishing her into the mattress, and whispered menacingly. "This will go much worse for you if you fight me."

He'd been drinking. His breath smelled like whiskey aged in a fish barrel. *Ew!*

Tally struggled harder, managing to free her legs but not her upper body. She tried to reach the flashlight she kept on the bedside table. It was lightweight, but big enough to give him a nasty conk on his head. Unfortunately, it was just out of reach.

She couldn't get his hand off her mouth to scream, and besides, the noise in the bar downstairs would drown out any sound from her room.

She struggled, this time freeing an elbow and jerking it backwards with enough force to elicit a hoarse curse as it struck his thigh. His hand tightened on her face. He said something else, but the blood pounding in her ears made hearing damn difficult.

Something cold and sharp touched her throat. Tally froze. He had a knife? The son of a bitch had a *knife* at her throat?

That's it! Tally pushed the weapon away from her skin, so furious, she didn't care if the sicko cut her in the process.

With almost superhuman strength, she shoved away. Free, she scrambled to her knees and then bounded to her feet to stand—no, *bounce*—on the sagging mattress. Vaguely, she heard the knife clatter to the hardwood floor as she grabbed him by the hair and shook him like a rat.

"Hurensohn!" she shouted in German. "You sorry excuse for a man." Shake. "*Kaproskilo!* Scum-sucking dirt wad." Shake. "Lowlife opportunist. You—"

"Mon Dieu!" The man grabbed her hands fisted in his hair. *"Merde."*

"Who are you? What are you doing in my room?" Tally paused, her fingers buried in his hair. Coarse, thin, oily hair.

Oh, gross. "What"—she held on, and shook him again—"do you want?"

"You are a dead woman," he said in gutter French. "A dead woman."

She yanked harder. "For a dead woman, I have quite a grip, don't I, you motherless bastard?"

"Let go or die."

"Let go *and* die, you mean. What do you want? What have I done to you?" She demanded, in French.

He shackled her wrists and threw her backwards. Tally landed flat on her back on the mattress, the man fell with her, crushing her chest. One arm was pinned beneath her own hip, the other was pinned by the weight of his body. She squirmed beneath him. He wasn't budging.

His hands came up around her throat. He was strong and determined. She gagged. Coughed. Gagged again. Brilliant lights starburst in the blackness of Tally's vision.

Her right hand was palm up, and she could feel his heavy erection twitch against her fingers. Oh, Jesus. Fighting to stay conscious, Tally tried to free either of her arms so that she could try to fight him off. Their combined weight made the task impossible.

With sheer gut instinct she closed her hand around the man's testicles and penis in a death grip. And squeezed with all her strength. The pressure immediately relaxed around her throat. She squeezed harder, digging her long nails into his flesh through his pants.

He screamed. High-pitched and loud. Still holding on, she levered her upper body off the bed. He was cursing in virulent French, bent over, trying to protect his privates while scrabbling for her wrist. Tally managed to get a two-handed grip on his body parts. As disgusting as it was, she wasn't letting go for anything.

His elbow smacked her check as he flailed around, in too much pain to be effective fighting *her* off. Good. She held to him as tightly as she could. Her hands numb with the pressure, her nails imbedded to the quick. There was no more erection of course, just a limp, disgusting noodle stretched to its limit. She was going to be grossed out as soon as she could figure out what to do next.

Oh, Lord. What *am* I supposed to do with him now? Staring blindly into the darkness, she shouted, "Michael! Help!"

Tally dragged the guy to the window like a pull toy. His language was blue and fierce, but of course, like any man, he followed his penis. She stepped outside onto the narrow wood lanai. The star-studded sky didn't give off enough light. But she saw that he was hunched over almost double, his hands clutched over hers, moaning in pain. Tally dug her nails in harder.

Below the balcony was Auntie's beautiful tropical garden. No stairs. So he'd come in through the bar and up the inside stairs. She gave a sharp twist. He screamed like a girl. "Tell me why you wanted to hurt me?" she demanded, trying to figure out what the hell to do now.

"I was looking for . . . money," he said in a rapid spate of French interspersed with much sobbing. "You will release my penis, and I shall go."

"And come back to rob me another time? I don't think so."

"*Non.* I will tell h—*mon Dieu!* Release me, I beg this of you."

Because she obviously couldn't stand there forever gripping the man's balls, Tally let go. And while he was still moaning and hunched over hugging his privates, she pushed him over the balcony to the lanai below.

There was a thump, a loud rustle of foliage, and then silence.

Without looking down, she rushed back inside and slammed the French door behind her. Grabbing the rattan chair near the bed, she wedged it under the handles. Useless, of course. Anyone wanting to come in only needed to give a hard push and the chair would slide across the wood floor.

Tally fumbled in the dark for the flashlight she always kept beside the bed, then pulled the thin drapes closed across the glass door with shaking hands. With the light to guide her, she went across the room and turned the useless lock in the doorknob, then flicked on the overhead light.

Better. Much better. She peered at her throat in the mirror by the door. Her neck was already starting to bruise, and damn it, the son of a bitch had *cut* her. She felt sick to her stomach at the violence. Two near-death experiences since she'd been here was two too many.

This was a little more reality than she was ready for. From downstairs came the sound of people laughing, talking, having fun. She hesitated, almost scared enough to go racing downstairs in her jammies.

But not *quite.*

She pulled off her pj's, and dragged on a pair of camel linen slacks, and a tailored white linen shirt with natural bone buttons. Barefoot, she opened the door into the hallway. If it hadn't been for the stream of light from her room, the hallway would've been pitch-dark. She went back inside to get the flashlight. If need be, she'd use it like a club.

A quick glance to the left showed Michael's door ajar. Had he come upstairs yet or was he still downstairs drinking and carousing with the locals? He wasn't the type of man to go to bed at ten o'clock. At least not alone.

She hesitated. Michael, or downstairs?

Surely he wouldn't sleep with her one night, and bring Leli'a to his room right in her auntie's hotel the next? The thought of Michael Wright having hot sex with the beautiful Tahitian girl made Tally's stomach roll.

With the flashlight raised, she turned toward the stairs and the noisy barroom below. Grabbing the metal banister, she raced down the steep cement steps two at a time.

Wearing shorts, a sweatshirt, and his eye patch, Michael tapered off his nighttime run to a jog, then finally, a walk. He wasn't wearing his watch, but judging by the position of the stars, it was after ten. There was no moon, but the stars winked ice clear in the blackness of the sky.

The beach was at least three miles long. He'd run the soft sandy stretch five times at a dead run and was barely winded. No heavy pack. No combat weapons. No sweat.

Not bad for a man who'd sailed for eleven months and avoided dry land, barring necessities. With all the toys he had onboard, two global positioning systems, the radios, and phone, fax, and e-mail capabilities, other than supplies, he could do everything he needed to do from the open sea.

Michael stood with his fingers locked behind his head and stretched as he stared thoughtfully out over the ocean. His lips twitched as he pictured Tally earlier at dinner. Did she know what a mass of contradictions she was? Elegant and earthy. Sexy as hell, and prim. Volatile and icy.

He shook his head and lowered his arms, then turned and walked away from the few lights of the bar and marina. Down the long, suddenly too bright, expanse of the beach. Farther up, as the beach turned the corner of the bay, he'd be blocked by a convenient rocky outcrop. The lava rocks meandered along the coast, steadily climbing, and forming a wedge as gentle hills became the cliffs on the west, north, and south of the island.

Warm, fragrant air caressed his damp skin.

The blast on Arnaud's boat had been expertly set and discharged. It didn't take an underwater detonation expert to figure that one out. Bouchard *had* been on deck when she'd blown.

Coincidence? Michael didn't think so.

He wondered if the explosion was a plan gone wrong. Did the delectable Tally have a nice big life insurance policy? And what about the second man? Also missing. How had he figured into it?

The sugary sand beneath his feet retained the heat of the day. Michael picked up a small broken slice of shell and flipped it between his fingers as he walked. The shell broke like a promise in his hand. He tossed it aside and veered onto the hard-packed wet sand.

He clambered over the lava rocks to the beach of the tiny cove on the other side. It was clear from the watermark striations on the rocks that this small stretch would be under water at high tide. Presently, the surf lapped gently at the surrounding rocks, leaving a snowy expanse of beach exposed.

Michael reconned the perimeter and found the small mouth of a cave, or deep depression. Darkness prevented him from seeing more than a foot or so inside. He crouched low and brailed his way around the opening.

"Sonofabitch, a cave." The narrow fissure opened enough for him to stand without bumping his head. But without a flashlight it was useless going any further. He'd come back tomorrow in the daylight. The cave would be a strong possibility for Church's hidden cache. His heart sped up with anticipation. God, it couldn't be this easy.

And why not?

Church wouldn't expect his enemy to show up announced at his front door.

Michael backtracked until he saw the faint glow of starlight, then emerged into the fresh air. He dug his toes into the damp sand and stuffed his hands into his pockets as he stared out across the vast expanse of the ocean.

There was nothing malevolent about the water tonight. A transparent white sheen painted a shimmering path to infinity beyond the glassy surface. Tempting. Luring.

Deceptively benign . . .

Tied together by the six-foot line, he and Hugo sank deeper and deeper into the icy darkness. Their target, the hull of the Marie José, *three hundred yards away.*

Something brushed his leg. A curious barracuda. Michael checked the illuminated compass board. Target dead ahead. He tugged once on the line. Hugo tended to get clausty down here after about an hour, and they'd been down twice that. I'm good. You?

Hugo tugged back. Good.

With a quick thrust of his legs, Michael swam downward, shooting forward, Hugo right behind him. The ocean was unforgiving. Especially at night. There was only one way to do this: by the book.

But "by the book" was a slow, laborious process in the pitch-dark in forty-degree water.

It was a damn good thing he didn't have time to think about how miserable he was. Even with the insulated layer of water between his body and wet suit, he was freezing his ass off. He ignored it.

The sound of his front-mounted rebreathing rig throbbed in his ears. Two more hours, and they'd be outta here. . . .

Ah, Jesus. He jerked out of his waking nightmare, eyes narrowed on the distant lights at the other end of the beach. The sound of music and laughter from Auntie's outside bar drifted faintly on the sultry air.

Michael turned his head. Looked across the water.

Do it, asshole.

A *child* could paddle. For Christ's sake, the water wasn't anywhere near him and his heart was racing.

The man he used to be faced his fear head-on, and beat it all to hell.

The man he used to be wasn't a coward. . . .

What he wouldn't give to be that man again.

Sweating, shaking, Michael rubbed a hand across his face.

Just do it, man!

Before he changed his mind, he strode purposefully toward the gently creaming surf. He had two days to get over this once and for all. Two frigging days.

"Come on. Come on. Come on." His toes touched water. He stopped as if he'd hit a brick wall. "Shit."

The deadly beauty beckoned, mocking him with his own cowardice, tantalizing him with its allure, promising absolution and oblivion.

Tepid water lapped at his toes, then his ankles. He swallowed a couple of times, tried to get rid of the cottonmouth. It didn't work. A chill, deep and unpleasant, crawled across his skin. *All* his skin. His pecker shriveled up and crawled inside him.

He glanced up the beach. Not a soul in sight.

He scanned the water. No boogeyman.

He'd loved water all his life. Swum in it as a kid, made his living from it as a naval officer. Loved it like nothing else as a SEAL.

And, because of Trevor Church, feared the living shit out of it now.

"Hugo?" Michael addressed the starry sky. "Are you watching this and laughing your ass off?"

Of course Hugo Caletti wasn't laughing.

He was dead.

Michael had killed him.

Chapter Seven

The moment Tally burst through the door into the light, she dashed straight for the rest room, where she used gallons of hot, soapy water to wash her hands. She emerged feeling slightly calmer, her hands pink and stinging from the scrubbing. Hopefully all the guy's cooties were scalded off her skin. *Ew.*

"There my girl." Auntie swung around the end of the bar to give Tally a bear hug. "No good pretty girl go bed so early." She elbowed a skinny young man off a barstool and all but hoisted Tally onto the worn leather seat. "What you drink, baby?"

Tally flipped up her shirt collar stylishly to hide the marks on her neck, and took a quick inventory of the room, her heart still pounding uncomfortably. The entire front wall of the bar was open to the mild trade winds blowing in off the ocean, and she was grateful for the breeze. All her nerves were still jumping.

"A piña colada?" She cleared her throat and tucked her bare feet around the legs of the stool. "A piña colada."

She made a point of not making eye contact with the handful of men in the room. They were all strangers. Covertly, she examined the occupants one by one in the flyspecked mirror behind the bar.

Are you the one? Or you? How about you? None of them looked greasy, or in enough pain, to be the man she'd tossed over the balcony.

"My specialty," Auntie assured Tally, bustling behind the

ramshackle bar for the ingredients. "Your voice soundin' a bit rough. You comin' on a cold, baby girl?"

No. I was just strangled, Tally thought somewhat hysterically. "Just a dry throat," she assured Auntie. *Oh, damn.* Michael wasn't down here, either. Where could he have gone to in the middle of the night?

Leli'a's house?

Don't go there. Besides, it was none of her business, and she didn't need him. Did she? No. She didn't. "Have you seen Michael around?"

"He troubled, that boy."

"You mean he *is* trouble." She'd talk to Auntie about a better lock for her do—

"What the hell happened to your neck?"

His voice came from right beside her, and Tally gave a little squawk of surprise. He'd materialized as if by magic.

"My neck?" she repeated stupidly, her heart racing for a totally different reason now. It was a pheromone thing, she decided, some chemical imbalance in her brain that reacted so strongly to Michael's presence.

His sharp gaze locked on her neck. Tally wondered how he'd zeroed in on her injuries so quickly. He stood watching her, hands tucked in the pockets of his black shorts, dark hair ruffled. He looked . . . sinister. Dangerous. Lost.

His brows pulled together in a frown. "And why," he asked dangerously, "are you shaking?"

"I—"

"What you be drinking, handsome?" Auntie leaned her sumo wrestler arms on the bar.

"Whiskey." He didn't look away from Tally. "Straight up."

Tally turned away long enough to break the connection. She clutched the drink Auntie set on the bar in front of her. A tentative sip, and the icy cold froth slid down her throat like glory. She sighed in appreciation.

"My specialty," Auntie said with a wide grin. She poured, then placed his drink on the tiled bar. "Where you been, hottie?"

"Running on the beach."

Auntie looked horrified. "Alone? You walk magical moonlight beach all by your lonesome? This no good. Next time you take pretty girl."

He turned away from Tally to give Auntie a quick, flirtatious smile. "When we have some moonlight, I'll come and get *you*."

"No. This here the pretty girl for you." She pointed at Tally.

Wrong. I'm not the girl for you, and you are definitely not the man for me. Too bad my body refuses to get with the program.

Tally waited until Auntie shuffled off to serve someone else, then took a deep breath. "Michael," she whispered urgently, "you won't believe what h—"

"Here be my man," Auntie interrupted, dragging a small, thin man by the arm as though he'd bolt if she let go. They were Jack Sprat and his wife. "Henri Jeûner, this be Tallulah, Trevor's o—Trevor's daughter—and her friend Michael. What you last name, hottie?"

"Wright." Michael glanced away from Tally's throat to greet the other man, then back again like a tracer bullet.

"Enchanté, mademoiselle." Auntie's Henri looked a lot like Sammy Davis, Jr. His accent was pure Maurice Chevalier, and for a second, Tally's heart stuttered. The man in her room had been French. Henri wasn't the man, of course; he was substantially cleaner, less robust, a foot shorter, and his accent was far more elegant. His brown eyes sparkled up at her as he bent to kiss her hand—an old-fashioned gesture Tally found charming. Or would have, at any other time. Right now she wanted to talk to Michael.

"Are you from Saint-Pois?" Tally asked in French, recognizing the slight regional inflection.

"*Mon Dieu!* Sourdeval, practically next door!" Henri burst into a spate of colloquial French, delighted when Tally told him she and her mother had spent several weeks in a village nearby when she was a child.

"You have come to see your papa." Henri reverted back to English. "He will be most surprised."

"No, he won't." Tally nibbled on the chunk of pineapple Auntie had used to garnish her drink. It was more tart than sweet and made her blink and purse her mouth. "He invited me."

Henri shot a fleeting look at Auntie, who shrugged. He said only, "Then he will be *most* happy that you are here."

Tally glanced up at Michael to see if he'd noticed anything strange about that little exchange. But the couple was on his blind side, and he wasn't looking directly at them, so he'd missed it. He'd moved closer to brace his hand on the counter behind her, his arm across her back. His breath ruffled her hair. If she turned her head a bit more she could bury her nose in the crisp hair on his bare chest. The man never wore enough clothes. She liked that about him.

Auntie shuffled back behind the bar, and Henri stayed long enough to suggest some local sights for them to explore. Nothing was any great distance, he told them. The waterfall on the other side of the lava field was worth a visit. Auntie, he assured Tally, would be happy to pack a picnic for them.

"They seem sweet together." Tally watched the other couple exchange a brief kiss before Henri went off to sit at a table outside with several friends.

"At least you've stopped shaking," Michael said flatly. He looked disreputable with his unshaven jaw, shaggy hair, and that sinister black eye patch. Tally was oh so tempted to fling herself into his arms and demand he take her back onboard the *Nemesis* and sail into the sunset. "What gives?"

"Some guy came into my room. He scared the bejesus out of me."

"What the hell did he want?"

It was going to sound overly dramatic or stupid when she said it out loud, but she said it, anyway. "I think he was trying to kill me."

"What?"

"He tried to—"

"Jesus. I heard you." He brushed aside her upturned collar with both hands. His warm fingers traced either side of her throat as he said in a deadly voice, "The son of a bitch put his hands on you."

"Well, yeah." Now that Michael was pissed off on her behalf, Tally felt much better. "He was attempting to strangle me. He also had a knife."

"So I see." He touched the small cut with a gentle finger, the look in his eye murderous. "Could you I.D. him if you saw him again?"

"You bet," Tally told him, pleased with herself. "He'll be the one limping, holding his . . . privates, and pulling a face like this." She screwed up her features in a parody of extreme pain.

Michael snorted a laugh and shook his head. "Kicked him in the balls, did you?"

"No, actually—" She made an upside-down claw of her right hand and made a wrenching motion.

Michael winced, then chuckled. "Jesus. I'd've given cold, hard cash to have seen that."

"Yeah, well, it wasn't quite so amusing when he was in action in the pitch-dark."

"Poor little bear, he really scared the crap out of you, didn't he?"

His sympathy almost undid her, and her eyes stung. Forcibly resisting the urge to rest her head on his chest, she blinked back tears as she pushed the wild tangle of her hair out of her eyes. "I threw him over the balcony."

"Yeah? Good for you."

Tally sipped the last bit of froth from the bottom of her glass, then held up her hands in a pseudo karate chop. "Better not mess with me, I have lethal weapons."

He smiled. "Amen, sister."

Michael wondered if she realized how pretty she was when the hectic color fired up her incredible blue eyes. Probably not. If the pulse at the base of her throat always beat that fast, she was on a fast track to a heart attack.

Unfortunately, he was starting to see hidden, and unexpected, depths in Tally Cruise. Rather like the beauty of a pearl, her luster was deep and subtle. And damn it, now that he'd noticed, it was hard to understand how he'd thought her plain when he'd first seen her.

He wanted to find the son of a bitch who'd hurt her and break him into several small, jagged pieces.

Which had absolutely no bearing on his prime directive.

Vengeance.

Her first mistake had been sleeping with him. The second had been drinking that third piña colada. She'd never had more than one cautious glass of zinfandel in a sitting in her life.

Whoa. Were the stairs always spongy? Tally tested the cement surface with her toe. Yep. She kept a tight grip on the wrought-iron banister and dragged herself up the narrow stairwell to the upper floor. Where her room was located right next door to the I'm-no-hero pirate with the sexy eyes. *Eye.*

Since she was feeling no pain, thanks to the anesthetizing effects of Auntie's yummy drinks, the small nick on her neck barely smarted.

She opened the door cautiously and, squinting, took a quick visual inventory from wall to wall before stepping inside, and closing, and *locking,* the heavy door behind her. The lamp beside the bed cast few shadows. There must have been a 250-watt bulb in it, and the white flowers on a fuchsia cotton shade did little to dim the bright, rosy glow reflected off the white walls.

Not bothering to wash her face—something she knew she'd regret come morning—she stripped and put on her favorite pajamas. Then fell nose first onto the snow-blinding bedspread as she hung over the edge of the mattress and peered under the bed.

No boogeyman. Whew.

She flopped back, spread-eagled, across the queen-size bed.

This trip was proving to be a smorgasbord of new experiences.

Near drownings.

Mind-blowing sex.

One-eyed pirates.

Mind-blowing sex.

Three-legged cats.

Un-*be*-lievable mind-blowing sex.

Stinky intruders with knives.

She frowned. Had she already mentioned sex?

Fab-ulous sex.

Piña coladas, and numb tongues.

Covering her eyes with her arm, Tally debated getting up to hang up her clothes. It seemed like an awful lot of tr . . .

It felt like seconds later when she jerked awake. For a moment she lay there on her back, wondering what had woken her. Not the soft, sibilant murmur of voices from downstairs.

Someone breathing.

She froze in place. The small hairs on her arms prickled. Her pulse raced, her muscles tensed as fight-or-flight instincts kicked in.

Not again, you bastard. Not again.

Cautiously, she inched her arm away from her face. The room was pitch-dark. No million-watt bedside lamp. No night-light by the door.

Don't freak out.

Before the panic attack got ahold, Tally flew off the bed, hit the floor running, and wrenched open the . . . *unlocked* . . . door to her room. Heart pounding, she slapped a hand on the wall and used it to brace herself as she raced down the equally dark corridor to Michael's room next door.

He might not consider himself a hero, but right now he was the only game in town. If nothing else, he was big and solid.

Tally burst through his door at a dead run.

Other than the blinking outline of the mean-eyed cat snoozing at the foot of the bed, the room was empty.

"Unless you can turn into something useful, you're no

good to me," she told Lucky. Not bothering to close the door, Tally made a screaming uie, and charged down the dark corridor. She did a running jump, a don't-step-on-the-cracks, scaredy-pants jump across her own doorway, and charged full tilt toward the stairs.

Disorientated by the dark, breathing as if she'd run six miles instead of six yards, she groped for the metal handrail. Light. She had to get into the light. Now.

Body vibrating with urgency, she found the handrail and stepped down . . . a hard shove caught her between her shoulder blades. . . .

Tally went cartwheeling through the thick darkness.

"Honey, you need a keeper."

Once he'd scraped her off the cement floor of the bar and taken her into a back room where Auntie had a narrow daybed tucked into a corner of her small office, Michael had checked her over. After falling ass over teakettle down a staircase, she was fortunate nothing was broken.

Tally tentatively wiggled her nose between two fingers, her blue eyes crossed as she tried to see the tip. "I think my node ith broken."

"It's not. Which is amazing, considering your speed when you came through that door. You're lucky you didn't break your neck."

She would have hurt a hell of a lot more if the door had been fully closed. As it was, she'd tumbled, screaming at the top of her lungs, through the partially open door. Her momentum had propelled her like a rocket. Wearing a dazed expression, and a pair of powder blue man-style pajamas, her unceremonious arrival had caused quite a stir among the few remaining late-night diehards. Several of whom were now crowded in the doorway, watching them. Michael would bet any one of the men outside would've liked an opportunity to run his hands over Tally Cruise's slender body.

She rose up on her elbow, glanced toward the door, then said with quiet urgency, "Michael. That guy came back. I heard him . . . breathing. I ran like hell, and when I got to the head of the stairs"—she shivered, her breath coming fast and uneven—"the son of a bitch *p-pushed* me."

"Calm down. You're hyperventilating."

"Of course I'm hy-per-ven-til-at-ing! S-Someone is—someone tried to—"

"Tally?"

She sucked air. "Wh-Wh-a-t?"

"Take a slow, easy breath, honey." Her pupils dilated as their gazes clung. Her blue eyes were too large, glassy and unfocused as she struggled to catch a real breath. A clammy film of perspiration glazed her skin.

His fingers tightened on her shoulders. "Easy. Try to relax." He stroked his hands soothingly down her arms. Her muscles were tight as bowstrings, fragile.

Michael took her face in his hands. His thumbs brushed her tear-damp cheekbones. She was gasping, couldn't catch her breath, her heart going nineteen to the dozen. From the looks of it she was in for a full-blown panic attack.

"Breathe with me." Michael placed his hand on her chest, fingers spread. Beneath his palm her heart flub-dubbed like a trapped bird. "In . . . slow. Out . . ."

She grabbed his wrist. " 'n't *breathe!*"

"Yeah, I see that, sweetheart." Hell . . . He slid his arm around her back and pulled her against him. His open mouth came down on hers. For a second she struggled, then became pliant in his arms as he breathed with her, gradually slowing his own breathing down until she matched his, and they breathed in unison.

After a few minutes she was so into the kiss, she forgot about breathing. Only then did Michael raise his head. "Better?"

"Much." She gave him a tremulous smile that went straight to his heart. "But you wouldn't be nearly as convenient to carry around as a brown paper bag."

He huffed out a laugh. "Did you hurt yourself barreling down the stairs at ninety-nine miles an hour?"

Tally rubbed her forehead and shook her head. "I must have rubber bones. I think I bounced."

He said nothing for a moment as he stared at the livid marks around her slender throat. The marks had darkened considerably in the last few hours. The imprint of two large thumbs showed clearly against the soft pulse at the base of her throat.

Fury rose like a black tide inside him. Some son of a bitch had put his filthy hands on her. *Hurt* her. Michael gently pushed her sweat-damped hair off her chalk white face. "You slid in like a ballplayer going for first base." Her pretty eyes were cloudy, and bewildered by the violence. And damn it, Michael was pissed. *That* ticked him off more than anything. She was zilch to him.

They barely knew each other. She was nothing more than Church's daughter. A pawn. A means to an end.

"We'll get to the bottom of this." He kept his voice soothing instead of murderous. "Whoever it was, probably wanted mon—"

"Here, baby girl, you take two of these. How you feel now?" Auntie had returned with a glass of water and a pill bottle.

"Thanks." She managed a smile for the other woman as she took the bottle and glass. "I'm sure I'll be fine after a good night's sleep." She grimaced. "Though how I'll manage that, I don't know. Every time I go to my room—" She handed the glass of water to Michael, shook a couple of Advil onto her hand, then took the glass back to gulp the water. "Thanks." Her smile was crooked. "You give new meaning to the words 'mouth-to-mouth' resuscitation."

"It's a gift." He didn't want her to thank him, or look at him with trust. But one look from those baby-blues and he almost forgot his own name. "Need help getting upstairs? Want me to get a big stick and come with you?"

"I'd love you to get a big stick. Then you could shove it up his—"

"Who *he?*" Auntie demanded, eyes narrow, beefy arms akimbo.

"Some guy tried to rob Tally in her room."

"Did he hurt you, baby?" Auntie demanded, coming to take Tally's chin in her hand. "Hoo-ee. That sumbitch give you bad bruises!" She shook her head in disgust. "It be those seasonal sailors comin', goin'. Bring boats in, havta hang around waiting to take 'em back out. Nothing better to do than drink—which is mighty good for Auntie—and steal from my customers, which is bad! The bossman get back, he gonna hear from Auntie, quick-quick! Enough bad stuff. You hear?"

"I hear you," Michael said grimly, helping Tally to her feet. She still looked chalky, which made the emerging bruise on her cheek look even darker. "Let's get you settled, before I start asking questions."

"Yes. Good. Get our girl in bed. We ask questions." Auntie put a beefy arm around Tally's narrow shoulders and led her through the door. "Out of the way, you!" She pushed through the men crowded outside. They scattered like chickens before a fox. "Business is now closed. Go home. Henri? You close up and lock that door."

"Now you," she told Tally, "just scoot upstairs and take nice hot bath, then Auntie give you a good, deep-tissue massage. Get those nasty knots out. You see. In morning you be fit as a fiddle. Henri? Make it quick-quick!"

"A hot shower would be great," Tally said. "Thanks for the Advil . . . oh. The light in my room's burned out. Do you have a bulb I can take up?"

Auntie bustled off behind the bar for a bulb. Tally looked pale, and fragile. She also looked damn delicious to Michael in those pale, soft pajamas covered with little yellow flowers. Not that tailored pajamas on a woman appealed to him. He usually preferred his women in nothing at all. Tally looked too virginal and ice princess-ish for his tastes.

And he wanted her more than his next breath. Damn.

Michael walked over to the counter and picked up the beer he'd abandoned when she'd crashed through the door headfirst to land practically at his feet.

He took a sip. Warm. "Go ahead. Turn on the light in the hall. I'll bring it up when I come."

She held a hand casually over the empty buttonhole on her pajama top. As if he hadn't already noticed the button was missing. As if he hadn't inadvertently seen a curve of small, plump breast when she'd been lying down.

As if her slender arm across her chest prevented him from seeing the outline of her body through the thin cotton backlit by the light in Auntie's office.

"I'll wait." Tally held on to the doorknob without opening the door. "I'm in no hurry."

He saw the nervous rapidity of her breathing and the tantalizing throb of her heart in the hollow of her throat. He wanted to put his mouth there. He wanted to put his hands on her. Instead, he chugged the last inch of warm beer, then crushed the can in his fist.

She wasn't his problem.

Tally took the proffered carton of lightbulbs from their hostess and hugged it to her chest.

Michael held the can tighter. A shield between himself and the woman with fear in her clear blue eyes. Damn. "Want me to come up and look under your bed?"

She didn't hesitate. "Please."

Michael held the door to the upstairs rooms open for her. The stairwell was dark, as was the hallway above. He flicked the switch a couple of times.

"Wait here." He handed her the crushed beer can and took the lightbulbs. His knuckles accidentally brushed against her small breasts. She drew in a breath and held it.

He released the door, waited a second or two for his eye to adjust, then sprinted silently up the steep cement steps to the floor above.

None of the upstairs lights were on.

Not over the stairs. Not in the hallway. Not in her room.

Her bedroom door stood wide open. The shutters blocked any starlight. The small shell night-light he'd seen when he'd searched her room that morning was gone.

He entered cautiously. Empty. The room smelled faintly of Tally's perfume. A hint of tuberose, and the floral shampoo he'd seen in their shared bathroom down the hall, mixed with the iodine scent of the sea.

Her room was set up exactly like his. Wood floor, queen-size bed, small bedside table, and a lot of violent pink. He strode to the table and removed a bulb from the pack. After the experiences of the last couple of days, it was no wonder she was freaked out. She'd probably woken from a dream, found the light burned out, and panicked.

Michael reached in to remove the dead bulb . . . there was nothing in the socket.

Chapter Eight

Half an hour later, Tally emerged from the bathroom. Since she'd never been beaten up, she wasn't positive this was what it felt like afterward. However, considering the aches and bruises her assailant had inflicted, she figured this kind of discomfort was in the ballpark. A hot shower had helped dull the aches; walking into her brightly lit room helped even more.

Seeing Michael Wright sitting in the chair under the window didn't help one bit. "What are you doing in here?" She realized she was clutching the front of her pajama top where the button was missing closed in her fist like a maiden aunt. She dropped her arms to her side and relaxed her tense shoulders.

She knew without looking that the thin, frequently washed cotton clung to her damp skin. She thought longingly of her nice, thick velour robe back in Chicago. She thought even more longingly of being in Michael's strong arms.

Auntie's gazillion-watt bulb purged the shadows from the room. The only remaining dark spot was the pirate seated by the window. Enigmatic, intense, he personified shadow.

"I found this under the table." Michael held up a small, nasty-looking knife. "Tell me about him."

Tally sat on the bed with a thump. She closed her eyes, trying to remember what he'd felt like, the space he'd occupied. "He seemed to be about eight foot ten. In reality, he was probably about . . . five six, seven. Solid. Balding. What hair he had was greasy and thin . . . French. Somewhere in the south, close to Spain, I'd guess."

"That's impressive."

Pleased, Tally smiled. "I don't want you to think I'm just a pretty face."

"Honey, the way you handled that guy convinced me of that. Nobody downstairs fits that description. I checked the shrubs below the lanai—nice shot, by the way—he landed hard, but judging from his footprints, managed to limp away. So the question is, what was he doing in your room?"

She scrunched up her face. "I'd swear he said he was here to *kill* me." Tally held up a hand. "Okay, not *swear.* I thought that's what he said. At first. But it seems *so* illogical, so far-fetched, I dismissed it." Her fingertips automatically went to the necklace of bruises. "Until he put his grubby hands around my throat."

"Not so illogical if you throw the explosion of the boat, and the death of both Bouchard and the crewman, into the mix," he said flatly.

"Oh, God. I thought that, too, but I didn't want to say it aloud." She pulled her pillow onto her lap and rested her elbows on it. "I thought *maybe* . . . but then, *why?* And *who?* It seems too ridiculous for words. He must've been looking for money. My traveler's checks, jewelry. As Auntie said—a lot of transients to-ing and fro-ing the boats for my father." She narrowed her eyes. "Right?"

"*Someone* was in here tonight. The bulb didn't burn out. It was gone. So's your night-light. Which means that either you were unlucky enough to have two visitors, or your inept knife-wielding assassin came back for another try. What about your jewelry and money? Still here, or gone?"

She slid off the bed. "God. I hope he took every dime." She was an adult, with access to credit cards, and to all manner of assistance should she need it. The panicky feeling faded a bit. But she knew it was crouched deep inside her, ready to spring forward and attack without warning. If the thief had wiped her out financially, she'd deal with it.

"You do?"

"Hell, yes. That means he was here to take *stuff.* Stuff can be replaced."

As for the man with the magic lightbulbs, her *non*-hero, all she knew about him was his proclivity for garish Hawaiian glow-in-the-dark shorts, and his name. And she couldn't be sure "Michael Wright" *was* his name. He had a nice boat. But as far as Tally knew, he *could* have stolen her traveler's checks.

If he looked like a pirate . . . Lord. She was getting paranoid. "I'll check later."

"Honey, you don't have anything I want." His lips moved in an unnerving parody of a smile. "Check now."

You don't have anything I want? Swallowing hard, Tally reached down at the head of the bed and grabbed her cosmetic bag. With trembling fingers, she pulled out the jewelry pouch and opened it. "Maybe it wasn't flashy enough for him."

Michael took the pouch and looked inside. "Understated. Elegant. Expensive." He glanced at her and handed it back. "Very . . . you."

She didn't know whether to be insulted or flattered, so she ignored his assessment. The wallet was easier. She fanned out just over three thousand dollars in traveler's checks. "Guess he didn't like my money, either. Traveler's checks are so, so understated, elegant, expensive, and so me."

Her attempt at levity fell flat. Her mouth went dry, and she felt the blood drain from her head. "This is not good."

"Don't be too quick to jump to conclusions. If he *did* want to kill you, he was a lousy assassin."

"Oh, thanks. I've never rated incompetence highly enough. I feel so much better now."

"This is a pocketknife, honey. If he was serious, he would've had something bigger and sharper. And he'd've done the job without waking you."

Tally put a hand up to her throat. "Thanks. I think."

"My guess is he was here to rob you and couldn't find the goods. You woke up and scared the crap out of him, and he was trying to frighten you."

"He succeeded, thank you very much. Why did he come back, then?"

Michael put his hands behind his head and whistled out a

breath. "Hell if I know." The hair in his armpit was dark and silky.

Oh, Lord. How could a man's armpit be sexy? She dragged her attention away from that body part. But there were other, even *better* things to look at. His broad chest. His muscular arms. His mouth . . .

God, she was glad he was here. How casual he was. All tanned, hairy skin and insouciant relaxation. Tally perched on the edge of the mattress, one big, stretched nerve.

She straightened her shoulders, uncertain whether she should pull on something over her pajamas or act as though she were properly dressed for company. With perverse disappointment she realized her state of undress didn't seem to bother him at all. But it bothered the hell out of her. Knowing he was three feet away, and she wasn't wearing any underwear under her pajama bottoms, made her hyperconscious of body parts she'd told to go back to sleep.

"Walk me through this one more time. What happened before you fell?" Michael asked, his tone cool and meditative. There was a quality in his stillness that unnerved her, although she couldn't think why. If he were any more laid back he'd be in a coma.

She noticed a small, pale, crescent-shaped scar just above his left nipple. She could only see it because the light was so bright. He also had a genuine six-pack of banded abdominal muscle that moved gently as he breathed. Her mouth went dry. He'd asked . . . ?

"Something . . . someone . . . woke me. The room was pitch-black." There was something far too . . . *immediate* about him. Something far too elemental, too visceral. Unfortunately, there was also something secretive about him—the haunted look in his eye, the bitter twist to his mobile, unsmiling mouth—that called to her, even though she was smart enough not to let it show. It was a ridiculous and unfounded physical reaction to a total stranger. Tally ruthlessly tamped down the bubbling cauldron of emotion. *I said no. I mean no,* she reminded herself.

"I ran," she said with spurious calm, finger-combing her short, damp hair off her face. "I felt a hand on my back before I fell."

There was a brief knock at the door; her uninvited guest rose. Tally backed up. Auntie shuffled in with a sunset orange beach towel over one shoulder and a bottle of oil in her hand. She looked from one to the other. "I come back later."

"No, come in," Tally said quickly. "Michael was just leaving."

"Sleep good, hottie."

" 'Night, ladies." Michael gave Tally a look that said they weren't done, then closed the door quietly behind him.

She let out a gusty sigh, and Auntie grinned. "He be one hot potato that one. Okay-dokey. Your poor, sad muscles are gonna be lovin' this. You get on the bed. On your tummy. Auntie fix good. You see."

Tally obediently lay on her stomach on the cool sheets, her head cradled in her arms. Auntie lit a candle and placed it on the table beside the bed. It smelled of vanilla. Next, she turned off the bright lamp, plunging the room into flickering shadows. Not Tally's optimum comfort level. Especially now.

Auntie patted her stiff shoulder. "You gotta relax, baby girl. Take your top off," she instructed. A click, and soft music played from the bedside clock radio.

Tally stripped off the pajama top and settled facedown on the mattress. How long could a quick massage take?

She heard the creak of a metal cap as Auntie opened a bottle, then the sound of oil being rubbed between her palms. The fragrance of mint filled the air as Auntie placed her strong hands on Tally's back.

"Now you close your eyes, and listen to the nice music. Feel Auntie's hands make everything better." For such a heavy woman, Auntie had a firm, but gentle touch.

Tally closed her eyes and tried to push everything else out of her mind. The music was soothing, and the feel of Auntie's hands moving down her spine felt great.

Michael stood on the lanai and watched as Tally relaxed under the older woman's skillful hands. *He* wanted to be the one touching her, stroking her smooth, golden skin. He felt like a kid standing outside the candy store. Everything he wanted was in that candlelit room. He could protect her better if he were right there with her.

He stepped quietly through the door into the room. Auntie glanced up without surprise. Her hands kept moving as she tilted her head, indicating the bottle of oil beside her on the small wicker table.

Michael smiled as he poured the mint-scented oil between his hands and came up beside Auntie.

She stepped out of his way, lifting one hand off Tally's narrow back. Michael placed his in the spot she'd just vacated, and ran his thumb up Tally's spine.

Tally moaned. "Oh. That feels wonderful."

Auntie grinned up at him and lifted her other hand in the air. Michael replaced her hands with both his, and pressed down on Tally's spine. He heard the soft brush of Auntie's callused feet as she went to the door. Felt the faint rush of warmer air as she opened the door into the hallway.

The door closed silently, leaving him alone with Tally in the candlelit room, soft music playing, and her half-naked.

He shifted a knee onto the bed, then straddled her without touching. She stiffened, her smooth brow puckered in a frown. He gently massaged her shoulder, and ran his thumb over the twin ridges between her eyes. She sighed and relaxed as he ran his thumbs firmly down the shallow indentation of her spine.

His fingers splayed across her narrow, lightly tanned back glistening with oil. He kneaded down the tight muscles in her back all the way to the low elastic waistband of her pajama bottoms.

She moaned low in her throat. "Mmm. That feels amazing"—she paused—"Michael."

He chuckled, running his fingers up her back and under

her hair and rubbing her neck until she groaned low in her throat. "No surprises, huh?"

She buried her face in her arms, so her voice was muffled. "I felt the changing of the guard."

"I must be losing my touch."

"Your touch—oh, yeah, hmmm, right there—is terrific."

"This is supposed to be relaxing and you're tensing up. Listen to the music and just feel."

She wasn't going to relax just because he told her to.

Michael smoothed his hands in a circle over her shoulders.

Tally sighed. "Tell me a deep, dark secret," she demanded softly, her voice thick and on the edge of sleep.

Her skin beneath his hands was fine-grained and as soft as a child's. Her back was narrow, fragile—and, damn it, bruised. "What kind of deep, dark secret?" The combined fragrances of the vanilla candle, mint oil, and Tally's own unique scent filled Michael's senses and went straight to his head. And lower. He was rock hard. All he had to do was flip her over. He was poised right over her. God. How easy to slip into the welcoming heat of her . . .

"Something you've never told another living soul," Tally said dreamily.

His life was full of secrets. Most of them deep and dark. He realized he was caressing more than massaging, and found a tight knot under her shoulder blade to work on.

"This isn't the moment for deep, dark secrets," he told her thickly. "Unless you'd like to share?"

She sighed into her arms, and her body turned fluid under his hands. He ran his palm down her sides, and his fingers brushed the plumped-up swell of her breasts.

"I don't have s"—she sucked in a breath—"secrets. Deep, dark or other-otherwise."

"Yeah? Must be nice. Ask me another time."

"I will. Tell me—"

"What?"

"About you," she finished.

"What do you want to know?"

Michael fanned his hands down the small of her back, then swept them under the elastic of her pajamas. Her behind was as sleek and toned as the rest of her. Instead of protesting, Tally melted into the mattress with a sigh. "Favorite food?"

"Mexican."

"Mine too. Favorite color?" She was starting to sound almost drugged with exhaustion. It had been a hell of a night. She needed to sleep.

But damn it, he didn't want to stop touching her. "Blue," he said gruffly. The clear, unflinching blue of Tally's eyes.

"Favorite music?"

"Eighties. You?"

"Jazz."

"Hmm. Favorite Christmas?"

"The year before my mom died. I was eleven. Yours?" He slipped the loose pants down her hips and stroked her butt. No massage, just a gentle stroke of his fingers across the twin mounds of her sweet ass. He felt her shudder between his knees, and wanted to fall on her like a starving man.

"Boarding school. Switzerland. I was thirteen, and had my first best friend. Sandra Klein. Yours?"

"Best friend?"

"Hmm."

"Hugo," he said hoarsely. "My best friend was Hugo Caletti."

"What happened to him?"

"Who said anything happened to him? He's great. Lives in Peoria with his wife and three kids." *I wish.*

"Did he die?" Tally asked gently.

Michael looked down at her narrow back through a filmy haze. "Yeah." He swallowed the lump in his throat, and wondered why, all of a sudden, he wanted to spill his guts. He wasn't a man who liked to talk about himself. Especially to a woman. Hell. Particularly, *this* woman. "You could say that. Yeah. He died." He sure as shit didn't go easy into that good night. *Christ, don't go there, Lieutenant.*

"I'm sorry." She reached over her shoulder and clasped his fingers in hers.

He swung his leg over her and off the bed, pulling away from her. Physically as well as mentally. "You need to get some sleep."

He didn't run for the door. But he moved damn fast.

"So, how far is this famous waterfall?" Michael asked the next morning. He had to hand it to Tally: The woman had amazing resiliency. The marks on her throat made *him* furious every time he looked at them, yet she was her bouncy, happy self. If he hadn't seen the very real fear in her eyes last night, he'd imagine nothing untoward had happened.

He hadn't slept more than a couple of hours himself. Saying Hugo's name out loud had been a new kind of torment.

"About a mile that way." Tally gestured toward the lava field ahead. "According to Auntie, it's about half a mile beyond, and to the left"—she grinned—"of the tallest palm."

He made a concerted effort to push the darkness away. "Great directions."

"Perfectly clear to me. Look"—she pointed—"you can see the top of the palm way over there." On the edge of the lava field, the lush tropical vegetation rose in gentle folds up the hill. One tree stood above the rest. A perfect landmark.

Michael carried a hamper filled with god-only-knew-what from Auntie's kitchen. Certainly enough food to feed half a dozen people by the weight.

The sky was overcast, the air muggy. Coupled with a sexy as hell sheen of perspiration, Tally wore a pink tank top tucked neatly into a pair of khaki shorts. On her feet were sensible hiking boots and matching pink socks. Today she'd left off the makeup. Either in deference to the heat, or in the mistaken belief that she appeared less attractive without it.

"Do you think it'll rain before we get there?" she asked, looking up at the sky.

"Probably. So. Do you have a significant other back in Chicago?"

"Jealous?" she teased.

Michael slapped a hand over his heart. "About to throw myself on my sword."

There was silence as they picked their way over the hard lava.

He glanced down. She was trying not to laugh, her blue eyes bright with merriment. "What?" he asked.

She made a zipping motion across her pursed lips.

Smiling, he pulled her hands away from her face. "Spit it out, lady. You don't want to know my methods of interrogation."

She giggled. Not like a child, but like the vibrant woman she was. The husky, joyous sound rippled across his skin like a cool breeze. "I was going to s-say—I was going to say—I've *seen* your mighty sword, Sir Black Bart, and I'd recommend you not"—she went off into peals of laughter—"n-not contort yourself."

Michael shook his head, smiling at her silliness. Desire for her burned hotly through all rational thought. He didn't want to *like* her, for Christ sake! "Gives new meaning to the words 'go f—' "

"Nuh-ah." She reached up and put a hand over his mouth. "Be good."

He kissed her palm, then lowered their hands, twining his fingers with hers. "I'll be as good as gold."

"Ha," she scoffed, but continued walking, their hands swinging between them like two teenagers on a date.

He hadn't held hands with a girl in years.

"Boyfriends?"

"A few. Nothing serious. You?"

"Not for a while."

"Ah."

He glanced down at her. "Ah?"

She made an "erase that" motion with her hand. "Ever been married?"

"Engaged. Maria Hammon. Lasted seven months. She left me because I wasn't good enough for her." Tally shot him a look, and he smiled. "I thought you'd like all the details."

She laughed a throaty, sexy as hell laugh that went through him like fine wine. "You are so full of it. Those were *bones,* not facts. Did you just make Maria up on the spot?"

"Scouts' honor, she left me for the local postmaster. They probably have six kids by now."

She was still smiling. "Were you a Scout?"

"Of course, an Eagle Scout, no less. I have the merit badges to prove it."

"Like what?"

"Liiike—Massage 101 through 125."

"You aced those, I bet. Did you practice on little Girl Scouts?"

"Only if their mothers were there," Michael told her with mock solemnity. "Then there was Camping Without Being Eaten Alive By Mosquitoes—"

She laughed. "Would that be the CWBEABM badge?"

"Yeah. That's the one. And the ICSFTMB. Which was a biggy."

"ICS—what?"

"I Can Swim Faster Than My Brothers. Got that one at summer camp. Of course it helped that I was bigger and older, and they didn't know we were in competition."

"You're crazy about them, aren't you?"

"My brothers? Yeah."

"Tell me about them."

"Sure," Michael said easily, "but another time." He'd already shared more of himself with her than he had with any other woman.

"No more nocturnal visitors?" The oppressive heat reminded him of his trip to San Cristóbal last year. He was counting the minutes until he could blow something up and get rid of this adrenaline buildup.

"No, thank God."

He'd known the answer before he'd asked. They'd both stayed awake last night. Alert for signs of more intruders, Michael had kept the door to his room wide open. The flimsy locks were useless. Tally's lights had remained on. He'd sat on the darkened lanai outside her room, and watched over her through the night. Dozing on and off. He was trained to sleep lightly. She hadn't slept at all.

It showed in the circles beneath her pretty eyes.

It was fortunate that this op would end tomorrow. It needed to be over soon. He was becoming dangerously fascinated by Trevor Church's daughter.

Despite the lack of sleep the night before, he felt energized. Pumped. *Hell.*

Horny.

Michael was confident he could make her change her no-sex rule with very little persuasion. Every time the lovely Miss Cruise looked at him, he read desire in her eyes. She hadn't denied it, either, which made him want her even more. He could break through that thin veneer of obstinacy in a heartbeat.

Hell, he should. He needed her to trust him, to depend on him. When push came to shove, he wanted her to choose him over Church, and he wanted to rub her father's nose in it.

Thinking about the gentle swell of her breasts in those virginal pajamas made him hard.

Damn it to hell.

He wasn't modest about his sexual prowess. He'd traveled far and wide, and his sexual experience was pretty damn vast. It was something of a hobby of his. A considerable portion of his studies had been more cerebral than physical. Several of his mentors had studied in the East, and although there were only so many body parts—what someone with the right knowledge could do with those parts was downright incredible. And Michael *knew* his way around a woman's body. *Well.*

He would've utilized every nuance of his expertise to get Church's daughter into his bed.

Hell, *she'd* made the preemptive strike.

Which dovetailed rather nicely with his newly formed plans.

Except she wasn't particularly his type. He preferred

women with a little more meat on their bones, preferred redheads to brunettes, preferred dark eyes to light . . . but one thing he *did* like about her was that there was no pretense. Sex had been the Band-Aid for her fear. She admitted enjoying it. She didn't need a Band-Aid anymore. End of story. There'd been no pretence, no coyness, no evasion.

She was streamlined and would be defenseless when he put his mind and, modesty aside, his extensive talents toward seducing her.

In all things, "control" was the operative word for Michael. Control and patience. He'd shown control by not returning to Paradise Island directly from the hospital. He wasn't going off half-cocked. He'd used his infinite patience to study his prey, to recon the island, to meticulously and thoroughly rehearse in his mind exactly what he was going to do. And how he was going to do it.

"This way," she pointed, "or that?"

"That."

Tally Cruise's presence sweetened the pot. Unfortunately, she'd damn near blown his mind. The moment her hot, avid mouth had welcomed his, Michael had forgotten every damn thing he knew about control.

She'd managed to sneak under his skin in a matter of days. Who the hell was in control here? His brain or his penis?

They veered off the beaten path onto the solid folds of *a'a* lava.

"That must be the famous high-tide blowhole Auntie told us about." Tally nodded at the gap in the lava.

Unimpressed—it wasn't high tide—Michael glanced at the opening in the rock as they passed. Behind them, the hillside sloped gently down to the beach and marina. He was more interested in things connected with that than coming up into the hills.

Yet there was a small chance that what he was looking for was up this way. Unlikely, but possible.

"So, Miss Tally Cruise. My life story is now an open book. Tell me more about you."

Heat radiated off the lava rock. Michael, too, wore sturdy boots. Without socks. He hadn't bothered with a shirt, either, and the slight breeze felt great as it dried the perspiration on his skin. "Start with your name. How'd you get a name like Tallulah?"

Their gazes met, and Michael was pleased by the sexual pull he felt. "If one can call the *Reader's Digest* version an open book," Tally groused. Her pupils dilated, but she kept eye contact for several seconds. "Okay. My turn. I was born in London, at the home of one of my mother's friends, and she named me."

Good girl, come into my lair, Michael thought. "Your mother or her friend?"

"Her friend. My mother didn't have an easy time of childbirth. She sort of . . . tuned out for a while," Tally said. *Like, twenty-seven years.* "When she got back, Aunt May had named me Tallulah Greta." She laughed. "You can imagine how *that* helped me in school."

"Got back from where?"

"Got back—oh, she went to meet Trevor in Tokyo a few days after I was born. Of course the birth certificate, et cetera, had to be completed. They weren't going to wait forever after all."

"Not even a few days? Or was it weeks?"

"Try a year."

"Your mother left a newborn with a friend for a year?"

"Aunt May was a very *good* friend," Tally said, smiling as she glanced around. "Should we go this way? It looks shorter."

"Sure."

"My mother isn't particularly maternal, I can't fault her for that. I was very well taken care of while she was gone. She made sure I had the best of everything. Her obsession, of course, was for my father. If he whistled, she was there."

"What about you? Did he whistle for you, too?"

"Off and on. He wanted to meet me, see how I was doing. At least that's what my mother insisted. Frankly, I'm not so sure that was true. He wasn't particularly thrilled with how I turned out."

"Why not?"

"Bev is drop-dead gorgeous. She used to be a model—could *still* be a model, if she chose. Trevor is handsome. Movie star handsome."

Michael turned to look at her. "Am I missing something?"

"I don't take after either of them. Bev always says her only child is a changeling."

"Christ, you seem amazingly well-adjusted for a woman with such shallow, self-serving parents."

Tally laughed. "Bev would've happily paid for my therapy if it was needed. Fortunately, I'm pretty well-grounded."

"Other than being scared of the dark." With one finger, he tucked her hair behind her ear. "Did you go to regular school?"

"Mostly boarding schools—plural. She couldn't always leave me with friends, no matter how good a friend they were."

"Where's your mother these days?"

"In Kenya, with friends. Safari. We don't stay in regular contact, although she'll call or e-mail occasionally. I can find her on e-mail if I want to. Of course that doesn't mean she'll reply. We talk at least a couple of times a year."

"Jesus, I can't imagine that kind of relationship with my family. My mother died when I was pretty young, but my father and I are close, and so are all of my brothers and our sister. My grandmother stepped in and took to raising us. God, I miss that old battle-ax. Talk about an iron fist in a velvet glove.

"Did you happen to notice the painting on the *Nemesis*? The cabin in the woods?"

"I did, yes. It's beautiful."

"Yeah, I think so. My sister, Marnie, painted it. It's the cabin my grandmother owned in the Sierras, where we used to spend our summers."

She smiled. "Sounds like a happy childhood."

"The best. I'm sorry yours wasn't great."

"It was fine. Unconventional, but interesting." Tally smiled. "Honestly, I didn't tell you all that to garner sympathy. I had a perfectly happy childhood. And look at me. I'm all grown up and reasonably normal."

"Yeah, all things considered. Beautiful, impulsive, intelligent, and charming. I'd say you turned out better than they had a right to expect."

"Thank you, sir. Listen, that must be the waterfall."

"Or rain," Michael said as the sky opened. They were drenched within minutes.

"Liquid sunshine." Tally laughed, twirling around, arms open, head tilted up. She stopped spinning and staggered, dizzy and giddy with sheer joie de vivre.

Michael dropped the picnic hamper at his feet, then caught her by the shoulders to steady her. Their eyes met.

"I don't think you should kiss me." Her hands rose to his shoulders, then slid around his neck. His skin was hot, slick with rain. She felt the flex of his muscles as her hands glided over the column of his neck so she could tunnel her fingers through his hair.

He dipped his head, his mouth a breath away from hers. "Is it okay if you kiss me?"

It took her a moment to remember she was the one who'd instigated the no-hands rule. "One wouldn't hurt. Would it?"

Michael's chuckle sounded rusty. "Can you eat one peanut?"

"Sure." Tally rose on her tiptoes to reach his mouth. "I do it all the time." It was *chocolate* she had a problem with. And Michael was dark and rich and decadently tempting.

His mouth closed the scant inches between them and came down on hers.

Because her own blood was racing, because her own heart beat a million miles a minute, Tally expected, *wanted,* the kiss to be hard. What she got was a gentle exploration. His kiss was slow, languorous. As if they had all the time in the world. As if they were in a quiet bedroom, lying on a soft bed. Instead of standing in the rain, on a hard lava bed, in the middle of earth and sky.

At the first feel of his tongue parting her lips, Tally's body went to fever pitch, and her heart beat triple time. So much for good intentions.

He used one large hand to expertly position her head at just the right angle for the most powerful impact. Tally almost sobbed with anticipation. His tongue explored the inside of her mouth, and she engaged it in a war for supremacy. She needed him to match her own hunger. Instead, he was taking his own sweet time, and in the process, torturing her.

Slow—oh, so slow. Nothing she did seemed to rush him. Her tongue challenged his to combat. She felt his laughter as a deep vibration against her chest. She clamped her arms more tightly around his neck. Using both hands, she positioned his head where she wanted him. But Michael realigned their bodies to his own liking.

Tally almost shot out of her already too tight skin. God. The man knew how to kiss. It was almost as though they'd each started on a different radio frequency and slowly, slowly, agonizingly slowly, he was bringing her current into alignment with his own.

He was good. No, he was a *great* kisser.

The scent of his skin, musky, intoxicating, filled her senses. The feel of his rough, unshaved cheeks against the soft skin of her face made her blood flow through her veins like liquid fire.

Her bones felt as fluid as melted butter, her muscles tense with longing. She was wet where the rain hadn't touched. Her heart accelerated, and she couldn't tell up from down. She wanted his hands on her breasts, but when she made a move to withdraw her own arms from about his neck, he pressed her closer, not allowing her to move.

He captured her face between his broad palms and kissed her deeply. Thoroughly. He nibbled her lower lip, took a small stinging nip, then laved the spot with tender sweeps of his tongue. Tally rubbed her aching breasts against his naked chest, feeling his crisp hair through her wet tank top. Her nipples ached. She couldn't wait another second for him to touch her. She managed to free her arms from about his neck and, with spread fingers, slid her hands down his chest.

His flat nipples were as hard as her own, and she groaned into his mouth. The small disks peaked when she stroked his chest as she wanted him to stroke hers. The brush of the back of her own hands on her nipples inflamed her further.

Tally couldn't stand it. She was almost jumping out of her skin.

Michael lifted his head, and like a metal shaving to a magnet, Tally found herself trying to direct his lips back to hers. He took her shoulders in a gentle grip, his hands warm on her bare skin. "I can respect your 'no,' honey. But you have to give me a break here for a while."

"I wanted—would've—"

"Your body and your brain need to be in accord if we ever sleep together again," he said softly, cupping her cheek and brushing her flushed skin with his thumb. Tally almost melted. "Just say the word. I'm ready."

Tally's eyes dipped to the enormous tent his erection made in his thin cotton shorts. She looked up at him. "You're an amazing man, Michael Wright."

He bent to pick up the hamper, and on the upswing pressed a quick hard kiss to her slightly parted lips. "Say the word soon, honey. I'm not *that* good."

"You know what?"

"What?"

"I think this is one of the best days of my life."

"Getting a kiss in the rain?"

"That, too." Her eyes shone, brilliant blue; her dark lashes spiky. Her lips were blush rose from his kisses, her cheeks flushed. "You know that Christmas Eve feeling? When you're anticipating what will be under the tree? The feeling you get even though you pretty much know what will be there—but there's a chance, vague . . . *maybe,* but a chance nevertheless that something . . . magical will be there in the morning waiting for you. That's how I feel right now." She laughed up at him and pushed his damp hair off his forehead.

"That my life is suddenly . . . oh, I don't know . . . *ripe* with possibility. Rich with anticipation." She closed her eyes and drew in a deep breath.

Michael wanted to reach for her. Instead, he stuck his fists into the pockets of his shorts. "Did you change your mind about sex?"

Those brilliant blue eyes opened. "I wish it were in me to have a fling without guilt, but I'm not that sophisticated enough. My father'll show up, and you'll be long gone. No, as much as it pains me to have to repeat myself, as much as I'm tempted, the answer is still no." She looked at him under her spiky lashes. "But you can kiss me as often as you like. Unless that's too hard on you," she grinned, "as it were."

"Honey, I'm a man, not a boy. If you want hands off, and only kissing for the duration, that's fine with me. I enjoy kissing you. Now, let's head off and find this waterfall while I rein in my libido."

With a wide smile, Tally took his hand. "You're a good man, Charlie Brown."

"Don't bank on it," Michael said, dead serious. But he liked the feel of her small hand in his, and let her hold hands with him like kids as they hiked up the trail.

It was clear Tally suffered from good girl conflict. She wanted sex, she just felt she *shouldn't* want it. Getting her back in his bed, getting her under him again, wouldn't take much. A gentle nudge, a few more passionate kisses, and she'd fall like a ripe, juicy peach right into his hands. Right where he wanted her.

The waterfall *was* dangerously romantic. A glittering silver ribbon of water dropped thirty feet into a small pond surrounded by lush vegetation. The air smelled fresh, and green.

The ground was spongy from the rain, and Tally was blissfully, gloriously happy to be alive. "What do you think?" She cast a sideways glance in his direction.

"Wanna get nekkid and play water games?" He reached for her.

"Oh, no, you don't." She laughed, walking backwards to avoid the gleam in his eye and his outstretched arms.

"I warned you about waterfalls being dangerously romantic."

"I don't think romance is what you have in mind."

"How do you know if you won't stand still?"

Tally continued laughing as she took another step back. Not very fast. She wanted him to catch her. Oh, hell, she was already in big trouble with this man. She stopped, and his arms slid around her. Michael jerked her up hard against his chest and crushed her mouth under his.

He tasted her smile and felt like a shit.

Behind her, the sylvan splendor of the waterfall rushed into an idyllic little pond. The shallow water glittered in the sunlight, promising untold delights.

Michael felt a rush of fury.

Blisteringly, *furiously,* angry that one more step closer to that water and he'd be sweating like a turkey before Thanksgiving.

And suddenly *incensed* that Tally found so much damned pleasure in simple things. The water. The air. The anticipation of connecting with her father . . .

Being with him.

The demolition expert who was about to blast her tidy, happy little world all to hell.

When his job here was done, the light in those pretty eyes would be extinguished. The sweet curve of her lips would be gone. That sheer joy would disappear from her step.

Despite last night, there was that bounce and a sparkle. She was happy to be alive. Happy to be here on her father's island. With him.

He didn't want sweet. He didn't want to taste truth and honesty when he kissed her. He wanted to obliterate the hope he saw every time he looked at her.

Shit. She didn't even have the weapons to resist him. Instead of shoving him away, Tally stood on her tiptoes and took all that he dished out. With—fuck it—*joy!*

Goddamn her.

He swept his tongue into her mouth with a vengeance, reveling in the taste and texture of her. He tunneled his fingers through her bouncy, happy curls and held her skull between his palms, slanting his mouth on hers for a better angle.

One of the men he'd offed in his long and illustrious career had been killed quite expediently by crushing his skull. It hadn't fazed Michael one bit. It had been war. Eat or be eaten. Was this any different? His fingers flexed on her fragile head. So easy. No fuss, no muss.

Why take on an added complication when he didn't need her?

She moaned. *Good,* Michael thought with grim satisfaction. *Be scared. It's gonna get worse.* She moaned again, and he realized incredulously that it wasn't because she wanted to be released. She was trying to get her arms up around his neck.

Didn't the woman have *any* goddamn survival skills?

And damn it, he *liked* kissing her. Liked feeling the quick flash of passion rising in her to meet him, fire for fire.

He could take her here.

Pull up the little pink tank top and cup her small breasts, taste her nipples.

He could push her down onto the sun-heated grass. Drag off her shorts, and screw her hard and fast. And Tally, daughter of his worst nightmare, wouldn't protest. She'd smile as she came.

He grabbed her wrist, and dragged her hand down his bare chest. Her fingers flattened, stroking, kneading like a cat on his already sensitized skin. Michael ruthlessly tightened his grip on the fragile bones of her wrist and continued the downward drag until her fingers passed his waistband and covered his hard-on.

She made a faint sound low in her throat, then her palm curved to cup his painfully hard erection. Michael shuddered.

Jesus, no. Be insulted. Pull away. Slap my face. Run, for Christ sake.

She fondled him; her inexperience showed, but didn't matter. In another second he'd go off like a teenage boy with his first girl. *No, damn you. No.* He pulled his mouth from hers and ground his teeth, on fire for her.

His placed a rough hand on her breast, felt the hard point of her nipple in his palm as she arched against him. Impossible to resist, he caught her mouth under his. His tongue dueled with hers, and she whimpered again. Not in distress; rather, it was a poignant sound of longing. Tally's fingers tightened around him, and he almost came.

He let her go abruptly. Almost shoving her in his haste to distance himself from the heat, the taste, the . . . *hope* of her.

Soft mouth red and damp from the force of his, she looked up at him, this daughter of a sadistic butcher, blue eyes filled with expectation, and goddamn it, *trust.* And Michael was glad he was accomplished at shielding his emotions.

"That *was* good," she said softly, raising her hand to touch his cheek. She smiled faintly and dropped her hand when he simply stared at her. "But not quite the kind of good I asked you to be."

"Yeah, sorry about that." He stepped away from her and wiped the back of his hand across his throbbing mouth. "I told you. I haven't had sex in a year. I was overcome by lust for your ravishing beauty." He said it with enough forceful irony, and watched the pretty pink drain from her cheeks, and the smile die in her eyes.

Without flinching she met his gaze. "Bull. If I believed you, I'd feel sorry for you. However, I don't think you allow anything to break that amazing control you seem so proud of. You knew exactly what you were doing, and you know why. What do you want from me, Michael?"

He let his gaze slide down her slender body, then raised his eye to hers. "Who says I want *anything* from you?"

"Other than sex."

"Other than sex," he agreed smoothly. "And since I can't have that, but you don't seem averse to kissing, what's the problem?"

"I don't know. But I'm sure there is one." A muscle throbbed at the base of her jaw.

"You're imagining things." He reached out and let his finger drift across her lower lip, still tasting her on his tongue. "We've seen the waterfall. Let's head back."

Chapter Nine

"I'm sorry," Tally told Auntie. "We didn't get to eat any of your lovely picnic." She set the hamper on the center table in Auntie's small kitchen, then leaned against the tiled counter and watched the older woman slicing fruit for a salad.

"Ua pola anei oe?"

"Aita," Tally answered absently. She *wasn't* hungry. Her chest ached. *He'd hurt her on purpose. Just a casually delivered verbal slap which had, unexpectedly, stung.*

Maybe Michael was one of those men who couldn't stand intimacy, and so he had pushed her away. If so, it didn't make sense. The most they could ever have was a fling, and she wasn't willing to go that route. He'd be gone in a few days, and she'd be busy with her father.

She scowled. If he'd been trying to get her to change her mind, it hadn't been in his best interest to tick her off and push her away.

So why had he?

"You be speaking Tahitian pretty good."

Tally smiled. "Ever since Trevor came here . . . I wanted to be ready."

"Is a long time," Auntie said. "More than ten year."

Tally shrugged. She didn't want to remind herself of how long ago she'd started preparing for this trip by learning Polynesian. Before Tahiti, her father had lived in France. She'd scrabbled to learn French fluently. There'd been Spanish, then Greek. She'd thrown up her hands at Chinese. She was prepared to visit him in any corner of the world.

Desperate to show him how well she could blend into his life if he so chose. Tally had wanted to be ready to come when he called.

And how exactly, she asked herself not for the first time, was she any different from her mother?

Perhaps she should've taken Bev up on some of those therapy sessions.

"Hey, you, baby girl. Come on back." Auntie shot her a glance. "*Eaha te fifi?* You be fighting with that hottie?"

Tally picked up a slice of melon and bit into the sweet green pulp. "We don't know each other well enough for that."

"You know plenty well, baby girl. I be telling you, he be troubled."

Tally shrugged and snatched up a small red berry, popping it into her mouth. "He'll be gone as soon as his boat's fixed."

Auntie glanced up. "You go with."

"Not in this lifetime," Tally said with a small laugh. "I have big plans, and they don't include a guy with no visible means of support. Nor one who carries his house around with him like a turtle." *Nor one who enjoys hurting me for no apparent reason.* She damn sure didn't need therapy for *that* decision.

Although she suspected whoever had attacked her was long gone. Hopefully. Maybe.

The yacht *had* exploded.

Yeah, but that didn't have anything to do with the guy in the next room . . . did it?

Damn it. She didn't know. All this stuff going on was far too pat to be coincidental. Yet, the idea of anyone wanting to kill her was equally far-fetched.

Until she could unravel what was going on, she preferred to think of it as one big coincidence. A cosmic joke. On her.

Auntie handed Tally a sharp paring knife. "Here. You cut. Like so." She showed her the size she wanted the segments of pineapple. "Home be where the heart is."

Tally stole the first chunk. The crisp fruit was sweet and

tangy. Juice ran down her chin, and she swiped the back of her hand across her mouth. "Hmmm. I heard that one, along with, 'It's just as easy to marry a rich man as a poor man.' "

"You looking for *tané* with big *moni?*"

"Money isn't the issue." Tally kept her head down and sliced pineapple. "I'm looking for a man who stays in one place. No traveling. All done. Do you have anything else you'd like me to—"

"I take now. Good job." Auntie scooped the luscious combination of fruits into a huge pottery bowl. "*Ava* go with *tané faaipoiro* where he go." She waddled over to the ancient GE refrigerator in the corner. Two swift kicks with her bare foot at the base of the fridge popped the door open. She placed the bowl inside and closed the door with a swing of her generous hip. "What difference water or dirt?"

"First of all, we're *not* husband and wife. Second, I've done enough traveling. I like to stay home. Have a garden. Get a dog."

"Here, cat," Auntie said as Lucky entered through the open door and limped across the worn linoleum, tail waving like a banner behind him. "You have."

Lucky made a beeline for Tally, and wound around her ankles. But the second she crouched down to pick him up, he hissed, and laid his ears back. His back arched, and he fell over, then lay there as if he'd done it on purpose. He glared at her from his prone position. Shaking her head, Tally picked him up and set him back on his three legs. The second he was on his feet, he hissed and narrowed his eyes.

"You're behaving like an idiot, you know that?" *Just like your master.* Tally gave Lucky's head a quick rub before she rose.

"Cats are too independent for me." And perverse. Just like Michael.

"Home be where the heart is," Auntie said firmly as she wiped down the counters. "Only three thing happy girl need." Auntie counted off on her stubby fingers. "Something to do.

Something to look forward to. Someone to love. You got. You be happy. I make poi for party later. You go swim. Lie on beach. Dream of love."

Tally didn't particularly want to dream about love, but the beach sounded like an excellent idea. "Hey, Lucky, you poor, disreputable-looking critter," she said to the sleeping cat at her feet. "Want to go to the beach with me?"

Brian's people had already fixed the holes in the hull. Clearly the movers and shakers on the island wanted Michael gone ASAP. The *Nemesis* was berthed on one of the side wharfs, and Michael climbed aboard. The clouds had burned off, and the sun shone brightly overhead. The sky was a brilliant blue. And he was in the mood to punch something. *Somebody*. Energy to burn, and no damn way to burn it. He plucked aside the elastic holding his patch and rubbed at his skin.

He didn't want to think about his aborted morning. *Asshole! I'm losing my grip if I can't handle one small woman, for Christ sake!*

In the good old days he would've dived overboard and swum ten miles. Instead, he dropped to the deck for a push-up marathon.

"One. Two . . ." He counted off. Half the anger this morning had been directed at himself. *Ten. Eleven.* Hell, 99 percent of it. *Fifteen. Sixteen.* Partly because he'd taken one look at the small—Christ, really small—body of water up at the waterfall and he'd almost passed out at the thought of getting in it. *Twenty*. Even with Tally. His damned stupid male pride had balked at Tally seeing his weakness. And, like a jackass, he'd taken it out on her. Which made him a prince among men.

Michael wondered, when he looked back on *these* days, what he'd call them? The shit old days? The screwed-up old days?

Or would he be around to wonder anything at all?

"Forty-two . . . forty-three . . ."

Damn it all to hell, inactivity was eating him alive.

Until arriving on Paradise Island, the last few months had flown by. He'd gathered every iota of intel available on Trevor Church. To heighten his chances of success, Michael had called in favors from his navy contacts, and mined his brother's antiterrorist agency, T-FLAC. The only thing he didn't know about Church was whether he took a leak five times a day, or six.

And where the hell he'd stashed the arms and munitions he'd sold to terrorist groups.

Michael was ready. More than ready . . .

"Sixty-two . . . Sixty-three." Church's buyers were due on Thursday. It was now Wednesday. All his ducks were in a row, but one.

He had twenty-four hours to find the ordnance, do what he needed to do, and wait for Church. And he had to do it in full view of anyone interested enough to be watching.

There were some extra-special party favors in Church's stash, making the bidding for this particular cargo hard and fierce, and extremely competitive.

The buyers would fly into Paradise late tomorrow. Possibly with Church on his private jet. The shipment was large, heavy, and volatile. They'd need a tanker to transport it away. The tanker couldn't get into the marina. The channel was too narrow. Which meant they'd anchor beyond the reef and ferry the boxes out.

A laborious . . . "Hundred-twenty . . ." and time-consuming endeavor. They'd need muscle and time. He'd already searched the large Quonset building used for dry dock. No evidence there of what he was looking for.

The marina had emptied out since last night. Several small sailboats, probably owned by locals, bobbed along the wharf. All the big, expensive vessels, like the *Mangusta,* were gone. Michael frowned, because if the boats were gone, then so was most of the muscle needed to do the transfer on Friday.

Arms burning, endorphins pumping, he leaped to his feet and went below. He grabbed a soda from the fridge, popping it open as he closed and locked the door to the galley behind him, then drew the small blue curtain across the windows.

Michael gulped the fizzy soda, then rubbed the cold can across his sweaty chest. Thanks to his brother-in-law Jake's sleight-of-hand inventions, the *Nemesis* could've sailed yesterday, even *with* those fist-size holes he'd made in the hull.

Those had taken a full day to repair. Now it was lunchtime, and the workers had disappeared like smoke. He had a couple of hours to look busy, then he'd go for a run and the hellish long walk down the beach.

He checked methodically to see that none of his fail-safe precautions had been breeched. "Thanks, Jake, my man." The guy was a master at disguising the obvious.

He spent several more minutes rechecking everything, then unlocked the door and climbed into the wheelhouse. He chose a nice big hammer from the tool kit he kept in a locker. Useless for anything he'd need to do serious repairs on the boat, but it was suitably noisy.

All he had to do was make it sound good. He picked an unobtrusive spot inside a cabinet and started slamming the hammer against the wood, heedless of the crescent-shaped marks he left behind. He just wanted to make a showing, and it allowed him to sound very busy.

For almost a year he'd slept when exhausted, ate when hungry, and quite literally sailed into the sunset. Despite the loss of an eye, he was as healthy as he'd ever been.

Having his health didn't give him back who he'd been before Trevor Church had turned his life to shit. He was no longer a Navy SEAL, so what did that make him now?

Being a Navy SEAL wasn't who he was . . . Michael paused to wipe sweat from his face, then took the blue handkerchief out of his back pocket, twirled it, and tied the narrow band around his forehead to keep the sweat out of his eyes. *Eye.*

Would this hollow feeling in his chest ever leave? Because, of course being a Navy SEAL *was* who he was. In his heart. His soul. His gut. With every fiber of his being. He missed what he no longer had. A feeling of purpose. The camaraderie. The knowledge that he was making a difference.

The severed limb of his life ached with a phantom pain that nothing could assuage.

Bottom line. No eye, no career.

Not with the navy, anyway.

Perhaps when he'd completed this op, he'd consider his brother's offer to join T-FLAC.

His baby sister, Marnie, had married Jake Dolan, and at least one of the Four Musketeers, Kyle, was probably married by now, too. One down, two brothers to go. Kane and Derek. Michael counted himself out of the happily-ever-after scenario.

He'd thought about it once with Maria. Briefly.

But after she'd left, the urge had faded. He'd had his career. He'd had a good life and a great, close-knit family. And he had terrific friends. He hadn't needed anything, or anyone else.

Then he'd crossed paths with Trevor Church.

His life was FUBAR.

His family couldn't reach him.

He'd lost an eye, and most of his courage.

And he'd killed his best friend.

Other than that, things were fine, just fucking fine.

Meantime, he had a boat to pretend to repair. He gave a satisfyingly loud whack to the inside of the cupboard. The blow vibrated up his arm. It felt so good, he whacked it again. And again.

Unbidden came a flash of Tally out there on the lava field this morning. His verbal assault had been bloodless and painfully direct. His own damn fault for allowing her to get close. He didn't know which made him feel worse: the hurt in her eyes, or the total absence of joy that had been there only moments before. It was as though a candle flame had been snuffed out. Bullshit. He was getting maudlin for no reason.

She was an adult, damn it.

He slammed the hammer down on the wood so hard, the clawed head flew off. Michael nearly lost his good eye as the metal shot past, missing his cheek by an inch. He swore virulently.

Hell. It didn't matter. He resumed his countdown. Twenty-four hours. Twenty-four fucking hours. He could keep his equipment in his pants and look for the ordnance.

He thought of Tally's narrow, bare feet with fire-engine red polish on her innocent toes last night. And her mouth, with that short upper lip, the full curve of her lower lip, and got hard.

Yeah. He was still a fully functioning male. BFD.

But not with her. If he had sex now, he wanted it with someone nasty. Someone who would give him hard, down and dirty, raw sex. With no pretense. If he had sex now, he'd want the woman to be big and meaty. Someone who'd want it as bad as he did and then go away.

If he had sex now, he'd empty himself, and maybe, just *maybe,* find a few moments of peace.

If he could work up the enthusiasm.

Tally Cruise wasn't his type. Not by a long shot. Too delicate. Too uptight. Frankly, she would be too much work for far too little reward, plus she'd expect too much in return.

Michael spent the next hour doing busywork, fixing things that really didn't need it, trying to keep his brain too busy to wonder what Tally was doing. His stomach rumbled. He'd screwed up their picnic lunch earlier, and now he was hungry as hell. He debated going back to the bar for a meal. Not yet. He wasn't hungry enough to face the elegant Tally and the hurt in her eyes.

Hell with it. He'd work himself into exhaustion, and when dusk fell he'd take the long walk down the beach.

He felt a faint give and rock of the *Nemesis* as someone

boarded. Light footfalls brushed across the deck. He cocked his head.

Not the elegant Ms. Cruise. These feet were bare, calloused. Tally was no doubt off somewhere shoring up her wounded pride and trying to figure out how to make lemonade from the lemon that was him.

"*Avatea.* I bring for you the Coca-Cola."

Michael glanced over his shoulder. *Well, well, well.* He straightened and turned. Leli'a. Niece of Auntie. Now *here* was a pair of hungry eyes that knew exactly what they were offering.

Long black hair flowed over plump shoulders bared by a teal and white pareu snugly wrapped around the girl's voluptuous body. She was quite beautiful and knew it. She wanted something, and *Michael* knew it.

"Thanks." He took the can and leaned back against the teak rail to open it. The soda was warm, but he was thirsty enough to drink it, anyway.

"Auntie say I bring." Black eyes sparkled as she gave him the age-old up and down. "*O Leli'a to'u l'oa* . . . Leli'a my name," she repeated in English. "You like?"

"I remember." Mildly amused, Michael drank the warm soda. "A very pretty name. Is Auntie really your aunt?"

The girl shrugged. "Auntie everybody auntie."

Over Leli'a's shoulder, Michael watched Tally pick her way across the street from the bar and head toward the beach. She'd changed into mint green shorts, and a skimpy little tank top. From this distance, she appeared cool and, damn it, unaffected. The woman always wore too many clothes. And when that thought occurred, the next was getting her out of them.

Shit.

" . . .with me?"

Michael glanced at the girl beside him. "To?"

Leli'a's lush lips tightened. "To the *ori* . . . dance. For Auntie's birthday. Tonight. I ask."

Now, here was an opportunity for raw, uncomplicated sex. So how come he wasn't jumping at the chance? His gaze drifted from Miss Plump and Ready to Miss Wounded Eyes, and he had his answer. "Honey, I'm ten years too old for you. At least. Don't you have a boyfriend?"

"I have, yes. *No.*" Pride, then denial. "No boyfriend."

"Thanks, but no thanks." Michael didn't bother to soften the rejection. He didn't have the time or inclination for childish games. He wasn't here to make some lovesick swain tow the line for this little coquette, nor was he going to be used for her teething.

For a few moments he lost sight of Tally as she skirted a clump of shrubs and sea grasses and headed down the slope to the sand.

"I appreciate the drink." He handed her back the empty can. "Now I've got work to do." Tally's dark hair shone in the sun as she stepped onto the soft, white sand and headed along the waterline.

"You be having the sex with Arnaud's wife?" Leli'a followed his line of sight, then glanced up at him, dark eyes flashing.

"Arnaud's *wife*?"

"*E oia,* you not know this?"

"No," Michael said flatly.

"Is good. Fix boat quick, quick. Take her far away to New York City. Nobody want here."

Arnaud's wife. That put a different spin on things. Goddamn it. "Why's that?" he asked tightly. *Arnaud's* wife, *for Christ sake.*

Leli'a gave an eloquent shrug. "Nobody like. Man want girl he can find in sheets. She be too skinny. And *very* ugly."

Ah. "Is that why you pushed her down the stairs last night?" Michael asked blandly. "Because she's skinny and ugly?"

"It dark. She clumsy and stupid. Fall down stair all by self."

Yeah. Right.

But that didn't explain the Frenchman with the knife. Or

why Tally hadn't mentioned the small detail of a husband when she'd asked him this afternoon if *he'd* ever been married.

As his sister, Marnie, used to say when she was a kid, "The thick plottens."

Tally removed her sandals, carrying them in one hand as she strolled down the beach. Beneath her shorts and tank top, she wore her swimsuit. In her bag she carried a towel, a can of soda, an apple, and her book.

She wasn't going to give the pirate Michael Wright one more thought this afternoon. She'd already decided what to do about his stinky attitude. But that was for later.

She'd find a shady spot near those rocks at the end of the beach, settle in, and veg out with her book for the rest of the afternoon. It was probably a couple of miles, at least, but although the sun was high and hot, a pleasant, balmy breeze ruffled her hair. She'd given up on keeping the sleek, sophisticated hairstyle she usually preferred in Chicago. The damp sea air and hot weather brought out the curl, no matter what she did.

She paused, lifting her sunglasses to look out across the sea. Breathtaking. She and her mother had come to Tahiti looking for Trevor when Tally had been about eleven. They hadn't found him, of course. He'd remained well-hidden, almost under Bev's nose. Tally had spent her days alone on the beach, her nights watching movies in their room as her mother had scoured the bars and hot spots. Tally's more vivid memories were of that hotel room and how lonely she'd felt, rather than the color of the surrounding ocean.

Because of being dragged around as a kid, Tally had deliberately avoided overseas travel as an adult. Silly, really, but she'd consciously wanted to purge the smell of desperation and sadness from her life that had come from traveling with her mother.

But this was different. Different not only because she was here as an adult, but because Trevor had, at last, *invited* her.

Tally felt a rush of pleasure, and with a laugh spun around in a little dance of joyous anticipation. Oh, she couldn't wait to see her father.

Her childhood memories were of a huge man, strong as he lifted her over his head. She remembered the sound of his voice on the phone, telling her about faraway places and grand adventures. Perhaps she'd built a little on those images. What the hell? She was no longer that starry-eyed optimist—

She laughed out loud. Yes, she was.

He'd made no bones about disliking kids, but she'd grown up. There was so much she wanted to know about him. So much she wanted to tell him about herself, her life. Twenty-seven years of anticipation pulsed and glowed like the angel at the top of the Christmas tree.

Even though Trevor had sent her the airline ticket to come to him, she'd tried to caution herself not to expect too much. Years of disappointment warned her to keep her hopes and expectations in check. Between visits with her father, she'd embellished her mother's opinions about Trevor Church until he was some sort of godlike creature. Tally had built her father up in her mind to heroic proportions. Her expectations had always been unrealistically high, so it was natural that by the time she saw him again, she'd been doomed to disappointment.

But there was a huge difference between trying to bond over a meal every couple of years and being together for a week or more. Tally was determined to take this opportunity, and to view her father through the eyes of an adult. If they didn't like each other at the end of this vacation, then they didn't like each other. So be it. But she was going to give this her best shot and keep an open mind.

Tally inhaled a deep breath of salty fresh air and sighed it out. Life was good.

Despite that man coming to her room and scaring the bejesus out of her, this was turning out to be a great vacation. The weather was glorious. The island idyllic. A handsome man was attracted to her, she was giddy with delight at the prospect of flirting with him later, and right now she had a picture-perfect beach all to herself.

Oh, yes. This was turning into a vacation to remember. She wasn't going to miss a single second of it.

Gulls, white-breasted and noisy, wheeled in a cloudless blue sky above the marina. Michael was there, she knew, fixing his boat.

But she wasn't going to think about him. She refused to think about the way he made her laugh, or the mocking slant of his mobile mouth when he talked about himself. She refused to think of how gentle he could be, or how tender. And she absolutely refused to think about the quick flash of fear she'd seen in his eye before he'd verbally slapped her. Probably just her imagination.

Still, she'd wanted to draw him close and hold him in her arms to comfort him. Silly, Michael Wright gave every appearance of a man capable of taking care of himself.

Which didn't mean she couldn't want to hold him and . . . do things to him, anyway.

Tally lifted her face to the sun and spread her arms wide, inhaling deeply. Could it get any better than this? The hot sun on her skin, the intoxicating fragrance of water and flowers. The sound of the balmy breeze combing the palm trees.

Heaven.

She opened her eyes and removed her sunglasses to gaze across the bay. Turquoise and aquamarine hardly described the incredible clarity and color of the water. She dropped the glasses with her bag and shoes on the sand, then waded ankle deep in the foaming surf. The water was slightly cooler than the air, and silky against her skin. Wavelets lapped gently at her feet, burying them in sand. Something touched her ankle. She glanced down and watched a blue, pug-nosed fish with what seemed like upside-down fins and a bright green patch on its side swim across her instep. Enchanted, Tally froze as several bright yellow fish frolicked in her shadow in the gently eddying water around her.

"Hang on, guys," Tally told the fish as she pulled her feet out of the sand with twin *plops*. "I'll be right back to play."

She moved her bag and shoes farther up the beach and took out her towel and spread it on the sand in the shade beneath a palm tree. Then quickly stripped down to her swimsuit.

The blindingly white sand stretched out on either side of her. Inland, the beach disappeared into sea grasses and tangled tropical vegetation in infinite shades of green. Stately palm trees marched along the ridge, their fronds crackled in the errant breeze. With loud squawks and high *ke-ke-kekyeks,* gulls and terns bickered above the reef where the calm sea formed frothy breakers over the coral.

With a laugh, Tally ran headlong into the water.

She came up wiping her eyes and spitting out salty water. Even though she'd swum several hundred feet out, the water came barely to her waist, and was so crystal clear, she could see her pale feet on the bottom. Smiling, she wriggled her toes to tempt the tiny fish swimming around her legs.

A prickle of awareness made her glance up.

Wearing nothing but bright purple shorts and a blue bandanna tied around his forehead, Michael stood, arms akimbo, on the beach watching her.

He'd heard her laughter, faint on the breeze, all the way up at the marina. As alluring as Lorelei, as tempting as Eve. He'd found himself loping down the beach toward the sound before he'd given the action much thought.

Before she'd noticed him, he'd stood on the very edge of the surf and observed her as she played in the water. Envious of her freedom to swim unafraid. The yearning to join her formed a terrible ache in his chest. Tally suddenly represented everything he couldn't have. And, damn it, he wanted it. Needed it, more than he wanted to admit.

His fingers twitched with the need to thread them through her short silky hair. He wanted to lose himself in the taste of her. Wanted to draw his mouth down her body. He wanted her eager to take anything from him. And then beg for more.

Who was to say he couldn't have that? If it didn't bother her that her husband had just died, why the hell should it bother him?

She was his for the taking for one more day. After that . . . he'd get over it.

She wore a plain, dark blue one-piece. She was too thin. Not a bad shape, but too damn thin for his tastes. Her breasts were too small, yet he wanted to put his mouth on them. Her hair was too dark, her mouth too big, and her attitude too damn . . . happy.

None of which accounted for his boner as he watched her frolic about in the surf like a child. He knew the second she spotted him. The laughter died. The smile on her soft mouth faded, and she froze like a Saudi in the gun sights of his MP5.

"There's nowhere to go, sweetheart," Michael said softly, mockingly, as she looked about almost desperately.

The straightening of her slender shoulders was infinitesimal, but he was trained to see nuances. Michael envied her the ability to wade through the shallow water with such ease . . . except for that little dip when she couldn't find purchase on the moving sand underfoot.

She'd better not go under. There wasn't anyone around to save her skinny ass.

"You better not be here to mess with my afternoon, Black Bart," she said from yards away.

"Huh?" He tried to gauge her mood. She didn't look particularly murderous, but she wasn't smiling, either. Which, he was learning, wasn't a good sign. "We've been invited to a party," he said, not knowing what the hell she was talking about but wise enough to shut the hell up.

"We?" She eyed his electric purple shorts. "Do you have a mouse in your pocket?"

"We were both invited," he said, his voice cool and ironic. "If you'd prefer to go on your own, feel free."

Tally did *not* want to be standing there, water dripping down her creamy, olive skin, swimsuit glued to her body. And he only knew that because her gaze lingered on her towel. Which he just happened to be standing on. She brought her attention back to his face. "What if I'd prefer not to go at all?"

"That would be kinda rude. It's Auntie's birthday."

"For real? Hmm. Who's going to be there? I thought just about everyone left early this morning." She gave him a suspicious look. "It's not going to be a party for two, is it?"

"Auntie said she felt like dancing. Ask her."

"As a matter of fact, she did mention something about a party earlier."

"Fine. Let's talk about Arnaud."

She shot him a startled look at the non sequitur. "Did they find him?"

"Not that I know of."

She frowned. "Why do you want to talk about him, for heaven's sake?"

"Why didn't you tell me you were married?"

"I'm not."

"Widowed, then."

"I've never been married. And if I had, I can assure you, Arnaud would have to be the last sperm-producing Homo sapien left on the planet for me to even consider it. What on earth gave you the idea he and I were married?"

"Leli'a."

"Auntie's niece?"

"Yeah."

"How weird. Why would she say something like that? Oh, let me guess . . . we're talking about *Arnaud Bouchard* here. If there's an angle, he'll find it. She probably pressed for a ring, and the slime told her he was already married. What a jerk."

And, annoyingly, Michael thought, *what a frigging relief.* "She's the one who pushed you down the stairs last night, by the way."

"*She* did? Why? What *is* that girl's problem?" Tally shook her head. "Now all we have to do is figure out who the guy was."

"I imagine he's long gone with the crews who left this morning."

"You think?"

"Yeah."

Her shoulders relaxed. "Another blight removed." She tilted her head, the sparkle dancing in her eyes. "Are you over your snit?"

"Snit?"

"This morning."

He glowered. "Men don't have snits, for Christ sake."

"Okay." Her mouth twitched. "Are you feeling better now?"

What was it about her, anyway? Michael wondered sourly. Aside from those huge, *happy* blue eyes. And her bee-stung mouth. Her ass was great. But, hell, she was *miles* away from being beautiful. So how come he kept forgetting that?

Damn it. What man could resist her effervescence? A disgruntled growl rumbled in his throat. "You don't want to mess with me, lady."

"No? Why not?"

"Because," Michael said roughly, shoving his hands deep in his pockets so he wouldn't grab her. *Because I'm going to annihilate your father. I'm going to use you to get to him, and you'll break in the process. I'm going to stomp on all your sweet little dreams and aspirations, and crush them to dust. Run, Forrest, run.*

"Because I'm a mean son of a bitch, and you shouldn't have a damn thing to do with me."

Her wet hair was slicked back off the pure oval of her face. Without the soft, curly distraction, her eyes appeared enormous, and very blue against the backdrop of the sky. "Hmm."

Jesus, wasn't she listening? "You're going to get hurt."

"After sleeping with you *once?* Okay, three times, but it was one night, for goodness's sake." She bent down and picked up her sunglasses, which she slid onto her nose. Damn. Now he couldn't see her eyes.

"So, you think you can break my heart in a couple of days,

do you? Get real. You're great in bed, but not *that* great. Women have flings all the time, and walk away unscathed. Why do you imagine I'm any different?"

"You are."

"No, I'm not."

"Yes, damn it, you are."

Tally laughed. "Thanks for thinking about my delicate sensibilities, but you don't know me. I promise you, I'm a lot tougher than you think."

"You aren't tough at all."

"Ha. Try breaking into my room with a pocketknife and say that."

"Jesus, Tally. Listen to me—"

"Get over yourself, Black Bart. I'm having a fabulous vacation. I told you. If you're here to bug me, go away." She glanced down at his feet. "May I have my towel, please?"

"What can I say to—"

"See this?" She drew a line with her toe in the sand between them. "This is the line of death. Cross it, and you're toast."

"I'll take my chances." He stepped on her line, and brushed a finger across her shoulder. "You're getting pink. Too much sun." It was a blatant lie. Her skin was already turning a golden brown, and felt as smooth and soft as velvet. He saw the gentle swell of her breasts above the modest edge of her swimsuit, saw the nervous rapidity of her breathing, and knew he was in deep, deep trouble.

"I don't bur—" she licked her lower lip, and those blue, blue eyes lost focus as he trailed his fingers up the slender plane of her throat.

A beat too late, she retreated a step.

He advanced, his hand still on her, unable to resist the temptation.

The pulse at the base of her throat syncopated with his own heartbeat.

She took another small step back . . . and stumbled in her own footprints in the sand behind her.

Michael allowed himself a ghost of a smile as he shot his hand up to grasp the back of her head, keeping her from falling. Drawing her closer.

Her scalp felt warm beneath his hand, and her wet hair curled around his fingers. She felt curiously fragile beneath his touch as she stood there without moving, her gaze fixed on his face.

"I guess neither of us listens very well, do we?"

"Guess not." She trembled when he ran his other hand up her back. Past the nominal barrier of spandex, to smooth up bare skin. Her lids lowered, ridiculously long lashes fluttered like a Victorian maiden about to be ravished. He knew she was afraid to let him see the sheer panic in her expression.

Brave little Tally.

Brave, but too slow.

She should have run for the hills.

Now it was just too damn late.

Chapter Ten

Michael lowered his head and put his mouth on hers. Desire shot to his groin, sweet and sharp. He increased the pressure, and her mouth opened eagerly beneath his. She tasted of pineapple. Temptation. Desire.

And worst of all, she tasted of trouble.

Michael slid his hands down her sun-warmed arms to capture her wrists, then slowly pulled them up and around his neck, until their bodies were flush. He wanted to groan with the pleasure of it, but tamped down the sound, knowing if it escaped, what was left of his self-control would follow.

He slowly captured her mouth, slanting his head to draw her tongue inside. She whimpered. Her nipples hardened against his chest as her slick, delightfully inept tongue tried to keep pace with his.

He'd always enjoyed kissing. Considered himself pretty good at it. But, God . . . kissing Tally was *amazing*. This foreplay was almost as good as the main event. Almost.

He felt the brush of her fingers against his neck, then fisting into his hair as he increased the pressure of the kiss. Asking more. Taking more. She drew him closer, tighter, against the gentle curves of her body, her nails flexing on his skin.

He could slide his hands down the modest neckline of her swimsuit, pull it aside, and cup her small, perfect breasts. He wanted to taste her nipples, salty from the sea. He wanted to push her down on the sugary beach, there in the brilliant tropical sunlight, and plunge to the heart of her.

He resisted the siren call, even as it enticed him, calling

him to drown in the sheer, scented beauty of her supple body. And the promise of forgetfulness, for even a heartbeat, of what he was going to do to her when her father arrived. Hell. He released her abruptly, dropping his arms to his sides as he took a step away from her.

"Not bad," he drawled, shoving his hands deep into his pockets to keep from grabbing her again.

Her eyes narrowed. "Not *bad?* You rat, you *did* come down here to tick me off and ruin my afternoon didn't you?"

With a shake of her head, she planted both hands on his chest and shoved him out of her way. She walked around him and bent to pick up her towel, shook out the sand, then cocked her head to look at him. "Well, your reverse psychology isn't going to work. Personally, I thought it was slightly better than not bad. *Slightly.*"

She wrapped the towel around her body like a clumsy pareu, and picked up her things, holding them bundled in her arms. "Not that I'm an expert on these things, but don't be so hard on yourself." She patted his arm with mock sympathy. "With a little practice, I bet you could improve. Come and find me when you feel better able to put some real effort into the project."

"I feel just fine," he said through his teeth.

"That's a shame. If you're feeling good now, there won't be any real improvement. Will there?"

"Tally, Goddamn it—"

"Is it that time of the month when you're just feeling low-down and cranky? Poor baby. I've heard exercise helps. And lay off the caffeine."

Without waiting for his response, Tally turned on her heel and strode briskly down the beach toward the marina. Back straight, head high, she waved to him over her shoulder.

Michael huffed a laugh. Damned crazy woman. He shook his head, then licked a finger, in the air, and sketched one point to the lady.

Although it was only early afternoon, and he preferred limiting his activities to darkness, he turned to jog down the beach in the opposite direction. The fun and games with her were amusing, but he had a job to do. And this was a perfect opportunity to scout out the cave he'd seen yesterday. He'd spent precious hours watching over Tally last night when he should've been searching. She was safe enough in broad daylight. Not that he thought the guy who'd attacked her was still hanging around, but better safe than sorry.

Michael scaled the boulders near the point and dropped down on the other side. The stretch this side was shorter and narrower than the other. He'd already done a recon of the area, and knew the strengths and weaknesses of the perimeter. The natural basin created by the rocks, beach, and sea offered complete privacy.

He scanned the cliff to his right. Because of the jaggedness of the rock and the angle of the sun, it was hard to tell, without scaling the face, exactly what was a cave and what was shadow. He'd start with the small opening in the base.

It was hellishly narrow, and a tight fit. He had to slide in sideways, but the height was ten feet or more above his head. About fifteen feet in, the narrow slit opened into a room approximately twenty by fifty feet. Michael paused, letting his eye adjust to the dimness.

Size-wise it would be a perfect spot to store the stolen arms and ammunition. Cool, and well-hidden. Easily accessible because of the slope of the beach and deeper water. Unfortunately it would also be *flooded*, come high tide. Not to mention it would be restrictive, if not downright impossible, trying to carry anything in or out through that notch-like opening. The ordnance would be in large wooden crates.

Damn. He narrowed his eye as he scanned the gloomy interior.

There, in back. His heartbeat quickened. He moved in, his attention focused on a couple of darker areas. *Yes!* There. A couple or three openings that looked like natural tunnels in the side walls. Narrow and—he shoved an arm in one—could go back thirty more feet, for all he knew. He'd come back and check those later. He moved around the room, considerably darker in back, to make sure he wasn't missing anything.

"What *have* we here?" Man-made stairs, roughly cut in the rock.

Damn. He wished he had a flashlight. He'd come back with one later, but for now he bounded up the uneven steps. He had to slow as they took a sharp and dangerous turn, then another. The higher he climbed, the lighter it became and the more his anticipation grew.

"Are you seeing this, Bud?" he asked Hugo, grinning at the ceiling. "Oh, man." The cave was three times the size of the one below, and flooded with sunlight.

Almost every square inch of it was filled with wooden crates.

He'd found the ordnance.

Michael pushed his way between the crates to the opening looking out over the sea. Christ, how easy was this? The aperture was perfectly angled as to be almost invisible from below. But at high tide, a ship could come right below the mouth, the crates could easily be rolled down a ramp right onboard. No fuss, no muss.

His pulse raced.

Filled with elation, Michael moved through the boxes again, this time his hand lingered almost affectionately on the splintery pine as he passed through the man-made canyons.

He'd set the charges tonight while everyone slept.

He jogged down the stairs and out into the sunlight, feeling light for the first time in a year.

Michael did a high victory jump, and punched the air with his fist. "Hoo-ya! Hugo, my man. We're in!"

The sun seared his shoulders, the hot sand burned the soles of his feet. Life was good. Revenge would be sweet. Goddamn it—he was king of the world. Able to leap tall buildings, yada, yada, yada. He grinned.

A cave. Perfect.

The explosive charge would be contained. The C4 would take out every last piece of crap within the rock walls, and chew up half the cliff face in the doing. Anything that survived the initial bang would be wasted by the ricochet effect.

The disposal of Church himself would be one on one, and a lot more personal.

Now, there was just one more small task before he headed back.

He looked out over the calm water, and the jubilation of only minutes ago faded. His heartbeat slowed to a familiar thud. Thud. Thud.

Shit.

The sand was cooler where it was wet as Michael approached the lacy foam trimming the waves. He didn't bother looking around. He knew no one could see him back here behind the boulders. And hell, fact was, even if they could, who the hell cared? Doing a final visual check was one more displacement activity he used to delay the inevitable.

The sapphire water was deeper because of a sharp drop-off close to shore. Great. He didn't have far to walk before he freaked out.

He paused, drew in a deep breath. Centered himself. He could do this. Goddamn it. He *had* to do this.

While the French Polynesian sun beat down on his head, Michael remembered a rainy summer's day in the Sierras. All four boys were determined to teach their seven-year-old sister how to swim. Marnie had been more than enthusiastic, despite her bad heart.

The river had been fairly deep, but sluggish. Michael had jumped in first, ready to catch his sister. Kyle had instructed her how to hold her breath; Derek had grabbed her skinny little arms and demonstrated how she was supposed to move. And Kane had run around screaming like a wild Indian, and dive-bombed the water, splashing them all amidst shrieks of laughter.

God, he'd fearlessly loved the water, even then.

Michael scrubbed his jaw, his throat tight as he stared unblinkingly at the placid skin on the water.

"Hugo? Help me out here, Bud. Help me so Church doesn't win. Again."

He could do this. He could. Just a second. That's all he needed. A second submerged. Christ, he *could* do this. He drew in a ragged breath.

"One-two—" He took off running. "Three," full tilt. "Hoo-yah!"

The water felt as cold as ether on his shins. *Jesus.* It clawed at his calves like icy knives. His brain went numb with terror. Felt like a heart attack. Fear—intense—debilitated, paralyzing. Couldn't breathe. Couldn't think. Couldn't even fucking run.

"Hugo. For God's sake, man . . ."

They were like two halves of a whole. Together since basic training, together through Hell Week and BUD/S. Inseparable. Invincible. The best of the best, and cockily aware of it, too. Even in the pitch-dark, Michael was as aware of Hugo as if they were holding hands instead of tied together on a six-foot line. They knew each other's moves so damn well, it was as though they shared a single brain. One mind. One thought. One goal.

Only the two of them had been inserted for this extremely dangerous op. The Marie José *had been pirated by Trevor Church, a modern-day buccaneer who'd become the scourge of French Polynesian waters for years. There wasn't much a single government could do about him. He did his dirty work on the high seas, and out of territorial waters. But this time, he couldn't be ignored. He'd progressed from minor infractions to the big leagues. He'd hijacked an enormous shipment of weapons being transported from Santiago. There was enough ordnance on board to blow away a large chunk of the Orient, for which it was headed.*

Right now the ship was riding anchor hundreds of miles from any inhabited islands as Church awaited the buyers. Intel had reported the terrorists would be there tomorrow. Noon. When they arrived, the Marie José *would be a dimple in the ocean.*

Hugo signaled. Target. Dead ahead . . .

Michael blinked back the clausty darkness and cold and shoved them back into memory.

The sun beat down on his head, the light breeze felt chill on his sweat-drenched skin. He extended his right foot; one more large stride and he'd be thigh deep. He could do this, goddamn it. He could do this . . . light-headed enough to pass out, he jerked the leg back in place.

He'd made it knee-deep before admitting defeat. Sick to his stomach, he stood there like a statue, the ocean sucking at his legs like some vile creature determined to drag him below. As if the sea had let him go once before and it was still trying to make up for the mistake. He felt sick, dizzy with fear. His body drenched in sweat, his heart manic. He forced himself to stay there. Knee-deep in the crystal-clear water. Counting each frantic heartbeat.

After ten, agonized minutes, Michael allowed himself to turn tail. He trudged out of the viscous water, almost blind with fury and despair.

He'd sailed on the son of a bitchin' sea for ten freaking months. *Dared* it to take him. Laughed at its power over him. And in the end, the vindictive bastard always won.

He dropped to his stomach on the hot sand.

Push-ups.

Five hundred.

Penance for the faint of heart.

Two. Four. Six . . .

At first, he imagined the high-pitched scream was in his head . . . he paused on the upswing . . . and heard it again.

He was at a full-out, dead run before he realized why.

More effective than a cold shower, a corpse lying on the sunny, tropical beach had knocked Tally's raging hormones into unconsciousness.

Her scream still throbbed in the air around her. Throat raw, she stared down at the body she'd literally stumbled across as she'd been picking up shells on the water's edge.

Well, that was the last time she'd go splashing through calf-deep water without watching where she was going. She'd been so busy obsessing about Michael's weird mood, she hadn't noticed a thing until the dead body had thumped hard against her legs.

The scream had been purely involuntary.

While her eyes were still trying to understand what she was seeing, her brain kicked her legs into high gear. She dashed up the beach as if it were a great white snapping at her heels.

The tide pushed the dead man after her in some sort of macabre chase. Unnerved, Tally clapped a hand over her mouth and sank down onto the hot, dry sand several yards up the beach. Her gag reflex worked overtime no matter how often she swallowed.

Get a grip, for heaven's sake! The poor guy is dead. He can't hurt you, she told herself, unable to tear her gaze from the body trapped in the shallows.

It was Lu, the kid who'd crewed for them on the *Serendipity.* Tally recognized his tie-dyed T-shirt.

Stand up. Walk away—one foot in front of the other. Get help. Get someone. No. Get Michael, he'll know what to do.

The body—*it was easier to think of Lu this way*—must have washed onto the beach with the incoming tide. Facedown, his black hair drifted gently about his head with the lapping waves. His hair looked so delicate, it almost distracted from the hole in the back of his head.

Almost.

His lifeless hand beckoned with the rhythm of the sea. *Come here. Help me.*

Tally swallowed hard, hummed a bit, then, "Oh the shark has . . . pretty teeth, dear," she sang as she kept vigil over the boy's body. "Lies a bod-y, oozing life. Some . . . one's sneaking round the corner . . ."

"Jesus, that's morbid. Give it a rest, would you?"

She shrieked and clutched the base of her throat as she spun around. Big, strong, I'm-no-hero Michael, in his fluorescent purple shorts.

Yes.

She noticed he was covered in sand. Sugary white dusted his taut, tanned muscles, and sparkled from the hair on his chest. While she was braving floaters, he'd taken a nap on the beach.

In a demonstration of remarkable maturity, she refrained from jumping into his arms like a motherless monkey—but only because she didn't think she had the strength to run. She staggered to her feet, but stayed where she was, feet planted. A corpse bobbing nearby.

"This is why you screamed?" he demanded. "The guy's already dead."

"T-This is Lu."

He glanced at her. "Lu who?"

"The guy who crewed for us on the *Serendipity* the other day. That Lu."

"Looks like he's been in the water a while."

"Since Monday?"

"Oh, yeah. Gunshot, point-blank. From the back."

"Somebody shot him? Oh, God, poor kid."

"At least he didn't drown," Michael said with no inflection, glancing at the obvious exit wound. "This was quick."

"I'm sure he's very grateful."

"How many people were on the *Serendipity* that day?" Michael asked from his crouched position beside the body.

Tally wanted to grab him by his hair and pull him back. She stared at his broad, scarred back. "Only the three of us."

"Did you shoot him?"

"Of course no—oh, crap. Arnaud!" Her heart did a double thump and then sped up. "Why? *Why* would he do something like this?"

"A very good question. Too bad we can't ask him." Michael sounded savage.

Tally dragged her attention back to Michael's face. *Talk. Then you'll stop thinking.* "You walked right by him—how could you *not* have seen him?"

He shrugged. "Lucky, I guess. Come on. Let's go alert whoever needs to know. Poor bastard's not going anywhere."

The sun's heat did nothing to ease the chill crawling through her bones into every single cell in her body. Tally shivered from the inside out.

"Where's your stuff?"

"Huh? Oh." She waved in the general vicinity behind her. She hadn't realized she'd dropped everything until he asked. Michael left her to walk over and snatch up her belongings.

She drew in a breath. Arnaud was the obvious culprit. But what if he wasn't the one who'd shot Lu? He was, after all, also dead. Who else was out on the water that day? Michael Wright, that's who. He'd got on her case about not heading in because of the typhoon. But he hadn't headed in either, had he?

What if *he'd* blown up the *Serendipity*? What then?

Tally shivered. Oh, God. None of this made sense. Why would *Michael* do something like that? He *couldn't* have shot Lu. He'd been too far away. . . . But why would *Arnaud* kill the boy?

The unrelated events of the last few days suddenly felt extremely related to Tally.

The boat blowing up. Arnaud's death. The man in her room. A push down the stairs. Now, poor, dead Lu with the back of his head blown away.

And beside her, at every bizarre turn, a sexy, one-eyed man.

Tally snorted. She was letting her fertile imagination run wild with possibilities. All she needed was a one-*armed* man, then she could be a TV show. Oh yeah, it was way past time to get a reality check.

Michael returned with her clothes and tote. He handed her the bag, and wrapped the towel around her shoulders. With a slight shake of his head, he shoved his hands deep into his pockets.

He let his gaze drift down the length of her body, from her wildly curling hair, down her towel-covered chest, along her bare legs, to linger for a second on her bare feet and sand-clenching toes. "Let's get you back to Auntie's," he said flatly. "I think you're in shock."

Had he seen the question in her eyes? She held her breath and felt the burn of that one-eyed inspection through every atom of her body. *Oh, God, he's potent.* Tally shuddered. All her emotions were going haywire, and there didn't seem to be much she could do about it. She took a step away from Michael. Ha! As if *that* would help.

"Shouldn't w-we . . . ah . . . pull him farther up the beach?"

"Tide's going down. Come on."

Just the brief brush of his hands as he pulled the towel around her shoulders set her pulse into overdrive. Tally adjusted the towel in what she hoped was a suitably casual gesture.

Oh, God. Oh, God. Oh, God. Who to trust?

He turned and started walking down the beach. She gathered the edges of the fabric in a white-knuckled fist, and pretended the towel wrapped around her was a comforting hug.

Chapter Eleven

"Auntie, give the lady a brandy," Michael commanded the moment they walked into the bar. "Make that two."

Auntie glanced from Michael to Tally and back again. "My specialty. Comin' right up, you bet, hottie."

"Here or out there?" he asked.

Tally glanced around. "Outside. Thanks," she said as Auntie slid two half-filled Coca-Cola glasses across the tiled bar. She caught Michael's eye and raised an eyebrow at the size of the shots Auntie had poured.

"You need it," he told her. "Let's sit."

"Eaha te tumu?" Auntie demanded, scanning Tally's face. Tally figured she probably appeared as pale and freaked out as she felt.

"The matter is she just tripped over Lu's dead body," Michael answered for her. He took both glasses and jerked his chin, indicating Tally walk ahead of him.

"Lu drowned?" Henri asked, coming up beside them and walking to a table out on the lanai, followed by Auntie carrying the bottle of brandy.

"Shot," Michael said flatly, scanning the audience for reaction to his statement. "Point-blank. Back of the head." He made no attempt to lower his voice. Within seconds, his announcement had the desired effect. A crowd collected around them.

He handed Tally her glass. "Take a slug."

She took a giant gulp and nearly gagged. It tasted like nail polish remover, but she figured it was medicinal, and took another sip, then shuddered as it bit all the way down.

Henri crossed himself. *"Mon Dieu."* Auntie plopped the bottle in front of Michael, then flopped down heavily beside Henri. Her husband took her hand and kissed it absently. "This is very bad. We've never had a murder on Paradise."

Several locals were seated at a table nearby with Auntie's niece, Leli'a, and two other island girls Tally hadn't seen before. A group of men gathered at the bar to listen as Michael walked them through the events. Tally drained her glass and pretended she was listening to the synopsis of a movie. Better that than close her eyes and see poor Lu with his brains leaking out of that big hole in his head.

Tally shuddered, grabbed the bottle, and poured another hefty dose of medicine, then took a healthy gulp and shuddered again.

As soon as Michael finished the story, Auntie wrapped Tally in a bear hug. "Poor baby girl. This bad magic, this. Have another drink. Something powerful and tasty?"

"No more, thanks," Tally said quickly, remembering the effect of three, no four, piña coladas the other night. God only knew what effect swigging brandy like water would have.

Her shakes had subsided, but she still felt sick to her stomach every time she thought about Lu. Poor, poor kid.

"You not be knowing that boy." Auntie tucked Tally's hair behind both ears, and cupped her cheeks in cool hands. "No be worrying. You go upstairs, lie down, take nap. Then dress pretty for Auntie's luau. You see, everything be fine and dandy."

Somehow Tally didn't think anything would be *fine* again—certainly not for the guy with a big hole in his head. She caught Michael's enigmatic look over Auntie's broad shoulder.

"Henri, you take Palaki and Feilo, and go quick-quick beach, get boy. Tomorrow you take home to Fatu Hiva."

"I'll go with you." Michael rose and started to follow

Henri and the two young men. At the edge of the lanai he paused and turned to look back at Tally. "Later."

She wasn't going anywhere; suddenly she was exhausted. She barely noticed when Auntie grabbed the brandy bottle off the table, then shuffled off behind the bar to pour drinks. Leli'a sauntered over to slip into the chair Auntie had just vacated.

"You be going back New York City now, *e oia?*"

"I live in Chicago," Tally told the girl absently. What did he mean later? Later what? Later they'd finish the kiss? Later they'd discuss the sudden appearance of the body? Later they'd go to the party together?

Lord, the last thing she felt like doing tonight was attending a party.

"Same," Leli'a said crossly. "You go. Nobody here want."

Tally stared at the girl. "Well, thanks for the warm welcome, but I'm not going anywhere." Any woman with big boobs, a tiny waist, and long, silky black hair shouldn't, couldn't *possibly* be jealous of someone as flat-chested and plain as herself, Tally thought. Unless . . . "Do you like Michael?" she asked carefully.

The girl's big brown eyes went wide. "Michael? Him?" She thumbed over her shoulder toward the beach, then shook her head. Her long hair flowed over her naked shoulders like liquid licorice. "Too old. Too poor."

"Too poor?" Tally asked, amused at the avaricious gleam in the girl's eyes. "Hmmm. I see. Well, if it's not Michael, why do you want me to leave? I'm only here for vacation, you know. Just a few weeks and I'll be gone."

"You like Michael?"

"Yeah, I do." Far too much, in fact. And if most of the men working for her father had left to deliver boats to buyers on other islands, then there was no one around to work on Michael's boat, and if there was no one around to work on Michael's boat, then he wasn't going to be leaving anytime soon. She took a mental breath at the litany.

All of which meant she either had to withdraw her line of death, or she'd have to find a chastity belt.

"Nobody else?"

Unfortunately not. "Nope. Nobody else."

"Nobody else," Leli'a repeated as a warning.

"Right," Tally said with as much seriousness as she could. "Your boyfriend—*boyfriends*—are safe from my wicked wiles. I'm a one-man woman."

Which was completely pathetic, and also rather alarming to discover.

Because, unfortunately, her mother had been the same way. And look what *that* had got her.

"Will you be at Auntie's birthday party?" Tally asked the girl.

Leli'a gave her a hostile look. "*E.* I dance."

"Great." Tally smiled, choosing to ignore the younger woman's venom. "You have such pretty hands, and I'm sure you're a wonderful dancer. I look forward to seeing you perform."

Oh, those nasty green pangs of jealousy. Tally had been all but invisible as a teenager. Makeup, deportment, and, most of all, *attitude* had helped bring her out of her shell. She'd been plain as dirt, painfully shy, and the new girl wherever she went. The older she'd gotten, the easier it had been to pretend she had some sort of grip on this man-woman thing. Ha!

Leli'a didn't realize what an arsenal she had in her voluptuous figure and those flashing eyes.

"I'm going upstairs." Tally rose from the table. In the distance she saw Michael and the other men returning from the beach, carrying the blanket-wrapped body between them. She rubbed the chill from her arms.

"See you tonight, Leli'a." Tally waved to Auntie, then opened the door to go upstairs to shower and change.

Besides, upstairs was as far away from Michael as she could get at the moment, which was definitely a good idea. Putting a little physical distance between them might be a good idea.

He couldn't have shot poor Lu, but could he have been

responsible for the explosion on the *Serendipity*? Tally thought about it as she went upstairs.

Not likely. While Michael Wright looked dangerous, he was so laid back, it would take an act of Congress to get him motivated. No, she didn't think her pirate was responsible for the explosion.

Thank God.

She pushed open her bedroom door. A nap, a couple of hours of oblivion, sounded pretty good right now.

Light streamed through the shutters she'd left open in her room before heading down to the beach. She blinked. Then blinked again before comprehension dawned.

The tropical sun shone through the windows, and illuminated utter chaos.

Her room was completely trashed.

"Oh, for Pete's sake!"

Clothes and personal items had been tossed about like children's toys. The sateen lining of her suitcase and garment bag had been shredded; the leather sliced. Even the mattress had been mutilated, and hung half off the bed, the sheets cut through to the ticking cover.

That damn Frenchman had come back.

And *this* time he'd taken scissors, or a knife, to every garment. Even the soles of her shoes had been pried apart and split open.

"Damn it! Not my favorite red sandals!"

Tally gripped the doorjamb in a white-knuckled fist, and tried to take in the carnage.

Suddenly, Michael Wright looked a lot safer than being alone up here.

"And then it hap-pened," she sang under her breath as she quietly closed the door and raced downstairs.

"Michael?"

He sat at a table on the lanai, shooting the breeze with the guys he'd helped with the body when she burst through the door from upstairs.

Michael glanced up as though he'd just seen her. He'd *felt* her presence, and one look at her ashen pallor told him that Tally had yet another problem. The woman was fraught with them.

She hadn't showered or changed yet. The beach towel remained firmly tucked under her arms and secured between her small breasts. She was barefoot, sand dusting her feet and legs. He glanced from her legs to her face—paler than the glistening sand clinging to her skin.

"Now what?" he asked warily. Christ, what next? An ax murder?

"May I talk to you privately for a moment?"

She actually spoke without moving her mouth. Her teeth were clenched so tight, it was a wonder she could draw a breath. No screaming hysterics for Tally. And if she was this scared, any moment now she'd burst into song.

"Sure." He pushed away from the table. Taking her arm, he felt the fine tremor traveling across her skin. He ushered her through the bar, grabbing the bottle of brandy and two glasses as he passed through. He pushed open the French doors to the enclosed, private lanai and headed for a small, round table in the shade of a flowering frangipani.

"Sit down before you fall down." He set the glasses on the table and uncorked the bottle. "What happened?" He poured her a healthy slug and handed her the glass. "Find another body?"

"Not yet, but the day is young." She sat down with a plop and scowled at him before picking up the glass and draining its contents. Her nose was a little pink from the sun, but beneath the unnatural pallor a golden tan was coming along nicely. Her dark hair was a silky tangle about her face, and her blue eyes looked a little haunted.

"That French guy came back and ransacked my room while I was at the beach. Damn. Damn. Damn. Everything is shredded and tossed on the floor like a mixed salad. And I was having *such* a good day. This is *really* ticking me off."

It struck him that, far from being afraid, Tally was furious.

Michael leaned against the wall beside her. "What makes you think it was the Frenchman?"

She frowned. "Who *else* could it be?"

The culprit, he strongly suspected, was sitting on the front lanai, her feet on a chair, chatting and laughing with her girlfriends. He'd smelled Tally's perfume on the girl the second they'd come up from the beach earlier. "I'm presuming that was a rhetorical question?"

"Not if you can answer it."

"Let me put it this way," Michael said. "I think this problem needs to be addressed by Auntie."

"Since it's *my* vacation wardrobe that's been slashed to shreds, I'd say this is a problem that should be addressed by me." Tally pushed her curly bangs out of her eyes. "This is giving me the willies. Michael, there are less than twenty people out there. One of them hates me enough to cut up all my"—her eyes narrowed as she glanced in the direction of laughter from the front of the bar—"that little brat!"

She turned to look up at him. "It's Leli'a, isn't it? Why on earth would she do something so vindictive? Just because she's jealous? Of what? Who? I don't get it. I should march out there and turn that little juvenile delinquent over my knee. Damn it. Besides everything else, she chopped up two pairs of my Manolo Blahniks."

Michael bit back a smile. "What the hell is a Manalow Blanick?" She was working herself up into a fine fury, and it was fascinating watching the thoughts drift across her features like gathering thunderheads.

Tally rolled her eyes at him. Damn, she was cute. "Shoes, Wright. *Shoes.* My passion, and my downfall."

He wanted to be her passion. Because he sure as shit was going to be her downfall. *Hell.*

"Yeah, well, be grateful that (a), you weren't *in* them when they were slashed, and (b), that the culprit was *Leli'a* and not your knife-wielding assassin."

"*He* didn't so much as touch my Blahniks. If he had, I'd've done worse than grab his privates and toss him over the lanai. I would've—"

"Yeah, I shudder to think. Shoes can be replaced. You can't."

Tally shoved her chair back. It screeched across the tile floor. With blood in her eye, she hitched the towel more securely around her chest.

"Now where are you off to?"

"I'm about to have a little chat with Tahitian Barbie out there."

Michael pushed away from the wall and followed her. "I'd hate to miss this."

Tally used both hands to push her way between the double French doors. She entered the bar like a gunslinger at noon and looked around. Only a handful of men remained. "Where's Leli'a?" she asked Henri, who was talking to a couple of guys playing chess.

"She went home, I think."

"Which is her house?" Tally asked pleasantly.

Henri glanced from Tally to Michael and back again. "The small pink one. What is it you—"

But Tally was gone, long, bare legs striding across the lanai, around the side of the hotel, and up the shell path.

By the time Michael caught up with her, she was pounding on the bright blue door of Leli'a's cottage.

"She's either stone deaf, or not here," he told her patiently.

"If she's smart," Tally said through her teeth, "she'll be on her way to Fatu Hiva or Bora-Bora. Preferably swimming. In shark-infested waters. With a small, bloody cut she got from the scissors she used to chop up my clothes!"

She closed her eyes, and inhaled slowly, deeply, and let her fist drop to her side. The towel slipped, revealing the top swell of her breasts. She struggled to maintain her poise. But the pulse in her throat beat harder. Michael wanted to put his mouth on the uneven pulse, to feel the beat of her heart against the tip of his tongue.

"It's unlikely she's left the island. She's got to be around somewhere."

"Yeah," Tally said with relish. "She can run, but she can't hide. Come on, let's go back." She turned back to the path, picking her way carefully over the sharp bits of shell and gravel in her bare feet.

"Leli'a was not home?" Henri asked, glancing up from scrubbing the counter.

"No. I'll catch her later," Tally told him calmly. Although Michael was walking behind her, he could tell her jaw was clenched. Her lightly tanned shoulders were stiff with fury as she pushed open the door.

He raised a hand to the older man—he'd talk to him later—and followed Tally back to their original spot on the back lanai.

She sat down and folded her arms on the table, pleats of exhaustion and annoyance between her eyes.

"Why don't you go up and grab a nap in my room?"

"I don't need a damn nap," she said irritably, then rubbed her forehead. "Sorry. I shouldn't be snapping at you. I don't have a single intact item of clothing left, thanks to her. Damn, and double damn."

"I think you should go and stay up at the house. Put a little distance between you."

"I'm not going to let that little brat scare me, for goodness's sake," she said indignantly. She tossed back an inch and a half of brandy without a blink.

God, he loved when her eyes lit up and flashed with annoyance. Her cheeks were no longer pale, but flushed. Michael felt an overwhelming urge to pull her into his lap and nuzzle his mouth against her soft, warm skin. Instead, he shoved his hands into the pockets of his shorts.

"I'm fine here until my father gets back. Besides," she said almost wistfully, "I'd feel really uncomfortable up there by myself."

Michael almost offered to accompany her. God. Wouldn't *that* be sweet when Church returned home? "Your choice. When's he due back?"

"Arnaud said Thursday." She hitched the towel up a little higher, then rubbed a hand across her face. "Darn it. What am I going to *wear?*" She looked at him and gave him a slightly loopy half smile, which cut to his gut. "Stupid, I know. But I want this meeting tomorrow to be *perfect.* And it's already screwed up because I don't—never mind. It's pointless to get myself in a knot about something I have no control over."

"There's sure to be something at the General Store."

"Right." She brightened. "I'll ask Auntie to open it for me later."

"She runs the store, too?"

"Haven't you noticed? She runs everything around here."

"You're going to have to tell her about Leli'a."

"I will. After Leli'a and I have our chat. I have to tell you, this has been one exciting vacation so far," Tally said dryly. "Beside a scissor-wielding teenage mutant Barbie, there's the *Serendipity* blowing up, a stinky guy with a knife. And now poor dead Lu." She rolled the glass between her palms. "All roads point to Mr. Slime himself. I'd just love to know what Arnaud was up to."

"And Leli'a."

"Yeah—thank God she didn't find my necklace."

"Only because she'd never think to look in the toilet tank."

Tally's eyes widened, "Michael, you rat," she choked back a laugh. "What were *you* doing looking in the toilet tank?"

"Maybe I wanted to hide my jewels."

"I am *so* not going to touch that line," she said with a small smile. There was a look of strain in her eyes. She *had* been through a fair amount in the last couple of days. A hell of a lot more than anyone could expect on an island paradise.

"I'd hate to lose those pearls." She played with the glass, turning it in circles on the damp ring it left on the table. "My father gave them to me for my twenty-first birthday. Not only are they very expensive, but they have a lot of sentimental value for me."

"Did you actually check to make sure the pearls were still there?"

Tally frowned and shot to her feet. "No. I didn't. Wait here. I'll be right bac—"

"No, *you* wait. I'll get it."

Henri came outside a few moments later. Tally wondered if Michael had sent him out to watch over her while he was gone. While unlikely, it was a nice thought.

"Auntie says you should eat," Henri said, dark eyes twinkling. He placed a platter of small pupus on the table, then sat in the chair Michael had vacated.

"Oh, Lord." Tally eyed the appetizers with a small shudder. "Thanks, but I couldn't eat now if I tried. My tummy is churning."

"A bad thing this. Perhaps this is not Lu? The man's face was not recognizable, after all. Perhaps a fisherman's dispute? But what was a fisherman doing so close to our shore? The fishing here is not so good. Pearls. None." He gave a Gallic shrug. "A man in the wrong place, at the wrong time, it appears."

"No, it was Lu. I recognized the clothes he was wearing when we were onboard the *Serendipity* the other day."

"I wouldn't worry," Henri said, reaching for a shrimp puff. "This bad situation has nothing to do with you."

"I sincerely hope not." Should she voice her suspicions about Arnaud to Henri? Tally had no idea what kind of relationship the two men might have had. If they'd had any relationship at all. And what difference could it make now with Arnaud gone, too?

Henri motioned to her almost empty glass. "Would you like me to bring you a soda instead?"

"No thanks." Tally smiled. "I don't think I need the caffeine rush at the moment. How long have you been here, Henri? Were you born in Tahiti?" she asked in French.

He helped himself to a bite of *poisson cru,* raw fish in lime juice. *"Non,"* he said in his native language. "My parents come to Bora-Bora for the pearl trade when I was a boy. They eventually went back to France. I remained. I did a little of this, a little of that. When I met Malie, she was married to another. I waited." His eyes twinkled. "Not so patiently, until she realized she was married to the wrong man."

Tally smiled. "And how long ago was that?"

"Twenty-four years. Twenty-four *good* years. The best. We were never blessed with children of our own. We came to Paradise, to take care of Leli'a, when Auntie's youngest sister died." While he talked, he polished off the pupus. "When she left for school, we opened the hotel to give us something to do other than make love all day." Henri grinned.

Michael stepped onto the lanai. The two men exchanged glances, then Henri pushed himself up with his hands on the table. "Better go back in and see what the boss wants me to do," he said with a lugubrious sigh.

"Thanks for the snacks," Tally said dryly, handing him the empty plate.

"No problem. I'll tell her you enjoyed them."

Still smiling, Tally glanced at Michael as he pulled out a chair and sat down. "Find my pearls?"

"No. They're gone."

Chapter Twelve

"This never happen before," Auntie complained, huffing up the stairs with a handful of large, plastic garbage bags. She shuffled into Tally's room and started stuffing one of the bags with bits of leather suitcase she found on the floor, her mountainous bottom, draped in grape-colored cotton, pointed to the ceiling, her voice muffled by her own large breasts. Tally wondered how the poor woman could breathe in there. "I no like this nonsense. No, I surely do *not*."

"Thanks for the garbage bags." Tally tried to take them. Auntie held on. "There's no need for you to help. Michael's coming back to help me get everything cleaned up—"

"I no like some no-good travelin' *tané* comin' into my place of business and messing things up." Auntie righted herself, her face flushed and screwed up in anger.

Until Tally knew, 100 percent, that Leli'a was responsible for the damage to her room, and for stealing her pearls, she bit her tongue. "I'm sure you ar—"

"I'll be finding that—a *hi'o!*" Auntie held up a scrap of Tally's underwear. The pale pink cotton had been sliced into shreds. "What doin' *this* for? You tell me that? *No te aha?* Make no sense."

Tally reached for the bag the older woman was dragging about the room. "Let m—"

"Here, you take." The woman shoved the crackling plastic at her. "Auntie get new sheets. Fresh outta the bag from Sears catalog. Downstair. I be quick-quick."

Michael flattened himself against the door as Auntie stomped past him.

"I see we got some garbage bags," he said laconically, stepping into the room and surveying the damage. "No sign of Leli'a. But then she can't have gone far. Stop being so damn finicky. Everything's trashed. Toss it in here and we're done. Did you tell her Leli'a did this? And stole your necklace?"

She felt sick about the necklace. "No."

"Why the hell not?"

"Because I'm not one hundred percent sure she did. I'll have a little chat with the juvie first, *before* I involve Auntie."

"You'd probably cut the baby in half, too. Just to be fair. Fine. Your call." Michael scooped up the rest of her clothing off the floor and stuffed it into the bag. "Any of your clothes left intact?"

"Nope." Her fashion-conscious soul cringed at the desecration to her carefully selected, high-end wardrobe.

"Go into my room, help yourself to anything that'll work. My mast came in. I'm going down to the marina to work on the boat for a couple of hours."

Tally smiled. "What size bra do you wear?" She rather liked the idea of wearing Michael's shorts and T-shirts.

He walked up to her and dropped a quick kiss on her mouth. "Honey, leave off the bra. You don't need one. Besides, I like knowing you're naked under my clothes."

He started for the door, paused, and came back. He didn't touch Tally, but it was as though he'd tossed a sensual net over her as their gazes locked.

"You need to rethink your line in the sand, sweetheart. I find I'm not that patient after all."

The e-mail from his brothers was waiting for him on his computer when Michael went belowdecks.

Ah, the miracles of modern technology. The Musketeers could find him damn near anywhere. The message was brief, and pithy. Their code a mishmash of things each had learned over the years, and only the four of them could understand.

He'd kept them off his back for the last month. They knew *what,* and *how,* but he refused to tell them *where.*

He stood for a moment, scanned the missive once more. His brother Kane, he suspected, had sent this. Methodical, orderly Kane's renowned patience must've come to an end. Probably aided and abetted by his twin, Derek, and stirred up by Kyle. And the only reason they'd be *this* hysterical was if *Jake* had spilled his guts. Dolan fit into the family like the fifth finger on a glove.

Damn.

No way was Michael letting Church anywhere near his brothers. No fucking way.

Life was fragile. Death final. The double-edged sword of guilt and survival wasn't going to touch the people he loved most in the world.

He swiftly tapped out an equally cryptic response. Then routed it through various addresses, and set a time delay on it. They'd receive it on Friday morning. By then it would all be over but the shouting.

That done, he quickly assembled what he needed. He'd come to Paradise loaded for bear; everything from a little bang, to a giant big bang. He'd lucked out. Church's stash of ordnance was in such a confined space, it wouldn't take much to do a spectacular disposal.

It was its own self-fulfilling prophecy. Michael liked the poetic justice in that.

He slung the MK 138 satchel charge canvas bag casually over his shoulder, went topside, and locked the door behind him. The door wasn't meant to keep anyone determined out—but he'd know if anyone other than himself opened it. No one had boarded the *Nemesis* all day.

SEALs had the ability to travel very light, and very fast. He had to get from the marina to the cave, set the detonating timer, and be back in time for Auntie's luau without anyone noticing how long he'd been gone.

He guesstimated he'd been gone four minutes by the time he hit the beach. The sunset was spectacular, brilliant, and gaudy.

He ignored it as he jogged the three miles to the cove, the forty-pound satchel charge riding comfortably on his back.

The cliff face glowed devil dog red in the dusk light. Michael removed the pack, withdrew a small powerful penlight, and slipped into the fissure.

It was twenty degrees cooler inside, the dark welcome. The anticipation that had hummed through him for months blossomed into a sensation that was almost orgasmic in its intensity.

"This big bang is for you, Bud."

God, Hugo had loved to blow things to hell and back. Matter of fact, so did he. Michael grinned. The narrow beam picked up interesting side passages, but he didn't waste time exploring.

He jogged across the sand to the back of the cave, then took the stairs two at a time, zigging and zagging his way to the top. As were most things in life, the rough-cut steps were easier to navigate with a little light.

The chamber was bathed with an eerie orange-red glow from the hovering sun. The crates were stacked six deep from floor to ceiling.

Four months ago, Church had pirated a vessel innocently disguised as a tanker, bound for a small African nation. How Church had discovered the vessel was carrying this amount of high-tech weaponry was still a mystery.

With a few well-placed people, he'd overtaken his quarry, boarded, killed all thirty-eight crewmen, and then made the tanker *Cheung Hu* disappear into thin air.

International intelligence—hell, entire *countries*—continued to search for the *Cheung Hu.* Good guys, as well as bad, would trip over their own protocol to get their hands on the ship's cargo.

And here it was.

Michael set the canvas sack on the floor and moved between the boxes, looking for a good spot. If, for any reason, anyone came up here before the transfer, he didn't want them stumbling over the bag.

It was all here. Stencils on the crates designated the contents in military jargon. CAR-15s, M16s, rocket launchers, all the necessary ammo. His heart pumped hard and fast when he saw the pièce de résistance, the pulse generator.

The pulse generator was state of the art. The power behind this machine, if the damn thing worked like they claimed, would be off the charts. Uncle Sam would've liked a look-see, but Church had obviously offered it to the highest bidder. Michael was here to see that none of them got what they'd requested from Santa.

Jesus. He rested his palm on the crate, and closed his eye. Logic had told him Church would keep this baby as the trump card. The high-bidding tangos must've negotiated the pulse generator into the deal.

The difference between Michael and the rest of Church's pursuers was that he'd known where to look.

He'd recognized Church's work. Many modern-day pirates kidnapped their victims, or set them adrift in one of the life boats, tied up, but relatively unharmed. Church's M.O. was to brutally murder the crewmen before loading the bodies on one of the lifeboats.

He took sadistic pleasure in his work, and it showed. No one was safe. He took boats of all shapes and sizes, either selling them, or using them in his piracy business with deadly effect. No one saw him coming. He was far-reaching in his target of cargoes. Be it ordnance, oil, or sugar. He'd discovered weapons when he'd taken the *Marie José* last year and it had already become a lucrative branch of his thriving operation. Church had quickly made a name for himself.

Terrorists had a voracious appetite for weapons and explosives. Church made their dreams come true. He delivered what they wanted, when they wanted it. He had the attention of every major power in the world. So far, he hadn't been caught.

Tahiti was well off the normal beaten track for pirates. Paradise was the perfect spot to bring the ordnance, hide it, send out for bids, and wait.

No hurry.

Lieutenant Wright would've done it by the book, captured him, and brought the sonofabitch to trial.

Michael was going to write the end to Trevor Church once and for all. By fair means or foul. Whatever it took . . .

. . . and, as Church had done to Hugo, smile while he offed him.

Michael found a nice little hidey-hole between two crates of stick dynamite, neatly boxed against the east wall. It was a tight fit, but perfectly obscured, even if someone did make a last-minute inspection before the buy.

He returned to the top of the stairs and brought the satchel back with him, squeezing between the rough wood crates before hunching down awkwardly to tuck the shoulder bag into the space between the boxes.

Normally he'd prime with a nonelectric blasting cap on the end of a section of time fuse, or use Primedet, but in this case he wanted more than an hour or so. He wanted *twenty-four* hours.

He set the timer for seventeen hundred hours on Thursday. The handshaking would happen Thursday evening after everyone arrived. The transfer was scheduled to take place Friday morning.

Timing was everything.

He and Jake had worked on this for days. Once set, there was no going back. No "Mother may I?" No room for error. On Thursday at five in the afternoon, this cavern was going to blow, and with it, Church's ordnance, his clients' faith in him, and half the frigging cliff-side. Nothing anyone said, or did, could change the course of events.

The explosion would trigger every intelligence community with satellite access.

It had to be this way. Church had powerful means of persuasion.

Michael had caved once.

He wouldn't do it again.

He paused with his fingers on the mechanism and smiled grimly. Even if things turned to shit, and for some reason he *didn't* exterminate Church, there was no one on the planet, himself included, who could turn this baby off now.

Knowing it was unlikely for anyone to see the dark green canvas bag, he nevertheless spent another precious twenty minutes efficiently rigging a set of phony M700 fuses, tangles of wires, and enough smoke and mirrors to keep anyone busy from now until seventeen hundred hours on Thursday, trying to disable his handywork.

One last check.

Everything in place.

No room for error.

Perfect.

He rose from his cramped position. A feeling of completion descended over him. For the first time in nearly a year, the forces wailing inside him stilled, and a familiar calm settled. Soon Hugo would rest in peace. Soon.

One more timer to set . . .

Then time to party.

Michael spent a couple of extra minutes standing on the beach, watching the approach of a tanker far out at sea. No coincidence, the tanker was arriving to remove Church's prize. Because of its size, it would probably drop anchor beyond the reef in readiness for the transfer on Friday morning.

Michael grinned as he walked around the hotel and headed back toward the sound of drums.

"Sorry, pal. You're shit outta luck."

The setting for Auntie's luau was the area behind her hotel. The watermelon and mango color of the setting sun illuminated the tropical clearing surrounded by lush vegetation and tall coconut palms, making everything look almost surreal and otherworldly. Flame trees, in bursts of fiery red, breadfruit trees with their large, delicately etched leaves, and brilliantly hued bougainvillea mingled with lacy green and yellow, big-leafed vines and other flowering shrubs to make up three sides, while the ocean and the Technicolor sky made a dramatic backdrop for the fourth.

The perfume of camellias, frangipani, ginger, and jasmine combined in a thick, heady fragrance, assaulted already overloaded senses.

The Garden of Eden.

Michael wasn't a fanciful man, but the brilliant colors of the evening sky and exotic flowers, coupled with the rhythmic beating of the drums, were enough to give any man pause.

He stepped into the clearing. Tiki torches dotted the wide circle, dancing flames ebbed and rose with the warm trade wind drifting off the water. A band, made up of several local men, filled the sultry air with the tinny twang of a ukulele, and the compelling rhythm of guitars. His blood, already pumped with adrenaline, picked up the driving throb of the *fa'atete-*, and the bass of the *pahu* drums.

Time to seduce his enemy's daughter.

Colors seemed brighter, the air smelled sweeter, and the musical notes blended into a rich, powerful resonant pulse that had his blood racing. All of which merged into a seamless, exotic tapestry.

"Hooie! Here we be, hottie." Auntie waved from the sidelines.

Surrounded by baskets and coolers, it looked as though Auntie had settled in for a month.

He leaned down and gave her a peck on her mint-scented check. "Happy birthday, beautiful. How's it going, Henri? Tally?"

Michael took the vacant plastic lawn chair on Tally's right. His blind side.

"What you be wanting drink, piña colada? *Hinano?*"

"Hinano." He opted for the local beer, and accepted the icy bottle Henri excavated from the ice chest. "Thanks."

"You be wanting that drink now, baby girl?"

"Sure, why not?" Tally caught Michael's eye as she

glanced over at Auntie. She'd tucked a bright yellow hibiscus behind her right ear.

Michael gave the flower a nod. "Know the significance of that?"

"The significance is that I have a flower behind my ear."

"Right ear means you're taken."

Her blue eyes sparkled, but she kept a straight face. "Yeah?"

"Yeah."

The flame red monstrosity Tally wore slipped off one creamy shoulder. She hitched it back with a small grimace. Florid yellow flowers, as big as dinner plates, sprouted all over the muumuu. The garment was large enough to drown her slender frame. But the unintentionally low neckline, ruffle and all, displayed a delectable amount of her small bosom, and the golden tan she'd developed this afternoon.

Michael leaned over the arm of his chair. "Been shopping, I see," he whispered.

She gave a choked laugh, and turned to whisper back. Her nose bumped his face. Instead of pulling away, she nuzzled her nose against his check. "I think Auntie and I could both fit inside this thing."

She smelled of tuberose and toothpaste. "Hmm. I'm thinking maybe you and I could both fit in there."

Tally smiled. "In your dreams, sailor."

Yeah. And those dreams were hot and sweaty and heart-pounding. "Why didn't you grab a pair of my shorts, or just wear a T-shirt over your swimsuit?"

"Auntie wanted me to—"

"Hold still."

"Why?"

He stroked her cheek with his fingers. Her skin felt smooth and silky, and warmed under his touch. "Your hibiscus has ants."

Her lips twitched. "It does not. I checked before I put it in my hair."

"There was one little soldier marching ri-ght across here."

She turned fully to face him. "Michael, I've been th—"

"Here come the dancers. Save it till later."

Her sigh was more drama than disappointment. Outwardly, she was her usual serene self; inside boiled the hot-blooded woman he wanted to get his hands on. And his mouth, and his . . . hell. He could almost taste her rapid heartbeat. He saw it pulsing hard and fast at the base of her slender throat.

His cock twitched to life.

Michael dragged his gaze away from the sight of Tally's life force and tried to focus on the activities in the clearing. But like a bloodhound, he could smell her there beside him.

Tuberose, innocence, heat.

He closed his eye.

Hell, she could wear the all-encompassing *hijab* and *burqa* of Arabic women, and he'd *still* want her.

One shrug and that stiff cotton monstrosity she wore would pool around her slender hips. Michael kept his attention fixed on the dancers who'd just pranced onto "center stage," a grassy circle inside the tiki torches.

For the next twenty-four hours he'd indulge his senses with sweet Tally.

"Okay. That does it," Tally said, furious as Leli'a and four other girls lined up in front of their audience. "She's wearing my pearls!"

Clad in short, scarlet and white pareus tied at the hips, matching bikini tops, and wreaths of ferns and flowers in their long dark hair, the women looked like a Kodak moment. Leli'a undulated her hips to the chanting and music. Ripe and sensuous, confident in her allure, Auntie's niece looked right at Michael and smiled. Tally's opera-length black pearls were wound twice around her neck and swayed with the movement of her body.

Tally's next thought was, *And keep your sneaky eyes off* Michael! And the heat of *that* thought surprised her.

She gulped down the last half inch of colada, and reached for the pitcher on the table beside her.

Auntie tapped her forearm. "Not be drinking too much lovely rum, baby girl. You like *ori* and music. Make blood flow hot and happy. Not needing alcohol. Make new memories tonight. You see."

Well there was one memory *Leli'a* wasn't counting on. Tally coming after her with blood in her eye. The little thief was prancing around in front of God, her aunt, and Tally, wearing stolen property. Un-fricking-believable.

Tally set the pitcher down. The entire setting was giving her enough of a buzz. Her blood raced through her veins like hot lava, and she was ready to jump out of her skin. Auntie was right: Alcohol was the last thing she needed.

"This spec-ta-cu-lar dance," Auntie told her, rough palm firm on Tally's arm as if holding her in place. "Call *o'te'a amui*. The *tané* will come next." The beat of the drums and rhythmic chanting grew louder and louder. The girls undulated to the rapidly increasing beat and were soon joined by the men.

Auntie *had* been holding her in place. Wise woman. An hour later, Tally had cooled off, a little, and she got her chance for a private conversation with her mutilating thief. The girls stood giggling under the trees as she strolled over.

"You and I are going to have a little chat, young lady." Tally took Leli'a's arm and walked her firmly away from her friends. When the girl refused to budge, Tally gave her arm a little jerk and all but dragged her out of earshot.

"*Haere tatou!* Let go!" Leli'a tried to shake her off. Tally held on tighter. "What you want?"

"My necklace, for starters. Good God. Are you really this amoral that you don't *care* that I'm standing right here while you're wearing it?"

The girl gripped the double strand in a tight fist at her throat. "My necklace. Give to me by Mother. Got from *her* mother, and *her* mother."

"You are so full of crap. My father gave that to me years ago. Hand over my necklace, toots, or I'll tell your aunt you were the vandal and thief in my room this morning."

The girl tossed her liquid black hair over her shoulder, rather like Miss Piggy. "Go to hell."

Tally narrowed her eyes. "And that you're the one who pushed me down the stairs the other day."

"Prove it."

"Give Tally back the necklace, Leli'a." Henri emerged from the trees.

Leli'a turned her glare from Tally to Henri. She went into a spate of Tahitian too fast and colloquial for Tally to grasp more than the gist. But then she didn't need to understand a word to follow the conversation. Leli'a wasn't about to part with Tally's necklace.

Henri was adamant.

Finally, Leli'a ripped the necklace over her head, tears of rage in her eyes. "I *hate* you," she spat, throwing the priceless gems at Tally's feet. She turned and ran past Henri, almost knocking him over.

"I am very sorry about that," Henri said gently. "She is young, and angry. She'll get over it."

Tally crouched to pick up the pearls. They were warm and smooth. She rose with the string draped over her hand and glanced toward the trees. Leli'a had disappeared.

"Henri, Leli'a was the one who destroyed my room." Tally saw that Henri had already figured that one out. She frowned, truly puzzled. What had she done to make the girl hate her so much?

Henri fell into step beside her. "I apologize for her rudeness, and for the damage she did to your possessions. But it is not *you* personally, my dear. She is a teenager. She sees a successful, attractive woman. Self-possessed, independent, and she wants to be like you. My Leli'a has a long way to go, I'm afraid. Don't take it personally. I will speak with her when she calms down a bit. In the meanwhile, Auntie will help you put together a new wardrobe."

Tally almost groaned. She'd chosen her clothes for this trip with infinite care, every item designed to make her appear to be what she thought her father wanted her to be. Now she was reduced to greeting him in an Omar the Tent Maker muumuu.

Oh, brother.

Chapter Thirteen

"I see you got your necklace back. How'd it go?" Michael asked Tally as they strolled through Auntie's garden back to the main house after the party. The darkness was redolent with the scent of night-blooming jasmine and the spicy fragrance of frangipani. Overhead, stars glittered, icy and brilliant white in the velvety blackness. The narrow shell path necessitated them walking close together. Michael could've dropped back, but preferred to stay beside her. Every now and then he felt the graze of the stiff fabric of her muumuu, or the brush of her soft skin against his bare arm.

"Weird." Tally frowned. "She neatly managed to turn everything around, so I felt that somehow stealing the necklace was *my* fault." Her eyes shimmered in the moonlight as she looked at him with a wry smile. "How can I be so damn furious with her, and feel sorry for her at the same time?"

"Beats the hell out of me. I thought I'd have to get in there and pull you off her."

"Really?" Tally grinned. "Did you think I was going to beat her up?"

"You could've taken her easily."

"Don't think it didn't cross my mind," Tally said dryly. "But what would be the point?" She rubbed her upper arms with both hands. "I don't think I've ever had anyone look at me like that before."

"Like what?"

"Like"—she caught herself and shook her head—"never

mind. Auntie will talk to her. She's obviously an unhappy kid. There's not much I can do about what she did to my things. Thank God it was only *things.*" She clasped the pearls over her heart as she walked. "I'm glad I got these back. They mean a lot to me."

"She wasn't going anywhere with them."

"No, but it was pretty darn bold to wear them like that right in front of me."

"She obviously wanted to let you know she had them."

"And now she doesn't."

He smiled at her pithy tone. "Find anything besides that stunning ensemble at the General Store?"

Tally held out a handful of fabric at her hips. "This or a *pareu.*"

"I vote for the *pareu.*" Michael paused. "Or nothing at all."

"I think that look would have limited appeal."

"An appreciative audience of one is all you need."

Tally didn't say anything to that as they crossed the lanai and entered the open French doors into the empty bar. Most of the lights were off, and the room was dim and moody.

"Want a drink before we go up?" Michael asked.

"No, I'm going to call it a night. This has been a full day, to say the least."

No shit. "I'll come up with you." He opened the door to the stairs. Tally remained beside him on the stairs. The smell of her—roses and warm woman—was mouthwateringly delectable.

Hunger, surprising and sharp, clawed at him.

He didn't have to work hard to imagine her naked despite the miles of starched fabric flowing around her. The image of Tally's slender body was firmly imprinted on his synapses.

He put a hand on her shoulder to stop her entering her room even though the door had been left open, and the brilliant light beside the bed was on.

He liked the feel of her beneath his hand. Spare. Taut. Nothing wasted . . . "Me first."

"Have at it." She waved him in, then leaned against the

doorjamb while he searched the room. Not much of a challenge. The closet was empty of clothes, let alone a lurker. The new mattress on the bed had been freshly made up, sans the bright cotton throw. The neatly tucked blanket exposed the bare wood floor. The damn light was bright enough to send a lighthouse warning to neighboring islands. "All clear."

"So I see. Thanks." She walked into the room, absently rubbing her forehead.

"Headache?"

She gave him a wan smile. "As I said, it's been quite a day."

"How about another massage?"

She shook her head. "I'll take a rain check. I'm already on overload."

She did look beat, but Michael still wanted to get his hands on her. "Sure?"

"I'm convincing myself I am."

"The door downstairs is locked. Leave your bedroom door ajar. I'll hear you if there's trouble."

"Hopefully, there won't be."

"Yeah, hopefully. 'Night."

"Close the door behind you. Yes, I'll open it again when I go to bed," she said before he objected.

"Want the bathroom first?"

"Thanks."

Michael saluted her, then shut the door behind him and stood for a moment in the well-lit hallway. A feral smile curved his mouth.

Point and counterpoint.

Tally showered in the old, claw-footed tub, then went back into her room. Michael's door was ajar, and she hurried into her own room and shut the door.

A few minutes later she heard the shower running again. Oh, boy. She squeezed her eyes shut. He was naked in there. Gloriously, magnificently *naked.* He'd be all gleaming, tanned skin, rock-hard muscles, and rock-hard . . . Tally groaned.

She saw, in her mind's eye, the runnels of soapy water trail slowly down his chest. The satin gleam of wet, tanned skin. She imagined him running his hand briskly over his body as he soaped himself . . . and then replacing his hands with her own, and imagined the skim of her own hands down the hard plane of his belly.

Soapy. Smooth. Slippery.

Tally leaned against the closed door and cupped her breasts, then pressed down firmly with her palms. Her hard nipples ached. Not for her own touch, but for Michael's. She was in big trouble here. No matter what she'd told herself, the last couple of days had been little more than prolonged foreplay. She was in a constant state of readiness.

Determined to rein in her lascivious thoughts, Tally shook herself free of thoughts of Michael, and started getting ready for bed. Her favorite blue jammies had been a casualty of Leli'a's temper tantrum. Rather than sleep in the scratchy muumuu, she traded it for one of the white T-shirts Michael had given her this afternoon.

Because she didn't like the constriction of anything around her neck when she slept, she'd cut the neckband off the shirt. The stretched neckline slipped off one shoulder as she applied moisturizer to her face. Tired but wired, she was about to burst out of her own skin. Damn. Maybe she should've taken Michael up on the offer of the euphemistic massage.

Sometime between the kiss on the beach and finding Lu's body, Tally had decided she wanted to sleep with Michael again. Life could be so short. Why deny something they both wanted?

She was a big girl. She didn't need the promise of a ring on her finger to enjoy great sex.

On the other hand, given the tumultuous events of the day, her judgment might not be so hot.

She checked the night-light by the door, and turned off the bedside lamp, then stood, staring out the window at the reflection of the moon on the water. Down the hall, the shower turned off. No doors opened or closed. She didn't hear any footsteps. Lord, the man was quiet. She tried to imagine what he was doing in his room. She could see the square of light cast by his window as it fell across the lanai outside their rooms. The slight breeze ruffling the fern fronds didn't reach inside the room.

Tally opened the French door to the lanai, hoping to draw in cooler air. She breathed in the fragrance of the tropics before stepping cautiously onto the slatted boards of the balcony. If she'd been back home in America, where every craftsman had to answer to half a dozen governing boards, she'd have felt a great deal more confident on what looked pretty darn rickety.

The light next door turned off. " 'Night, John-Boy," she said under her breath. A large, comfortable-looking rattan rocking chair hunched in the corner of the lanai. She made her way across the splintery boards and sat down. The chair creaked as she pulled her legs up beneath the T-shirt and rested her chin on her up-drawn knees.

A soft, rolling meow sounded, and she glanced down to see Michael's cat looking up at her.

"Can't sleep, either?" she asked softly. Green eyes stared back unblinkingly. Tally curled her legs to the side and patted her lap. "Let's not go through your entire repertoire of hating me, okay? One creature a day is about my limit. Come up here and pretend to be civil."

Lucky narrowed his eyes and cocked his head as if he understood what she'd said. He jumped lightly onto her lap. "There's a good boy."

Tally lay a tentative hand on the cat's head. His short fur felt soft beneath her fingers. He butted his head against her hand with a low growling purr of pleasure, then sinuously draped his body over her thigh. The weight of the cat felt comforting in her lap.

"I think I'm going to get a cat when I get home," Tally told Lucky, scratching him behind his half-chewed right ear. She rested her head against the wing of the chair and felt a familiar hollow ache in her chest. Felt the longing deep inside.

She was lonely. Aching to have a connection. To someone.

"I'm hoping it's with my father," she told Lucky. "It's strange, you know. I don't call him anything when I talk to him. Not Trevor, or Father, or Dad. Not that we talk often, God knows. We're like strangers, really. Maybe I want too much from him. Maybe I want too little. What do you think? Too much? Yeah, I was afraid of that." She stroked her fingers down Lucky's supple back. "Too many commercials with pretty families all looking happy, that's my problem. I know that's not reality, but there's always been that stupid little part of me that wanted to sit at the breakfast table with my parents and siblings and pass the English muffins."

She had plenty of friends, several of them close. Her best friend, Marty, kept telling her she'd feel better if she got laid more than once every five years. Tally smiled. Not quite the same.

She knew all the pop psychology about absentee fathers and lack of love. But, damn it, she was twenty-seven years old. When was she going to get over the feeling Trevor had abandoned her? Lots of women didn't have fathers, and they turned out pretty normal and well-adjusted. *She* was normal and well-adjusted. For an adult woman who wanted her daddy.

Why did she want this relationship so badly?

Everything else in her life was great. Good job, great circle of friends, a beautiful condo, nice clothes . . . okay, her love life was flat, not fluffy, but all *that* would take to fix was saying yes, instead of no, when someone asked her out.

Tally rubbed Lucky's neck. "How about this?" she said softly to the disinterested cat. "I see how things go with Trevor in the next couple of days. Either it'll be great, or it'll be a bust, and I'll go home to my life and give up the idealized fantasy once and for all. That sounds reasonable, doesn't it?"

Lucky, limp as a noodle, snored.

. . .

He could hear her out there.

The chair creaking each time she moved, her soft voice as she talked to Lucky, and of course her under-the-breath singing. Stretched out naked on the sheets, Michael stacked his hands under his head and hoped for a breath of air to cool off his shower-damp body and raging libido.

He wasn't going to cool off lying on his bed alone. He got up and pulled on a pair of shorts, then stepped through his open French doors onto the moonlit patio.

His neighbor was singing, "I'm going to wash that man right outta my hair," very softly. Michael shook his head at how off-key she was. "You've had a full day. Why aren't you sleeping?"

She gave a little shriek. "God, you scared me. Why are you lurking?"

"I don't lurk, I prowl. It's too hot to sleep." He'd been in hotter places and had slept just fine. "Are you okay?"

She shivered in the heat of the night. "I can't stop thinking about that poor man."

"Your first corpse?"

Tally Ho gave him a wry look. "There aren't that many in my line of business."

"Guess not."

"Not *your* first dead body, apparently."

"Guess not."

The T-shirt had slipped off her shoulder. Her skin looked translucent and pale in the moonlight. Michael wanted to touch his mouth to the curve where her shoulder met the swell of her breast.

He'd wanted women before. Hell, he'd wanted women *badly* before. When he returned from an op, he was always horny as hell. But this . . . this pull with Tally was different. Not quite as easy to tag and file. Yeah, he wanted to fuck her brains out, and come back for seconds. And thirds. But he also wanted to delve into what made her so damned happy. So accepting of what life dished out. He wanted to know what she was thinking when her blue eyes got that faraway look. What she dreamed about when she curled on her side asleep.

He wasn't sure he liked that she was getting under his skin. Or that he might, somewhere in the deep, dark, murky depths of his subconscious, not want her hurt. Even if it was by him. Especially if it was by him.

He refused to have second thoughts. Tally Cruise had been dropped into his lap for a reason.

Vengeance.

But there was nothing saying he couldn't take what was being offered.

"It's a little cooler out here," Tally said softly.

He smelled her floral shampoo on the balmy night air. The scent of her shot in a direct line from his nose to his dick.

He strolled over and leaned against the railing, his back to the ocean, his arms extended and braced on the wood railing on either side of him. "Yeah," he said dryly. Sweat collected in the small of his back.

Tally looked up at him, eyes narrowed. The pulse in her throat made Michael feel like a vampire; the urge to sink his teeth into her soft, delectable flesh was almost overwhelming.

She stroked Lucky's arched back. The cat subsided once again, his head hanging off Tally's knee. Moonlight shone on her face and picked up small circles of light on the pearls she wore around her neck. He glanced into her room, lit by the glow of her night-light. Her bed hadn't been slept in.

"How long have you been afraid of the dark?" he asked softly.

She did a small self-conscious shrug. "It's so irrational. I've had this stupid phobia since I can remember. I have no idea why. It's just always been . . . there."

"Irrational or not, phobias aren't stupid."

She smiled. "I bet you've never been afraid of anything in your life."

"You'd bet wrong."

Her smile slipped. "Seriously?"

"Dead serious."

"Will you tell me?"

No one knew. No one. Logic had nothing to do with it. Irrational fear was just that—irrational. Hell, he was embarrassed by the fear, embarrassed he hadn't been able to conquer it. Humiliated that he couldn't get the fuck over it. Now. Today. Yesterday.

"I'm shit scared of the water." Where had that come from? He stared at her sitting there like an angel in the moonlight, and wondered what magic spell she'd cast that had him admitting his deepest, darkest nightmare.

"But you live on a boat," Tally pointed out softly. "Why?"

"Because I won't let the fear win."

"That's incredibly brave."

"No, it's not," Michael said, his voice suddenly raw. "It's incredibly stupid. Every minute of every day I'm waiting for the ocean to take me. I can't even goddamn go swimming anymore, for Christ sake."

"Oh, Michael."

"No different from your fear of the dark, Tally. No different. Except I should be able to overcome it, and for some damn reason I—can't. I just can't."

"What happened?"

None of your business. None. Of. Your. Damn. Business. "My best friend . . . drowned." *Blood and guts, and bits and pieces of Hugo floated in the inky water of his mind's eye.*

"Hugo?"

Jesus. How did she know—hell. The other day when he'd spilled his guts. "Yeah. Hugo."

"Were you with him when it happened?" Her gentle blue eyes captured his and wouldn't let go.

"Oh yeah," Michael said thickly. "I was right there."

"And you did everything in your power to save him, didn't you?"

"It wasn't enough."

"Somehow I'm sure your friend would disagree. If it had been humanly possible to save him, you would have."

"Moot now. He's gone, and I'm paying for my mistake." Michael shook off the black despair he always felt when he thought of Hugo. "Let's not waste a pretty moonlit night talking about past mistakes.

"I can practically hear your mind working. Still worried about this meeting with your father?"

She shrugged, and his T-shirt slipped a little farther down her shoulder and caught in the bend of her elbow. "I want too much, I think." Her skin had the same sheen as the pearls.

"What do you want from him?"

"Love. Acceptance . . . acknowledgment." She exhaled softly and ran her fingers down the filbert-size beads. "I can't seem to get the little girl waiting at the window separated from the woman I've become."

"Some men have no interest in kids. Sounds like your father is one of those guys." Michael kept his tone impersonal. He'd rather talk about her angst than his own. And the sad truth was, many men had no interest in becoming fathers but they made kids, anyway. He felt a sharp pang. He missed *his* dad. They'd been close . . . before Church screwed over his world.

"Intellectually, I know that. We've certainly never been close." She gave a small laugh. "Okay, that's an understatement. I've seen Trevor exactly sixteen times in my entire life. Mostly when I was a kid, and only then because I was with my mother when she'd track him down. A couple of times I met up with him in Vancouver. Once in London. I more or less forced the meetings. Stupid, huh?" She twined the pearls around her hand.

"Want to hear something terrible? My father isn't a very nice man. He treated my mother like crap, and he's pretty much ignored me my entire life. On the rare occasions we've met, it was awkward and uncomfortable. I know it, and yet I still believe that because we share blood, there should be some sort of . . . bond. A connection. *Something.* I *want* us to love each other, because parents and children *should* love each other.

"When I got the ticket to come, I forgot all about reality. Illogical, I know. If the bond isn't there, it just isn't there, no matter how much I want it. But there's nothing wrong with wanting to give it another shot. Right?"

"Maybe it'll work out." *Church "wasn't a very nice man"? Jesus. No shit.* "When did you say he'd be back?"

"Tomorrow afternoon sometime. God. I'm excited, and nervous, and"—she gave a small, choked laugh—"terrified. Must seem strange when you're so close to your family."

"Used to be."

"Did you have a falling out?"

"No."

"Do they know where you are?"

"Only which hemisphere."

"You're not terribly talkative, are you?"

"Not usually, no. And particularly not at two in the morning." He'd said far more than he'd wanted to, and felt raw and exposed because of it. There was every likelihood she'd use the information to stab him in the back if the opportunity presented itself. He was a fool.

"Go to bed, then. I was perfectly happy out here by myself."

"No, you weren't. You were wishing I'd come out here and ravish you." Michael crossed one foot over the other, and spread his arms wide on the railing behind him. He remained quiet, and the silence stretched until she hurriedly filled in the void as he'd known she would.

"I was?"

"Sure." Michael watched her pale hands smooth Lucky's coat. The cat was dead asleep. *She* was wired.

"If you know this, then why aren't you doing it?"

"You were going to tell me something when we were out at the luau. Wasn't this it?"

"Oh, boy," she said with a small laugh. "Are you psychic?"

The heated look she was giving him made Michael's blood race. Mesmerizingly beautiful in the moonlight, Tally's eyes glittered, and her soft mouth begged to be kissed. Michael dropped his eyes down the length of her. His white-knuckled fingers gripped the wood railing when he saw, beneath the soft cotton of his T-shirt, her peaked nipples, hard and needy.

When she came to him, he wanted her to come all the way. "And?"

Her eyebrows shot up. "And? And I changed my mind about the line of death. I *want* you to cross it."

No slow build-up. No prevarication.

So Tally. "Yeah?"

Her smile widened. "Yeah." She carefully plucked Lucky off her lap, uncurled her long legs, and stood. She set the limp cat on the seat of the chair. "I've been wanting to kiss you again, all day," she admitted, closing the gap between them.

His arms trembled with the urge to grab her. His mouth salivated to taste her. The wood grain of the railing etched into the tight grip of his palms. "So have I." He kept his voice mild. "No wonder neither of us could sleep."

Tally lifted both hands to his face. Not that Michael was going anywhere. His feet were glued to the floor.

Her slender hands felt cool and smooth on either side of his face, her touch light as she explored the angles of his cheeks, his nose. A finger traced the line of elastic that ran over his right brow and disappeared into his hair.

"My wounded warrior." Her body brushed his as she rose onto her tiptoes and gently touched her mouth to his. The touch of her lips was as soft as a butterfly's kiss, as maddening as an unscratched itch, as electrifying as the first time he'd taken a girl. His body tensed in anticipation.

Michael held himself taut as she explored his face with her sweet mouth. Her breath smelled faintly minty from toothpaste.

The gentle pressure of her unbound breasts tantalized him

as she pressed her upper body against his bare chest and rubbed against him like a cat.

"Michael." Her breathing quickened when he released his grip on the railing to wrap his arms around her slender body. He used both hands to grip her bottom through two thin layers of cotton and pull her tightly against him. She trembled, her arms tightening around his neck.

"Michael," she repeated, her breath a soft sigh as she offered up her mouth.

But he was beyond *soft.* Beyond *tentative.*

He crushed her mouth under his and tasted her with the passion he'd kept banked all evening. Hell, for *days*.

After a small eternity, he dragged his mouth away from her for a few seconds. They were both breathing hard. "Be sure this is what you want, honey. Be *damn* sure." His voice was thick, hoarse, unrecognizable.

"I am. It is."

He needed them horizontal, *now,* but the taste of her drew him back for one more sample. With his hand at the small of her back, Michael pulled her tightly against him, drawing her up, and slanting his mouth down on hers with fierce hunger. He swallowed her soft moan.

Openmouthed, Tally returned his fervor, her tongue dueling with his. Michael controlled the urgency by sheer mind over matter. He was ready and primed for action. He wanted to be inside her now. Hard and deep. But it wasn't himself he wanted mindless. It was Tally.

He withdrew his mouth from her hungry lips and tasted the damp skin of her jaw, taking gentle little love bites along the way. Her body vibrated against his. She moaned, and he bit down on the thudding pulse at the base of her throat. Her fingers flexed on his chest as he sucked, and her nails scored his skin.

He cupped the front of her slender neck in his hand, over the bruises that son of a bitch had made on her. Stroked her neck with his thumb. "Know what this is called?" He drew a line with his palm. Down her chest, between her breasts.

"Torment?" she panted through gritted teeth.

He tried to slow his own breathing. It wasn't easy. "Energy meridian."

Her laugh mingled with a groan as his hand glided down her belly. "Please! S-S-ave the textbook f-for lat-ahhh."

He cupped her mound through two frustrating layers of fabric and felt the heat of her. Her hips followed the movement of his hand. Too hot. Too soon. He shifted gears. Up again. His thumb and fingers spanned her stomach, slid over the thin material of the T-shirt, and traced over her rib cage.

"The Chinese," he told her, punctuating his words with small bites on her bare shoulder, "discovered this line, running down the center of your body—" He nuzzled her neck. Her nails dug into his chest, then one hand slipped around to his back and tried to pull him closer. He gave her shoulder a sharp nip with his teeth. "It's supposed to be incredibly sensitive—"

"Oh, God. It *is*."

"—and runs from here"—he nibbled her lower lip—"to here." He trailed his fingers down her body and across her mound. While his hand petted her below, he shifted his mouth to her ear, nibbling and laving until she shifted mindlessly between his hands.

"M-Michael?"

"Mmm?"

"We-We're on the balcony."

"Mmm."

"The s-same one I threw th-that guy over. Remember?"

He raised his head an inch and, remarkably, wanted to laugh at her vehemence. His lips twitched. "And?"

Tally covered his hand and pressed it hard against her damp heat. "And let's get *on* with it!"

"Or you'll toss me over the side?"

"Yes!" She thumped her forehead on his chest. "If we don't make love soon I'm going to jump right out of my skin."

"I *am* making love to you."

"Inside."

"The room?"

"Me!" She threaded her fingers through his hair, grabbed him by the scruff of his neck, and pulled his face down. "You're at my mercy, Black Bart," Tally growled, nose to nose. "Have your wicked way with me, or suffer the consequences."

He captured her mouth under his and swung her up into his arms without breaking the lip lock. More by instinct than anything else, he carried her down the lanai, through his open door and into his moon-bright room.

Michael placed one knee on the rumpled sheets, then lowered her onto the mattress.

She reached for him. "Hurry."

He gently captured her wrists, then guided her arms over her head, stretching her body out before him like a banquet. "The last time we made love, it was in the dark, and in a hurry. Let's take our sweet time. I like delayed gratification," he told her, his voice rough with need. "There's no deadline. Is there?"

"Are you crazy?" Her hands flexed restlessly under his. "I'm *dying* here."

Michael chuckled. *"La petite mort."*

She lay on his rumpled sheets, half on her back, half on her side, her arms above her head, a scowl on her face. "Not yet. And there's nothing *little* about it! *Mich*-ael!"

Ah, Jesus. He could eat her in one bite. He didn't remember sex being *fun*. Torturing Tally, seeing her eyes haze with pleasure, intensified his own enjoyment a hundred-fold. He spread his legs to ease the pressure on his balls. It helped. A little.

"I have a real problem with the amount of clothing you insist on wearing, lady." On his knees, Michael threw a leg over her to straddle her narrow hips. He released her wrists, and started sliding the oversize T-shirt up her legs. He took his sweet time, enjoying the way her eyes glazed, and her lips parted on a silent sigh as she watched him. "And since by rights this T-shirt is mine, I'm taking it back."

She grabbed his wrists, stopping the progress he was making to get her naked. "I have a terrible confession to make."

"I know you're not a guy," Michael assured her.

Tally's deep, throaty laugh was wicked and sexy as hell. "That *would* be awkward, but no." As if she couldn't help touching him, she skimmed her palms up his forearms, then down again. Her touch was maddeningly feather light. "I-I well, I—"

"Spit it out, I can take it."

She chewed the corner of her lip and gazed up at him, the devil in her eyes. "I'm wearing your underpants, too."

"Jeesus, Tally!" Michael groaned, bending down to bump his forehead on hers. His hand skimmed up her smooth thigh, then across the narrow span of her belly until he found the slit in the underwear.

Chapter Fourteen

Michael's hand felt cool against Tally's warm skin. She tilted her hips to encourage his fingers, and her chin to capture his mouth. "Hmmm," she sighed, a low hum of pleasure as his palm skimmed across her tummy, and his mouth connected with hers. His tongue was hot, slick, hungry.

While he kissed her, she tried to push down her underpants—his underpants—but Michael put a warning hand over hers, and lifted his head a fraction of an inch.

"Hey," he said hoarsely. "Get your hands back where I put them."

She wiggled her bottom. The hand he'd slid inside her underwear skimmed a little closer to where she wanted it. "You're not the boss of me," she told him breathlessly.

His chuckle sounded strangled. "Pretend I am for a while."

She hesitated, then returned her arms to the mattress above her head, and shifted a little more onto her back to give him better access. "Hmmm. Then do I get my turn to be the boss of you?"

He smiled against her mouth. "Oh, yeah."

She ran the tip of her tongue across his smile, and enjoyed his responding shudder. "Okay."

"Good girl."

"Girl? Oh, boy," she groaned as his fingers skimmed her wet heat. "*That* feels great. Ahhhmm. Don't push your luck, p-pal," Tally warned, spoiling her severe tone with a moan. She shifted under him. "Can I sit up a bit?"

"No. Why?"

"I don't have any cleavage when I lie flat, that's why."

"Your concern is premature." He nibbled her lower lip. "I haven't got up that way yet. Besides, cleavage is overrated. More than a mouthful is a waste."

Tally went deaf as Michael slid his fingers inside her. He duplicated the movement of his fingers with his tongue in her mouth until Tally didn't know if she was coming or going. The sensation was like the sea, as wave upon wave of sensation bombarded her senses. The waves gathered, and crested closer and closer until she squirmed beneath his touch. Wanting less. Craving more.

"Wait. W-Wait. Wa—" He silenced her with another kiss. His touch was so sure. So exactly . . . right, that in seconds, her entire body clenched, then exploded in a mind-blowing orgasm.

"Wow," Tally managed when she floated back to earth.

"Enough chitchat." Michael slid the hem of the T-shirt up her legs. "I want my clothes back now."

Tally waved a weak wrist. "Take 'em."

As he took his sweet time gliding the soft fabric up over her hips, he moved backwards to straddle her knees.

She shifted so she lay flat on her back, itching to touch him. She'd get her revenge. *Later*. Moonlight sheened his shoulders and the muscles flexing in his arms as he crouched there, poised over her like a temporarily tame, black panther.

He paused to brush the string of pearls off her chest. They coiled in a warm heap beside her throat. Tally closed her eyes as Michael's slightly callused palms skimmed over her peaked nipples.

"So responsive." He leaned down, and drew his tongue over her nipple. When she arched her back, he took the tight bud into his mouth and sucked hard. Sensation shot from her breast to her hoohoo in two seconds flat. Tally about came off the bed.

It was several seconds before she noticed that he'd pulled the T-shirt over her head and had tossed it aside. Tally sighed. "*Now* we're talking."

Michael chuckled as he slid his body against hers, and lay beside her, skin to skin. The hard length of his erection pulsed against her thigh.

She licked her lip, and sucked in a breath. "You have a-amazing con-control."

"You ain't seen nothin' yet," he promised, his murmur low. He picked up the string of pearls and wound it in a figure eight around her breasts. Since there wasn't much of a mound to hold them in place, the warm strand slithered across her skin making her shiver with anticipation. She didn't have long to wait. Michael's hot mouth closed over one nipple while he manipulated the smooth beads around her other breast in a maddeningly erratic motion that had her almost jumping out of her skin.

Just as Tally got used to one technique, the suction of his mouth changed, and he laved her nipple with heated licks interspersed with hard, mind-blowing sucks.

She didn't know where her nipple stopped and Michael's mouth began. Her body was already beyond reason. All she could do was accept. And feel. And burn.

The pearls glided across her skin as they uncoiled from her breasts and traveled down the center of her body. Strangely cool and warm, erotically smooth and sensuous as each individual bead rolled across her sensitized skin and made her body tremble.

The wet suction of his mouth skimmed the shallow valley between her breasts, then latched on to the other nipple.

It was sweet agony, and she almost sobbed, the sensation of his avid mouth overwhelming. "Please. Please. Ple— What—"

While his mouth distracted her, Michael spread her thighs wider, then was very busy with his hand as he methodically inserted the pearls deep inside her. She hadn't even realized that somehow he'd taken them from around her neck.

Tally writhed on the bed. The sensation was alien . . . not uncomfortable, but . . . different. The string was a thousand miles long. And Michael was *slow.*

"Michael—" she began doubtfully, not at all sure she liked the sensation of the foreign objects inside her, filling her.

"Trust me," he whispered darkly, then lowered his head once more to suckle her. Tally almost forgot what else he was doing.

The last few inches of the strand tickled across her belly before they, too, were tucked deep inside her.

Michael lifted his head to watch her. "How does it feel?"

Oh. It felt . . . odd. "Full. Strange. E-erotic."

He kissed her mouth as if he was starving for her. "How about now?" And he started removing the pearls with agonizing slowness.

The sensation took Tally somewhere she'd never been before, somewhere dark and forbidden. She fought against it, bringing her hands up to try to push the intrusion away.

Michael was relentless. He used his free hand to capture her wrists, then held them there, flat on the mattress above her head. When her legs shifted restlessly, he threw a leg over hers to pin her to the bed. Even trapped as she was, Tally went wild as each pearl slid free, gliding, bumping along the bud of her sex. Pushing her higher, higher. Tally's head thrashed on the mattress, and she fisted her hands in the sheet.

Michael stopped. "Trust me?" he whispered seductively. There was a thread of tension there, a banked emotion she couldn't quite grasp.

Tally tried to catch her breath, which came now in shuddering gasps. "Come to the dark side, Luke . . . yes. No. All right! Yeeees."

Michael's chuckle vibrated against her throat. The smooth beads rubbed against the very heart of her. Shocking. Electrifying. A glorious, delirious urgency consumed Tally. Her heels dug into the mattress, her hips rocked as her body clenched. She began to whimper as the sensation overwhelmed her. She couldn't. Take. Any. More—

The sensations swept over her. Overwhelming in their intensity. She tried to pull away from them, even while her body arched in response to the drag of the necklace against her most sensitive flesh. She felt the kiss of each individual pearl. Each delicate, maddening, intimate, kiss.

Her head thrashed, and her body bucked.

Michael didn't stop. It was as if he knew she couldn't take any more, and he was relentlessly determined to prove to Tally she could.

He kept up the steady extraction, letting the beads do their magic as they were withdrawn inch by agonizing inch.

When she begged him to hurry, he kissed away her protest. When she wanted to bring her arms up to push him away, or to draw him close, he imprisoned her limbs.

She made a broken sound, and fought the build of sensation. Afraid to let herself fly into that darkness. Afraid to let go of everything sane and familiar. Then she had no choice.

The orgasm came harder, sharper than the last. And went on and on and on as Michael tormented her, withdrawing those damn pearls . . .

One.

Agonizing.

Bead.

At.

A.

Time.

She cried out his name in a long, heartfelt moan as she came. And came. And came.

Michael gathered her in his arms, feeling the shudders that still gripped her body. They were both slick with sweat. He ached from prolonged denial. But he'd achieved his goal.

She trusted him.

He let her doze in his arms, skin glued together, for fifteen minutes. Then he started again. She gave a sleepy protest when he ran kisses down her center meridian, and closed his mouth over her swollen folds.

She threaded her fingers in his hair as he cradled her hips in his large hands and brought her closer.

"There are no more O's in me, you know," she told him weakly. His tongue pushed inside her, and she moaned long and low. "Okay. M-Maybe *one* mooore—" She went over the edge.

While she shuddered and fell apart in his arms, Michael slid his body over hers and sheathed himself in her slick heat.

His body bucked and jerked with the intensity of the mating. It took mere seconds for him to come. His groan of sheer ecstasy could probably be heard in Bora-Bora.

After several minutes he rolled over, taking Tally with him. Still hard, still joined, he ran his hand down her sweaty back.

"That's it," Tally moaned. "Uncle. White flag. Pax. I give up."

Her skin quivered as his hand moved down her back. He stroked the baby-soft skin on her bottom. "Yeah?"

"Yeah." She kissed the side of his neck. "No more. I can't move a muscle."

He flexed his PC muscle. She went still. He did it again. Tally gave a choked laugh, "Obviously you can, Man of Steel. If you have one ounce of energy to leap me in a single bound, have at it." She rested her head on his chest and closed her eyes. "Wake me when you're done."

"Sure," Michael lied, rolling her over and plunging deep. She was as pliable as C4, and just as combustible when she sprawled bonelessly beneath him. She didn't open her eyes as he moved slowly. But the more he built the waves, one on top of another, the more she participated. She opened her eyes to glare at him. "No fair."

"I never said it was equitable, did I?"

She wrapped her arms around his neck and dug her heels into his butt, and held on.

Together they flew over the edge of the world.

Since they were the only UTD/SEAL team inserted, Michael and Hugo each carried several limpet mines attached to a simple harness on their backs. Although the mines contained very little explosive, it would blow them to smithereens if they weren't careful. They were very, very careful.

They'd also brought along some C4, with a waterproof M-60 underwater lighter, and a timer fuse as a chaser. They were loaded for bear and loving it.

Although Michael couldn't see Hugo in the dark, he could imagine Hugo's grin.

His friend's favorite saying was, "There are very few of life's problems that can't be solved with high explosives and a big bang! Hoo Yah!"

Ahead, the shadowy bulk of the Marie José.

Hugo is going to get his heart's desire, *Michael thought, mentally grinning at his friend's enthusiasm. This was going to make one helluva nice bang. All they had to do was plant the explosives, detonate them, and get the hell out of Dodge before the bad guys knew what hit them.*

Piece of cake . . .

Fresh from her shower the next morning, Tally finger-combed her hair and watched Michael and several men hoist the tall mast on the *Nemesis*. Wearing another of Michael's T-shirts, and a ragged pair of orange shorts, she stood on the upstairs lanai and looked out over the marina.

Ye gods. What a night. She ached in places she didn't think had names. She smiled, wondering how Michael felt this morning. She'd eventually had her turn to be the boss of him, and he'd begged for mercy. Twice.

It had taken forever to wash the pearls. Of course she'd been wearing them at the time, and Michael was finicky about cleanliness. Tally held on to the wood railing, almost melting at the blurred memories of last night. She got wet just thinking about it. About him.

She tried to shake off the sensual lethargy. That was then, and this was now.

Unlike her limp self, Michael had seemed tense, on edge,

this morning when he'd leaned over to kiss her before leaving. Could it be that he was feeling a little of what she was feeling? Separation anxiety? She smiled wistfully.

Not likely.

She suspected the prolonged stay on Paradise was stretching Michael Wright's limit for being in one place. It was clear he was ready and rarin' to be off on his next adventure.

How long after the last of the repairs to his boat were complete would he stay? An hour? A day?

It was barely nine in the morning. Feasibly, they'd finish securing the mast long before afternoon.

He knew her father was arriving late today. They'd talked about it last night. Michael knew how eager she was for this meeting to go well. He knew the emotional investment she'd made.

Would he stay to be with her? To see how things worked out with her father? Or would he decide it was past time to move on, kiss her good-bye, and wish her luck?

She ran her fingers through her drying hair again, and tried to focus on the more immediate and the mundane.

Her clothes situation was pretty dire. She didn't want to meet her father dressed in a pair of Michael's fluorescent shorts, nor did she plan on wearing island garb for their first meeting in six years.

"If I sewed, which I don't," she told Lucky, who sat in the chair licking himself, "I'd make something elegant out of my drapes, like Scarlett O'Hara." It was a good thing she didn't have to depend on her nonexistent seamstress skills.

Fortunately, she'd remembered that she'd stuffed her shorts and tank top in her tote at the beach. Along with a pair of sandals and a small, emergency makeup pouch of basics. "At least I won't look completely awful."

She'd washed the shorts and top and hung them over the back of the chair to dry.

Anticipation hummed through her. Anticipation for the meeting with her father this afternoon vied with thoughts of last night, and Michael. Neither man gave her enough mental peace to wait passively. She needed action.

Tally paced from one end of the balcony to the other and back again.

Oh, God! She'd done something really, really stupid.

She was afraid she'd fallen in love with her vacation fling.

Not just stupid. *Exceptionally* stupid.

She hadn't asked him to stay once his repairs were done. But if she did . . . would he?

If she herself wasn't so tense about this upcoming meeting with her father, Tally was sure she would've asked Michael to stay for a few more days. And yet what would she achieve in the long run? Nothing. Eventually he'd be on his way, "seeing what he could see" around the world. With no desire for a home, and no need for a destination.

And eventually she'd go back to Chicago.

Their lovemaking last night had been magical. She'd relished the hours they'd spent in his bed. Making love without restrictions, expectations, or boundaries had been incredible.

But falling in love with the man had been the ultimate folly.

"He's the wind, and I'm the earth." And while he would skim across her surface, he'd never settle. Tally turned to look at Michael's cat. "Pretty poetic, huh?"

Lucky looked at her under his upraised leg, then went back to his ablutions.

She returned to her view of Michael working on his boat. The boat which would take him away from her, and out of her life, within hours.

Her heart ached, and her eyes stung. He'd never made any promises. It was her own foolishness that had gotten her into this emotional mess.

From her vantage point, and from this distance, she couldn't see details, like the sweat gleaming on Michael's brown skin, or the way his muscles moved as he worked, but she could use her imagination.

"What am I doing up here, longing to be with him, when I

could at least be down there with him?" she asked the disinterested cat. "Wanna come with me?"

Lucky rose, stretched, and gave her an unblinking green stare.

Tally tried to pick him up, but he flattened his ears and arched his back. "Make up our minds if we're friends or not, Cat. Fine. Follow me if you want to, or don't—"

A glimpse of a shiny blond head on the beach caught Tally's eye, and she turned for a better look. It looked like—no—yes! "Arnaud!"

Without giving it much thought, she shot through her room and raced downstairs.

As she tore through the bar, Auntie gave her a startled look. "What you bei—"

"Going for a run, maybe a swim. Be right back."

"The hottie say you be staying right . . ."

Her words faded as Tally raced across the shell path and down the small grassy incline to the beach. Arnaud, if it had been Arnaud, and not some sort of reflection of the sun off the rocks, was gone.

"You're losing it, Tallulah." But she kept up a steady loping pace as she ran on the hard-packed sand at the waterline.

Only one person on the island had that pale, bright blond hair. Arnaud. The slimy turd.

By the time she arrived at the rocky outcrop a few miles down the beach, she was out of breath, sweaty, and doubting what she thought she'd seen. She scrambled over the rough *a'a* lava, anyway.

On the other side, a small inlet, a miniature of the larger beach, was surrounded by rough rocks. The tide was coming in, and the beach was just a sliver of pale, exposed sand. Tally scanned the area—

"Oh, shit. Not again!"

In the shadow at the base of the cliffs lay the crumpled form of a man. His back was toward her. He wore the ubiquitous khaki shorts and T-shirt of half the island's inhabitants.

She hesitated, looking around quickly to see if the assailant was laying in wait hiding, for his next victim.

Her.

The cove was quiet. Not another soul around. And there was a possibility that the guy was just sleeping on the beach. Yeah, right, while the incoming tide sucked at his ankles. Not.

Tally ran over and fell to her knees behind the man. "Don't be dead. Don't be dead." She placed her hand on his shoulder covered in a wet, sandy T-shirt and gave him a little shake.

"Wake up, okay? I've had my fill of things that go bump in the night already." The guy half-rolled, and she recognized him immediately. It was Brian, the Australian, from the marina.

He wasn't going to wake up.

He was stone-cold dead.

Chapter Fifteen

A shadow fell over her as she crouched over Brian's body. "Oh, thank God, I was just c—" Tally turned, expecting to see Michael.

"Arnaud!" She jumped to her feet, heart sinking to her bare toes. She'd followed him to get answers, but now that he was right in front of her, she'd lost her enthusiasm for explanations. What she really wanted was distance. Until she learned differently, Arnaud Bouchard was her number one suspect in the murders of both Lu and Brian.

She stood three feet away from a killer. This was not good. The curve of the island hid the cove from view of the marina and hotel several miles away. As far as Tally knew, the two of them were here alone with nothing more than a dead body between them.

"I am so glad to see you," Tally lied cheerfully, mouth as arid as the sand behind her. She hoped to God that Arnaud wouldn't notice the rapid pulse beating at the base of her throat. "We—I thought you'd drowned. Where on earth have you been?" She kept her tone light with effort. Given more than two seconds to think about it, chasing after Arnaud had not been the brightest idea in the world.

For a mad few hours, way back in the mists of time, she'd thought Arnaud Bouchard's Nordic good looks and slight French accent the sexiest thing since sliced bread. Until she remembered that she hated white bread, sliced or otherwise. They'd slept with each other for almost the same reason: to stay in Trevor Church's orbit. Each thought a relationship between them would cement their places. In fact, Arnaud had *proposed* to her the next morning without a spark of passion or even liking in his ice blue eyes. It was only after she reminded them both that she was pretty sure Trevor didn't give a damn about her, one way or the other, that Arnaud had come to his senses.

On those rare occasions Tally actually thought about it, the memory gave her chills.

Blond hair gelled to perfection unruffled by the ocean breezes, khaki slacks neatly pressed, and an open-necked black shirt, Bouchard appeared the epitome of a *GQ* model. All that marred the perfection was the angry red stain in his tanned cheeks, and the vein throbbing in his forehead.

Arnaud grabbed her upper arm and shook her. Hard. "What the fuck are you doing here?"

She licked desert-dry lips. *Oh, God. Michael, where are you?*

"Hey. Don't get all pissed off at me. I'm the one you left for dead, remember?" She yanked her arm from his clutches. "I saw you out the window a few minutes ago. Of *course* I followed you. Geez, Arnaud, I thought you were a ghost when I saw you. I think I deserve some explanation for why the boat blew up, and also why you didn't have the courtesy to let me know you made it."

Arnaud stood between her and the rocks. How to get around him without being obvious? She *had* to mention Brian. The dead body was like the two-ton elephant in the living room everyone pretended not to see. "In the meantime, we have more pressing business. I think Brian"—*Is dead, Jim, dead*—"must've drowned. Shouldn't we go and get hel—"

Arnaud stepped between Tally and the open stretch of beach. This time when he grabbed her arm, he almost yanked her off her feet.

"Hey! Get your damn hands off me." She tried to shake him off; his grip tightened, and her heart skipped a beat.

"What are you doing here?" he demanded, ignoring the rest of her babbling.

Okay. That hadn't worked. "Damn it, Arnaud. I want some answers. How did the *Serendipity* blow up? Hell, *why* did it blow up? How did you manage to get off without me seeing you? And what about Lu? Why did you—"

"Shut the fuck up." Arnaud drew back his arm and struck her across the face.

The force of the slap sent Tally stumbling backwards. Her bare heel collided with Brian. She tripped over him and landed on her butt in the hot sand, one leg draped over the dead man's waist. *Oh, God. Oh, God.* She lifted a shaking hand to her hot cheek and scooted out of range.

Anger warred with pure, soul-numbing fear. "What is *wrong* with you?" Tally shouted. "Are you on drugs or something?"

Arnaud strode around the body and jerked her to her feet. She slapped at his hand. Gone was the suave charmer who had served as her father's right hand. In his place stood a man with chillingly dead eyes, and an agenda of death. The alarm bells in her head clanged with deafening clarity. Tally tasted the metallic tang of fear in her mouth. Adrenaline raced through her, causing every fight-or-flight signal to tangle in a scary mess inside her.

"I told her I didn't want you here. Incompetence must run in your family, for Christ sake!" He was almost dragging her across the sand. Away from the marina. Away from help.

Away from Michael.

He was heading toward the end of the small cove. As far as Tally knew, the only thing beyond this point was a rocky cliff face, and a lot of water. She dug in her heels. "I'm not going mountain climbing with you."

"I was about to drag my old chum, Bri, a little farther out so the tide could do my cleanup for me. Grab his leg and help me pull him over there."

"Are you out of your mind? Jesus, Arnaud, *listen* to yourself!"

He backhanded her.

Her eyes filled with tears of rage. She swung at him blindly, and missed. His arms were longer than hers, and she couldn't get close enough to make a connection.

"It wasn't a request. Grab his leg. Now."

Tally wedged her feet ankle deep into the soft sand. "No. In fact, *hell* no. Lift that hand to me again, and you'll regret it."

She tasted blood in her mouth, and swiped the back of her hand across her split lip. Arnaud jerked her by the arm. Tally let out an earsplitting scream for help. He hit her again.

"Michael!" she yelled at the top of her lungs. Arnaud slapped a hand across her mouth and tried to drag her.

Tally kept her feet planted. He jerked her off-balance, as she struggled and wriggled to get in a few hits of her own. *Oh, damn. She was such a girl.* Why hadn't she had brothers to teach her to fight? She lunged out again, connecting with his ribs.

He grabbed a handful of her hair and held her away from him. Tally grabbed his thick wrist with both hands and tried to break his hold. The bastard was pulling her hair out by the roots. She dug her long nails in as hard as she could.

Arnaud threw her aside like a rag doll. Without her hands to protect her fall, she dropped to her knees. Hard. She lifted her head, spitting out bloody sand.

"You're going to regret this, Arnaud. You are going to regret this big time!" It was the most ridiculous, and childish, of threats. He was far stronger and more determined than she was. He could do pretty much anything he wanted to her. Her mind raced like a gerbil on a wheel. What to do? What the hell to do?

She felt around in the sand for a rock, a stone—hell, a seashell, anything she could use as a weapon to defend herself.

"What? Gonna haunt me, Tally?"

Haunt? The blood drained from her head, then took up a frantic beat in her ears. She sat back on her heels. "You won't kill me." *Yes. He will. Of course he will.*

He stopped to look at her. "You've got more fucking lives than a goddamn cat. Hell yes, I'm going to kill you, you stupid bitch. But not here. I don't want Daddy falling over you until I'm good and ready for the big finale."

"Are you going to tell me *why?*" Tally asked calmly, heart racing. "In mystery novels, the killer always bares his soul before he kills his victim."

"You read too much."

"How about a little clue?"

"How about shutting the fuck up so I can hear myself think?"

He'd apparently done enough thinking already. "Let go. You're breaking my arm."

His fingers tightened cruelly. "In a few hours you won't be feeling any pain at all."

Keep him talking. "Come on, Arnaud. At least tell me why?"

"What the hell difference does it make?" he sneered, hauling her to her feet. "Let's see." He rubbed his chin as he pulled her toward the rocky beginning of the cliffs. "Save the girl, and lose millions. Kill the girl, and get away clean. Hmm, real hard choice. I know. Kill the girl. And for God's sake, spare me and don't start singing. For old time's sake, I'll make it quick."

"Damn nice of you." Her mind was going a mile a minute. While her brain reconciled this Arnaud with the Arnaud who'd worshiped at her father's feet, she was slowing him down by literally dragging her feet. Tally leaned more and more of her body weight away from the arm he held. Her shoulder joint screamed for mercy. Her heart pounded. His large hand held her upper arm so tightly, he was cutting off her circulation. She considered dropping and rolling. There were a few rocks on this part of the beach. But better a few bruises than dead. She waited for just the right moment.

If Arnaud managed to get her beyond this small cove, there was a pretty good chance he'd make good on his threat.

Never leave one crime scene for another. Thank you, New Detectives on the Discovery Channel. Great advice. Her heart was pounding so fast, it felt like there was a rabid animal scrabbling around in her chest. Her breath hitched. She was about to have a full-fledged panic attack.

Help . . . I need somebody . . . Help, not just any . . . booody . . . HELP! "Why would you kill Brian? Wasn't he your friend?" *And why do you want to kill me?*

"I needed Brian for a while. Our partnership didn't suit him. He failed to understand that we *both* needed to be dead to make this work. He thought he could screw with me and walk away."

This *had* to be about money. A great deal of money. "What did you do? Rob my father? Have you been skimming money from his business?"

He smiled, but it didn't come close to reaching his eyes. "That's how it started. A little here. A little there. Hell, old Trev has enough to share."

"But you got greedy."

"He's getting old. Soft. He refuses to take an early retirement."

"So you're going to kill everyone on the island? To prove *what*, for godsake? That you *can?*"

"You were supposed to be dead. I wasted a beautiful yacht for nothing, goddamn it!" He jerked up hard on her arm, making her scream with pain. Agony shot through her shoulder, and her hand went numb. She swung with her other arm in a futile effort to connect. Her swing went wild.

"You would have been dead, I would have been dead—" Arnaud continued furiously. "What the hell are you? A cat with nine lives?"

"If I saw you, someone else must have," Tally pointed out breathlessly.

"If they did, nobody will tell. Except for *you.* You piss me off, Tally, you really do."

"Gee, Arnaud, I'm not feeling particularly warm and fuzzy about you, either. Here's a plan. Why don't I stroll back to Auntie's, and keep very quiet about your miraculous resurrection, and you go your merry way?"

"Because your father and my buyers are arriving in a few

hours, and you have to be gone before they get here. I don't want you opening your big mouth and blabbing to your father about things which don't concern you. You know me. I don't like little loose ends. Everything needs to be neat and tidy."

"Fine. Let me save you the trouble." She tried to turn out of his grasp, but he held on more tightly. "Let me go, and I'm outta here. For heaven's sake, Arnaud, I can't believe anything is worth killing three people for." *Especially if I'm one of the dead people.*

"You have no idea *what* your father does, do you, you skinny little hag?" He laughed. "Taking over Church's business is worth killing a *hundred* people for. A thousand, a—"

"I get the picture," Tally said dryly. "Hag" was a little harsh, even for a killer. "Arnaud, listen to me. Do you really think my father will be pleased when he arrives to find me bloating on the beach?"

"Get a fucking clue. He thinks *I'm* dead. And he has no idea you're even here!"

"Of course, he does. He's the one who invited me."

"No, he didn't."

"Who did?" she asked with dawning horror. "You?"

"We were having a bit of a problem offing you in Chicago."

"Offing?" God. She was in the middle of a *Sopranos* episode. They were at the far end of the cove. She couldn't match him in strength. She had to outwit him. Hard to do, when her brain was a gibbering, screaming blob of fear.

"It was supposed to look like an accident. A fall in front of the train. A trip down the stairs in a dark movie theater. But you appear to have rubber bones, and the devil's own luck. Never mind. Apparently, if I want the job done right, I'm going to have to do it myself."

"I agree a hundred percent."

"You do?"

"Hell, yes." Tally twisted and, with the full strength of her body behind the blow, kneed him in the groin.

Miraculously, it was a direct hit.

With a girly scream, Arnaud fell to his knees, clutching his balls. She kicked him again. Hard. This time on the thigh. He fell to his side, howling, curled in a fetal ball, his hands between his legs.

Tally started sprinting back toward the marina. Back toward Michael and safety. She made it halfway to the other side.

Arnaud tackled her from behind. They went down in a tangle of arms and legs. He pinned her upper body with his chest, and her flailing legs with his own.

Struggling to push him off her while attempting to draw air into her lungs, Tally managed to scream at the top of her lungs. Her cries for help were cut off when Arnaud slammed his forearm across her throat. She gagged.

"Shut the fuck up, bitch."

Not having a choice, Tally complied, but she sure as hell wasn't going to lie there with him on top of her for any longer. She grabbed handfuls of sand and aimed for his eyes. That didn't deter him much.

He rolled off her and jerked her to her feet. "One more sound out of you and I'll kill you right here. And, believe me, I'll enjoy every second." He dragged her toward Brian's body. "Grab his legs and help me."

Tally stood her ground. "Go to hell."

This time, Arnaud punched her. The blow to her jaw snapped her head back, and it was only his grip on her arm that prevented her from falling backwards.

Blood flooded her mouth. "Fine. Go ahead. Then you'll have two bodies to drag wherever. But I refuse to help you. And I'm sure as hell not touching your friend. I didn't even like him when he was alive."

"The only damn thing you can do is to help me hide Brian, and die without me having to expend too much energy."

"Fuck you." Her jaw throbbed, and her lower lip felt bigger than one of Arnaud's promises. The skin on her upper arm leeched white from the pressure of his fingers, and the pain radiated all the way to her shoulder.

Arnaud jerked her after him, then flung her down to the

sand. Tally went sprawling, a hard rock under her left hip. She slid her hand beneath her body and tried to pry the rock free.

Arnaud removed a gun from the waistband of his slacks at the small of his back. Tally's gaze was drawn to the disproportionately long barrel of the nasty-looking weapon. The smooth rock beneath her refused to budge. She lifted her body a little for better leverage, and tried to get a better grip on the slippery surface.

Arnaud checked to make sure the silencer screwed correctly into the barrel, then raised the pistol and leveled it at her head.

The fist-size rock came free. Tally closed her hand around it. With blood in her eye, she rolled over, scrambled to her knees, and lunged for Arnaud's legs.

Her shoulder hit him mid-thigh. The gun went flying, discharging a harmless, almost silent, shot into the air.

Until this trip, she'd never been in a fight. Never feared for her life. Desperate to survive, Tally started throwing punches. She didn't give a damn about finesse, or even accuracy. As long as some part of her made contact with some part of him, and made it *first,* she considered herself fortunate.

Fist. Rock. Fist. Rock. Bite whatever came close enough. The son of a bitch wanted to kill her. She refused to die without a fight.

Arnaud slugged her hard and fast. He and Tally were matched in height, but not in body weight. His punches hurt like fire. Blood trickled down her chin. Sweat ran into her eyes. Every time she hit *him,* it hurt *her.*

She managed to sink her teeth into his shoulder, biting down as hard as she could. He bellowed with rage, and tried to throw her off. While he was concentrating on her terrier hold on his shoulder she brought her knee up and slammed it into his groin again for good measure. It seemed as though her jaw were locked as they went down, Tally on top this time.

Not releasing her bite on the meaty part of his shoulder,

feeling his blood slowly fill her mouth, Tally punched, kicked, and struggled against his hold.

He brought both hands up to her throat and squeezed.

The bright sunny day faded almost to black, and she unclamped her jaw to drag in more air. He shook her like a rat and rolled on top of her. "I take it back. It's not going to be quick."

He squeezed her throat with a slow, consistent pressure. Tally's eyes rolled back in her head. Unconsciousness lapped. Gagging and fighting to stay alert, she realized that if Arnaud thought he'd subdued her, he'd probably release her. Tally closed her eyes and went limp. It was hard to do. Her body was struggling for a small sip of air, and she was almost out. But she managed to lay flaccid and unresponsive between his hands.

Gradually his fingers eased their grip. Tally fell back on the sand, remaining limp. Arnaud's hands loosened around her throat.

"Jesus. If there's a way for you to fuck with my life, you'll find it, won't you? Stay unconscious until I get b—"

With a last burst of energy she brought her arms up between Arnaud's, and surprised him enough to shove her palm up, and under his nose. She had the satisfaction of hearing a distinct crunch as she broke his nose. Blood spattered her arms. She shoved his arms aside as he made a grab for his face.

"You bitch!" He slammed his arm across her already bruised throat. Tally bucked, kicked, and punched as they rolled across the beach in a macabre deadlock.

Suddenly there was someone else on top of them. The hope that it was Michael was snuffed as Tally realized the "trois" in their "ménage" was Leli'a.

"You two-timing son of a bitch!" Leli'a straddled Arnaud's chest. Tally rolled aside as the Tahitian girl pummeled her lover.

Saved by the belle, Tally thought wryly, staggering to her feet. Arnaud covered his head as his girlfriend yelled obscenities, and tried to explain that far from having wild monkey sex with Tally, he was attempting to kill her. Apparently honey-lips wasn't going for it.

Tally didn't waste time eavesdropping. She ran. And ran like hell.

Michael.

Michael.

Michael.

Up and over the rough *a'a* rocks as if jet-propelled, Tally scaled the mountain between herself and safety, feeling no pain.

She clambered to the top, and glanced back. The couple continued rolling around, spraying sand and obscenities.

Tally almost tumbled down the other side, ignoring the scrapes and cuts from the rocks on her already battered body.

Michael.

Michael.

Michael.

She hit soft sand, and paused a second to drag in a ragged, gasping draft of air. She could do this. It wasn't *that* far. The beach stretched out before her. White and pristine. Paradise.

A million miles before she was safe.

Tally shuddered, wishing she were telepathic. If she were, Michael would know she was butt-deep in alligators, and would come charging down that unspoiled stretch of sand, waving an Uzi in one hand and a . . . some other dangerous weapon in the other.

She wanted the Terminator on her side, damn it.

Unfortunately, Michael was probably stretched out in the sun, taking a nap.

Chapter Sixteen

Michael loaded supplies onto the *Nemesis,* and kept an eye on the beach where Tally had gone for a morning run. Damn, he couldn't believe she had that much energy left after their sexual marathon. The woman was one surprise after another.

This time when he glanced at the spot where she'd disappeared an hour and a half ago, he saw her racing back toward the marina.

He straightened, angling his head for a better look. She was running, all right. But with a distinct limp.

Hell. Now what?

Resigned, he grabbed a clean rag and mopped the sweat from his face before jumping down onto the dock and striding toward the beach path. Old instincts snapped to life. The hairs on the back of his neck stood straight up. In his SEAL days, he'd learned to trust that feeling, and he didn't stop to question it now.

The closer he got, the faster he moved until he was flat-out running.

She looked like hell. This was more than a fall, more than a simple accident. Her face was battered, blood ran freely down her chin, pooling at the base of her throat. Rage fueled him, and at a dead run now, Michael reached her halfway down the beach.

Someone had beaten the shit out of her. She wasn't looking where she was going, and almost ran into him. He had to grab her upper arms to keep her upright. "Tally?"

She looked up, blue eyes dazed with shock. "Mi—" Her eyes rolled back in her head, and she slumped into his arms.

"Ah, Jesus, honey." Scooping up her limp body, he scanned the beach behind her. No one there. The incoming tide had already obliterated her footprints in the sand.

What the hell was going on?

Goddamn it, he didn't have *time* for this. Much as he wanted—hell, needed—to backtrack her steps, guns blazing, there wasn't a damn thing he could do without leaving Tally lying unprotected on the beach.

If she'd shouted for help, he hadn't heard her over the racket he'd made loading boxes and water tanks onboard. Shit.

He scanned the area again. No sign of anyone. He turned and loped toward the marina, Tally in his arms. Whoever was doing their best to kill his wo—to kill Tally—was going to have to go through him to get to her. And considering that his life might not be worth shit in a few hours, that wasn't an encouraging thought.

What to do with her? He glanced up at the hotel. Auntie? No. He didn't know who the hell to trust except himself. No one was around. They'd gone inside in the heat of the day. He hitched her limp form higher in his arms and jogged to the *Nemesis*.

It wasn't easy getting aboard with her, but he was damned if he'd let her go, even for a few minutes. He glanced at her face as he cast off one-handed. Still out. Shock? Serious injury?

Fear pounded in his chest to the rhythm of his heartbeat. "Get inside," he told Lucky, curled asleep on deck. The cat rose and stretched, then darted between Michael's legs into the wheelhouse. "Nice to have someone who listens to me," Michael muttered as he strode into the wheelhouse and started the engine, Tally still in his arms.

He negotiated the jetties and the channel at dangerously high speeds. He needed to check how badly she was hurt, but couldn't tied to the marina where anyone could board before he could protect her.

She moaned in his arms.

"Hang on. Almost there."

" 'K." It was clear she had no idea what he'd just said, but she laid her head back on his chest and scrunched her eyes closed. Obviously in pain.

Michael blocked out the sight and the sound of her distress. There wasn't a damn thing he could do to help her until they were out on the open sea, where he'd have a shot if anyone approached in another vessel.

He skimmed the northern point and motored a couple of miles behind the island, where no one was likely to spot them unless they were mountain climbing. Once there, he dropped anchor and set a few of his brother-in-law's toys to alert him of an approaching enemy. The ship secure, he took Tally below to his cabin.

He laid her carefully on the bed, then sat beside her and reached for her tank top. "Now, let's have a look at you."

She was sweating. Sweating more than the high room temperature warranted. He could see the frantic pounding of her pulse at the base of her throat, and she was struggling to drag air into her lungs.

Michael recognized the symptoms immediately: panic attack, coupled with shock. He tried to help her sit up. Almost as though he were holding her down instead of helping her, she struggled to get free. Tally swiped her arm across his body, and tried to jettison herself off the bed. She tried to talk, but she was breathless, incoherent. She gave him a beseeching look, her eyes panicked with the attack.

"Easy, honey. Easy. Here." He braced her narrow back with one arm and held his splayed hand over her midriff. "Inhale from the pit of your stomach. Slow and easy. That's a girl. There you go. Slow. And. Easy. Just. Like. That." He breathed with her, deliberately setting a regular rhythm until her breathing slowed to near normal.

He brought his hand up and massaged the tense muscles in her neck. Jesus, she felt fragile. She had such a mouth on her, he sometimes forgot that she was just a little bit of a thing. A strong wind could blow her over. And from the look of her, something a hell of a lot stronger than wind had had a go at her.

When he found the fucker responsible for hurting her, there wouldn't be a spot in hell hot enough for him.

Eventually her breathing evened out, and he helped her lie flat again. "How you doing?" Her breathing was still a little ragged around the edges, but she had it under control.

"Okay, thanks."

"Let's see what we're dealing with here," Michael told her, suddenly aware her hand was clenched around something. "Open your hand, you're bleeding—what the hell?"

Her fingers were stiff and cramped around the object. Michael helped her peel her fingers away.

They both looked at it. Tally glanced up with a puzzled frown. "I thought it was a rock. What is it?"

Michael took the smooth, flat object from her hand. The black box had a small LCD touch pad, and was about the size and shape of a TV remote control. "Where did you get this, Tally?"

They both looked at it. She glanced at him with a puzzled frown. "I picked it up on the beach. Why? What is it?"

"It's a remote control." It belonged with the pulse generator that Church was planning to sell. God, this was sweet.

"Oh." Tally lost interest and closed her eyes.

Michael set the box on the bedside table.

First things first.

He pulled the blood-spattered tank top over her head. She wore no bra, and her pale pink nipples peaked in the wash of air. He made quick work of stripping her naked.

He glanced up to find her watching him, her eyes large and very blue in her battered face. Sick to his stomach at the violence done to her, Michael needed to get the hell out of here and pound someone's face into the dirt. Then he wanted to stomp what was left of the sonofabitch to dust.

"Jesus."

She was a mass of bloody scratches and contusions.

"Bad, huh?" She ran her tongue gingerly across her swollen upper lip. "You should see the other guy."

"I intend to," he said grimly. "Who'm I looking for?" He rose and covered her with a blanket.

"Arnaud killed Brian."

Michael turned. "He's alive."

"Unfortunately. I found Brian on the beach. Not that I was looking for him. I'd seen Arnaud from my window and had run down to the beach to try to talk to him." She gingerly touched the cut on her mouth. "He wanted me to help him move the body. As if I would. He must be a few bricks short of a load." The bravado huffed out of her. She looked very young and afraid. "Michael, all the accidents I had in Chicago . . . they weren't accidents. Neither was the explosion of the *Serendipity.* He wants me dead. Me *and* my father."

Fuckwad, Michael though grimly, *and I want him dead. Him and your father.* "Bastard," he said. Bouchard was ten pounds of shit in a five-pound bag, and Michael wanted at him so bad, his molars ached. His insides twisted with the necessity to go back to shore and finish the dirtbag off. But Tally's needs were top priority right now.

Unable to sit still, Michael walked into the galley for supplies. He ran warm water in a bowl and came back. He set the water and supplies on the bedside table, then drew the blanket out of the way.

He started carefully washing the blood off her face. "What's his story?"

Tally winced as he dabbed at the drying blood on her lip. "He's been stealing from my father. He wants to take over my father's boat brokerage business, and Trevor isn't ready to retire yet. God, I don't know." She looked up at him, her eyes haunted. "He tried to kill me, Michael." She shuddered and squeezed her eyes shut, then opened them again, the fear still in her gaze. "He tried to *kill* me. He wants me *dead.* What have I done to warrant that kind of hatred? I don't understand any of this."

"He didn't say anything else?"

"Lots of really complimentary stuff." Her sarcasm made

him feel better. She might look like hell, but she was still Tally. "But he never did get around to saying exactly why he was so bent on killing me."

"Christ. You must have a hell of a life insurance policy."

"Not that great, and I can promise you, Bouchard's name is nowhere on it."

"Who, then? Your father?"

"My two goddaughters. If I were to die, everything I own goes to my best friend, Marty's, two girls."

Michael bet whatever Bouchard was up to had everything to do with Trevor Church. The man had a knack for bringing out a person's homicidal tendencies.

"Sorry. This is going to hurt." He dabbed the wet cloth on the cut on Tally's forehead. She remained stoic beneath his hand, but he could tell by the way the skin beneath her eyes flinched it hurt like hell. His jaw hurt from grinding his teeth, but he kept his hands businesslike and gentle.

The bastard had really done a number on her. Michael was more concerned with the look in her eyes and her bewilderment than with the numerous scrapes and scratches on her otherwise creamy skin. She had a fat lip, but the bleeding had stopped. She bore faint finger marks on her throat—Bouchard would pay for those—and had a knob rising on her forehead.

"Get these panic attacks often?" he asked, running his hand through her dark, silky curls to massage her scalp. She leaned into him, trying valiantly to regulate her breathing.

"I used to get them a lot as a kid." She dropped her head to give him better access to her neck, her breath still a little huffy. "Not so much anymore. They're terrifying. I hate having them."

"Why don't you take something for them?"

"I thought I'd grown out of them. Damn, I'd *hoped* I'd grown out of them."

"I'd say circumstances lately have helped bring 'em back with a vengeance."

"No kidding! God, I should write my memoirs when I get

home." She rotated her neck, and he continued stroking until he felt her muscles ease a little.

"You want to know what it feels like?" Tally asked, rubbing her clammy forehead against his chest like a cat. "It's as if you were dead asleep, and woke up in the middle of the night to find the monster under your bed standing right *there.* Looking at you. About to eat you whole." She shuddered. "You *know* monsters don't exist, but your body does that whole fight-or-flight thing."

Monsters existed, all right. You just had to know where to look. "Floods your system with adrenaline," Michael murmured. He surreptitiously glanced at his watch. It felt as though a full day had passed, but it was barely eleven in the morning. Sunlight from the porthole filtered through the blinds, striping the bed and Tally's smooth, olive skin.

Smooth skin that was bleeding, abraded, and bruised. His jaw ached with suppressed anger. "How you doing now?"

"Okay. Thanks."

He tossed the rag in the bowl of water. "I think it would be quicker, and more efficient, if you took a shower. Half the beach is glued in the blood on some of these cuts and scrapes. Stand under the spray for a while, soak everything clean. Then I can see to doctoring up the damage."

"Good idea." Tally struggled to sit up.

"Want me to come help you?" Michael asked, helping her swing her legs over the side of the bed.

"Yes." Her lopsided smile was like a punch in the gut. "But there isn't room for both of us in there. I'll be okay. Ow. Ow. Ow!" She limped over, and opened the narrow door into the head. Even her small, heart-shaped ass had a bruise and several scrapes on it.

He clenched his teeth. "Use plenty of soap."

She gave him a weak salute before shutting the door. A few seconds later he heard the shower turn on.

Michael looked at his watch. Christ, the timing couldn't be worse. Church would be arriving soon.

What the hell was he going to do with Tally? He grabbed up the control detonator and took it topside.

The original plan didn't seem nearly as appealing as it had several days ago. She'd already been beaten to a pulp physically. Was he really so far gone he'd use her to make what he'd planned for her father that much sweeter?

Shit. He rubbed the back of his neck and looked around, trying to decide where to secure the control. Man. He was tempted to throw the sucker far and deep. But one never knew when something like this might come in handy.

He opened the hidden compartment where he'd secreted the satchel and set the small box far in the back. No one would find it there.

She was humming in the shower. Not a happy tune. An off-key, rather pathetic little dirge that, inexplicably, made him want to laugh. He shook his head.

She hadn't been part of his original plan. It would be simple to exclude her from the updated version. He didn't need her. He didn't *have* to use her. Fuck. He didn't *want* to use her. Simple as that. It would make him no better than the piss-faced bastard who'd tried to kill her.

Michael took what he needed from the first-aid kit and laid the supplies on the table with a surgeon's precision. Next, he needed ice. And plenty of it.

A towel wrapped around her, Tally emerged from the shower ten minutes later, damp and dewy. Her nose was pink, her eyes a little more puffy than before. The adrenaline still pumped through her system.

He scanned her pinched features as he handed her a can of cola. "Take a shot of sugar and caffeine."

"Thanks." Her fingers trembled slightly as she took the can. She might be scared out of her gourd, she might've bawled in the privacy of the shower, but she wasn't going to fall apart like a wet Kleenex.

She chugged half the can, then rested the cold metal against her swollen lip. "I didn't notice before—you're all dressed up."

"Jeans are dressed up?"

"On you, yeah. What's the occasion?"

"Only thing clean in my wardrobe." The long pants and untucked Hawaiian shirt would soon cover an arsenal of weapons. Now that T-Day had arrived, he'd be loaded for bear. "Come back here and lie down."

She put the can down on the table. "You know what I'd really like before I do?"

"What?"

"I'd like you to hold me. Tight."

"Honey, I'm scared I'll hurt you."

She slid her arms about his waist and pressed her face against his chest. "You won't hurt me. And I don't care. I just need to know I'm alive." She used one hand to unbutton his shirt, then rested her hot cheek against his bare skin. Michael felt the dampness of her tears, and wanted to howl.

Very carefully he wrapped both arms around Tally's slender body and pulled her as close as he dared.

She lifted her face, and he placed his mouth on hers. Gently, softly.

Tally stood on her toes for better access. He slid his tongue inside the warm cavern of her mouth, and resisted pulling her up hard against his body as he felt her moan vibrate from her lips to his.

The towel, wrapped around her, slipped to the floor. Instead of touching her bare body, Michael cupped her face in both hands. Her skin was baby smooth, warm to the touch, and damp from her tears. He ran his thumbs across her cheekbones and gently swirled his tongue around hers. Tally pressed closer, returning the kiss with more urgency. He tried to slow it down. She'd taken a real licking, and he was afraid he'd hurt her more than she was already.

She slid her hands up his back, giving him goose bumps as she rubbed her palms erotically up and down under his shirt. Her mouth slid from his, and she peppered his chin with kisses. "Make love to me, Michael."

"Tally—"

"Please?" She stepped away from him. Gloriously, un-self-consciously naked, Tally took his hand and led him back to the bed. "I want your hands on me. I want to feel the way you make me feel. I want to wipe away the fear."

"Making love isn't going to make that go away."

"It will for a little while."

Michael allowed her to draw him onto the bed. Tally wiggled down to lie flat, and he braced a knee next to her on the mattress. "Don't let me hurt you."

"You won't. Come to me." She held up her arms, and he lay down beside her, wrapping her in his strong embrace.

Her heart swelled with emotion strong enough to bring tears to her eyes. She pressed her face to the center of his chest, breathing in the musky, familiar smell of him, feeling the steady beat of his heart against her cheek.

Oh, God. I really do love him!

She snuck a small taste with a snake-like dart of her tongue. His skin was salty. She experimented with a longer lick. Deliciously salty.

Moisture pooled between her legs. She lifted her face and searched for his mouth, kissing him with growing desperation. She wanted to consume him. She wanted him to consume her. Their tongues twirled and stroked, imitating the mating dance, until Tally had to take a break for air. She sucked oxygen into her lungs, her face buried against his neck, and blindly reached for his belt buckle.

Which happened to be undone, thank you very much, saving her a step. She skimmed her palm down his washboard abs, down inside the front of his jeans. From smooth, taut skin to crisp hair. He sucked in a ragged breath as her fingers slid under his BVDs to close around his pulsing shaft.

"It's mind-boggling that something this size can fit inside me so perfectly," Tally told him, her eyes gleaming avariciously. That look made him pulse and twitch in her hand.

He wanted a glib comeback: "One size fits all." His heart

refused to lie. They were perfect in bed, and if he lived through one more day, he'd miss her for the rest of his life.

Tally wiggled down to lie next to him, arm draped across his chest as she started kissing him. Anyplace she could reach was fair game. She licked and nibbled on his earlobe, loving the way his body shuddered. She nipped and tasted the muscular curve of his shoulder and the smooth skin between shoulder and neck.

And all the while the lady had her small hand neatly tucked down his pants. Michael just about came up off the bed as her fingers slid over the head of his penis and, finding moisture there, used it to lubricate her hand's slide and glide. She saw a muscle twitch in his jaw as he gritted his teeth. She met his gaze and gave him a slow, wicked smile, increasing the pressure until his eyes almost crossed.

"I figure," Tally told him with a saucy smile, "as long as I'm holding on to your dipstick, I am the boss of *you*."

Michael chuckled as he skimmed his jeans down his legs, kicked them to the floor, and then turned back to Tally. She was more than ready for him. Slick and wet, and close to finishing without him. "Hurry!"

He handed her a rubber. With trembling fingers, Tally glided the lubricated sheath over the head of his penis, then unrolled it down the curved length.

He wasted no time. As soon as the job was done, he slid over her and, with one hand, guided himself, with excruciating slowness, deep inside her, before he supported his weight on his arms.

Tally tilted her hips, then sucked in a breath. For a few seconds, neither of them moved. The sensation of Michael filling her, stretching her, was so sweet, the feeling so sharp, she couldn't bear to move.

"Okay?" he asked.

In answer, she drew up her knees and felt the glide of him deep inside until he almost touched her cervix. Tally muffled a scream of pleasure against his shoulder.

He stroked slowly, once, twice. Her body clenched, and

she dug her nails into his back as every particle of her body coiled tight as a spring. Tighter. Higher. *Impossibly* higher.

She wrapped her ankles around his hips, and felt the bunch and clench of his butt under her heels as he pistoned his hips and nailed her to the mattress.

Her release was stunning in its intensity; Michael covered her mouth with his and swallowed her scream.

In the next instant, his body stiffened, every muscle rigid. He wrenched his mouth away from hers and, head back, grit his teeth. Tally held tightly on to his bucking body with her arms and legs as he came.

She slept against his side, their slick bodies glued together. Michael resisted cupping the gentle swell of her breast, pressed against him, and looked at his watch instead.

Twelve-thirty.

He couldn't lie here all day. He had things to do and places more important to be. And he knew Tally could have no part in any of it.

It was too damn late to ship her off to one of the neighboring islands. He ran through who was left on the island. Anyone he might trust with her safety.

Auntie and Henri.

Maybe.

Dare he risk her safety, perhaps her life, on a "maybe"?

Hell, no.

He stroked her hair off her face, and she woke up immediately and gave him a soft smile. "Is it morning?"

"It's lunchtime, same day. We need to be heading back in."

Her eyes clouded, and she gave him a worried look. "I've got to tell you, I don't feel really great about confronting Arnaud again. He wasn't kidding around. If it hadn't been for Leli'a thinking we were having sex on the beach, I'd be a floater like poor Lu. And Brian."

"If I showed you how, do you think you could handle the *Nemesis*?" The idea was preposterous. Fatu Hiva was several hundred miles away across open water.

"Handle it to do what?"

"I think you should go to one of the other islands until you can get a flight out."

"As much as I'd love to take you up on the offer, there're two things preventing it. One, I haven't a clue how to steer a boat. Two, I'm here to see my father." She rose and went to dig through his clothes for something to wear.

She found a pair of black shorts and a black T-shirt. Held up a clean pair of BVDs and, when he nodded, pulled them on.

Seeing Tally in nothing but his underwear made Michael hard all over again. She pulled the black shorts up her legs, covering the sight, then yanked the T-shirt over her head.

"I didn't come all this way to not see him. Whether my father expects me or not, I'm here now. I think—God, I *hope*—Trevor will be happy to see me. I have to find out."

"Will you at least agree to stay aboard the *Nemesis* while I search out Bouchard?"

"Gladly."

Michael still weighed the risk of trusting Henri to get her away safely. Goddamn it. He shouldn't have been such a stubborn, self-serving prick. He should've gotten rid of Tally from the start.

He stretched above her head and opened a narrow door in the teak paneling she hadn't noticed before, and removed an object. "Know how to use this?"

Tally stared at the big black gun, making no effort to take it. The weapon looked far too at home in Michael's big hand. She glanced from the gun to Michael and back again. "Not only do I not know how to use a gun, I *wouldn't*. I hate those things."

"Let's go topside. I want to show you how to use it. If Bouchard comes anywhere near you, point and shoot."

"Better show me how to pull the trigger with my eyes closed," Tally said with a grimace. "I don't think I can actually shoot anyone. Okay, maybe Arnaud. Unfortu—"

With a warning look, Michael clamped a hand across her mouth. She stared up at him wide-eyed, heart in her throat, as the lights flickered, then dimmed, then flickered again.

He brought a finger to his mouth for silence, then jabbed it toward the deck above their heads. "Someone's coming," he said on a mere breath. The lights flickered faster.

Tally listened. She couldn't hear a thing.

She'd never seen him move so fast. In seconds he had another gun in his hand, as well as other assorted weapons. She stared at him.

Who was this man?

Not the lazy sail bum she'd thought.

This Michael was cold-eyed and efficient as he checked his weapons. His eye narrowed, his jaw tightened. Tally decided if she were a bad guy she'd be running for the hills about now. He didn't so much as glance at her as he swiftly opened the same hidden locker, and removed a knife in its sheath, and strapped it to his ankle beneath his jeans.

He tucked another gun into the back of his waistband, under his loose shirt, and motioned with the one in his hand for her to go back into the bedroom. "Lock the door," he mouthed.

Tally darted into the stateroom, watching his stealthy progress across the galley for a second or two before she softly closed the door. And locked it.

Chapter Seventeen

Michael stood in the wheelhouse of the *Nemesis*. The sleek Italian lines of the hundred-foot Mangusta motor yacht looked familiar as she cut through the water on a fast approach starboard. Michael didn't need to see the name on the prow. They'd been refitting the *Beautiful Dreamer* the day he'd arrived on Paradise. She now sported a discreet gun deck, and four high-powered speedboats hanging from the lifeboat stations.

Because of his brother-in-law's electronic genius, the *Nemesis was* capable of outracing the twin-engine, 1,450 HP diesel engine of the motor yacht. *Just*. But *Beautiful Dreamer* was too close to make a clean getaway. And those gun turrets were a hefty deterrent.

Shit.

There was only one reason the other vessel wasn't opening fire.

The pulse generator detonator.

Arnaud would have searched for the device on the beach. Not finding it, he would have realized Tally had picked it up. And since Michael had Tally onboard with him, the bad guys wouldn't blow up the *Nemesis.* At least not until they had the detonator in hand. As long as he and Tally knew the location of the control device, they had a chance of staying alive.

Unknowingly, Tally had saved their asses.

Michael opened the door from the wheelhouse. Arms crossed, he waited for their arrival with forced casualness.

The *Beautiful Dreamer* was a sight to behold as she approached, her white paint gleaming in the sun. Michael had visited a friend on his Mangusta years ago, and now he tried to visualize the interior floor plan and deck configuration as he waited.

Two men efficiently sent over grappling hooks, pulling the two boats snugly side by side. The deck of the *Beautiful Dreamer* loomed several feet above the deck of the *Nemesis*.

A familiar, and welcome, feeling of calm anticipation filled Michael. The same sensation he'd always had when inserted on a mission and the shit was about to hit the fan. Damn, he'd missed it. He hefted the CAR-15 comfortably in his hand. Not making an aggressive show, but not bothering to hide it, either.

Michael recognized the seven men on deck. All local island guys. Honor among thieves. They were heavily armed with MP5s, and stood like cats at a rat hole waiting for him to make a move. They'd have a long wait. He'd played in ball games much rougher than this.

"What's up, guys?"

"Mr. Bouchard wants to talk to you," Palaki said, not meeting his eye.

And Michael wanted to talk to him. With his fists. "Yeah?" he said casually. "Well, here I am. He can talk to me anytime."

He kept his back to the wall of the wheelhouse. The odds were the shits, but he'd been in worse situations and lived to tell the tale. The only difference was that *this* time he had a distinct blind side. He angled his head for the best visibility.

He could get off several rounds, and kill a few of them, but by then he'd be a sieve. They wouldn't kill him until they had the info they wanted, but they didn't have to give him a great quality of life until then, either. Under normal circumstances he'd take his chances. But right now there was too much at stake.

Because once they got through with him . . . there was nothing to keep them from going after Tally.

"Where is he?" Michael asked, not lowering his weapon.

Feilo, who also refused to meet his eye, gestured to the other boat. A slithery chill went through him. He'd rather face a dozen blazing guns than cross the few feet separating the two vessels.

"Fine. Tell him I'll put the coffee on, he's welcome anytime."

Palaki waved his weapon. "He say you come. Now."

A quick glance up showed the muzzles of half a dozen weapons pointed at his head.

Stalemate.

Michael considered his options. At least if he went aboard the other boat he'd be able to keep Bouchard in his sights. And away from Tally. He strode across the deck.

Feilo and another man dropped a lightweight ladder, climbed down, then stepped across, clambering over the railing of the *Nemesis.* Michael obligingly handed them his CAR. And raised his arms when told. They searched his body for more weapons, and while they'd stripped him of the gun in the small of his back, they didn't go down far enough to discover the knife sheathed on his left ankle.

"Where's Tally?" Feilo asked.

Michael shrugged, one leg over the teak rail. Jesus, the few feet separating the vessels looked a million miles wide, and the lapping water in the valley between the hulls beckoned. "How the hell am I supposed to know?"

Michael blocked spatial distance and took the leap to the rung ladder. It clattered against the Fiberglas hull of the *Beautiful Dreamer*. Michael hung there, over the hypnotic lure of the water a dozen feet below. He hauled himself up the cold metal rungs, then tossed a leg over the railing and landed on the deck of the other vessel, bathed in an icy sweat, but on two feet. *Hoo-yah.*

He didn't see the guy on his left, who delivered the hard blow to his head. By then, it was too late.

. . .

Tally strained to hear what was going on up on deck. She couldn't hear a damned thing. Where was Michael?

She held the large black gun in her hand. He hadn't had time to show her how to use it. Although the operation seemed basic—point and pull the trigger—Tally was pretty sure there must be more to it than that. On the other hand, if it were much more complicated, every redneck in the United States wouldn't have a gun rack on his truck.

Without moving her hand, she tried to see if the gun had a safety catch on it. It didn't appear to, but then, damn it, she had no idea *what* a safety catch *looked* like. Even if she figured it out, she wouldn't know if Michael had it ready to shoot, or if she'd have to . . . Tally groaned. If nothing else, the thing looked big and scary.

The *Nemesis* rocked, and she froze, staring at the locked door. She cocked her head as she heard the soft susurrus of voices.

Her heart sped up. *Arnaud.* It had to be Arnaud who'd come aboard. The bastard.

Thank God Michael had taken a gun with him. Arnaud was a bully, but she bet he would back off considerably if faced with another man carrying a weapon.

A few seconds later she heard several sets of footsteps on the deck overhead, then those same heavy treads running down the stairs. Heart in her throat, Tally stood, lifting the gun in both hands and pointing directly at the door. It would probably look more effective if she could stop shaking. On the other hand, what man wanted to take a chance with a clearly nervous woman aiming a loaded weapon at him?

The footsteps crossed the salon. The handle on the cabin door rattled. "Tally? Are you in there?" The handle jiggled.

She didn't recognize the man's voice. An islander by the sound of him, and someone who knew her.

Friend or foe?

The handle rattled again.

One man said to the other in Tahitian, "She's in there."

Silence.

The gun wavered in her hands. Who knew a gun was so heavy? Tally raised it a couple of inches, and braced the back of her legs against the built-in bed behind her.

A loud crash indicated they'd hit the teak door with something heavy.

Tally stared at the huge crack they'd made in the door.

"Kick it again," came the order in Tahitian. "Hurry."

"Michael?" Tally yelled. Just in case he was with them out there. She didn't want to shoot him by mistake.

"He's not here," the man said in English. "Come out. Mr. Bouchard wants you."

Mr. Bouchard's *had* me, Tally thought furiously. "I like it just fine right here. Tell him to go to hell."

Another kick to the door. The crack lengthened.

Tally checked to make sure the gun was still pointed more or less level. She closed her eyes reflexively as she pulled the trigger, then screamed with surprise at the loud retort, and the impact of the recoil. She fell onto her butt on the mattress behind her with a thump, and the automatic fired several more shots, up the door and then into the ceiling.

Annie Oakley she was not. Her ears rang, her hands were numb, and her heart was doing triple-axels. She opened her eyes in time to see two guys breaking through what was left of the door. Her satisfaction at seeing one of them clutching his bleeding arm was short-lived as they charged her. They didn't have far to go.

Two-fisted, she raised the gun.

Michael was gone.

Arnaud would kill her if he got his hands on her again.

Tally pulled the trigger.

She heard a loud thud as one man hit the floor.

Oh. My God. She'd shot someone. She couldn't think about it.

Run like hell.

Where?

No idea.

Bleeding copiously from his arm, the first guy she'd shot jerked her off her feet before she could get by him. He plucked the gun from her numb fingers, then frog-marched her over the remains of the door, through the salon, and up the stairs. Lucky howled as they passed, then hissed and cried, and ran in circles around the guy's feet.

The man lifted his foot.

"Kick that cat," Tally told him, "and I'll rip your heart out through your nose!"

He pushed her up the stairs ahead of him, then slammed the door on the yowling cat.

Through the windows of the wheelhouse Tally saw a huge white boat looming above the decks of the *Nemesis.*

"Where's Michael?" she demanded, squinting as she was shoved outside into the brilliant sunshine.

"He and Mr. Bouchard are waiting for you."

That's what Tally was afraid of. "And?" she asked.

"Mr. Bouchard invited you to come aboard."

"And I'm politely declining. Go and tell him so."

"Tally, there you are," a nasal voice shouted.

She turned to the source, then glanced up. Arnaud looked down at her from several feet above the deck from where she stood. His hair and clothing were immaculate as always, but his nose was swollen to three times its normal size, and had already turned black and blue.

That made her feel better. She smiled sweetly. "Aw. Did I break your poor nose?"

"Bring her up," Arnaud instructed the bleeding flunky beside her. His blond head disappeared from view.

Tally estimated the distance she'd have to run to get away from this guy. Too far. The distance to the island? Too far. The chances of getting shot in the back while she did something that stupid? Good to excellent. "How am I supposed to get over there?"

He indicated the ladder. It looked spindly, and way too flimsy.

"I don't think it'll hold me," she said.

"Go."

She went.

As soon as Tally's head cleared the railing on the other boat, she saw not only Arnaud but Leli'a as well. *Oh, joy.*

"Thank you for joining us," Arnaud said civilly, as though he hadn't attempted to murder her a couple of hours ago. He and Leli'a sat at an umbrella-shaded table on deck having, of all things, lunch.

Michael lay on the floor nearby. He wasn't moving, and she couldn't see his face. Was he alive?

Her heart hitched. She forced herself to look away. Behind her, the man who'd accompanied her lifted the ladder to the deck.

She strolled over to the table and pulled out a chair. "Now why doesn't it surprise me you two are in bed together?"

Arnaud nodded to a hovering servant, and the man poured Tally a glass of juice. She ignored it.

"Where is the detonator?" Arnaud demanded.

Tally gave him a wide-eyed look. "What detonator?"

"The small silver 'box' you picked up on the beach."

"Ahh. That was a *detonator?* I put it somewhere safe. I didn't know what it was. I guessed it was valuable. But a detonator? Wow. What does it detonate?"

"Kill her and get this over with. When her boyfriend comes to, he'll tell us," Leli'a said coldly.

"My *boyfriend* won't tell you a damn thing," Tally told them coldly. *Wake up, Michael!*

"Did your lover tell you why *he's* here?" Arnaud asked.

"Because your goons knocked him over the head?" Tally asked sweetly. "What's the matter? Afraid to face him man to man?"

"Don't pussyfoot around, Arnaud," Leli'a said with distinct glee. "Tell her."

"Tell me what?"

"That Lieutenant Wright has been to Paradise before."

Lieutenant? Michael was a cop? Since when? And no, he

hadn't mentioned he'd been here before. In fact, he'd said otherwise. Tally remained silent.

"He and his Navy SEAL partner came here last year to destroy your father. Are you aware of that?"

Tally's mouth got drier. "No, but what has that got to do with anything?" *Michael was a Navy SEAL?* Little bits and pieces clicked into place like dominoes. *Oh. My. God.*

"I would imagine your lieutenant has returned to the scene of the crime, as it were. I do believe he's come back to kill Trevor."

Tally laughed. It wasn't exactly filled with wild mirth, but the idea was pretty damn far-fetched. "Michael is a sail bum. He would've told me if he'd been here before." *Not,* a little voice said, *if he planned to kill your father.*

"He used you," Leli'a said smugly, dark eyes flashing in triumph. "He fucked your brains out because he wanted to use you. Haven't you looked in the mirror lately? You're a skinny, flat-chested . . . *nothing*. Did you really believe for one second a virile man like *that* would spare a glance for someone who looks like *you?*" The girl laughed. "Give me a bloody break."

Tally's hand curled in her lap. How odd, her heart literally hurt. Ached. Silly, really. Of course she knew what she looked like. But she'd *forgotten* when she was with Michael.

He'd made her forget she was flat-chested, and plain.

She'd forgotten, because when he'd looked at her with hunger in his eye, she'd *felt* beautiful.

But she'd be damned if she'd give this little bitch the satisfaction of knowing her barb had hit home. "Gee, Leli'a, sounds like you're jealous to me." Tally flicked a glance at Arnaud. "What's wrong, Arnaud? Not enough for her, either?"

He flushed under his tan. The stem of his wineglass snapped between his fingers.

"For heaven's sake." Leli'a waved for a servant to remove the glass from Arnaud. She gave Tally a withering look. "Don't sit there all pale-faced and wounded. You're a big girl.

I'm sure the sex was more than delicious. Consider yourself fortunate he fucked you, *whatever* the reason. Girls like you don't get the opportunity that often, I'm sure."

Leli'a crossed her legs and lit a cigarette. She inhaled, then blew the smoke at Tally. The breeze wafted the smoke over Leli'a's hair, and she fanned it away impatiently.

Tally gave her a cat-got-the-cream smile. "Eat your heart out, you silly little girl. The sex was delicious. Unfortunately for you, you'll never know firsthand. Arnaud is—what—twenty-five years older than you? Old enough to be your father, in fact. Skinny, flat-chested, pitiful me has had them both, and news flash: I got steak, and you got the toy in a Happy Meal. Guess big boobs and miles of hair don't count for as much as you thought they did, huh?"

Leli'a started out of her chair. Arnaud put a hand on her arm. She subsided, glowering like the teenager she was. "Now that we've got that out of the way, where is Arnaud's detonation device?"

Tally, still trying to assimilate Michael's betrayal, shrugged. If Arnaud shot her right now, she doubted she'd feel anything. She was numb.

"Don't be so damned impatient," Arnaud snapped to the girl. "They must both know where it is. We take no chances." He motioned for one of the men carrying a gun. "Bring him round. Dear Tally needs motivation to jog her memory."

Michael was alive. *Thank God.* Tally leaned back against the soft cushions as though she didn't have a care in the world. "I believe those earrings you're wearing are mine. Hand 'em over while we're waiting, toots," she told Leli'a, who was wearing a green cotton sundress, high-heeled sandals, and Tally's favorite silver-and-emerald earrings.

"Tell me what you did with my pearl necklace before we kill you," Leli'a snarled in response, her pretty face pink under expertly applied makeup. The island girl was gone completely, Tally suddenly realized. This self-possessed young woman was not only well-dressed, and perfectly groomed, she also spoke perfect English.

"Hmm. No more pidgin English, I see," Tally said absently.

Michael wasn't coming around. Arnaud got up from the table to hassle his men. Tally dragged her attention back to Leli'a. "What happened?" she asked. "Did you take elocution lessons this morning?"

Did Auntie know her niece was plucked-eyebrow-deep in Arnaud's business? God. Was *Auntie* involved in all this? And Henri?

Michael lay insensate on the deck, while Arnaud and two guards crouched over him, presumably trying to decide how to get him to wake up.

"I had a better education than you did," the girl told her coldly. "Twelve years at San Souci in London."

"They might've taught you to speak the Queen's English, but that didn't help with your klepto problem, did it?" Tally said. One of the men had thrown a pitcher of water over Michael. He wasn't moving. Oh, God. Perhaps he *was* dead.

Leli'a leaned over the table. "Let me explain something to you, *toots.* My great-grandfather brought those pearls up one at a time from the reefs of Bora-Bora more than seventy years ago. He had them strung in Paris for my great-grandmother. They've been passed from each generation of women in my family. *My* family, you bitch. Not yours. The pearls are mine, and always have been."

Tally frowned. "Are you saying my father stole them from your family, then gave them to me?"

"I'm saying *my* father stole them from me to give to you," Leli'a said flatly, her black eyes watching for Tally's reaction.

Tally glanced over as another pitcher of water was thrown on Michael. Damn it. Why didn't he wake up? She glanced back at Leli'a. "I'm sure my father has a bill of sale. He gave them to me years ago. You would have been only a child then. Perhaps your father sold the—"

"You not very bright, are you, sista?" Leli'a mocked in pidgin English, switching back to her faintly accented British as she said venomously, "My father is Trevor Church."

Tally heard her quite clearly, but she said, "What?" anyway.

"He was living with my mother when you and *your* mother were in Papeete looking for him ten years ago. I am more his daughter than you could ever hope to be."

Tally felt as though she'd been punched in the stomach.

She didn't doubt Leli'a's claim for a moment. She and Bev *had* come to Tahiti years ago looking for Trevor on a flimsy lead. Tally remembered the long, lonely days, and even longer, lonely nights. Her mother's desperation. Her own yearning. They'd both hoped. And in the end they had returned home under another crushing, bitter disappointment.

God, what irony. She'd always wanted a sister. If only she'd known . . . and if she had, then what?

She reached for the fruit drink on the table, not caring what was in it, and chugged it down. She didn't taste it. Had her father left Leli'a behind when he'd packed a bag and gone off on one of his "business trips"? Had he taken the little dark-haired girl with him? Had Trevor cared about Leli'a, and *her* mother, more than he'd ever cared about Tally and Bev? Had he called, and promised Leli'a the moon, then delivered nothing? Had he told her half-sister he loved her? And meant it?

God. This shouldn't hurt so badly. It wasn't as if she and her father had ever had anything close to a relationship. But Leli'a had been with him for all these years while Tally had just dreamed of *seeing* him for a few hours . . . for those same years.

A nasty, overwhelming, jumble of pain, jealousy, anger, and hurt tore through Tally. She ached with her father's betrayal. To herself. To her mother. Dry-eyed, she stared at Leli'a. She must look like her mother, although now that Tally knew, she thought perhaps the Tahitian girl had the same slightly crooked smile her fath—that Trevor—sported. *Oh, God.* She needed to go somewhere quiet to assimilate this. To come to grips with it all.

One look at the triumph in Leli'a's eyes dissuaded her.

"Why would he steal the pearls from you to give to me? It doesn't make any sense."

"Because they are perfectly matched and priceless. And I was wearing them the afternoon he went to meet you for your birthday. He was angry with me. And he took them and gave them to you for spite. I want them back."

Tally had felt so grown up when he'd handed her the pearls over dinner. Damn it. She'd pretended he actually gave a damn about her. "I'll give you the pearls when we get back to the island," Tally told the girl.

She covered the horrible, burning pain in her chest with her hand. Her throat worked, her eyes stung. She blinked back the tears and forced the numbing pain somewhere manageable. She'd be damned if she'd cry in front of Leli'a.

"Tell me where they are," the girl said. "You won't be going back."

"Oh, for God's sake," Tally said, throwing up her hands. "Are you threatening me, too? What is it with you and Arnaud? Haven't you ever heard of discussing a problem without killing the person because they disagree with you?" Tally glanced over at Michael. His head and shirt, and the deck around him, were soaking wet. But he still hadn't moved.

Of the multitude of emotions rushing at her, Tally allowed anger to win out. "Whatever you two are up to, I just don't care. Got it? I don't *give* a damn. My—Trevor is expecting to see me this afternoon. If I'm not there, he'll want to know why. When I've seen him, I'll leave. Until then you're S.O.L."

She sensed someone behind her just as Arnaud's attention flicked over her shoulder. She tried to turn, half-rising out of the softly padded chair. She was unceremoniously shoved down by two rough hands on her shoulders.

"What the hell do you hope to achieve with this, Arnaud? Trevor is going to have your guts for garters when I tell him what you've done to me."

Arnaud laughed mirthlessly. "*Non.* I do not believe your father will care one way or the other."

Unfortunately, that was probably, and sadly, true. One of the men grabbed her arms and held her hands together as the other guy wound a thin, hairy rope about her wrists. "Ow, damn it. That hurts!"

"Tie her tightly," Leli'a instructed, sipping at a glass of wine. "Tighter," she snapped.

"You won't get away with this," Tally said furiously, hoping, praying Michael would wake up and save the day. This was not looking good. There was no point straining against her bindings, Leli'a had them tied so tightly, Tally couldn't feel her fingers.

"Auntie and Henri know I was here. People will talk. Trevor will kill you for this."

"He is *my* father. You think he has given you a moment's thought in the last twenty years? No, he has not. I am his daughter. I am the one he cares about, not you."

Direct hit. And it *hurt,* damn it. "I'm the one he gave the pearls to."

Leli'a hissed in a breath. "Where are they?"

"I forget."

"You stupid, bloody bitch. My father won't care when you die. He's never cared about you."

"Whether he cares or not, when he finds out I've been here, and then suddenly disappeared, he'll start asking questions. It'll be suspicious that we're all gone at the same time."

"Yes," Arnaud said pleasantly. "The staff is taking you and your lover to Bora-Bora to catch a plane back home. A romantic cruise to end a pleasant vacation. Nothing more. A favor for the boss's daughter. They will return, tell him they dropped off the lovers in Bora-Bora, and you won't be heard of again."

"And you don't think he'll be slightly put out I came all this way to see him and then didn't bother waiting for him to show up?"

Arnaud laughed. "I have worked these many years to impress upon your father how American you are—thoughtless.

Selfish. Inconsiderate. No, he will think nothing of this quite normal and inconsiderate behavior." Arnaud pulled a red grape off the bunch on his plate and brought it to his mouth. "Here are your choices, Tallulah. One, you tell us where the control is hidden. Two, you don't—"

"Good. I choose door number two."

Arnaud continued uninterrupted. "And we torture your friend here until you spill your guts." He nodded at one of the soldiers. The man drew back his booted foot and kicked Michael hard in the ribs. "Once more. No," he snapped. "Not forceful enough. Again." Satisfied, he turned to Tally. "Which is it to be?"

"Wow. Hard choices," she said, her brain going a mile a minute, and bile climbing her throat at Arnaud's casual brutality. If she told Arnaud and Leli'a she didn't know where the device was, they'd kill her and torture the information out of Michael. If she told them she was the only one who knew where it was, they'd kill Michael in a heartbeat. "Michael took it apart."

"Christ." Arnaud went pale. "Well, where the fuck is it?"

"I only know where my half is. Sorry."

"She's lying!"

Tally looked from one to the other. "If you think so, might as well kill me now. I'm not telling you. Isn't it funny how thieves and liars always expect the same thing from other people?"

Leli'a reached out and slapped Tally hard across the face. Tally's head bounced on the cushion behind her head, then she was up and out of her seat.

She might not have the use of her hands, but her feet were just fine, thank you very much.

She kicked Leli'a a hard whack in the boobs. The girl gasped as the impact knocked the air out of her lungs. She and her chair skidded across the polished deck and clattered to a stop against the railing.

Tally staggered back several steps to regain her footing.

"I'm *damn* sick of you people slapping me around. Knock it off!" She was panting, hard and fast. Damn it, her wrists felt like hamburger meat, her eyes were tearing, and Leli'a was screaming like a madwoman as two sailors tried to help her up.

Arnaud suddenly stiffened. Tally followed his gaze. High above them was the tiny speck of a plane, the faint hum of the engines carried on the breeze.

Trevor, Tally almost cried with relief.

"Leli'a, stop that goddamned caterwauling and get over here. Now." Arnaud rose and motioned impatiently to his men. "Take them below. I'll talk to them there."

Hurry, Dad, Tally screamed silently. *Hurry.* It was a testament to her terror that she had never called him "Dad" in her life.

Chapter Eighteen

Under the hull of the Marie José, *Michael carefully and efficiently removed the harness of the limpet mine on his back, knowing Hugo was mirroring his actions nearby. He pried the magnets from the steel plate which held each in position, then placed it against the steel hull of the vessel. Next, he removed the plastic explosive from its pouch and molded the C4 between his hands.*

He'd precut lengths of M700 time fuse and removed them from his pack along with the M-60 fuse lighter.

Ready to rock and roll.

A quick check of the Rolex on his board. They were right on the nose, time-wise. The wet sub waited a klick away, ready for extraction. The op had been textbook perfect.

Hugo tugged on the line.

Michael set his fuses, and pushed off.

Time to go home.

Suddenly, and without warning, bright light flooded the murky water. Michael blinked, and narrowed his eyes. The water was alive with bubbles, lights, and a dozen divers. The enemy was suited up, and armed to the teeth.

Michael and Hugo were outflanked, and way the hell outgunned. Michael signaled his intent, and slashed at the line between them, freeing them both. He signaled his next maneuver to Hugo, who, thanks to the near-spotlight brightness, was as clear as day, although he was already twenty meters away. The key was to take this unexpected fuckup and turn it into a victory.

Hugo signaled back.

As one, they swam directly at the biggest cluster of divers. Straight into the ambush, weapons drawn, thereby changing a defensive action into an offensive action. If they could pull this one off, they'd win. If they couldn't, they'd die trying.

His heart was beating loud and strong in his ears. The rebreather was getting a workout, but they were out of options. The first spear glanced off Michael's left thigh. Didn't hurt. He knew it'd made contact by the mist of blood around him. The water churned with the flash and dash of black bodies. Kicking, firing off their harpoon guns, thrashing about, wondering what the hell these two fucks were doing swimming at them instead of away.

Michael fired his modified Glock 17 from close range, and got a twofer. One guy behind the other. The two men jerked in unison, then separated to drift in the bubbles from their aerators. Plenty more where they came from.

The sound of the blood rushing in his ears, the thud of his heartbeat, made Michael feel gloriously alive. Hell. Invincible.

He saw Hugo out of the corner of his eye, weapon drawn, giving as good as he got.

Hoo-yah.

Michael fired off another round from the Glock. The enemy was close. Damn close. He whipped out his K-bar knife from its holster and went in. Up close and personal. Man, he loved this shit.

The water churned red. Auroras of light backlit the enemy divers. Everything happened in slow-mo. Hand to hand, nasty and messy. He cut one guy high on the shoulder, another in the throat. Some dude came up behind him, trying to pull off his mask. Michael moved like a great white, turning on a dime, flipping, and coming up behind him. In seconds, Michael had the bad guy's mask-hose cut. The guy drifted away as quiet as you please. Next?

Within seconds, Hugo was surrounded. The bad guys closed in for the kill. Michael streaked through the clouds of blood, straight for the kill zone.

The last thing he saw was Hugo's face. Fierce. Determined. Michael had a "come to Jesus" moment, and everything went dark.

"Michael? Wake up. Come on, wake up. We're in deep doo-doo here!"

Hugo?

"Michael!"

Tally. He groaned and squinted his eye open. They'd dumped him on the floor like yesterday's trash. Tally was on the bed, trussed up like a Sunday goose.

"Did the sonofabitch hurt you again?" Michael demanded, ignoring what was clearly a broken rib, and a mother of a headache. His hands were bound behind his back, then tied securely to his roped ankles.

"Let's put it this way: It's been an enlightening afternoon."

"Yeah?" He tested the strength of the bindings on his wrists. They'd done a damn fine job. "Could you give me a quick overview? I doubt we have much time."

"A quick overview?" Tally repeated, her tone way too mild. "Certainly. Hmm, let's see . . . Arnaud wants to take over my father's business. Oh, yeah, already knew that one. Turns out Leli'a is my sister—half-sister. You screwed my brains out for your own perverse reasons. Oh, yeah, and you're here to kill Trevor. Whose plane, by the way, is probably landing on Paradise as we speak. And in a while, Arnaud is going to persuade us, probably violently and painfully, to give him that control thingy. That quick enough for you?"

Tally turned her head so she could look him in the eye. "Oh, yeah, *Lieutenant.* One more thing. I'm glad you're not dead. Because, if we ever get out of this mess you've gotten us into, Ollie, I'm going to kill you myself."

"Jesus, you're bloodthirsty. Could we at least get free before you bump me off?"

"And just how are we supposed to do that?" she whispered hotly. "You're way over there, and I'm a little tied up myself."

There was a slight quiver in that bravado, but Michael blocked any feeling of sympathy. Time was of the essence.

Whatever the reason Arnaud was not down here beating the shit out of them, Michael was grateful, but their luck wasn't gonna last. He fumbled around, teeth gritted, until he could reach his ankle.

"Got fleas?" Tally asked sweetly.

"Knife," he grunted, as he managed to pull it free from the ankle sheath with his bound hands. He couldn't get enough give in the ropes around his wrists to cut them.

He felt the throb of the engines beneath the floor. They hadn't turned around yet—but if the positions were reversed, Michael would head out to sea. *Away* from the island. Away from Church.

"You're going to have to help me with this." Michael rolled over twice, hoping to hell he didn't puncture a lung with his broken rib, and came to rest beside the bed. "Any give in your bindings?" he asked.

"No."

He rolled up onto his knees. Jesus. They'd bound her wrists so tightly, her hands were bleached white, then they'd tied them to the railing that ran behind the bed. She was stretched out like a sacrificial lamb. Obviously in pain, she looked at him without complaint.

Michael leveraged his weight onto the bed. He was half on top of Tally when he landed. She grunted. He rolled to the side, then shifted onto his knees to bring his own bound hands level with hers. "Did Arnaud tie these?" Sadistic bastard.

"Better." Tally shifted uneasily as he positioned the small sharp knife between the rope around her wrists. "My new sister supervised. Arnaud was in charge of having *you* kicked back to consciousness. It's a good thing they didn't find the knife, otherwise you'd have to gnaw your way through the rope like the rat you are."

He glanced over his shoulder and cocked a brow as he sawed at the rope. She bit her lip and turned her head away. Michael could smell the soft fragrance of her hair. He concentrated on helping her work the ropes. Cursing silently at the tightness of the cords. That sister of hers was a vicious piece of work.

Tally closed her eyes and rested her head on the pillow. This was going to be a long process, so she might as well be comfy. "I told Arnaud you took the detonator apart, and we each hid half."

"Smart thinking."

"I thought so. What did you really do with it?"

"Tossed it overboard."

Tally stared at him. "Are you sure that was a good idea? What if we need it to bargain with?"

"The people we're dealing with don't bargain. Let's keep the truth our little secret."

"Yeah, sure. Fine." No surprise. Michael Wright was just chock full of secrets. "Could you hurry up? Arnaud flipped out when he saw the plane. I don't know what's going on out there, but I'll bet they're planning something unpleasant. Aren't you *done* yet?"

"Almost. Spread your hands."

As opposed to "spread your legs." She tried to separate her wrists. The rope held fast, but a few threads unraveled. Michael continued sawing.

At last Tally was able to break the last few threads binding her hands by snapping them. "I have mobility. Here, give me the knife," she whispered. She took the sharp knife and slipped it between his wrists.

He kept a steady tension on the rope to make her job easier. The ropes separated. He flexed his wrists before rubbing back the circulation. "Thanks." He took the knife from her and cut apart his ankles, then hers, then staggered off the bunk.

He looked around for a weapon and a way to block the door. There wasn't much.

The cabin was luxurious, and clearly only for guests. He removed several of the padded hangers he found in the locker, and used them as a makeshift wedge under the door. They wouldn't hold worth a damn, but they were better than nothing. All he had to defend them was the three-inch blade of his knife. He went back to the bed.

She looked up, her eyes cerulean blue and hot. "I hate you."

"Don't blame you."

"I'll never forgive you for using me."

"Hold that thought for twenty years. Okay?"

"How are we going to get out of here? There are at least ten of them and two of us."

"Our motivation is stronger. Come on." He hauled her off the bed, then caught her as her knees buckled. "Easy."

She grabbed his chest for balance. He hooked her chin with his hand and scanned her face. *Ah, hell, sweetheart, look at you.* She was battered and bruised, had a fat lip, the beginnings of a black eye, and the knot on her forehead was now purple and swollen. Damned if she wasn't beautiful, anyway.

Michael lowered his mouth and kissed her gently, running his tongue along the seam of her lips until her mouth opened beneath his. God, she tasted sweet.

Tally bit his tongue.

Michael winced and lifted his head.

"Do you have short-term memory loss?" she said without heat. "I hate you."

"I know." Michael took her hand. "The door's locked from outside, and there are a couple of guys standing guard." He removed the dubious deterrent of the hangers under the door and tossed them on the bed. "Go lie down in the same position, and scream bloody murder. Not too loudly. We don't want everyone in here. Just the guards outside."

Tally obediently lay down with her arms extended above her head and her feet together. Michael tossed a couple of pieces of rope over her wrists and ankles. It wouldn't fool anyone who gave more than a cursory glance. But a quick glance was all the time he needed. He stood where the open door would shield him, and nodded to Tally.

She was good. Her shriek was just sufficient enough to get the men's attention. Seconds later, the door burst open to reveal the two guards, one in front of the other.

"What are you yelling about?" one man demanded, pointing the business end of his PM5 at Tally.

"These ropes are tied too tightly," Tally said crossly. "My circulation's being cut off. Come and untie me."

The guy in front laughed. The guy in back had another problem as Michael stood behind him and put one arm around his neck, the knife to his throat. He didn't make a sound as Michael gave a sharp upward twist, snapping his neck.

At the same moment, Tally whined, "Hurry up!" neatly blocking the sound. She shifted impatiently on the bed, keeping her attention on the soldier.

Without a sound, Michael dropped the other guy to the floor and quietly closed the door.

"They look fine to m—" The rope covering Tally's wrists slid off. "Hey! What—"

Before the bad guy could get to Tally, Michael grabbed his shoulder and spun him around. In a quick, lethal motion, he punched him out. The man's eyes rolled back in his head as he toppled over onto Tally's leg.

She shoved his arm off her hip, then scrambled out from under him. "Nice work, Double Oh."

"Take his weapons." Michael was already bent over the man at his feet, stripping him of his weapons.

He glanced up. Tally held an MP5 between her fingers. "We never did get to that shooting lesson, did we?"

"Apparently experience is the best teacher."

"Here." Michael checked the weapon, then showed her how to hold it. "If anyone gets in your way, point and shoot. Accuracy won't matter if they're close enough. Stay close, and don't stop for anything. We're going for the stern boat portside. Let's do it."

"Back, left?"

"Yeah. Back, left." He opened the stateroom door quietly, stuck his head out, and checked the companionway. All clear. He pulled Tally after him.

Voices came from the salon. Arnaud, Leli'a, and several men. It would be nice if everyone was in there, but not likely.

He glanced back. Tally had her weapon pointed in the middle of his back. He turned slightly and nudged the barrel slightly to the side. Hey, he didn't mind getting shot, but he'd be damned if he'd get it in the back from a pissed-off lover when there were so many others waiting for a chance at him. He motioned Tally to wait, then moved stealthily toward the salon. The door wasn't quite closed. Inside, Leli'a sat on the sofa; he could just see her swinging foot. Three men lounged in the armchairs opposite, facing the woman, and talking to Arnaud, who must have been standing beside her.

Michael motioned Tally the other way, and they ran silently down the corridor. They headed for the aft stairs. So far, so good.

He and Tally charged up the stairs, taking them two at a time. There was a closed door at the top which he opened cautiously. He glanced around, and motioned Tally through.

His limited visibility had already proven to be a liability. Michael knew there were at *least* three more men somewhere, plus five or six crew members. He wasn't taking any chances. As much as he wanted to race across the wide, open deck to the speedboat hanging against the side, he took time for a thorough reconnaissance.

They had one shot at getting this right.

The sound of low voices carried in the balmy air. Two men. Ten to twelve feet away. He motioned Tally to close the door behind her and lock it, then held up his hand for her to stay put. She obediently crouched low in the doorway.

Michael snuck around the corner and spotted two armed men having a smoke as they checked out the *Nemesis,* which still rode anchor near the cliffs in the distance. They hadn't gone as far out as he'd thought. Excellent.

The men stood between him and the small boat they were

obviously not guarding. He tilted his head so he could see all the way down the deck to the prow. All clear.

Which didn't mean shit. The rest of the bad guys could be an inch out of view.

He slid the knife from the ankle sheath and checked the guys' shadows. The sun was slightly in front of them, casting their shadows toward him. Perfect. They wouldn't see him coming.

Stealthy as a cat, he shot across the few feet separating them. In a swift, silent move, he shoved the knife up high in the closest guy's kidney. The man dropped to the deck without a peep. By the time the other one turned, not even alarmed, Michael had the knife to his throat.

This dude wasn't going quietly. He spun around, weapon up. The moron had the safety on. He pulled the trigger. Click. He opened his mouth to yell a warning, but Michael's knife silenced him in mid-squawk. He gurgled, then dropped to the deck beside his friend, sightless eyes staring at the bright blue sky.

"*Sayonara,* asshole." Michael wiped the knife clean on the guy's shirt.

He kicked the start button to lower the small speedboat down the side and into the water. It was a slow process. While it winched down, Michael dragged the two guys by their collars, then hefted them one at a time and threw them over the railing into the wake of the *Beautiful Dreamer.*

He sprinted to get Tally. She was exactly as he'd left her. Pale-faced, wide-eyed, and clearly terrified as she lip-synced a song to keep herself busy. And sane.

He grabbed her arm, indicated she should stay low, and raced across the deck. She hesitated at the bloodstain on the deck, but Michael wasn't taking time for explanations. "Over the side, it's a small drop."

"Oh, my God," Tally said, horrified. "We can't swim that far." The island was five klicks behind them.

"Down there." He indicated the slowly descending speedboat. "Make it snappy, we have company. Here, give me that." He grabbed the weapon out of her hand, and she threw her leg over the railing as three guys came barreling down the deck toward them.

"Jump," he told her, then opened fire on the bad guys. Shit. He'd needed a couple of extra minutes to lower at least a couple of the other speedboats. He was out of time.

He heard the thud as Tally's feet gained purchase on the smaller boat.

The bad guys fired back. They were shitty shots; nevertheless, there was a hail of bullets as Michael threw his leg over the railing and paused to return fire.

"In the water yet?" Michael shouted, clipping one guy and dropping another. A bullet grazed his cheek like an angry bee. He jacked a round into the chamber of the Browning, fired off a few more rounds, and got a hail of bullets in response. Shit.

"A few more feet," Tally shouted back.

"Find the release knob on the dash."

"Got it. Now?"

"Now!"

He heard the splash, then the strident roar of the engine as Tally fired her up. Good girl.

He shot off another volley to keep the guys where they were. He was still shooting as he dropped over the side. Damn. Just like the good old days.

His landing left a lot to be desired. But he was in the boat and not in the water.

"Go. Go. Go!" Michael grabbed the wheel and hefted Tally across the seat. The small cigarette boat danced across the wake of the *Beautiful Dreamer* with a bone-jarring thump-thump-thump. There was no time for finesse. The boat was fast and easy to maneuver. He did a screaming uie, and took off across the water like a bat out of hell heading back toward Paradise. Behind them, everyone had arrived five minutes late to the party. He grinned as the bad guys yelled, and cursed, and fired at their spume.

"Hang on to something and don't let go," Michael shouted

as water slammed over the dash and sprayed overhead. The powerboat raced across the water as if it were dragging across lumpy cement without shocks.

A shot slammed into the dash right between them. The next bullet hit the windshield with a loud *crack!* The impact spiderwebbed the Perspex, reducing visibility to zilch. They were flying blind. So what else was new? He was getting used to that.

"They're coming after us," Tally yelled. He twisted around. All three of the other cigarette boats were in the water, and right on their ass.

"Shit. Stay down. Stay down!" Holding on to the shimmying wheel, Michael brought his foot up and kicked at the windshield, using his full weight behind the blow. The windshield severed off the front of the boat, bounced off the seat tops, and careened in the sea.

Water sprayed over him. But at least he could see.

Another volley of shots.

And then an answering shot from directly behind him. Michael glanced around. Tally crouched in the back, firing in the general direction of the mother ship. She wasn't going to hit anything, given her inexperience and their speed, but it was a deterrent. "Good girl."

Every few seconds she'd fire off another round. "They're gaining on us."

"Think you can hit it?"

"From here? No way. God, Michael, they're closing in on us. And *they* do know how to shoot."

"Don't panic. Use your bullets sparingly. We're well ahead of them. How many on board the closest one?"

"Four. Guards, I think."

"Jesus, they're multiplying like flies. We weigh less. We'll go faster. Give them another blast and, for God's sake, stay low!"

She stayed low and managed another volley of shots. "They're gaining on u—ow!"

"Jesus. Were you hit?"

"No, sorry. I bit my tongue. Just drive, would you?"

In the distance, Michael made out the green peak of the volcano forming the bulk of Paradise Island. All they needed was ten minutes or so on dry land before the goons arrived. No one at the marina to block their way. And a faster boat. And no interference. Yeah. All they needed was a frigging miracle.

Out of the corner of his eye he saw the nose of the other boat. Almost neck and neck. Jesus. Without slowing down, he turned and fired a barrage of shots. Several at the men, several at the engine. One guy screamed as he fell overboard. A bullet ricocheted off the side of the other boat. A hit, but no cigar. He hoped like hell their boat stayed on course. He had no choice. They were close enough for him to see the whites of their eyes, their directive was to kill.

"Get down. Get down!" he shouted at Tally. She needed no more urging. Between the over spray and the increasing barrage of firepower there was nothing she could do but keep her head low. Michael turned to make himself as small a target as possible. He was a better shot than the three goons in the other boat, but eventually he was going to run out of bullets.

Like right now. *Shit.*

"Here." Tally was flat on her stomach between his feet. She held up the CAR. Michael grabbed it and fired a volley of two-fisted shots. He winged one guy, and the other fell overboard like his friend. Two down, two to go.

He accelerated. The boat was going flat out. Shaking with the increased speed, it skimmed over the water, leaving the other boats to battle their wake.

"Get up here." He shouted over the hellacious noise the two engines made, and the hard, brutal slams as they took the waves head-on.

Tally staggered to her feet, more crouching than standing. "Grab the wheel and stay on course."

She braced her legs on the seat, leaned back, and clutched the wheel in a white-knuckled grip. The muscles in her slender arms strained. She gritted her teeth and held on, her expression grim. He repositioned her hands for better control, then crawled to the back of the boat. He whipped the canvas cover off the Rocket-Propelled Grenade—the RPG—bolted to the back.

The RPG launcher was top of the line, U.S. issue. Michael could've kissed it. If he'd had time. Locked and loaded. *Hooyah.*

He fired. The grenade went wide as they slammed down a trough. They fired back with their own RPG.

"Incoming. Hold on," Michael yelled, as their boat skittered across the water with the impact. Tally struggled to maintain control. Michael got off a few rounds from the MP5, until Tally realigned them. He wasn't wasting the grenades if there was no chance of a strike. The boat slid to port, then starboard. It jumped and jived, slamming up, then down. He didn't waste time telling Tally to hold it steady. She was doing the best she could. And her best was damn good.

She finally had it. The little boat slammed down hard, then continued in a direct hell-bent-for-leather path toward the marina.

Michael braced his feet and repositioned the RPG. Fired again. Direct hit. The boat blew, blooming like an orange rose on the frothy white water of their wake.

There was a second speedboat right behind it. The driver did a slick evasion tactic and was coming at them fast, guns blazing.

"Go, go, go!" Michael yelled at Tally as he got off a shot that clipped the prow of the other boat. Chunks of white Plexi flew into the air. It took a licking and kept on ticking, closing the distance between them. Reinforced. They were used to getting shot at.

"Marina?" Tally shouted.

"Beach," he yelled back. "Hang on, I'm coming."

Their speed, and her inexperience would land them nose-deep in Auntie's kitchen. He used the spent MP5 to jam the trigger mechanism of the RPG launcher. The result was a hail of grenades. Although the other boat wasn't being directly targeted, it was a handy-dandy deterrent.

He climbed over the seats and stood behind Tally. She leaned in to his body as he grabbed the vibrating wheel, and they held on to it together for a few seconds. "Got it. Get down."

She sank to the floor and scooted from between his feet in the narrow space under the dash.

Marina dead ahead. Michael veered off to the left and headed for the small cove near the base of the hills. Right now he needed cover, and God only knew who was waiting for them at the marina.

Tide was in. The water was fairly deep, covering at least half the beach. He powered down, slowed marginally. "Get ready to bail."

Tally staggered to her knees beside him.

The nose of the speedboat bit into the sand. The back end came up, vibrated, then slammed with a bone-jarring slap back in the shallow water. The engine screamed a protest as Michael shut her down. "Go!"

He grabbed her hand and pulled her over into the surf. The water hit him mid-thigh; Tally staggered in waist-deep water. "Where are we going?" she demanded breathlessly, clinging to his hand so hard, his fingers went numb.

She shot him a quick glance. His face was hard, his jaw locked. He had the strangest expression on his face. "Were you hit?" she demanded, scanning his taut features, then running her gaze down what she could see of his body.

"I don't have time to deal with this shit," he muttered under his breath. "I'm fine. Come on."

Oh, God. Oh, God. Where *could* they go? Arnaud and Leli'a were crazy enough to kill them in front of everyone. She didn't trust this man with her heart, but she did trust him to keep her safe until they could . . . what? Get help? From where? Leave? How? It seemed pretty damn hopeless to

Tally. But Michael was crouched low and running across the soft sand, and she didn't hesitate to follow him.

She skinned her knee as he hauled her bodily up and over the rough rocks. "Where are we going?"

"There's a cave up ahead. Move it!"

A cave? She hesitated. Oh, no. No way. Too small. Too dark.

"Don't think about it," Michael said grimly, not letting go.

They rounded the corner at a dead run only to be brought up short by the sight waiting for them at the mouth of the cave.

Tally almost collapsed with gratitude. "Daddy!"

Chapter Nineteen

With a relieved sob, Tally ran toward her father, who stood watching the drama play out in the company of a dozen men. He held a hand up to stop her, then instructed several of his men to take care of their pursuers who were circling in the surf nearby, like sharks waiting for the kill.

Her father asked no questions. As the other boats aimed for where they stood on the beach, Trevor's men opened fire. Tally flinched as she saw the face of the driver seconds before a bullet hit him in the forehead, leaving a small, neat, black hole. She looked away and shuddered at the casual violence.

Without a driver, the speedboat went up the side of the rocks at full-throttle. Bodies flew as the boat looped, ass over prow, and landed upside down in the surf like a pregnant turtle.

Tally turned away and looked at her father, trying to reconcile this man with the person she'd seen in London several years ago. He'd changed, and not for the better. Or perhaps she was suddenly seeing the real man.

Trevor Church had always been large, tall, and robust, but in the last few years he'd packed on a good fifty pounds, which strained his white shirt across his belly. The shirt was open to mid-chest, exposing a glint of gold chains against his tanned chest. Fleshy jowls hung from his square jaw. The change made him appear dissipated, like a man who spent too much time hovered over a whiskey bottle. He'd shaved his head, and now sported a small gold earring in his left ear.

Emotion poured through Tally at the sight of him. Hope. Pain. Anger. Relief.

Before she got near the small cluster of men, Michael grabbed her arm and pulled her back sharply. Off-balance, her body slammed into his chest. "What are you doing? Let go." She tried to tug herself free.

Michael pulled her up hard against him with one arm around her waist. She felt the steady thud of his heart against her shoulder. "Stay with me," he said grimly.

Tally wriggled to get free. "Don't be silly. That's my fathe—"

"What the *bloody hell* are you doing here?" Trevor Church demanded, his British accent crisp and as cutting as broken glass. Eyes distant, mouth grim, he remained where he was.

At her father's words, Tally stopped struggling out of Michael's hold. "I—what?"

"I can't believe your stupidity. Why are you here, Tallulah?"

His reaction wasn't unexpected, but her heart pinched all the same. Tally lifted her chin. "Gee, it's good to see you, too."

"I repeat. Why are you here?"

"You know, I've been asked that question so many times, by so many people lately, I'm beginning to think I'm just not welcome," Tally said tartly. She and Michael weren't touching, but she could feel him right behind her, only inches away.

Her father scowled. "We meet where and when *I* say. You have never been welcome here." He glanced past Tally and smiled unpleasantly at Michael. "Came back for more, I see, Lieutenant. This time will it be my daughter you kill instead of your partner?"

"You're a real prize, Church."

"And you're a dead man." Trevor jerked his head, and his goons strode forward. Three circled behind Michael, one roughly grabbing hold of Tally's arm.

Michael's arm tightened about her waist, pulling her hard against him. "Tell your people to back off," he told her father.

"Or what, Lieutenant?"

"Or someone is going to get seriously hurt."

"Are you going to stand there using a woman to shield you?"

"This has nothing to do with Tally. Tell your apes to back off, then let her go. This is between you and me. No one else."

"As much as I'd relish finishing what I started last year, Lieutenant, I don't have time today." Church jerked his chin.

His men grabbed hold of Michael from the back. Tally felt his body jerk, and heard his grunt of pain as he was hit from behind.

The man beside her tried to pull her free, almost ripping her arm out of its socket.

"Hey! Do I look like a damn wishbone?" Tally twisted and kneed the man holding so tightly to her left arm. With a shriek he doubled over, holding his groin. She jerked herself free of Michael's hold and stepped away from him, then glared from him to her father, encompassing all the men in their audience. The testosterone level in the air was as thick as pea soup.

At the end of her emotional and physical rope, Tally snapped. "Stick a fork in me, guys, I'm done. I'll just stand here and watch while you shoot one another. Last man standing can help me get off this damn island."

"You'll do what you're told," her father said.

"Or what?" Tally countered, planting both hands on her hips and glaring at the man she'd waited so long to see. "You'll kill me? Big deal. Right now, a bullet to the brain sounds like a vacation!"

"Tally."

"Shut up, Michael," she snapped, never taking her gaze off her father. "I've been burgled, choked, pushed down stairs, nearly strangled, chased by a speedboat, shot at. Who knows what's next? If you think you can scare me now, *Daddy,* you don't know me any more than I know you."

For one split second, she thought she saw a flash of—

something, was it pride?—in Trevor's eyes, but by this point, she couldn't have cared less. "So tell you what. Why don't you just have one of your goons shoot me now. Or better yet, give me the gun. Your guys keep screwing it up!"

"Damn it, Tally."

She spared Michael one quick glare. It had taken four men to hold him. They had his arms strained behind his back in what looked like an extremely uncomfortable position. "I am not speaking to you."

"Lucky man," one of her father's henchmen muttered.

"If you're not going to shoot me, color me gone." Tally turned as sharply on her bare heel as sand would allow and started down the beach. As tempting as it was, she didn't run. She pulled back her shoulders, lifted her head, and kept her eyes focused on Auntie's hotel in the distance. One phone call would bring the charter plane back. All she had to do was put one heavy foot in front of the other and keep walking.

Tally couldn't tell which hurt more, her battered and bruised body, or her heart. She was one giant ache from head to toe, inside and out. But beyond the hurt, she was extremely pissed off. The brilliant white beach ahead blurred, and she angrily dashed the moisture from her eyes.

Neither man was worth crying over.

One of her father's men came up behind her swiftly and jerked her off her feet. She stumbled in the sand. "Let go of me," she snarled, trying to twist out of his hold. His fingers gripped her upper arm where she had bruises on top of bruises. She turned to her father. "Tell your goon to let go of me. Right now!"

"Where do you think you're going?" He might have been talking to a stranger for all the emotion in his voice and features.

"Why the hell do you care? I've been walking without assistance for twenty-seven years. I can certainly do so now. Believe me, you don't need to have me escorted off your precious island. I'm more than happy to go. Thanks for the familial welcome. I feel warm and fuzzy all over. Good-bye."

"Take them up to the house until I decide what to do with them."

"Trust me," Tally said coldly, "*you* don't need to decide anything. I'm leaving."

Her father, flanked by his men, walked up to her. He paused to rake his gaze from her head, to her toes, and back again. He shook his head. "Pity you didn't get Bev's looks."

"I'm surprised you remember my mother's name. She wouldn't look twice at you now, Jabba the Hutt. Eat your heart out."

He hit her.

She fingered her bleeding lip. "I guess we're both disappointed."

Four modified golf carts waited on the other side of the rocks. Church and one of his men got into the first one; the rest of the crowd filled the remaining vehicles. "You drive," the goon told Michael, and motioned with his weapon for Tally to get into the passenger seat.

Michael shot her a glance. For all her bravado, her face was pale, her jaw set. Here was a woman about to blow.

Behind them sat two men, Uzis trained on the backs of their heads.

"Drive," the back, left goon ordered. Michael engaged the stick, and the convoy headed across the beach.

The fact that he had no weapons was no big deal. He could make a weapon out of a paper clip. And, fact of the matter was, he'd been prepared to die completing this last op.

Tally had put a whole new spin on things.

He might've been prepared to die. But he found himself vehemently opposed to any more harm coming to Tally.

It was hotter than hell. The sun bounced off the white sand, causing shimmering mirages in their path, reminding him of the op in Somalia back in '93. He'd had backup, weapons, and a hope of getting out alive. Right now, things weren't looking so hot.

Sweat ran down his temples. He wiped his face on his shoulder as he drove, keeping both hands on the wheel in plain view. Tally's hands were clasped so tightly in her lap, her knuckles shone white.

Michael glanced at her pale face. Jesus, she'd been thrilled about the invitation, and even when she'd learned it had all been a ruse, she'd still been delighted to be here. She'd anticipated a happy reunion with her father. He'd watched her flinch with each verbal bullet from Trevor Church.

Damn, he was proud of her chutzpah for returning fire.

The idea that such an unfeeling, callous bastard could've fathered a daughter as warm and caring as Tally was inconceivable.

The tide was coming in, which narrowed the beach to a white strip. They traveled in silence along the dappled shadows under the tree line at the back edge of the sand, where there were more rocks and roots to contend with.

Past the marina. The *Beautiful Dreamer* was sailing into port. Michael wondered absently how Church would react to the news that he and Tally had absconded with the detonator to the pulse generator. If nothing else, it would buy them some time.

"Don't slow down," the man behind him snapped.

Michael took the buggy over a gnarled root protruding from the sand. The vehicle shuddered and shimmied over the obstacle. "This thing isn't qualified for the Indy 500, pal."

He guesstimated the boat would dock in twenty minutes. He eased the cart onto the shell path in front of the hotel. There was no sign of either Auntie, or Henri. Hell, Michael wasn't sure whose side they were on, anyway.

The higher up the base of the volcano they traveled, the more dense the vegetation. The English Tudor–style mansion rose above a garden running wild with tropical plant life. The sun was high in a cloudless blue sky, the heat shimmering and reflecting off the stark white walls of the house.

"Stop here," the guy behind them instructed, rapping the back of Michael's head with the barrel of his weapon. "Keep your hands where I can see them, and get out."

Michael brought the vehicle to a halt. There wasn't much

time. Church would want them out of the way before his buyers arrived. It was a given *this* time he'd kill Michael. He wouldn't give him a second chance to get away. Not with this many guards and firepower. Not with this much at stake.

Regardless, Michael had to figure out a way to get Tally to safety, preferably off-island, before that happened. Bouchard and Cruella De Vil's arrival might facilitate her escape.

Church and his men entered the house. The front door yawned open in expectation. Michael stepped out of the cart and waited for Tally. He brushed her arm as she came around the front of the vehicle, and she flinched as though he'd poked her with a cattle prod. Head high, she preceded him up the shallow front steps and through the carved wooden front door.

He wanted to touch her. To reassure her. But of course he was the last damn person she'd want reassurance from. And frankly he couldn't tell her much. "Run like hell, honey," seemed inadequate for their circumstances.

Two men came up from behind him, holding him until the other cart arrived, then accompanied by six bodyguards, Michael strode up the stairs and followed Tally into Church's house.

The dim, cavernous entry hall felt cool as they crossed the green-and-white-checkered marble floor. Tally waited for him beside a pair of ten-foot-high mahogany doors guarded by two more of Church's little army.

Her eyes met his, then she turned and went through the door one of the men shoved open.

They walked into the English study, which was done in dark woods and plush jewel-colored velvets. Although unsuited to the tropical climate, everything Church had imported from his home country was top of the line. The large room looked as contrived as a stage set, and as inappropriate as a hula dancer at high tea.

Church stood with his back to them looking out the window.

Michael glanced around, assessing everything in the room

as a potential weapon. On their left, ceiling-high bookshelves were filled with heavy, gold-etched, leather-bound books. A large library table. A ladder. Plenty of throwable knick-knacks.

"Did you hope some of your decorator's class would rub off on you?" Tally asked her father sweetly.

Church turned from the window. "Sit down and shut up. Don't take your eyes off either of them," he instructed the six men who'd accompanied them silently into the room. "Not over there. Right here." He indicated the two low-backed chairs before the desk. Michael followed Tally, and they sat down. The men closed in behind them, weapons trained on their heads.

"A hell of a family reunion," Michael said, crossing his ankle over his knee. The desk was a couple of feet away. It appeared heavy and solid, but with enough force, Michael figured he could kick it hard enough to pin Church to the wall.

"Think I'll pass," Tally said flatly. "This whole armed-guard thing is ridiculous, you know. I don't want to be here. You don't want me here. What's the point?"

"The point is, your presence has put me in a tenuous position. I have guests arriving any minute. I have to decide what to do with you before they get here."

"I have several suggestions," Tally said flatly. "None of them involve sitting here with six guns pointing at my head."

"She's right." Michael wished to hell he could see out of his left eye. He knew the guy was right there, inches away, but he would've liked to *see* him. With this much firepower up close and personal, there was no way he was going to make a move without ending up dead. He had two things to accomplish before that happened: Church and Tally. He settled back in his chair, relaxed, but ready. "This has nothing to do with your daughter. Let her g—"

The door behind them slammed open.

"Papa!" Leli'a came tapping into the room accompanied by Bouchard. The gang was all here.

"What are you doing out of school?" Church demanded furiously. His face was red with temper. Things were obviously not going according to plan.

The girl's steps faltered. "I graduated months ago." Under her petulant tone was a tremor of fear.

"Go back to London until I tell you differently." He looked over Michael's head and motioned to one of the armed guards. "Get rid of her."

"No, Papa, wait. We have something important to tell you."

Church gave Bouchard a curious look. "I thought you were dead."

"A misunderstanding. They have the detonator for the pulse generator," Bouchard said as quickly as pulling off a Band-Aid. His voice was nasal because of his broken nose, which had swelled nicely and was black and painful looking.

Church's attention flew first to Michael, and then to Tally as he half-rose from his chair. "Impossible."

"She stole it, then gave it to him," Leli'a offered helpfully. She came and sat on the edge of her father's desk, a few feet from Tally. The two women eyed each other like two lionesses over a kill.

Church sank into his chair. "I don't bloody well have *time* for this shit," he told Bouchard, who hadn't moved from his position by the door. "How *you* died and were miraculously resurrected is another big question mark. But that can wait. Where is the detonator now?"

"They have it," Bouchard said.

"So *that's* why you're here," he said to Michael. "You knew about the weapons sale." Church's face and bald head were red with fury. No one outside his own circle was supposed to know about this deal.

"That's one of the reasons, yeah."

Church shot a glare from him to Tally. "Give me my property."

Tally glanced up at Michael. "Do you have his property?"

"No."

She looked back at her father. "Neither do I. Weapons sale?" Tally asked Michael. "What weapons sale?"

The guy on Michael's left was fascinated by the conversation, but his weapon was pointed unwaveringly at the middle of Michael's head. Good to know. "Your father's brokering arms deals with terrorists now."

"What's that got to do with brokering boats?"

Michael snorted. "The boats are stolen, the owners killed, and your father makes a tidy profit—Right, Church? You've heard of chop shops back home?" he asked Tally. "Well, Daddy Dearest here has the boating equivalent."

Tally looked from Michael to her father. "Is this true?"

"Small potatoes," Church told her. "Selling arms to my clients is far more lucrative. More entertaining, too."

"You're nothing but a crook," Tally said flatly.

"Watch that mouth," Church told his daughter. "I'm a businessman."

"And making a lot of money at it, I'm sure. Is that why Arnaud is trying to double-cross you?" Tally asked with false sweetness. "His bizarre behavior is starting to make sense to me now. Might as well 'fess up, Arnaud. He blew up a boat, and almost killed me, so *you'd* think he was dead. Then he was going to show up, and—what, Arnaud?"

"Don't listen to her fucking lies," Arnaud said hotly. "I was trying to retrieve the detonator for the pulse generator. For you. For the sale this afternoon."

"I trust no one. Not even you, Arnaud." Church opened a drawer and removed a Smith & Wesson, which he held casually. "Do you think I wasn't aware of what you've been doing in my absence? I've known for months you were planning a coup. Therefore I knew as soon as I heard the news of your death the reports were greatly exaggerated." The gun pointed at Bouchard. "The question is, should I give you one more opportunity to show your loyalty, or should I just do what is expedient and kill you now?"

"None of that is true," Arnaud said rapidly. "None of it. They are lies. We both have enemies—"

"Oh, shoot. I was hoping I got a vote," Tally told her father. The Smith & Wesson swung toward her. She gave it a dismissive glance, making Michael chuckle. "More power to you if you believe him. But I wouldn't turn my back on him if I were you." She shifted a little closer to Michael, her bare arm brushing his.

Listening to the conversation, Michael resisted touching her as he acclimated himself with the room. To his right, Leli'a had slid off the desk and made herself comfortable in one of two large armchairs. Bouchard was now on the sofa, a marble-topped coffee table in front of him. The window behind Church's desk was covered in floor-to-ceiling burgundy velvet drapes. Behind Tally, six armed men and a double door of solid wood. Outside, at least a dozen men armed with M16s and CAR-15s.

Fuck. He missed binocular vision. He missed Hugo. He had neither. And the man responsible for his losses smirked at him from behind his desk as he pointed a gun at his own daughter.

"My buyers will be here soon." Church glanced at his watch. "Very soon. Where is my detonator?"

"Didn't he just ask us that question?" Tally wanted to know. "News flash. We're not telling you. Live with it."

While the crates and boxes of weapons and ammo were a hell of an incentive to any terrorist group, Michael knew the pulse generator was the real cause for the fast and furious bidding. No doubt, Church would receive an astronomical amount. But without the detonator, the sale would be a bust. No one wanted a weapon of mass destruction lacking an "on" switch. Pity.

Which was why Bouchard had been on the beach with it this morning. The man with the detonator called the tune.

And despite what he'd told Tally, Michael had the detonator. He'd left an encrypted message for his brothers. They'd find it and know what to do with it when the time came.

"Did you ask your trusty right-hand man over there where it is?" Michael indicated Bouchard. The lamp on Church's desk was heavy brass. He measured the distance. Nine feet. Seconds.

"How would I know?" Bouchard demanded.

"Because you had it with you on the beach this morning. You remember. When you tried to kill me?" Tally answered sweetly. "What were you doing with it, Arnaud?"

"I was bringing it back here for safekee—that's none of your business. She claims," he told Church, "they divided the device, and each hid half."

"Impossible," Church snapped, looking from one to the other with a deep scowl.

"Bummer, huh? Who knew something *that* important could be so carelessly dropped?" Tally asked, shaking her head in feigned amazement. "If I'd known it was so important to you, Arnaud, I'd have reminded you the minute you took your hands off my throat."

"You stupid bitch!" Leli'a stalked across the room and shoved Tally in the chest with the flat of her hand. "You don't see? Nobody wants you here. Nobody. You are nothing to us."

With gritted teeth, Tally shot to her feet and planted the heel of her hand on her sister's forehead and gave a good shove. Leli'a staggered backwards. "You know, even for a pain in the ass, you're a real pain in the ass. Knock it off," Tally said in a deceptively cool voice.

"There's nothing here I want. Have at it. You all deserve each other. And frankly, I deserve bet—push me again, and I'll break those fingers," Tally snarled as Leli'a shoved her again.

"That's enough, Leli'a. We have more pressing problems than your petty jealousies. Go. Check something in the kitchen. I'll have to delay the buyers from inspecting the merchandise until I can figure out what the hell this one-eyed moron has done with my detonator."

With a pout, Leli'a headed for the door. "She's not so smart if she brought your enemy with her, is she?" she said, standing at the open door.

"It doesn't matter who brought whom. They'll both be dead

soon. You could be, too, so I'd advise you not to piss me off any more than you have already. Close the door behind you."

The door slammed.

Church inclined his head to a guard just inside the closed door. "Take this one to the waiting room." He indicated Tally, who was standing in front of her chair. "I'll call when I want her brought back."

Michael wasn't letting Tally out of his sight. God only knew what those goons out there would do to her. Even a blind man could tell her father didn't give a flying fuck about her. The trickle-down effect was clear. Just look at the way Bouchard had treated her.

"Thank you," Tally told Church. "I'm quite capable of removing myself from your august presen—damn it, let go!" She tried to shake the man's hand off her arm.

"I have business to conduct with the lieutenant. I'll call you if I need you."

"You need her now," Michael said flatly. "If she isn't alive, and where I can see her, I don't talk."

The door opened. Cruella was back.

"Henri left to pick up your guests," Leli'a told her father. "They'll be here in half an hour. Have they told you where it is yet?"

"Get out," her father snapped, rising to his feet. He crossed to her and jerked her by the arm until he could stare down into her face. "This has nothing to do with you. I wouldn't have this problem if you'd minded your own fucking business and stayed where I'd put you."

"I couldn't stay in school forever, Papa. I knew you'd want me here now that I—"

"That's something you and your fool sister have in common, Leli'a." He shoved her away, then slapped her with unconcerned brutality. Her head jerked back as she stared at him with wide, dark eyes. "You have the small brains of a woman. Women weren't designed to *think.* Women are for fucking. Nothing else."

He strode back behind his desk. "Do something useful. Remove the cover from the second drawer in the credenza behind you."

Despite her reddened cheek, the girl shot her father a triumphant look, but Michael saw a dose of fear in her dark eyes. She removed a folded drop cloth from a drawer, then shook out the white plastic sheet and dropped it to the carpet.

"In less than half an hour my buyers will be here," Church told Michael, indicating Leli'a should spread the cloth over the carpet as he was talking. "I can kill Tallulah now, or you can tell me where my detonation device is." He looked at Tally. "No hard feelings, darling. But I can't entertain if your entrails are splattered all over my carpet."

Michael heard Tally's swift inhalation beside him. He didn't look at her. Hell, he *couldn't* look at her. "You're one sick bastard, aren't you? Here's a news flash, asshole. I'm the one who has your detonation device. Kill her, and you might as well kill me while you're at it. As long as we're both alive and kicking, you have a small chance of getting what you want. Kill her, and that's history."

"Excuse me. Do I get a vote? Because right now swallowing agonizing cyanide, or being chewed alive by fire ants sounds much more appealing than standing here listening to you guys!"

"Let's not waste each other's time." Church leaned back in his chair and steepled his fingers over his mouth. "You've gone to great lengths to return. You wanted revenge. You didn't achieve it. If I'm not going to get back the pulse generator detonator, what's to prevent me from killing both of you now?"

"Not a thing," Michael said mildly. The explosion would happen in—he tilted his wrist and glanced down—an hour and six minutes. Whether Church had the pulse generator detonator or not. Whether Michael was dead or alive. It made no damn difference.

"I should have killed you the last time you interfered in my business."

"It wasn't for lack of trying," Michael pointed out.

"Still," Church continued without pause, "I am curious as to why you brought Tallulah with you."

"You'll have to ask Bouchard."

Church glanced at his second in command. "So, you *did* invite her."

"No, Papa, *I* did," Leli'a said defiantly. "I wanted to meet her. I wanted to see if she was special. Or prettier than me."

"And to get rid of her once and for all," Michael said flatly.

"You stupid fucking bitch. All this trouble, and for what? Nothing! Get over here!" Church waved the gun at her, motioning her forward, and the girl moved closer. The white plastic sheet rustled underfoot.

Without flinching, Church aimed and fired, shooting his younger daughter between the eyes.

There was an abrupt, shocked silence, then Tally screamed as Leli'a crumpled onto the plastic sheet she'd used to protect her father's carpet.

"Oh, my God. Oh, my God." Tally pressed the back of her hand over her mouth as she stared with horror at the girl's body on the floor. A puddle of blood formed under Leli'a's head as she stared sightlessly at the ceiling.

Tally spun around to stare at Church. Blue eyes glazed with horror, white-faced, she struggled to get free of the men holding her. "You monster! You sick, despicable . . . monster!"

The phone on the desk rang. Ignoring Tally, Church picked up the receiver. "What is it? Are they here?" He listened intently, his attention now fixed on Michael. The color drained from his fleshy face. "Is that so? And . . . ? I see. How long? I will take care of it on this end." He paused. "Good. Send them in. Yes. That would be advisable."

Church put the phone down just as the door opened and four men stepped inside.

Michael glanced at them from the corner of his eye: low on the evolutionary scale, big and armed to the teeth.

Church's pissed-off voice demanded attention. "I've been

informed by my people that you have set a detonation device on my merchandise."

"Yeah. Imagine that."

"The device is apparently set to go off in little over an hour. My guests will be here in minutes. You will tell my associates exactly how to disable the timing device."

"If I could, which I can't, I wouldn't. Guess it doesn't matter if you have the pulse generator's detonator after all. It's all going to go kaplooie, anyway."

"Wrong, Lieutenant. You *will* disable your bomb, and return my detonator. Show him why, if you please, Mr. Griffith. Not the hands. We might need them later." He glanced up at the men behind Tally. "Keep her from interfering."

Two of them held her arms. She struggled valiantly in their hold. Even managed to bite one of them on the back of the hand. But they managed to contain her, and hold her away from the main bout.

Two burly apes grabbed Michael's arms, yanking him out of the chair. Before he was fully on his feet, Mr. Griffith punched him in the stomach. Michael's breath left him in a whoosh, and he doubled over like he was supposed to. He brought his head up sharply, butting the man hard in the chin. Griffith's teeth snapped like castanets. He drew back his fist and punched Michael in the solar plexus.

Michael twisted one arm free, and returned the body blow. The guard tried to regain his hold, but he was no match for Michael, who shook the other guy off and danced before the three of them, light on his feet, and a hell of a lot more motivated.

Griffith's foot came up to kick him in the stomach. Michael sidestepped, grabbed the guy's foot with both hands, and twisted. His own momentum flung Griffith over onto his back. Swearing and cursing, he tried to get up but slipped in the pool of Leli'a's blood on the plastic sheet. He went down hard.

A round of bullets shattered the front of Church's desk,

missing Michael's leg by inches. Slivers of fine wood flew like confetti. He heard Tally scream, and Church curse. "Stop shooting, you fools. I want him alive!"

A fist came in on Michael's blind side, but he blocked it with his forearm just in time. The impact made his arm go numb for a second. Someone came at him from the right. He lifted his leg and kicked the guy in the face. The airborne guard flew over Church's desk, scattering papers in his wake. Another one came at him. Michael swung a second too late. The guy used the butt of his CAR to slam a stunning blow on Michael's check. For a second, both eyes were blind. But that didn't stop him. He grabbed the weapon and dragged the guy closer, then flipped him over on his back and used the same method to coldcock him.

"Bloody hell! Hold him. Hold him," Church yelled. His men were running around trying to figure out how to reach him. Michael stood with his back to the desk, surrounded by three bodies and two chairs. The men holding Tally dragged her out of the line of fire. He got a brief glimpse of her terrified blue eyes just as a man flew across the back of a chair, directly at Michael's middle.

They went down together. Another guy tried to kick Michael in the head. He missed by a hair breadth. Michael shoved his arm into the prone guy's throat, and used his foot at an angle, aiming for the kneecap of the one standing over him. He kicked, and heard the crunch as the knee dislocated. The guy went down screaming.

The guy on the floor wasn't breathing too well. Michael pressed down harder. The guy's eyes bugged, and he clawed Michael's forearm, trying to break free. Michael leaned on him. His eyes rolled, and he was out.

Griffith was back. This time with reinforcements. It took four of them to hold him, but this time Michael wasn't getting free. Griffith had hands as big as hams. And he knew how to use them. Left fist, right fist. High. Low. Left. Right. The man was methodical and thorough.

Michael stood up as long as he could, then gave it up and dropped, curling into a ball to protect his guts from the kicks to the ribs that had him so stove up he couldn't breathe. And when he thought he just might die—it stopped.

He dimly heard Tally sobbing, begging her father to make them stop. Michael could've told her nothing short of death was going to satisfy her old man. "Barely alive" would do the trick as far as Church was concerned.

As long as Michael could manage to speak, and his hands were capable of disarming the detonator, the rest was up for grabs. They might've left his hands uninjured, but everything else hurt like hell. Guaranteed they'd cracked a couple more ribs. He pulled in a hesitant breath and winced as he exhaled.

Still on the floor, breathing ragged and shallow, he tilted his wrist. "One hour, thirty-one seconds. And counting."

"Perhaps we used the wrong incentive." Church's voice was just a little tighter. "Let us see how you react when you have to watch that same treatment applied to Tallulah."

Tally wrenched herself away from the man holding her and planted her hands flat on her father's desk. She leaned in. "Do you think he gives a damn what you do to me? He doesn't. He used me to get to you."

Church backhanded her.

Michael rose to a half-crouch and used his body weight and adrenaline rush to shove the desk. Church screamed as the heavy desk pinned him to the window like a butterfly on a pin. "Get him. Get him!"

Michael levered himself the rest of the way up with the help of the overturned chair, and grabbed a fallen CAR and held the men off. He could tell by its weight that the weapon was empty; but they didn't know that. Everyone froze.

"I hope," Tally said flatly, cradling her cheek, "that this is the part where you tell me you aren't really my biological father." Bouchard had come up behind her and had his arm around her throat. Off-balance, she held on to his arm to stay upright. Her red nails were dug deep into the man's skin.

Church tried in vain to shove the desk away from his thighs. "You, get over here and help me. If either of them moves, shoot to disable."

Everyone looked from Michael to Church. Michael smiled. "Try me." He pointed the CAR at the closest man.

The guy moved forward, calling his bluff. Shit.

It made no damn difference, because Griffith hit him on his blind side. Michael fell to one knee, blood running into his good eye. The room spun. Griffith hauled him to his feet, and he stood there, swaying more than necessary, then let his knees buckle. Griffith let him drop back to the floor. Michael fought to stay conscious.

Two guys stepped forward and started pulling the desk away from their boss.

"Take her to the caves. Do not," Church said harshly, "kill her. Do you understand me, Bouchard? Do *not* kill her. I want the Lieutenant here to know she is alive and in danger. It will keep him motivated to retrieve the pulse generator device and tell us how to turn off the detonator. We'll see how strong his resistance is when his lover is at ground zero. In the meantime, I want the munitions cleared. Instruct the men, *all* of them, to clear the cave immediately. See to it, Mr. Griffith."

"The tide isn't high enough yet," Griffith frowned. "Tomorrow morn—"

"We don't *have* until tomorrow." Church turned to Tally with fury. "If your lieutenant doesn't restore the pulse generator detonator to me *and* disable the bomb he's planted on my merchandise, then *you* will drown—if you don't die first in the explosion."

Tally turned to look at Michael. Her face was dead white, and a frantic pulse beat at the base of her throat. "Whatever happens, make him pay for this, Michael. Make him pay."

Their eyes met in perfect accord before her escort jerked her toward the door.

"Get him on his feet. Have Palei and Hanu escort our guest wherever he needs to go so he can do his job," Church instructed. "Griffith, gather your men, start clearing that upper cave. And as for you," he said to Bouchard, "you take her, and tie her securely in the lower cave.

"The clock is ticking, Lieutenant," Church said, turning to look down at Michael. He was smiling, and his eyes were as black and flat as a shark's. "Tallulah's life hinges on you doing both your jobs within the next hour."

"Get out." Arnaud grabbed Tally's arm and dragged her across the seat of the golf cart. The guard got out, spread his feet, then hefted his weapon, training it on them.

Tally dug her heels in the sand and leaned back against the cart. "Go to hell."

Bouchard pulled her to him, picked her up, and tossed her over his shoulder. She used her bound hands to pummel his back.

He grunted as he scrambled over the lava rocks with her dead weight. "I should've killed you when I had the chance."

"Yeah, well, now you have a baby-sitter to make sure you don't," Tally reminded him. The guard remained on the highest point of the rocks, watching them. The rifle trained on Arnaud's back. Which she just happened to be shielding.

Blood rushed to her head, making her ears ring as she hung over his shoulder like a bat. Arnaud clambered across the rough rocks and scrambled down. Where once there was beach, it was now thigh-deep water.

He grabbed her by the waistband of her shorts and tilted her upright. She dropped into the water feet first. It came well above her waist, stinging her cuts, and soothing the bruises.

"In there." He shoved her between her shoulder blades to walk ahead of him.

"In there" was an extremely narrow slit in the cliff face. Caves had a tendency to be dark. And dark was about the last straw she needed right now. She halted mid-stride. "No way," Tally said flatly. This was her absolute *worst* nightmare coming to life in living color.

"Walk in under your own steam," Arnaud snapped, "or I'll knock you out."

Oh, God. Neither was an option. She'd rather have been gutted like a fish in her father's living room than die in a dark place all alone. Not only would she have to go into a cold, dark place, but Michael couldn't tell Trevor where the detonator was, because he'd tossed the damn thing overboard. And he couldn't disable the bomb, because . . . oh, God. Oh. God. Oh, God. No one would ever come to find her. She'd die here. In the dark. Alone.

Her breath came hard and fast. Her heart raced, icy sweat sheeted her body. The tide relentlessly surged against her, pushing her closer and closer to that opening. "Arnaud, please . . ."

"Get inside." Arnaud punched her on the shoulder. "Now."

"There's no point to this, Arnaud. You heard Michael. Nothing you, or Trevor, can do will make him give you back that detonator."

"Trevor told me not to kill you. He didn't say I couldn't make you wish I had. Move!"

Her breath hitched as her heart started hammering painfully. *Not now. Damn it, this is no time to have a panic attack.* "I c-a-n't," Tally gasped, trying unsuccessfully to suck in air. *Too late.* The sunny day hazed as her vision blurred. "I won't . . . ki-ll me no-w. Because as . . . as s-ure as God made l-little green apples, there's no w-way I'll go in th-there."

Fatalistically, Tally observed Arnaud lift his arm. Then, in a blur of motion, he brought the butt of his pistol down on her temple.

Her world went dark.

Chapter Twenty

Tally's gaze fixed on the sliver, the *tiny* sliver, of buttery sunlight slicing through the solid rock wall in front of her. Her heart pounded so hard, it hurt, and she was breathing as if she'd just run a one-minute mile. And damn it, she couldn't stop shivering.

She concentrated on taking deep, even breaths. If she hyperventilated, she'd pass out.

OhGodohGodohGod. Arnaud, the bastard, son of a bitch, turd, had knocked her out. She hoped he'd ended up with a hernia carrying her inside. By the time she'd come to, he'd tied her bound wrists to a metal handrail in the wall and left her sitting on the carved stone steps at the back of the cave.

The step under her bottom was icy cold, and slimy with moss. The tide sent the wavelets lapping on a steady rise up the rough lava walls. The water she and the rat-faced bastard waded through had hit her mid-chest. It was deeper now.

Breathe in. Deep. Fill lungs. Hold.

Breathe out. Slowly. Empty lungs. Hold.

Tally bent her head and tried to gnaw through the ropes around her wrists. The hemp was wet, and tasted like . . . rope, and didn't give an inch. The rough fibers cut her tender lips and sore mouth. Panic leaked into her breathing. She took a couple of deep, quivering breaths, then bent her head and got serious.

If she didn't hurry, the water would keep rising. Her heart stuttered, then took up a frantic rhythm.

She suddenly knew exactly what *Michael's* phobia felt

like. As if with the dark she didn't have enough to contend with, now the very real fear of drowning reared its ugly head.

"Reality check," her voice echoed creepily across the water. "Even if Michael is capable of getting to me in time, he's not going to be able to swim in here to rescue me." His fear of the water was going to keep him out.

If there was a rescue to be made, she was going to have to do it herself. Dark or no dark. Deep, black water or not. If she wanted to see Michael again, she was going to have to figure out a way, and a *quick* way, to get the hell out of Dodge.

The stairs behind her must go somewhere. Hopefully somewhere sunny and bright. And dry. And as soon as she could chew her way through this rope she'd be up there in a flash.

But first things firs—

BOOM!

"You lying, fucking bastard! It was set to go off in an hour!" Church screamed, racing to the window to look out at the source of the noise.

"That wasn't the main explosion," Michael informed him calmly. "The door to your storeroom is now closed. My insurance. You won't be getting any of your crap out of there before the big boom goes off in"—he checked his watch—"fifty-seven minutes."

Tally's heart slammed into her throat. Ears ringing, heart pounding, she froze, her mouth on her wrists. Michael's bomb had gone off early. The horrific noise continued to ricochet off the walls for a few minutes after the blast, and almost, *almost* blocked the sound of crashing and bouncing rocks.

She looked around frantically, waiting for the sky to fall. Waiting for her life to flash before her eyes. Waiting to be dead.

The slice of filtered sunlight was extinguished.

Worse than death.

Dark.

. . .

Climbing over the rocks separating the cove from the beach, Arnaud's head jerked up at the sudden, deafening explosion. He spun around to look behind him, almost tumbling head over heels back the way he'd come.

"No! No! NO!" Bouchard screamed, clambering up toward the guard, who was still waiting for him, weapon drawn.

Huge boulders and rocks bounced down from the top of the cliff. They struck the face, breaking more rocks free. They landed with a thunderous impact that kept the ground shaking for a full minute. Arnaud and Church's henchman scrabbled for balance as the ground shook, and the rocks where they stood trembled under the impact.

As the dust settled, Arnaud's heart sank, and his fury rose.

The rock fall had effectively sealed the opening to the upper cave. No one was getting anything out of there now. Not for days. Maybe weeks.

Not enough time.

When the next explosion hit, it would impact on the munitions and weapons inside the cave, and the entire side of the cliff was going to end up in Bora-Bora. And, Bouchard thought furiously, take him, not thirty feet away, with it.

He spun around and rushed to climb down the other side as fast as his legs and arms could go.

He ran past the uselessly slow golf cart, ignored the terrified man behind him, and raced down the beach to safety.

It took Tally several minutes to realize the cave had stopped shaking. It was her body that still trembled. Bathed in icy sweat, her breathing came so fast, she wondered vaguely if she would pass out.

Daddy? Daddy. Let me out. Oh, please, let me out.

Algiers. A broiling hot summer day. The day before her fifth birthday. Bev had found Trevor in a seedy hotel on the waterfront. Tally was sticky and hot and thirsty after the long flight, and the smells and the noises of the city scared her. But she was happy to see her daddy. He gave her a noogie on top of her head, which hurt a little. Then he forgot about her. He was sorta happy to see her mom, though. He and Mommy kissed right there in the middle of the International Hotel lobby. Tally went to sit on a chair by the door. She made herself as small as possible, but kept watch on their suitcases. She knew people could steal other people's bags, and she was a big girl, and had to be responsible. After a while, they all went up to Daddy's room. Tally eyed the big bed longingly. She was so sleepy.

Daddy picked her up, and Tally laid her head on his nice, strong chest and closed her eyes. Now that she was with her daddy, everything would be happy again. He smelled good, spicy and sweet, and she breathed deeply. Content to be in his strong arms.

"She'll be okay in here for a while," Daddy said, shoving her into the closet. The door slammed.

She sat there on her bottom in the hot, stuffy, pitch-darkness. She was thirsty, and she hadn't been to the bathroom yet. "Daddy? Let me oooout . . ."

Over the sound of her own sobs, Tally heard every breath, and moan, and the creak of the bed as her parents had sex. Her hands hurt from banging on the door. She kicked with her feet, until her legs ached. Finally, cried out, she lay on the floor in a little ball with her face pressed to the crack at the bottom of the door. Mommy was going to be mad. Tally had wet her pants because she couldn't wait anymore.

Tally listened to the sounds of the shower running, and the toilet flushing. She called for her mommy. Mommy said, "Shhh, go to sleep," like she was really mad. Tally listened as they dressed for dinner, and listened to the scary quiet when they were gone. She heard them come back later, and the bed creaked some more. But they didn't let her out.

Tally huddled in the back of that pitch-dark closet all night, and all the next day. Until Daddy eventually packed his suitcase, and left. Her sobbing mother loaded her on a plane to go back home. Tally didn't mind going home. She didn't remember she'd been in the closet.

Until now.

"Holy shit," Tally said out loud, stunned by the suddenly crystal-clear memory. "Who knew getting beaten up, kidnapped, shot at, chased, tied in a cave, and damned-near drowned would shake *that* free?" These last few days had apparently served her better than a future of expensive therapy.

But if she was going to enjoy a neuroses-free life, she had better figure out a way to get free. Now.

"What's the collateral damage?" Church demanded into the phone, clearly talking to one of the men he'd sent to clear the weapons and ammunition crates.

With a worm's-eye view, Michael squinted through his swollen good eye as the man's feet moved from one end of the plastic sheet to the other. The men stepped over Leli'a's body as if it were no more than a piece of furniture.

"How long to break through?" Church paused. "Not acceptable. You have less than an hour. Take as many men as you need. But get the job done."

Jesus. Was Tally all right? Michael wondered, eyes closed. "Unconscious" might buy a little time to pull himself together. He'd survived worse and lived to tell the tale. This was different only in that Tally was the stake in this poker game. He hadn't been thinking about Tally when he'd set those explosives.

Now he was.

Church had ordered Bouchard not to kill her—which meant squat to a scum-sucking dickwad. Bouchard's plans included Church's early demise. What did he care about Church's orders, or Tally?

She'd be safe in the lower cave from the first explosion. The second explosion would wipe out everything on the north side of the island. In less than an hour.

Michael heard the faint hum of a golf cart coming up the shell path, and the murmur of voices. Buyers, or brute force?

The phone rang. Church listened, then threw the cell phone down on his desk with a clatter. "Is he awake?"

One of Church's men tapped Michael none too gently on his back. Michael grunted. No act. It fucking *hurt.*

"Get rid of her body. Now," Church instructed. "Do *not* release him," he told the two men holding Michael down.

He leaned over and slapped Michael's cheek, while in the background, plastic rustled as they carried Leli'a's body out. "Naptime is bloody well over, Lieutenant."

Michael opened his eye and stared up into the face of his enemy. "How does it feel to know you're about to lose everything you thought you had in the palm of your hand?"

"You'll eventually tell me what I want to know." Church nodded to the guy holding Michael's arms. With a sharp, upward wrench, the guy made Michael's shoulders scream with pain.

"You might want to imagine the water over Tallulah's head about now. Do you have the balls to out-bluff me, I wonder?" Church asked as he knelt down, then paused to run a handkerchief over his sweating face and bald head.

You're going to be sweating a hell of a lot more before I'm done with you, Michael thought, flexing his fingers behind his back. All in working order.

"Which will get her first?" Church mused, using a metal knuckle-duster to punch Michael in his cracked ribs. The room darkened around the edges. "Another explosion," Church continued conversationally, punching him again, "or will you let her drown?"

The image made Michael suck in air. Jesus. His worst nightmare happening to Tally. He couldn't go there. And he refused to let Church know he'd scored a hit. He shrugged. The casual gesture hurt like hell.

"Kill either of us and you'll be greeting your buyers with more than egg on your face, old man." He was fortunate the goons hadn't broken his legs. They'd certainly cracked a few more ribs when they'd used him as a punching bag. Michael breathed through the pain.

He'd had several broken ribs the second day into SEAL Hell Week, and he hadn't rung the bell then, either. All he'd had to do was concentrate on the end zone.

A quick memory of Hugo's face as he flew over that railing . . .

Michael was up, and on his feet, leaving the two men who had been holding him sprawled on the floor. He took the one closest to him out with a hard chop to his throat, and commandeered the guy's CAR-15 as he went down.

Church screamed bloody murder, calling in reinforcements. He ran around to the other side of his monster desk, jerking open draws and tossing papers as he desperately searched for another weapon. "Shoot him. Shoot him!"

Michael swept the heavy brass lamp off the edge of Church's fancy desk and held it in his left hand, the CAR in his right. He swung the lamp. It connected on the side of the second man's temple with the satisfying splat of a watermelon breaking.

Michael shot the second guy just as the door burst open. Half a dozen men poured into the room. They tried to surround him. Despite his injuries, Michael was as fast as he was determined. He got off a quick round, downing a couple of men on his blind side without really looking.

He did a high kick, landing his foot high in one goon's chest, and sent him stumbling over one of his friends on the floor. Michael swung his leg again, same guy, same place. This time, the guy went flying backwards, hit a chair, and lay still. Michael tossed aside the lamp and grabbed an M-16 rifle on the floor. Cool. Weapon in each hand, he suffered no pain, and felt like Rambo.

Hoo-yah!

A volley of shots tore up the mahogany bookcases across the room, scattering bits of paper and gold-embossed leather. He returned fire even as he spun on his heel, and vaulted over Church's pretty, burled-wood desk. Before Church had fumbled the Glock he'd found into his hand, Michael stood behind him, his arm around Church's throat.

A few morons tried to get off a few shots. The window behind his head shattered, and the rod holding the heavy velvet drapes crashed to the floor.

"Call 'em off. They're starting to annoy me."

"Don't shoot, you imbeciles." Church held up his hands. "Don't shoot."

"I'm going to kill you," Michael said against Church's ear. "And believe me, I'm going to enjoy every slow second before you breathe your last." He glanced up at the men scattered about the room. "I'll get to the rest of you later."

Michael wrapped his arm more tightly around Church's neck and pulled him off his feet. The older man was several inches shorter, and fifty pounds heavier. He tightened his elbow around the man's neck. Church grunted and tried to stand taller. He twisted, trying to reach Michael, but Michael didn't budge.

"I've wanted to do this since I met you, Church. For what you did to my partner, for what you did to me—"

"You killed your own partner by pushing him overboard. And it was your own fault that you got in the way of the bullet meant for him."

"But now that I've come to know you better," Michael continued, unfazed by Church's rationale and rhetoric, "I have an even more valid reason for wanting you dead."

"What's that?"

"Tally."

Michael jerked his forearm up with a twist, heard the satisfying crunch of snapped vertebrae, felt the sonofabitch go limp, then stood back and let Church's lifeless body fall across the scattered papers on his desk.

Shit. *Too* painless. *Too* quick. Too rushed. He'd anticipated a bigger rush. More satisfaction. He hadn't known how much more important choosing life would become. Footsteps . . .

Michael glanced up.

The buyers stood at the door, weapons drawn, taking in the carnage.

Michael's frown turned to a laugh. "Jesus. Am I hallucinating?" he asked as the two men strode into Church's office, bypassing the bodies on the floor.

"Two of them aren't on the plastic," one of them observed, British accent wry. "You've gotten sloppy, Wright."

"Hunt St. John, you son of a bitch. What the *hell* are you guys doing here?"

"Never knew a SEAL to let well enough alone." Dare poked at one of the men sprawled on the floor. "This one's still breathing. May I?" Without waiting for permission, he tapped the guy, then looked up, his scarred face beatific. "T-FLAC to the rescue, my man—"

"The hell you say." Michael pushed Church's body off the desk. He needed the support for a moment. "Since when does T-FLAC tread on Uncle Sam's toes?"

"Since we offered to come in, politely as you please, and close your Mr. Church down." Huntington glanced at Darius. "Didn't his brothers say he was ass-deep in this?"

"Yeah."

"There you go." Hunt hitched the knee of his navy slacks, and sat on the arm of a chair. "We have a message for you from said brothers: 'Come home.' "

Michael felt a rush of gratitude and relief. Damn it, even separated by thousands of miles, the Musketeers came through for one another. He'd underestimated his family. Thank God.

"Can you two yahoos do cleanup detail? I have a little errand to run."

Dare began stripping weapons from the bodies and gently sliding them across the floor to make a pile. "Don't know why we should have to clean up your garbage, Wright. You had all the fun."

Michael grinned, despite the pain in his split lip, and strode to the door, making a concerted effort not to limp. "I presume you have backup?"

Dare admired a rifle he picked up. "This is pretty. I'm keeping this one." He looked at Michael. "We kinda like backup. Unlike some branches of the military."

"This op was strictly unofficial. I'm not a SEAL anymore," Michael pointed out, reaching for the door handle.

"Should have fully realized your resources, old chap," Hunt said quietly, getting up to assist Dare.

"Hoo-yah," Michael said, grateful for the reminder. He'd used some of T-FLAC's resources, but none of their manpower. His brothers and brother-in-law had come through, anyway.

"I have a lady to rescue. Here"—he tossed Church's cell phone to Hunt—"stay turned. I might need to fully realize my resources."

They'd brought the *Nemesis* back into the marina. Michael made a quick detour. He couldn't afford the time, but he had to be prepared for anything when he got to the cave.

The second he boarded, he knew he wasn't alone. "Shit. I don't have time for this." He strode to an aft locker aft, opened it, and removed a Sig Sauer from a hidden compartment in back.

Armed, he opened the door to the wheelhouse, then shoved aside the door to the salon. With a howl, Lucky darted off the counter in the galley.

Arnaud Bouchard rose as Michael stepped into the salon.

"You're like a fucking cat, Lieutenant. Unfortunately for you, you just used up your last life."

Standoff. Both men were armed, determined, and dangerous.

Michael sighed. "Would you mind stepping to your left a few feet before we start spraying bullets around?"

"What?" Bouchard automatically stepped aside. "Why?"

"Because my sister did that sketch behind you, and I don't want to ruin it—thanks." Michael shot him between his startled eyes.

Not exactly satisfying, Michael thought as the man dropped to the carpet. But expedient.

Michael stood on the rocks and stared down at the water in the cove. He'd run the length of the beach as if death were on his ass. Knowing what he would find, and yet hoping—

High tide was in. The small crescent of beach was completely covered. Given another hour or so, and judging by the watermark on the cliff face, the ocean was going to rise another three feet—by which time the slitted entrance into the lower cave would be under water. And possibly blocked by falling debris from above.

He trained his eye slowly upward. The mouth of the upper cave was completely blocked. It would take a cleanup crew a month and a week to clear the rubble. He wasn't a demolition expert for nothing.

He'd done his job well. Too well.

Michael quartered off the cliff face, looking for a way in from the top. There wasn't one.

Right now, Tally was inside, in the dark, terrified out of her mind, probably singing at the top of her lungs.

There was only one way to save her: and that was for him to get in that swirling water.

He'd have to go in. He'd have to go under.

His mouth went dry, and sweat chilled his sun-warmed skin. His heart pounded so hard, he thought he'd pass out. He blinked back the black snow filling his vision.

It'd taken him a fucking *year* to have the guts to get in up to his waist. A year. One stinking, cowardly inch at a time. His ears rang with the force of his blood pounding through his veins.

Michael looked up at the blue sky. A sky the same brilliant color as Tally's eyes. *Ah, Jesus,* he thought, stunned by the lightbulb moment. *I love her, and my life will be shit if she's not in it with me.*

Hugo . . . help me, man, I've gotta save my girl. "No guts, no glory—right, Bud? Hoo-yah!"

He jumped.

The icy water closed over his head and it felt as though his heart stopped.

Michael saw Hugo's face as the props sucked him in—the water churned as the propellers picked up speed in slow-mo. White. Then frothy red. Hugoooo—

No! *Tally.*

Michael shook his head to clear the vision, his heart thudding in his ears as he broke the surface. He bit down on the fear—no time, no time, no time—and started swimming in strong strokes toward the opening. Two feet remained at the top. Twenty-four inches which were less than a handspan at their widest point.

The current pushed and pulled him, and he braced his feet on the rock. He filled his lungs. Emptied them, and filled them again. Then dived beneath the water and pulled himself along the canyon of the walls with both hands. Fallen rocks had piled at the base of the opening in an untidy heap. There was no getting to Tally without moving them. And moving them *fast.*

He spent precious minutes rolling the obstructions aside, shooting to the surface for air, and diving back down again.

All the while a metronome ticked in his head.

Tally. Tally. Tally.

Finally, he'd cleared enough of the debris to allow his body to pass to the inside of the cave. He surfaced once more, dragged in a lungful of air, then dived and immediately started pulling himself between the narrow walls of the fissure, scraping his hands on the jagged surface as he kicked his feet. It was a tight, claustry fit.

The moment he cleared the entrance, he broke the surface of the water and dragged in lungfuls of air, then started swimming toward the back of the cave. The ceiling, now only three feet above his head, seemed to press down on him. His chest was tight, his throat ached. But he was in the water and functioning, by God.

The air was charcoal gray, not quite pitch-black, but close enough, thick and stuffy, and damp with spray. Water slapped loudly against the walls, sucking and pulling as the tide rose.

Michael strained to hear Tally.

Silence.

No. No! NOOOOOOOO!

Chapter Twenty-one

With water lapping at her toes, Tally finally freed herself from the ropes. Heart in her throat, she groped her way up the spiral stone stairs. "Sun . . . shine on my shoulders maakes me haaapy—"

The monster of her childhood lurked in the surrounding watery darkness, ready to pounce the moment her self-discipline faltered. "Sunshine on the water looks sooo lovely—" *Ha! Not!*

Her eyes had adjusted a little to the dark; it wasn't quite as impenetrable as she'd first thought. And the higher she climbed, the lighter it became. She took the stairs two at a time, her hands braced on the damp walls as she ran.

She arrived at the top slightly breathless to find herself in a considerably larger "room" than the water-filled cave below. Two things made it preferable: It was slightly lighter. And it was dry.

Tally glanced around. So *this* was what all the fuss had been about. Wooden crates on top of crates on top of more crates. By the stenciled markings on the containers, it was clear what was inside. Enough munitions to make the IRA look like a Boy Scout troop.

She cocked her head. Under the swish of sloshing water was a faint noise—more a feeling than a sound. Her imagination, because she knew there was a clock counting down the minutes in here *somewhere?*

She zipped down the center aisle between the boxes, heading for the pinpricks of light indicating the way out. She imagined the water creeping up the stairs trying to find her. She wasn't hanging around. The rubble at the far end of the cavern shouted freedom, and by God she was getting out of here.

Come hell or high water.

Directly ahead, Tally saw the source of the earlier crashing and bashing. The entrance to the cave had been effectively sealed by the explosion. Stray shafts of sunlight speared through the rocks and boulders. The rocks and boulders that blocked her way out.

And somewhere in this lava rock warehouse was Michael's bomb, ticking away.

"Oh, I *don't* think so." Tally slid between the rest of the towering crates until she reached the debris blocking the mouth of the cave. She sized up the situation as she got closer. Beyond this barrier lay the ocean. It was high tide. She was probably about twenty or so feet above the water-filled cove. Feasibly, if she could clear a big enough space, she could wiggle through, jump down into the water, and not break her neck.

Or . . . she could stay right where she was, kiss her butt good-bye, and pray.

Easiest decision of her life.

Tally started grabbing rocks as fast as her body could move. Grab. Toss. Grab. *Wrestle.* Toss. Drenched with sea-water and sweat, she got a good grip on another huge chunk of broken cliff. At the rate she was going, she'd have this pile cleared by her 102nd birthday.

If her situation hadn't been so dire, she'd bewail her ruined manicure. She started to laugh a little hysterically. God, this was bizarre. Here she was—she hefted a smaller rock and tossed it behind her—battered, beaten up, bruised, bleeding, and in imminent danger of dying, and she noticed she'd broken a couple of nails and her polish was chipped. "You've lost it, Tallulah."

She put her hands around a head-size boulder, one of the smaller loose chunks, and put her back into it. "Ninety-nine boulders and rocks on the wall, ninety-nine boulders and rocks. You take one down, pass it around—"

"Jesus, woman. You're hell on a man's ego, you know that?"

Tally stopped singing in mid-note and turned as Michael came into view at the other end of the corridor of boxes.

Their eyes met, and they stood drinking in the sight of each other. His wet hair was slicked back off his face, and his jeans, dark and heavy with water, clung to his strongly muscled legs. Tally had never been so happy to see anyone in her life.

They looked like twins, their faces bearing black-and-blue badges of honor.

Tally's heart almost burst with love for him. Michael had come for her. He'd risked everything to come for her. He'd faced his fears, fought her father, risked life and limb, and shown up just in the nick of time.

Rescuing herself was ingrained, but, damn, it was a relief to see his battered face. They'd both survived. So far.

She tossed the rock she held into the pile behind her and grinned. "You're late, Double Oh."

"But not *too.*" Michael did a visual scan of her from top to toe and back again. That look wound around her body and heart like a warm caress.

"Forget trying to clear that mess. It'll take too long." He held out his hand. "Come back this way." Through the maze of boxes and back to the top of the stairs.

"Tell me you're going to turn off your bomb to give us more time."

"No way to turn it off. Move it, time's a wasting."

"How much time?" Tally wended her way between the boxes. Fast. The ticking in her head seemed much louder.

He hesitated. "Fourteen minutes."

Tally sped up, the imaginary ticking sounding like Big Ben. "How are we going to get out?"

"Swim."

Tally hesitated. "Right." The water downstairs was well

over her head. She was a fairly strong swimmer, under normal circumstances, which these weren't. But a diver, she wasn't. She met his eye as she got closer.

Despite his fear of water, he'd come. He'd battled his dragon to find her. She wouldn't let him—or herself—drown now, by giving in to her own fears.

Michael snagged her hand and tugged. When she was flush against him, he lifted her face with a hand scraped raw. "Trust me."

"Implicitly." That was the one damn thing she *was* sure of. Despite it all, she *did* trust him.

He brushed her mouth with his. "Let's do it."

They stopped at the waterline, which was now more than halfway down the stairs. Michael shone a mini Maglite down across the black water. Tally sucked in a sharp breath. It looked like miles to the other side. The darkness pressed in on her like a suffocating blanket, and her heart did a little flip of panic in her chest. She drew in a shaky gulp of air. "You know I'm terrified, right?"

Michael tucked a strand of wet hair behind her ear, his fingers warm and steady. "You're the bravest person I know, Tally. I've never seen anyone face fear with as much courage as you have." He stroked her shoulder—a light, reassuring brush of his hand, as if he couldn't bear *not* to touch her. "You're going to be fine. *We're* going to be fine. Work with me here, honey."

She swallowed hard and forced a smile. Getting into the deep water would be harder for Michael than fearing the dark would be for her. But he was going to do it without hesitation. Could she do any less? "Right," she said briskly.

He showed her how to use the small rebreather. "You'll only need it for a few minutes to get through the fissure. Okay? Don't panic. I'll be right here with you. Breathe easy. There you go. Ready?"

No. "As I'll ever be." Tally's hand was engulfed by his. She followed him into the water. Her skin crept at the thought of swimming across the enormous, *deep* expanse in the dark.

The water closed over her shoulders, and she treaded water. "Michael?" she said, her voice sounding as freaked out as she felt.

"Right here," he said, calmly drawing her closer to him until their legs brushed under the water. "If you can do it, sweetheart, so can I. Together. Let's go." He released her hand.

Now or never. Tally struck out. Under. Over. Under. Over. No style. No finesse. All she cared about was speed.

Kick. Kick. Over. Under.

She sensed Michael keeping pace with her.

The rock ceiling snagged her hair. *Oh. God. Oh. God.* The water was rising. They switched to breaststroke and kept going.

Tick. Tick. Tick.

It took years to reach the far wall. Breathing hard, she slapped a palm against the rough rock, and let her legs drop. Quivering, out of breath, terrified, she rested her head against the cold surface. She felt the thud and pulse of her heart behind her eyeballs.

Michael came up behind her, wrapped an arm about her waist, and braced her weight in the buoyancy of the water. He pressed his large hand against her diaphragm. "Take a breath and relax. We'll be through any minute."

She inserted the breathing device in her mouth, and turned so he could check it. He gave her the thumbs-up.

"I'll be right behind you. If you have any problems, signal." He smiled, and touched her cheek. "Let's make this snappy, honey. We've got things to do, and places to go. Ready?"

She nodded.

He tugged on her hand. "Let's do it." And he pulled her deep under the water. A gentle shove on her butt, and she was maneuvering between the narrow walls of the exit.

Instinct took over. The only thought in her mind was to get the hell out of there. And still, it was the longest "minute" of Tally's life. With Michael's guiding hand on her behind, she stayed calm enough to push herself through the water. The walls were too close together to swim. The murky water lightened, and Tally pulled harder, heading toward the sun-bleached water ahead.

She popped free of the rocks, kicked toward the surface, and emerged gasping to drag in huge lungfuls of salty air. It smelled sweet. The sunlight on her face was brilliant and was so welcome, Tally almost cried with gratitude.

"Don't stop now!" Michael yelled as his head broke the surface beside her. He struck out for the rim of rocks barely visible above the waterline to their left. Swimming side by side, Tally knew he was pacing himself to her speed.

Tick. Tick. Tick.

He finally streaked ahead, and reached the outcrop before she did, so he was already climbing out of the water as she arrived. He hauled her up and out, keeping hold of her hand to help her across and down the other side of the rocks with barely a pause.

The clock in Tally's head ticked louder. Faster.

Hand in hand, they raced up the beach toward the protection of the trees.

"Go. Go. Go," Michael yelled, running hard and fast through the soft sand, pulling Tally with him. Breathless, she clung to his hand and damn near flew across the beach. Sand clung to their wet feet and ankles like cement shoes.

BOOM!

The first explosion shook the ground. The percussion reverberated across the sand and water in waves. Even though she was expecting it, Tally shrieked and instinctively tried to look over her shoulder. Michael kept her running.

Just the appetizer.

Fifteen seconds to the big one.

His heels bit into the soft, dry sand, his long legs eating up the distance to safety. Tally's feet barely made contact as sand rooster-tailed in their wake.

A barrage of debris followed them. Rocks, boulders, sand, and vegetation rained down in a dangerous hail.

Fourteen.

Michael played dodge 'em, dragging Tally with him in a mad dash across the beach. "Move. Move. Move!"

Thirteen.

Almost carrying her because his legs were longer and stronger, he staggered as something heavy slammed into his shoulder. He almost fell, and this time it was Tally who jerked him upright. "Don't stop! Don't stop!"

Twelve.

Eleven.

He veered to the left, toward the tree line. *Ten.* His arm wrapped around Tally's waist, lifting her, propelling her along ahead of him.

Nine.

Eight.

Seven.

Their feet hit the shrubs and sea grasses. *Six.* Michael threw her to the ground behind a ridge of dunes and rocks. *Five.* He flung his body over hers, and covered her head with his arms.

Four.

Three.

Two.

BOOM!

The earth shuddered. Sand danced on the beach like fleas.

He buried his face against Tally's neck. Rocks and debris flew over them as if in the grip of a tornado. Her body trembled beneath his from the exertion of running flat out, and from his suffocating weight. Michael pressed down, covering as much of her body as he could.

BOOM! BOOM! BOOM!

He absorbed the sound, relished the percussion, as the mountainside blew up. The cacophony of destruction was music to his ears. And despite the falling crap bulleting into his back, Michael grinned in satisfaction.

When he was pretty sure the chance of shrapnel was gone, he enjoyed the silence, punctuated now and then with a loud crash, as more cliff broke free and fell with a tremendous splash into the ocean below.

As quickly as it had started, it was over.

Silence.

Blessed, triumphant silence.

"Omph," Tally said from beneath him.

Jubilant, feeling no pain, Michael rolled off her and jumped to his feet, pulling her up beside him. Sand, rocks, and bits of plant life dropped off his body. "Hoo-yah!"

"Is it over?" She brushed leaves and dirt out of her hair and stared at the raw scar on the cliff side.

He grinned. "Hell, no. It's just beginning."

"Crud," she said, dismayed. "What's left to blow up?"

Michael laughed, and wrapped his arms around her. "No more big bangs. Not that kind, anyway." He pulled her tightly against him, loving the tensile strength of her slender body in his arms.

He couldn't stop touching her. Her face, her throat, her hair. He brushed his mouth across her forehead, then just stood there, her body pressed to his, his arms wrapped around her, holding her close. "Jesus, Tally," he said thickly. "I was scared I'd be too late."

"And I was afraid Trevor would kill you." She slid her arms around his waist, her small hands on the small of his back holding tightly to his shirt. "I thought I was hallucinating when I saw you. I wasn't sure—I didn't think—"

"That I'd go in the water?"

She nodded. "I didn't expect you to. For me." She shivered, despite the tropical heat.

"The thought of losing you"—Michael buried his face in her hair, inhaled her scent, and closed his eye on a prayer of gratitude that was soul deep—"I would've walked through hell and back to find you."

She pulled back, looked up at him, and smiled as she cupped his battered face. "You *did,* Michael."

Yeah, he thought, he'd fought his own private hell. But had

he won heaven? "Let's head back to Auntie's and get you patched up and into dry clothes. It's been a hell of a day."

"Good idea." But she didn't move; she just stroked her thumbs across his cheekbones with a gentle touch. He saw pain and sadness in her eyes. "You conquered your dragon to save me," she said.

"I didn't have a choice." He reached up and caught one of her hands in his. "You were my touchstone."

Her lashes came down and shut him out. She released his shirt and stepped back, and his fingers lost contact with her skin. He felt bereft.

"Nice to know that I proved useful after all. Not quite what you had in mind, I know. But, hey"—she wrapped her arms around her waist—"it's unfortunate that Trevor didn't give a rat's ass about me. Think how much more fun it would have been if he'd given a damn."

Michael shoved his hands deep into the front pockets of his wet jeans so he didn't reach for her. He kept his gaze steady. "Just because *he* was an ass doesn't diminish in any way who *you* are, Tally."

"I know." She looked . . . lost.

No matter what kind of man Trevor Church was, and no matter that Tally *knew* it, Trevor Church had been her father. And Michael had killed him. *Hell.* He'd known this moment would have to come. He just hadn't been looking forward to it.

"I came here to kill him, Tally. No apologies. He was responsible for killing Hugo, for the loss of my eye, and consequently my navy career. And that was just the personal stuff. He was one of the seriously bad guys. Hell, I don't have to tell you what kind of man he was.

"You weren't supposed to be here. So, yeah, when I realized who you were, using you was in the cards."

"Understandable," she said reasonably as she watched him, head tilted. Waiting? For an explanation? A logical rationale? For him to walk away? To grab her and kiss her?

Shit. He was lousy at this man-woman stuff. Was she pissed? Hurt? Indifferent? "I didn't know you then," he said. The truth, no frills. Just the facts, ma'am.

"If you had?"

He hesitated. "I don't know," Michael admitted. "Getting Church was the only thing that kept me alive for so long—I don't know if I could have given that up. Even for you."

She plucked her wet and sand-crusted shirt away from her skin with a small grimace as she watched him. "If I'd known then what I know now, I wouldn't have asked you to."

"I couldn't take that chance. I did what I came to do."

"I'm glad you killed him. He was a sick, twisted son of a bitch." She started to walk down the beach toward Auntie's.

That had gone pretty well, Michael thought as he followed her.

There was probably a square inch on her body that didn't hurt, but Tally was hard-pressed to figure out where that might be. But the outside was nothing compared with how badly her heart ached. She'd learned a lot about herself in a short time. And one of those things was that she had a tendency to love where it wasn't wanted. She'd better learn to stop doing that.

"What now?" Michael asked, close but not touching.

What now? How like a man, after all they'd been through. Tally couldn't look at him. If she did, everything she felt would be right there on her face for him to see. Eyes front, one foot in front of the other. She refused to look at him. She refused to beg. And, damn it, she thought blinking rapidly, she refused to cry. "I'm going to do the only thing left to do. Call the charter company and see how soon I can get a flight out."

Michael put a hand on her arm. She stopped dead and tried not to react to his touch. Right. Like telling a match not to react to being struck.

"Come with me, Tally," Michael said urgently. "Come with me and be my first mate on the *Nemesis*. Let's sail across the world together."

Narrowed-eyed, she looked up at him. "What does being a first mate entail?" How had he gotten so close? Tally refused to step back, and stood her ground while her heart did a loop-de-loop in her chest, her palms suddenly sweaty. "What are you offering me? A job? Or an affair with sight-seeing privileges?"

He smiled. "Not a job. Not just an affair." A sea wind ruffled his drying hair. "We'll be lovers. Friends. Partners."

Her heart thudded. Disappointment warred with anticipation. "And when it's over?"

"It won't be."

"Why not?" She held her breath. *Don't get your hopes up, Tallulah. Pump that balloon too high and it's a long drop down to reality.*

His eye locked on her face. "Because I'm in love with you."

There it was. The brass ring. The words she'd waited most of her life to hear someone say to her. And the fact that it was Michael doing the talking only made them sweeter. Still, darn it, she wanted, *needed,* more.

The pulse at the base of her throat sped up. Her eyes scanned his features as if she were reading the secret of the universe in his face. "We haven't even known each other a week."

"So? In Paradise Island time, that counts for about twenty years."

Tally couldn't help but laugh. It was shaky, and hopeful. But still a laugh. "Is that like dog years?"

His lips twitched. "You have to admit, it's been a hell of a few days." He took his hands out of his front pockets and reached out to stroke her bruised and battered cheek. "I learned you this week, Tally Cruise. Learned you enough to know that I love you. Enough to know I can't imagine my future without you."

She grabbed his hand and held on to it with both of hers. From somewhere in the distance, she heard the shouts of the island people, probably running for the beach to check out the commotion. But it didn't matter. The only person in the world who mattered was standing right in front of her, looking less confident than he had since the moment she'd met him.

"Hmm," Tally said, watching him. He needed a haircut, his jaw was shadowed and prickly, and he looked as though he'd been in a war. Which he had. He was being so sincere, and earnest, she wanted to tumble him onto the beach and ravish him right there on the spot. Her thumbs moved over the back of his hand, and she saw hope spark to life in his one gorgeous eye.

"No kidding, it's been a hell of a week." She looked up at him so he could read in her gaze how she felt. "I came to Paradise looking for . . . family. A connection. And if nothing else—closure. I found you when I didn't even know I was looking for you."

"Tally—"

"I'm not finished—"

"No," he said, cutting her off. "Let me say this. I love your strength, your straightforward approach to life. I love your bravery, your willingness to see the good in everyone. I love your confidence in yourself, and your ability to cut any problem down to bite-size pieces."

"Michael—"

"I understand your need to be sure I'll keep your heart safe. And I will. But I'm willing to give you all the time you need to be sure I'm what you want. We can take as long as we like to head Stateside. We ca—"

Tally shook her head and laughed.

Stunned, he just stared at her. "You're laughing? I'm pouring my heart out here, and you're laughing?"

"You're preaching to the choir, Michael."

"Huh?"

Tally wrapped her arms around him and held on, knowing she'd finally found the one place where she belonged. A strong sea breeze buffeted them, but they stayed strong, locked together. Just as they always would.

"I love you," she said simply, honestly. "I love that you're a man of honor in a world with too little of it. I love that you love me exactly as I am. I love that I feel safe in your arms. And I want you to know that you'll always be safe in mine."

"Are you sure?" he asked, studying her features.

"Michael? Have I ever given you the impression I'm a woman who doesn't know what she wants?"

He exhaled, and a brilliant, blinding smile lit his face. "Nope."

Tally stood on her tiptoes. "Then kiss me, sailor, and let's take the long way home."

Chapter Twenty-two

Six Months Later

"Lucky, leave Duchess alone," Tally laughingly told the cat. "Look at him being territorial. Trying to oust a Great Dane, of all things. Silly cat, pick on someone your own size."

The huge dog shot her a grateful look, but the cat, with his ears back, snarled at Tally and went back to staring at the small pink bundle in her bassinet on the floor beside the dining room table. The baby cooed and smacked Lucky on the head with a little starfish hand. Lucky closed his eyes in ecstasy. He fell over, tail swishing back and forth, and purred loudly enough to be heard in the next room. Everyone at the table laughed.

Marnie, Michael's sister, smiled. "Duchess takes her babysitting duties seriously." The enormous dog did her best to guard her daughter from the furry intruder. Unfortunately, Lucky tried to scratch the dog's nose every time she came too close to her charge. The Great Dane lay as close as she dared, nose on her paws, brown eyes ever vigilant. "I think Lucky wants his own baby to look after."

"Lucky's going to have to wait," Michael said firmly, sharing a look with Tally, who gave him that sparkly eyed look he loved and, with studied innocence, wound her fingers between the long strand of lustrous black pearls around her neck while holding his gaze.

His own look promised retribution. Amazing that just a *glance* from Tally made his pulse race and his body hum.

Thanksgiving at his father's house in San Jose. And God knew, Michael was thankful. The people he cherished most in the world were right here. He let his gaze travel slowly down the table, his heart overflowing with love and gratitude.

His twin brothers, Kane and Derek. His sister, Marnie, and her husband, Jake Dolan. His brother Kyle sat beside his pretty wife, Delanie. The last time Michael had seen her, deep in the jungles of San Cristóbal, she'd been sweaty, pale, and terrified. Michael caught Kyle's eye over her head and shared a remembered moment with his younger brother.

What goes around comes around.

"Have you heard from the couple who ran the hotel?" Geoffrey Wright asked from the head of the table. Michael's father was holding hands quite openly with the woman seated beside him. Michael watched the byplay between his dad and Sunny Hamilton with interest. Sunny was an attractive blond widow who'd been their neighbor for thirty years. Michael felt guilty for being so caught up in his own drama that he hadn't noticed his father falling in love.

"Auntie and Henri are still getting over the loss of Leli'a. Her death struck them hard." Tally put down her fork and casually shifted Michael's hand off her inner thigh and onto her knee, where she held it. Firmly. "She was the daughter of their hearts. Even though she turned crazy toward the end, when she hooked up with Arnaud, they loved her deeply. They're still grieving."

Michael wound his fingers through hers, and Tally gave him that special smile that melted his heart and made other body parts hard. "They have you as a surrogate daughter. And that monstrosity of a house."

"You bet. They're *thrilled* to have Trevor's house as their new hotel," Tally said dryly. She'd inherited the island along with Church's bank accounts and all his legal businesses. Several hundred arrests had been made after following Church's paper trails around the world.

Tally had happily and willingly handed the whole mess over to T-FLAC for dispersal, and had made a tidy sum in the process. Then she'd turned around and donated all proceeds to a charity to help homeless and needy kids. She wanted absolutely nothing to do with Church or his money. Michael didn't blame her.

"Auntie's in her element, bossing everyone around, getting ready for visitors. And I've never seen Henri so happy. He hated what Trevor was doing. And now that it's over, Paradise can become a *true* paradise."

"Amen," Michael said. "They have the honeymoon suite saved for us anytime we want to use it."

"I'll pass," Tally muttered, shaking her head.

"So what's the deal with the island now?" Kane asked from the other end of the table. "Hand over those yams, bro. Now that T-FLAC's bought it, is it off-limits to tourists?"

"Damn straight, it is. I'll be using it for some of my training exercises." Jake handed him the steaming platter. "The terrain, while compact, will prove handy for an interesting variety of combat simulations. It'll also be used as an R&R installation for T-FLAC operatives and their families. Think you're going to need it soon?" Jake checked out his brother-in-law. "I notice you didn't waste time taking your bag upstairs this morning when you arrived."

Michael had seen Kane's bag in the entry hall, too. His brother was traveling light.

"I'm catching the red-eye later. But I might take you up on the offer sometime." To Michael, Kane's smile seemed strained, and he thought he saw a flash of something in his brother's eyes before he speared another slice of turkey and put it on his plate. "Pass the gravy."

"Are you going under?" Michael asked, locking eyes with his brother.

Kane took the gravy boat from his twin, Derek, and slathered gravy on to his third helping of turkey and mashed potatoes. He glanced down the table at Michael. "Yeah. But this assignment will be short and sweet. In, out, pass the beans. No fuss, no muss."

"Famous last words," his sister said, giving him a worried

glance. "Where are you going?" She sighed when he looked at her, one eyebrow raised. "Is it hot? Cold? Dry? Wet?"

Kane cut into the turkey slices on his plate. "Sandy," he said dryly. "Very, very sandy."

"Are you taking your camera?" his father asked. Michael knew how their dad worried when any of them were out of the country. Hell, *he* didn't like the Musketeers being out of the country much, either.

"I'm a photographer, Dad." Kane glanced up, saw his father's expression, and said quietly, "I'll be careful."

"See that you are," Geoffrey told him gruffly. Michael noticed that Sunny squeezed his father's hand. Geoffrey was used to what his sons did for a living. Didn't mean he liked it. It was nice to know that after all these years their father had someone to share his concern with.

"This is getting *way* too serious for our first family dinner in a year," Kyle told everyone firmly. "Have you heard the one about the CIA agent and the nun?"

When he'd finished the joke, Marnie threw a dinner roll at his head. His wife buried her face in her hands, and the rest of them laughed.

Michael leaned back in his chair, feeling as content and satisfied as Lucky looked sleeping on the windowsill in the sun. It was all so normal. So Wright.

He grinned and caught Tally's hand. She turned away from talking to his brother, Derek, who looked far too damn suave, debonair, and un-rancher-like for a cattleman.

"I love your family," Tally whispered as Michael brought her hand to his mouth and kissed her fingers.

"Good thing, because they're crazy about you." He and Tally had taken four months to sail back to San Francisco. Four months that had given their bodies time to heal, and their love time to grow. Michael hadn't realized how vast his capacity to love was until he met Tally.

Tomorrow all the ladies would go off and find *the* wedding dress. As far as he was concerned, Tally could wear a sack down the aisle next month and she'd still be beautiful.

"You look very handsome," she said with a soft smile and a loving light in her brilliant blue eyes, "but I miss the patch. Will you wear it for me once in a while, anyway?"

The doctor had been less than pleased that Michael had gone so long without wearing the prosthesis. He was coming to terms with it, and adjusting to his limited vision. "You like that pirate look, huh?"

"Only on you. Have I told you in the last eight and a half seconds how much I love you?" The pearls clicked between her fingers as she rolled the strand slowly across her chest with the flat of her hand.

Holy hell.

Michael rose abruptly to his feet. Stopped several ongoing conversations in mid-word. "Tally needs a nap. See you later." He hauled her up from the table and out of the dining room.

"You haven't finished your dinner!" Marnie yelled after them.

"Apparently they're moving straight to dessert," Kyle said with a laugh, pushing back his chair. "I'm turning the stereo up. Loud!"

Tally got the giggles as music suddenly blared from downstairs. They raced upstairs to Michael's old room, where they'd been staying since their return. He slammed and locked the door behind him, then pressed her against the wall and kissed her until they were both dizzy and breathless with need.

"They all know what we're doing in here, you know." Tally lifted her arms so he could pull off her sweater. He tossed it on the floor. Still laughing, she wrestled with his shirt and sent buttons bouncing on the carpet.

Trying to strip each other simultaneously, they fell onto Michael's bed, kissing, laughing, fumbling with buttons and fasteners. Tally tugged at his zipper, managing to pull it down. She slid her hand inside his briefs and wrapped her hand around his hard length.

Michael stripped her jeans and underwear down her legs, leaving her wearing nothing but the pearls and a smile.

"I can't wait. I can't wait. I can't wait," Tally chanted as they rolled together and bumped into the wall on the other side of the bed with a loud thump. Several of his boyhood swim trophies thudded to the floor.

They were both laughing as Michael slid into her wet heat.

Home, sweet home.

Hoo-yah!